T0146694

FACE OF THE
BELL
WITCH

FACE OF THE BELL WITCH

BOOK ONE OF THE MEDIUM SERIES

JERRY GUNDERSHEIMER

FACE OF THE BELL WITCH
BOOK ONE OF THE MEDIUM SERIES

iUniverse books may be ordered through booksellers or by contacting:

iUniverse
1663 Liberty Drive
Bloomington, IN 47403
www.iuniverse.com
1-800-Authors (1-800-288-4677)

ISBN: 978-1-5320-0221-2 (sc)
ISBN: 978-1-5320-0223-6 (hc)
ISBN: 978-1-5320-0222-9 (e)

Library of Congress Control Number: 2016913614

Print information available on the last page.

iUniverse rev. date: 03/10/2017

For Debbie.
Thank you for your inspiration, your patience,
your suggestions, and your love.
This story represents the first of many new adventures for us.
Thank you for believing in me.

Thanks to Susan McGinn
for the many hours you set aside to initially edit this manuscript.
Your attention to detail and the multitude
of excellent suggestions you made are greatly appreciated.

Thanks also to Lucinda Hauber
for your superb cover illustration.
I am grateful for the many revisions and alterations
you so kindly tolerated!

A very special thank-you to the editorial staff
at iUniverse.com
whose many hours devoted to the betterment of this manuscript,
along with their truly salient comments and suggestions
and tireless commitment to Face of the Bell Witch,
have helped make this the type of tale
I can truly be proud of.
You never wavered in believing in either Brody Whitaker
or in Jerry Gundersheimer.

1

TUESDAYS never went well for Lyle Trent. To most, Mondays were considered a scourge—days when fists were shaken and Murphy's law was invoked. But to Lyle, the youngest Trent, they were cakewalks compared to Tuesdays, which consistently brought him a dearth of good fortune, as every malady rained down on him in monsoons. Bills came due. Fevers flared. Pets perished or ran away. Car snafus were inevitable. Lyle had been dreading Tuesdays for years, but the one he woke up to this day—this one was an exception.

For it was on this Tuesday he was to help his brother, Teddy, pull off one final heist. Then he'd be free.

⌇

"Daaaddy! I can't find my sweater! I'll freeze to death running to the bus!" Abby Whitaker's muffled whine came from upstairs.

"Look on the hook behind your door, Abs," her father, Brody, shouted. His ten-year-old had a flair for the melodramatic—one of her endearing traits, actually.

"Got it!"

"Good girl! Hurry up! Come down and get this waffle inside you."

"She's lucky to have you, Giff," Susan Whitaker said from her perch on the counter beside the stove. She wasn't fazed by the waffle browning on the griddle directly beside her or the steam rising up around her face and penetrating her soft yellow curls.

Brody smiled at her, acknowledging the compliment, and then transferred the sizzling bacon onto his daughter's plate. He crossed over to the circular mahogany table and placed Abby's breakfast next to her glass of OJ, straightening the silverware beside it. "Hurry up, pumpkin," he called. "You're going to be late for the bus if you don't get a move on!"

"Coming, Daddy!" In no time, she plopped down in the chair, dropping her knapsack beside her and grabbing her fork. "It smells yummy, Daddy. Thanks!" She glanced at her father standing there in his bathrobe and chided, "You're *not* wearing those white socks with your slippers again, are you?"

Crimson filled in beneath his early-morning stubble. He improvised a semispasmodic jig, complemented by his melodic explanation: "Well, sugar pie, honey bunch—I just can't help myself."

She shook her head in mild exasperation, and in the span of a few seconds, half of her waffle disappeared from her plate, and her juice glass was firmly in her grasp. She gulped twice, drinking the majority of it.

"Whoa-ho, girlfriend. Come up for air!"

She stared at his dimpled chin for a few seconds, burped loudly, and giggled.

"Such the lady," he kidded, glancing over at Susan and rolling his hazel eyes.

Sitting there, legs crossed, Susan smiled at him.

Abby chomped into a crisp strip. "This bacon is sooo good! Thank you, thank you! It's just how I like it."

"You mean: not moving?"

She raised one corner of her mouth; that was all the reward he would receive for that retort.

"You're welcome, my princess."

"Your ... princess?" she challenged.

"Sorry. My queen," Brody corrected himself, bowing his sturdy, six-foot frame before her.

"That's more like it, sir." Abby tapped his broad, strapping shoulder twice with her fork-scepter.

"You're sooo much like Mommy," he chuckled, straightening her bangs and looking at her freckled face, her eyes so blue.

She chugged the rest of her juice, dabbing her mouth not quite so daintily with her paper napkin. "She was our queen, wasn't she?"

Susan's smile grew. She slid down from the counter and drifted toward them, resting just to Abigail's left.

He replied, "Yes, honey. She was." He looked at his daughter and saw her resemblances to Susan—her pert little nose, the natural wave in her hair, the high angles of her cheekbones, the twinkle in those impish cerulean eyes. "She was our everything."

A single tear spilled onto Abby's left cheek as she nodded in agreement. Susan bent over and kissed the droplet softly, spreading the moisture over Abby's skin. Abby turned her head sharply to her left and stared intently in the direction of the sensation, her hand gently wiping away the dampness.

Brody smiled at the cognition.

⌇⌇

When his alarm awakened him at 7:30, Lyle had long since decided enough was enough. His allegiance to Teddy had resulted in many scars—both outward and inward, of equal, substantial depth. His loyalty had certainly been risky, to say the least; foolhardy at best. Obligatory up to that point for Lyle, but no longer.

He was all too weary of simply falling into step behind his big brother, of catching the residue of Teddy's devastating draft. At long last, he felt entitled to jettison the chute that had repeatedly dragged him down the abrasive runway to an emotional halt for the last eight years—his finish line perpetually, tantalizingly in sight yet seemingly miles from reach. Lyle was going to follow through with this last heist and then inform his brother that it was their final hurrah in tandem. Lyle was retiring from the team; Teddy would have to go solo from then on out, like it or not. If he persisted in his criminal ways, they'd be his ways alone.

Lyle's focus shifted to the ceiling fan spinning above him—his own life circling in empathy of that endless loop. How he needed to alter the direction of his heretofore directionless existence. "Shit," he muttered to himself.

He swung his feet onto the cold hardwood floor and straightened himself up on the edge of the Goodwill-acquired mattress, scratching one armpit, then the other. He stared at his gaunt and disheveled self in the dresser mirror—the tousled sandy hair, the premature creases beside his sunken twenty-one-year-old eyes. He could count every single rib; he never used to be able to do that. But that was before the beer, pot, and women—and before aiding his brother in opening Pandora's box.

"Fuck!"

Gazing out the sunlit window, he knew he had to do it. After prepping himself for almost two weeks, he had finally corralled the courage to broach the subject to Teddy—he could not let the sun set without carrying out his plan. *It's now or never,* he assured himself as he stretched and yawned, his rib cage protruding even farther from his taut flanks.

Surely the revelation he was planning on unveiling to the source of his downward spiral would herald the beginning of more-promising things to anticipate on Tuesdays.

❧

"Time to go, my queen," Brody said, interrupting his daughter's trance.

Abigail tied the brown ribbons she'd brought downstairs with her onto the tail ends of her twin braids and straightened the beret on her head. She had a Girl Scout meeting right after school that day, and her troop leader, Mrs. Culligan, was going to bring her home. Ever since elementary school, she'd been best buds with Mrs. Culligan's daughter, Maddie. They'd risen together through the ranks of Troop 645, through thick and thin.

"You fed your goldfish, right?" he asked her.

"You betcha!" She saluted her father.

Brody helped his little girl put on her sweater and gather up her belongings. As they headed for the door, he noticed her turn once more and stare, yearning to see that which was unseeable to her. He guided her outside, gave her a kiss on the forehead, and watched her run to the curb.

"Don't talk to strangers while I'm gone," Abby playfully called to him.

"Sorry, force of habit," he chuckled as she stepped onto the riser of the yellow transport that would steal her away for another few irretrievable hours. "Bye, pumpkin!" he called while the doors indifferently squished closed. He waved good-bye as the school bus pulled away and moved down the tree-lined street, the fallen autumn leaves swirling behind in a colorful eddy.

As he was about to turn inside, he recognized a figure across the way that had been hidden behind the bus. The woman was dressed in a blue robe, white leather gloves, and a woolen hat, an unlit cigarette dangling between her lips. Tugging at her right wrist was a little brown-and-white dog on a braided leash. The woman took out her lighter to light the cigarette.

No, no. Don't do it! Don't do it! Brody pleaded silently. His pleas were in vain, though, as he knew full well she would continue.

As she bent over slightly to light her cigarette, the Pomeranian, suddenly feeling the slack, jerked the leash free from her hand and darted toward the street. The woman ran after her pet, her hat lifting from her graying hair and floating to the ground. She caught up to the dog in the street and scooped it up, scolding it and then clasping it firmly to her bosom while a silver minivan struck her from behind. Brody winced even though he'd seen this scene play out a number of times in front of his house, a different vehicle unknowingly participating each time. He could run to her, but she wouldn't be there when he arrived—she never was.

Shivering in the autumn morning air, he cinched up his robe and closed the door. Once inside, he turned his attention to clearing Abby's dirty dishes, rinsing them in the stainless steel sink and placing them in the dishwasher.

"You've done a good job with our little girl," Susan told him, coming closer.

His eyes moistened as he stared into the deep blue of hers. "I've tried. It hasn't been easy, without you. She misses you so much. We both miss you very much." He could almost smell her patchouli.

"She has you. She's good. And I'm right here, Giff."

Brody stared in her direction. She *was* here in spirit, and that comforted him. How he wanted to hold her, touch her! Had she not passed away so rapidly from pancreatic cancer five years before, he would have been able to.

And then she was gone.

Tucking in the second half of his shirttail, Lyle finally made his way into the kitchen. A brand-new face greeted him at the Trent table. A curvy brunette—her hair long and in tangles from a far-from-noiseless tryst with Teddy the night before—sat beside Teddy in her hot pants and tube top, applying some heavy paint to her pursed lips. Her feet were propped atop the edge of the table, her fringed beige suede shoes layered across one another. Lyle admired her shapely, smooth calves accentuating legs that didn't quit and launched an eyebrow in modest reverence to his brother's prowess. He grabbed a plate from the sink and whisked the remnants of a former meal off the chipped surface with his blue plaid flannel sleeve. "You save me some?"

Teddy pointed at the skillet on the stove, flashing the ample Gothic letters of his tattoo that read DESTINY. The letters were oriented so that they were upright to anyone at whom he flashed his fist. He had a similar tag spanning his left knuckles—ABSOLUTION. Both were souvenirs from his latest incarceration. He said apathetically, "You can head out now, Barbara."

The young woman stopped in midstroke of her lipstick. She stared at Teddy with her almond eyes wide open, head cocked, her loose curls dangling on that side. "Barbara? Are you kidding me?" Her curls bounced like limp springs, accompanying her vapid questions.

Bad move, lady, Lyle thought. *That sounds damn near like an insult. Unnecessary. And stuu-pid!*

Lyle knew that Theodore Rudolph Trent could be a mean son of a bitch. He had a hair-trigger temper plus a devil-may-care attitude—a very volatile, combustible combination indeed. And second-guessing one of his commands was an especially touchy pet peeve of his, setting him off like a firecracker.

Teddy stared back at her, daring her to venture further down that same path.

She took the next foolish step. "Barbara? Barbara? You're kidding me, right? It's Brenda. *Bren*-da." She glanced back into her compact mirror and raised her lipstick, unaware of the chain reaction she'd just set in motion.

Teddy backhanded her feet off the table, and she spun in her chair, facing him, shaken by the rapid, abusive move. He rose, assuming as menacing a posture as he could. "Look, Barbara, or Brenda, or whatever the fuck your name is—I said it's time to scram. Vamoose! Get your shit, and hit the road! *Comprende?*"

Trembling, she threw her lipstick, without twisting it closed or capping it, and her compact into her also-fringed leather purse. She cowered around her rude john to the kitchen doorway and wobbled away on her wedges through the living room. The money she was owed was no longer of interest—she just wanted out of there.

"And don't let the door hit you on your way out, *Bren*-da!" he yelled after her.

"Don't call me anymore, asshole!" She slammed the front door as she exited.

At the apparent disrespect, Teddy sprang up, but Lyle grabbed his arm.

"She ain't worth it, dude." He stared his brother down. He was the only person alive who could do so and get away with it. "They never are, man."

Teddy eased back down into his chair. "Damn straight, bro," he fumed. "Skanky *ho!*" he hollered in the direction of the departed trollop. He picked up the almost spent ketchup bottle, threatening to hurl it after her. But then he simply tossed it in the air, caught it, and slapped the bottom with the butt of his hand, trying to force the remainder of the contents onto his lukewarm scrambled eggs.

Hell, even the condiments ain't safe around here! Lyle thought.

Lyle had to sometimes remind himself that Teddy wasn't born with such a volatile temperament. In molding and shaping Teddy's demeanor, environmental stimuli factored into the equation more heavily than his roots, although this rotten apple didn't fall too far from the paternal branch of the family tree. He had been a well-tempered child up until a third-grade incident Lyle heard about firsthand from his brother. Landon Popplewell, a fifth grader, had shaken Teddy down for milk money—thirty cents—and then jumped him later that afternoon. Pinning Teddy and straddling his midsection, Landon had hurled insults relentlessly at his younger victim, each accompanied by a stinging slap. "What a pansy!" "C'mon, Trent—even girls fight back!" "Candy ass!" "Needle dick!" "You're such a loser!"

When Teddy had arrived home, wounded emotionally more than physically, he vowed to his younger brother that such humiliation would never be allowed to tarnish his ego again. Bulking and toning his physique became his obsession. He hung a speed bag in the garage, studied self-defense books, practiced martial arts, and lifted weights incessantly. One day, he had taken Lyle out to the garage and sliced the tips of their index fingers with a carving knife, demanding a blood oath that one day one of them would exact revenge upon the catalyst for Teddy's metamorphosis.

Teddy looked across the cramped room at Lyle. "Real looker for a hooker, though, huh?"

"Yeah," Lyle said snidely. "Cream of the crop." He added with a smirk, "Damn fine legs, though."

Teddy laughed. "They squeezed me like a fuckin' python!"

"You mean—a python fucking, don't you?"

He smiled at his little brother. "Yeah," he chuckled. "Good one, little bro, good one."

That brought a subtle grin to Lyle's face.

"Lyle, Lyle, crocodile! You ready, bro? You up for today?"

Lyle looked into his brother's stone-cold brown eyes. "Yep. Bring it onnn!" He then grinned, hopefully convincingly. He reached across the stove and flipped some eggs out of the pan with a flimsy spatula. Then he grabbed a Miller Lite from the fridge and sat down at the little round table. "So, let's run through this again."

Teddy arched a crooked eyebrow. "We went over it last night, brocephus." He shoved more egg into his mouth and then wiped the back of his hand across his mouth, knocking away the yellow morsels clinging to his short, bushy beard. "You forget already?"

"It's just my mind's racing, and I want it to be clear; that's all."

Teddy looked over his plate. "Okay. Here we go: We head south to Planter's Bank in Clarksville at 0800, just as that piece-o'-shit, good-for-nothin' sonuvabeeotch security guard opens up the door. We walk in behind him, and I'll take him down while you disarm him. Meantime I'm flashin' heat at the tellers and anyone else who's in the lobby, lettin' 'em know who's boss. You help me get everyone on the ground, and we make sure they know the risk-reward of bein' a hero. I'll grab the loot from the tellers while you watch for anyone who wants to, uh, challenge our authority." He locked eyes with Lyle. "You'll make sure we got everybody on the same page."

Lyle stared back, silent.

Teddy cocked his head. "Right?"

"Y-yeah, sure, sure," stammered Lyle, offering the required reassurance. "You know I will."

"Thass my boy!" Teddy grinned, three AWOL teeth having missed roll call. Poor dental hygiene combined with recent hand-to-hand combat had resulted in several casualties on the front line.

Lyle knew the whole story behind the absent teeth. Several weeks earlier at Big Jim Jennings' local poker parlor, Teddy had suffered a run of inferior hands to the tune of $2,250, a debt he'd yet to repay. Few debtors received a gratis week's reprieve from that bull moose; however, last Friday, Teddy divulged to Lyle that Jim had granted a brief continuance to the elder Trent—

all for Teddy's squandering a couple of three of a kinds, a full house, *and* a straight flush—but only after forcing him to ante up a pair of incisors, with a canine high. He'd been left spitting blood from his wounded gums while Jim, assisted by henchlings Tommy Madison and "Slots" Humphrey, goaded, "I got eyes, Trent; I got eyes. Don't you ever forget. You know I'll know when that money finds you. Don't you *think* about fuckin' with me—it won't be pretty. Not if you value the rest of your teeth, and what they're attached to."

It was high time for Teddy to change his tally, to get the heat off his back, and—with Lyle's help one more time—to provide them both some breathing room.

Lyle smiled back. "Yeah, man. Then what?"

"Then," Teddy continued, pointing his fork at Lyle, "then we hightail it with the goods down Hiter Street and head west on the other side of the Methodist church on Madison. We split, to be less suspicious, at the corner on Third. I head down Madison to Second, toward the river to Kline Alley behind the houses, where we parked the car. You go south with the bags down to Union Street and lay low behind the Dollar General. If someone makes you, pop 'em; if you feel heat, stash the cash where we can get to it later, after things cool down. I'll get to you as fast as I can, and we'll head home to divvy up the take, unless we gotta go back and retrieve it later. Got it?"

Lyle gulped another forkful of egg and washed it down with some icy brew. "Yeah, man. Real cool."

"Cool? Colder'n a witch's tit in a brass bra in January, brohaha." He smiled.

They laughed together.

Teddy polished off the last of his Miller. "Well, I guess it's time to get goin', ya think?" He got up and chucked his dish roughly into the sink, chipping that plate too. "Got any more of your brew left?"

Lyle downed the suds. "*Aaahhh.* Nope."

Teddy nudged Lyle with his elbow and grabbed a cold one from the fridge. He held up the bottle, twisted off the top, and asked, "Hey, man—you know why light beer is like screwin' while canoein'?"

Lyle sighed. *Another corny joke.* "No, man—why?"

Teddy grinned pre–punch line. "'Cause it's like fuckin' close to water!"

Lyle shook his head slightly and then turned away, not wishing to satisfy Teddy with his clandestine grin.

Nonplussed, Teddy growled, "All right, let's git 'er done." He chugged the beer as he traveled into the living room, belching proudly and pungently several times.

Lyle rose and followed.

Teddy shoved the magazine into one of the two AMT Hardballers he'd bought a few months back off his former fellow inmate Carlos Salazar. He chambered the first round and handed the loaded gun to Lyle. "Stick that where the sun don't shine, bro o' mine." He stood in front of the mirror hung beside the door, took the comb from his pocket, reslicked his hair, and then took a step back, admiring his reflection with a Fonz-like gesture: "Aaay!" His jet-black strands framed a moderately handsome face obscured beneath the scruff of coarse whiskers.

Lyle shook his head. He checked the safety of his gun, tucked it into the front of his jeans, and then yanked his leather jacket on.

"Got your mask?" Teddy asked.

Lyle patted the bulge in the front pocket of his coat. "Yep."

Teddy jammed the clip into his Hardballer and slid the gun inside his waistband behind his right hip. He handed Lyle a pair of latex gloves and stuffed a pair into his own jacket pocket. He felt for his mask and grinned. "Today's the day, eh, Lyle-o? Today we hang ten on the big kahuna. Our biggest ride yet. Ya up for it?"

"Ready and steady."

"Let's take the last train to Clarksville then," sang Teddy, a self-aggrandized aficionado of '60s and '70s classics. Still singing the old Monkees tune—popular in that neck of the woods—he walked outside first, the sunshine striking his still-bruised face. "Bee-yoo-tee-ful day, ain't it?" He took a deep breath, shut his eyes, and extended his arms in worship of the heavens. "Beee-yooo-teee-ful! *Um-hmm!*"

Lyle closed the front door. "Couldn't be better for a Tuesday," he deadpanned, stepping down the concrete steps and following his brother to the Oldsmobile.

⌒⍦⌒

Brody backed his silver Accord down the driveway and swung onto Maple Lane, heading toward downtown Clarksville. He had a bank errand to run and then a meeting with a Ms. Jennifer Connors afterward, producer of the local *Daily Show—Live* on WCVL-TV, Channel 13. She'd learned about him through a friend of hers and called him several weeks prior, to ask if he might be interested in doing a segment where viewers would contact the station to request a reading. He would keep his usual fee from the client for the arranged sessions, plus be paid an additional amount agreed upon with the station. The show's content and the details of the contract were to be discussed at the meeting.

"I don't know about this," Brody said as he drove.

"What have you got to lose, son?" his father asked. Walter Whitaker took a puff from his carved meerschaum pipe, the smoke exiting through his salt-and-pepper hair.

"You know, that thing …" Brody nodded at the pipe.

"Yes," Walter groused, "will kill me. Well, it did."

Brody shook his head. *Still stubborn, after all these years. Some things truly are eternal!* He chuckled.

"Look, son, it's a TV show—what harm could it be?"

"That's what you said about the pipe."

"Touché." He hung his angled, goateed chin in surrender.

"I've grown accustomed to my anonymity, my relative obscurity. It's comfortable. Just like that sweater you still sport, with the holes in it!"

"*Humph.*" Walter's barrel chest puffed again. "Your mother gave it to me, so hush! Say, son, you're getting along all right, aren't you?"

"What do you mean 'all right'?"

Walter removed the pipe stem from between his lips and released it in midair, where it hovered, still smoking. "Are you making ends meet?"

"Well," responded Brody, "pretty much. But there's always something extra that comes up: new sneakers for Abby, busted hot water heater, new carburetor. You know."

"Yeah, I do. I mean, I *did*. When your mom passed, I was in the same situation you are: single dad, raising a child with no assistance."

"Yes, and you really manned up, Dad. You were a great example for me to follow."

"Thank you. Brody, why not at least hear her out? You can always use a little extra moola, right?"

Yes, I can. Ever since he'd quit his day job at the bank to give his full attention to channeling spirits, it had been pretty rough. Even though his reputation had grown substantially in and out of town, the requests were still sporadic; they were never quite as steady as he'd hoped they would be when he'd first given his notice. In fact, he'd hit an unusually dry spell when Jennifer from the station contacted him with their proposal. Out of pride, he'd politely balked at first, but she'd persisted, following up rather opportunely after several more lean weeks for him—necessity dictated his change of heart and a more conducive reply. He had agreed to the meeting at ten to at least hear her out. "I suppose. Depends on what the bank says."

The objective of the bank errand was to determine if there was a need for him, at least part-time, in the loan department again. Pending that outcome, the possibility at WCVL might turn out to be a true godsend after all.

"Forget the bank. Listen to us 'deadbeats' instead, son. We're far more fascinating than any stodgy loan officer!"

Brody turned to look at his father. "Look, Dad, I appreciate your advice. I always do. And I appreciate your watching over us, along with Mom and Susan—"

"And Ruffy!"

"Oh, yes." Ruffy had been his childhood dog. "And Ruffy. But I really think—"

"Truck."

"What?"

"Truck." Walter nodded toward the windshield.

Brody glanced ahead and then stomped on the brakes. The Honda screeched to a halt. Brody's seatbelt restrained him, but Walter hung within the Accord's cockpit like a cabled Burl Ives parade balloon with a smoking pipe as satellite. The car halted mere inches from the trailer hitch of the bright-blue F-150 pickup paused at the stoplight in front of them. The driver swiveled his head to see who'd almost bought him a brand-new bumper and then spat his chew out the window. Brody stared wide-eyed at the near miss, panting heavily, and turned to face his father.

Walter snatched his pipe out of thin air, inflated a large puff between his ruddy cheeks, and blew the smoke in Brody's direction. Brody never smelled it; it neither irritated his eyes nor passed into his lungs as it wafted harmlessly, passively around him.

"Never underestimate the power of a spirit, son." He winked at his boy.

2

LYLE was nervous. He'd held up well on the drive down US Route 79 from Guthrie, but suddenly butterflies flitted inside. His nerves were suffering, unraveling—more impetus for change.

As they parked the Olds on Kline Alley, his stomach churned. He belched again, furnishing brief relief. Teddy put his hand on Lyle's left shoulder and squeezed it firmly, and Lyle felt his brother's impressive gold skull ring, with its angry ruby eyes, creating quite an impression, even through Lyle's heavy jacket. But he dare not flinch—that was a sign of weakness he was unwilling to display.

"You cool, bro-meister?"

"As a cucumber," Lyle lied.

Teddy laughed. "Thass my boy!"

One true redeeming quality could be ascribed to Teddy Trent: he was forever looking out for the welfare of his little brother, even if Lyle wasn't overly appreciative of the effort. In grade school, Teddy had made certain his weaker sib escaped the wrath of the bullies trolling the hallways and playgrounds. Rumor quickly spread that you'd better not jack with scrawny Lyle Trent, or one day you might be found like Paulie Wilson was—your nose crumpled halfway to your brain. The only detail Teddy had ever mentioned to Lyle, and him alone, regarding the incident was that it had been in retaliation for a wedgie Paulie inflicted on Lyle in gym class the previous morning—which happened to be a Tuesday. Alas, Paulie apparently hadn't been a recipient of the advice about avoiding Lyle, or maybe he just didn't care, thumbing his nose at the semiauthority of Teddy. Yet after the following day, Lyle had never been tormented again. And Paulie had never regained his sense of smell from that nose he'd so thumbed.

The brothers took off for the corner and made a right, striding down the sidewalk in front of the Centerstone–Oak Hill residences, heading toward the bank.

Teddy tapped Lyle on the elbow. "Hey, man."

"What?"

"What's the difference between a girls' track team and a tribe of pygmies?"

"Don't know. What?"

"No guesses?"

"Not a freakin' one. What *is* the difference?"

"Well," Teddy said with a grin, "one's a bunch of cunnin' runts …"

In a second or two, the leading punch line hit home, and Lyle gave in readily to the laugh.

Teddy tapped him on the elbow again. "Good one, huh, Lyle, Lyle, crocodile?"

"It was a pretty good one," he allowed.

As they walked farther along, Lyle's adrenaline began to counteract his heartburn, energizing his gait.

⌒⌒

Brody pulled the Accord into a spot marked EMPLOYEES ONLY, down the row, away from the front door of the bank.

"Well, here we—" Brody began, but Walter's spirit had vanished. He chuckled and glanced down to check his cell phone for any new calls. As he listened to the messages, he noticed two guys walk up to the entrance and test the handle. The front door was still locked, however. One of the men put his hands up to the glass and peered inside.

Typical early-morning walk-ins, Brody thought as he switched his gaze out the driver's window toward the drive-through lanes.

⌒⌒

Frank McGuire, vice president in charge of loans, sat at his desk on the outskirts of the wide, circular lobby, picking at the bounty of pill balls that dotted his sweater and tossing tiny wads of the wooly nuisances into the wastebasket beside his desk. He watched Tony Polino, the lone security guard who'd been with Planter's Bank & Trust for over a decade, polish off his jelly doughnut and brush powdered sugar onto his khakis as he traversed the travertine toward the sunlit entrance.

"Openin' up," the pudgy guard called out.

Frank glanced through the heavy bulletproof glass lobby wall of his office. Three of his tellers were busying themselves completing their respective drawer counts. At the front door were two shadows outside—a lone pair of customers waiting to be let in. The big marketing campaign looked to be off to a rather pedestrian start.

In his years at the bank, the only time Frank had ever seen Tony—an ex-cop and the son of an Italian immigrant—draw his weapon was when elderly Mrs. Gertrude Brooks had threatened the foyer employees because the coin counting machine was on the fritz, forcing her to resort to a manual tally of the $416 in change she'd hauled all the way from her Buick in a burlap sack atop her walker. She was convinced of a conspiracy and was relentless in her filibuster, ranting to the extent of actual terroristic threats against the machine's manufacturer. Her diatribe hadn't sat well with Tony, and he certainly didn't take kindly to her shaking her bony, arthritic fist near enough to his face that he couldn't possibly have failed to count her liver spots. Frank watched Tony warn her sternly but knew it had fallen on deaf ears—literally. So, in an attempt to frighten the woman into ceasing her tirade, the guard drew his weapon. The intended result was honored in spades by the spinster, who immediately fainted. Tony deftly caught her in midpirouette before her head struck the polished floor. Frank rushed over, and the two of them fanned her with a couple of spare Pendaflex folders. With Tony bending over her, she came to and abruptly punched him in the nose, bloodying him. As a result, Mrs. Brooks's account was summarily closed, and she was conducted to the police station a couple of miles away, where, for her performance, she had been awarded a brief booking in an iron-barred luxury suite, replete with a porcelain love seat and three squares a day.

Although Tony's nose had recovered, Frank knew that swollen pride took much longer to heal.

Tony tipped his cap to the tellers, crossed the variegated floor, and whistled while he tugged at the belted cluster of keys affixed to a stainless steel, retractable umbilical cord. Fumbling with the metal jumble, he located the one for the entrance lock and inserted it.

With the day's work beginning, Frank kicked his door closed and swiveled his back to the lobby, addressing an incoming phone call.

⁓

Lyle didn't notice the guard approach the glass, but he heard the door unlock. He waited for the man to finish fiddling with the bolt and move away from the entrance. With the only other person in sight parked a ways away, paying no attention to them, Lyle and Teddy withdrew their ski masks and tugged them snugly into place over their heads. They then snapped their gloves on, withdrew their guns, and stepped purposefully into the bank.

Inside, other than the tellers and the security guard, whose back was to them, the only person Lyle saw was a dude talking animatedly on his phone with his door closed, facing away from the lobby, oblivious to what was transpiring. The tellers were equally occupied, with their noses in their cash drawers.

The men closed in on the guard, and Teddy pistol-whipped him in the back of the head. Tony fell with a thud, his nose breaking as it struck the unforgiving marble. Teddy rushed toward the tellers as Lyle pulled the guard's gun out and stuffed it into his waistband.

Chaos ensued. One of the tellers screamed, raising her hands in the air; another fainted; the third reached underneath her counter, fumbling for the alarm switch.

Teddy saw her moving and snarled, "Uh-uh—don't do it, sister. Don't so much as twitch. I've got an itchy trigger finger, and it's itchin' for you." He crossed to her, pointing his gun at her face. Instinctively, she raised her hands. "Do as I say, and you'll all live through this."

She nodded.

Teddy asked, "Now tell me, sister, who's in charge?"

"You are," the woman coolly replied.

"Good for you, honey pie." Teddy flashed his sweetest gap-toothed grin and then called to his brother, "Get the keys, dude, and relock the door."

Lyle began panting heavily as he reached for the guard's belt and unclicked the key ring. His heart pounding in his chest, he looked across the lobby at the man in the office who was still unaware of what was going down.

Teddy moved swiftly along the teller windows, waving his pistol and barking, "You know what we came for; now fork it over. Put the cash in your bags, and set 'em on the counter. And no stupid moves—you'll appreciate the outcome much better if you cooperate, ladies."

The teller at the far end of the counter stuffed the banded bundles quickly into her bags, zipped the bags closed, and placed them at the front of her window, as she was told.

Meanwhile, Lyle was moving to the front door, peripherally aware of the fellow still distracted inside his transparent cubicle.

⌇

Brody listened to the last of the voice mails from potential clients and got out of the car. He shaded his eyes against the harsh glare of sunlight off the glass front doors to the bank as he approached. He opened the door and was stung inside the lobby by what his readapting vision afforded.

Tony was lying facedown a few yards away, a halo of blood having seeped from a wound on the back of his head. The two men he'd noticed out front a moment before had since donned ski masks; one was pointing a gun menacingly, shakily at him.

Both Brody and the man aiming at him stood there, neither offering a next move.

Brody broke the silence. "Hey, I don't want any trouble."

The gunman glanced over his shoulder at his accomplice and then quickly back to Brody. "Shut up. Shut up!" He nodded his gun barrel, and Brody reflexively crouched, assuming a subordinate posture.

The second gunman heard the shout and swung his pistol toward Brody as well. Then, seeing that Brody was adequately covered, he pointed it back at the tellers—Lucy, Alice, and Mary, whom Brody could see was sprawled on the ground behind the pedestaled counter. He hoped she was okay.

"Let's go!" the second gunman barked at the tellers through semiclenched teeth. "Get out here! Now!" The two women still on their feet obeyed, shuffling out from behind the counter. He ordered them, "Facedown!" The women quickly obliged. "Hands over your heads, and don't move a fuckin' muscle!" Once more they did as they were told.

Lucy whimpered, "Please ..."

"Shut the fuck up, lady! I'm not kiddin', and I sure as shit ain't repeatin' myself."

The robber closest to the tellers grabbed the money bags and loped over to his partner, checking the women for any unsolicited movement. "Get down, hero," he growled at Brody, placing the business end of his gun against Brody's forehead.

Feeling the cold steel, Brody sprawled there, motionless, with the smooth stone beneath his cheek and outstretched palms. "I'm no hero," he muttered.

"Damn straight, buddy," said the crook. He indented the muzzle of the gun firmly into Brody's temple.

"No, man. No need for that," the accomplice said. "We don't need to complicate this."

Lucy whimpered again, and the metal released from Brody's forehead as the crouching gunman jumped up and rushed over to Lucy. "I told you to shut up!"

Brody glanced up as the aggressive one raised his gun to strike the teller. The second one intervened, grabbing the other's arm. "Dude! Cool it, man. C'mon, leave well enough alone. Let's get the hell out of here while we can!"

Brody pressed his head back down. Everyone else on the floor remained quiet and still.

"Yeah, man. Let's go. Any of you move before we're outta here, and I'll rethink what my partner suggested. Understand?"

Not a sound.

"Understand?"

Silence.

"Good!"

"Yeah, good," the second one repeated. "Let's scram!"

The two men turned and fled the bank. Brody lifted his head again. As the door closed behind the two men, Frank McGuire finally revolved to face the lobby and then, seeing the individuals prone on the floor out there, vaulted from his chair and burst forth from his glass cocoon. He approached the closest person flattened out on his stomach. "What's going on here?"

Brody turned over and sat upright.

"Brody?" Frank then looked over at Tony lying unconscious on the opposite side of the central customer island, bleeding, and then his tellers across the lobby. "What the hell happened?"

"Two men robbed the bank. They just left with the money. And Tony needs an ambulance."

Frank nodded and then addressed the tellers. "Lucy," he asked, "are you all right? Alice? Mary?"

"Yes," Lucy said as she slowly stood up, shakily brushing herself off and straightening her silk blouse. "Alice and I are both fine. But Mary fainted, and Tony's hurt. Oh dear, I hope it's not his nose."

"I hope it's *only* his nose. Call 911, please," he said.

"Yes, Mr. McGuire."

He pointed to his office. "Use my phone."

Now that seemed appropriate.

3

TEDDY and Lyle raced away, tugging off their masks and gloves and stuffing them, along with their weapons, into their waistbands. Teddy passed the six money bags to his brother, who deposited them into twin sets of doubled-up Walmart sacks and tied the handles together.

They crossed Hiter and headed south toward the Commerce Street United Methodist Church, slowing their pace halfway down the block to avoid suspicion.

As they passed the church, Teddy looked at his brother and slapped him playfully in the ribs. "We did it, didn't we, brodacious?"

Refusing to flinch, despite the sting of the slap, Teddy replied, "Yeah, man. We sure did!"

"Fuckin' A!"

Their jubilance was short-lived, however, for a siren sounded a few blocks away, putting a damper on their celebration. They maintained their even pace—just two guys out for a stroll.

Teddy pointed across the street. "There's the Dollar General. You head around back, and I'll go get the car."

Lyle nodded and traversed the parking lot toward the store. He turned around and took a few backward steps. "Hurry up!"

"Yeah, man. Hang on. I'll be right back to get you. Don't eat all them groceries, now." He laughed. He took off his jacket and handed it to Lyle and then trekked down Madison, gaily swinging his arms and whistling. The plan worked—the lone pedestrian sauntering down the street in a plaid shirt was irrelevant to a passing patrol car.

◡ℳ◠

"Brody," Frank McGuire asked, "what did you see?"

"There were two guys. I couldn't see much because of their masks."

"One of them was missing a few teeth, the one who made me give him the money," Lucy said.

"How much did they get away with?" Frank asked.

"I'm not certain, sir. I was double-checking my count, but I know it was about eighty thousand, because you tripled our drawers for the new customer promotion. In the meeting last Friday you told us to expect a lot of new accounts this week with the hundred-dollar CD giveaway and to be prepared for more than the usual number of transactions."

"Yes, that certainly was my expectation. We'll have to shut it down now and put that promotion on hold. I'll have to check with corporate ... Alice—how about you? Any idea how much was in your drawer?"

"Much the same, sir. We were completing our counts when the robbers struck. I know they got somewhere in the neighborhood of seventy-five thousand from my drawer alone. And then there was Mary's drawer."

Frank shook his head and sighed. "Okay. I'll check to see how much should have been there. Ladies, listen—I'm sorry I was preoccupied and didn't see what was happening. I feel like a complete idiot. I really let us down."

Alice touched him on the sleeve. "That's okay, sir. We managed the best we could for the bank."

"I know you did, Alice. I have no complaint or criticism of how bravely you all handled yourselves; I'm just thankful you ladies are safe." He handed Alice his handkerchief.

The doors to the bank opened, and the paramedics sped through with a stretcher.

"Over here!" Frank gestured toward Tony, still facedown on the floor. No one had tried to turn him over for fear of a possible neck injury. The paramedics hurried to him and began their assessment.

"Is he all right?" Frank asked.

"Hard to tell," said the younger of the two. "We'll take all the necessary precautions for him. Possible concussion and broken nose from the look of things. Can't be sure. We'll stabilize him and get him over to Gateway. They'll take things from there."

In unison, they rolled Tony onto a backboard, carefully keeping his neck immobilized. On the quick count of three, they hefted the backboard onto a low-lying gurney and strapped him securely in. While one of the men administered to the unconscious guard, the other asked, "Is anyone else injured?"

"Well, sir," Lucy said, "Mary fainted behind the counter over there."

"Show me, ma'am."

Lucy led the other paramedic away to her fallen comrade as the police arrived.

On the far side of the Dumpsters behind the Dollar General, Lyle crouched on his haunches, biting his fingernails and glancing around for a hiding place for the loot. His brother's jacket lay beside him.

A metal door suddenly banged open, and squeaky wheels rolled down a nearby ramp. Lyle heard the Dumpster farthest from him slide open. He reached down for his gun, grasping its grip, and braced himself, those damn butterflies fluttering inside again.

As the Dumpster panel slid closed, Lyle improvised. He quickly covered up his weapon with his jacket, closed his eyes, and attempted to gain control of his rapid breathing as best he could, feigning slumber.

"Hey, mister, you can't sleep here," a youthful-sounding man said.

Something nudged Lyle's shoe.

"Hey, mister!"

Lyle was about to bolt when the young man said, "N-never mind."

Lyle heard footsteps retreating. He peeked between his eyelids, but whoever had accosted him was no longer there. The rear metal door banged closed once more. Nervously, Lyle glanced around, again looking for a place to stash the sacks. He tried to raise himself, pushing his left elbow against the concrete wall for support. A portion gave way, easing inward, revealing an irregular defect about a foot and a half above the ground—the sanitation guys must've been a bit careless one day with lowering that Dumpster. With some effort, he pushed the broken, nearly one-foot-in-diameter, roughly circular section of concrete inside the wall, where it remained level, resting on an aluminum cross strut. He reached inside the hole and eased the piece of concrete out, rotating it slightly and angling it in order to clear the freshly made opening. The empty space was slightly larger than what he required. It was certainly big enough to hold the merchandise and high enough for protection against the elements. Quickly, he pushed the Walmart bags into the hole and onto the ledge within. He replaced the concrete, lining it up meticulously so it resembled nothing more than a hairline crack to the naked eye, imperceptible in the facade.

His task accomplished, he sank back down on his backside and smiled.

The rear door to the store banged open again, loudly striking the aluminum railing. On instinct, Lyle sprang to his feet, snatching up Teddy's jacket, and began to sprint toward Union Street.

"Hey, you!" someone shouted behind him—an older, deeper voice—and then two loud gunshots sounded. A bullet whizzed past him, and he tried to glance over his shoulder as he ran. The second projectile struck him in the side and damn near kicked him to the asphalt. It burned! He reached his free hand around to the source of the pain and then retracted it, inspecting it. Blood! *Oh, fuck! I'm hit!*

"I'm callin' the police!" the shooter yelled.

"Fuck!" He cried out to no one but himself. *Oh my God, it hurts!* He kept running. The warmth flowed down inside his trousers, over his calf, into his sock. *I can't believe this shit!*

The world began to move differently to him—herky-jerky, exaggerated—as he struggled his way down the block across the street. He held firmly to the excess baggage; he dare not leave behind Teddy's jacket. Coming to a house in the middle of the next block, he had to plunk down heavily in its dense lawn, releasing hold of Teddy's jacket. He lay there a few feet off the sidewalk and the front walkway to the house, waiting to see if the Olds came into view.

Lyle was afraid to look directly at his wound but lifted his jacket high enough to see that blood was continuing to drain from it. Something was turning his blue plaid shirt reddish violet. *Ohhh ... Fuck! Fuck!*

The softness of the cool grass felt so soothing surrounding him. He stared at the sky and laughed. *So fuckin' typical*, he thought—the botched escapades his brother always goaded him into. For his bowing to Teddy's lead and instructions over the years, all he'd won was detention, then juvie, followed by a stint in the pen.

Should've stayed in bed today. He winced. All the would'ves, could'ves, and should'ves he'd hoarded over the years shuffled through his mind. Would've possibly skipped those six months in county. Could've maybe passed that employment interview at the crosstown Home Depot. Would've perhaps not been jilted by Lizzie Snowden that Tuesday night last spring. But when one associated with his older brother, hindsight was deceptively cruel and unforgiving—just like Teddy.

Lyle closed his eyes. He lay there for several minutes and then was startled by a succession of rapid, short bursts of air pressure escaping over to his left. He turned his gaze to see a sprinkler head pop up in the section of lawn on the opposite side of the walkway. Water sprayed forth. He was hopeful of catching a dab or two of the moisture, but all he felt was a drift of fine mist as the breeze wafted it across him. He wondered if the sprinklers would emerge from the patch of ground around him, dousing him. Too exhausted to really care, he worried over it and welcomed it at the same time. Whether he lived or died—or got soaking wet—at last he'd be free. He awaited the effluence of the sprinklers, trusting it would camouflage the moisture emerging from his eyes.

What a shitty day. I hate *fuckin' Tuesdays!*

The paramedics departed with only Tony; the women were treated and allowed to remain behind, shaken but recovering quickly. The police swarmed all over the lobby like ants over a broken mound. Cameras flashed, sketches were made, fingerprints sought, statements taken.

Officer David Jeffries was in charge of the investigation. Of Ashkenazic descent, Jeffries had a smoky complexion and dark, full eyebrows. On the force for two decades, he'd worked his way up from patrolman to master sergeant. With several commendations under his belt and his reputation for the dogged pursuit of justice, he was the logical choice in the department to be assigned anything out of the ordinary, such as this abrupt, brazen daylight heist.

As he jotted down notes, he directed the various activities. He then moved to recording the eyewitnesses' accounts. Having been made aware that Brody was the lone patron in the bank at the time of the crime, he decided to begin his line of questioning with him. "Uh, Mr. Whitaker?"

Brody turned toward the sound of his name, his gaze shifting down an inch or two to address the gentleman. "Yes, Officer?"

Sergeant Jeffries extended his hand to Brody. The policeman had a vise-like grip—the product of long hours in the headquarters' gym. "I'm Sergeant David Jeffries. May I ask you a few questions about what happened here?"

"Certainly, Officer. Anything I can do to help."

"Thank you." He removed a digital recorder from his pocket and began the interview. "Eyewitness Brody Whitaker, customer and former employee of the bank. Mr. Whitaker, how many people were involved in this robbery?"

"I saw only two, Sergeant."

"Were there any identifying marks you can recall on either suspect, sir? Scars? Blemishes? Facial hair? Tattoos? Piercings?"

"One of them had a couple of missing teeth," he said. "Nothing else I can say for sure. I was facedown most of the time."

"How about their approximate heights, weights, builds? Tall, short, lean, muscular, obese?"

"Well, again, it happened so fast I can't be certain, but one of them seemed close to five eleven, slender, say about one sixty or so. The other ... around six feet, two twenty, if I had to guess. They both had on leather jackets, both black—or one might've been a dark brown. I did notice them from my car as they were entering the bank, but honestly, I was paying more attention to my phone than to them. So again, I'm not positive."

"Did they use any identifications—names, nicknames? Any tip-off as to who they are or where they might be from? A regional dialect or accent perhaps?"

"No, they were quite careful to avoid using names. Nothing special about their speech patterns either. Sorry."

"That's fine, Mr. Whitaker. We're just trying to cover all bases."

"Of course, Officer."

"Anything else you can think of offhand, sir, that might be helpful to us in apprehending either suspect?"

Brody paused a moment, looking thoughtful, then answered, "The taller one with the missing teeth might've had a beard as well. I thought I could see a trace of it below his mouth, although it was hard to tell with his mask on."

"That's good, sir. That's very useful information. Thanks."

"You're welcome, Sergeant."

Satisfied he'd gotten everything he could from that witness, the detective turned his attention elsewhere.

⸎

Brody wasn't satisfied; he felt almost useless. He wished he'd had more to offer the officer. After all, he wasn't just some random bystander. He'd been employed there, helped grant loans to customers, and generated revenue for the company—he wanted those crooks apprehended. He felt a greater sense of obligation than a run-of-the-mill witness would have.

Frank McGuire walked up from behind him and touched him on the shoulder. "What brought you up here, Brody? You needed to see me?"

Frank was a middle-aged fellow with beady eyes and male pattern baldness. He stood only five five and compensated for his lack of height and hair by chasing skirts. Brody had vouched for his boss on one occasion that could have easily been construed as sexual harassment; the end result would've seen Frank being thrown ignominiously out on his keister, had not Brody verified his boss's side of the story. The same employee accusing Frank had made a pass at Brody the week before—the difference being that he'd rebuffed her.

Brody exhaled. "Yes, Frank. As a matter of fact, that's actually why I came here this morning. Great timing, huh?"

Frank exhaled. "What a mess, what a mess, all right. Hey, how 'bout a cup of coffee? I sure could use one."

"Please." He followed Frank into the break room and fixed himself a Styrofoam cup of java. He grabbed a container of cream and a stirrer and joined his ex-boss at one of the less-wobbly square tables.

Frank folded his hands in his lap. "What's up, Mr. B?"

Brody blew onto the surface of the coffee and took a sip or two. "Well, I know you know what I've been doing since I left the bank."

Frank lowered his voice, leaning in. "Conjuring the Devil?"

The VP was also prone to tasteless humor with an accompanying lack of timing, matching his woefully inadequate way with the ladies.

Brody gagged slightly on his coffee.

"Just kidding! Yes, I know what you've been up to. How's that working out?"

"Well … it isn't. At least, not yet. It takes a lot longer to establish oneself, I guess, in this business."

Frank stared at him. "Business is kind of dead, huh?" He grinned.

Brody grimaced.

Frank motored along. "Well, I guess it must be difficult to get established. I thought you might have a tougher go at it than you figured."

"Yes. Well, I was wondering if you might need me here for a while. Part-time? To help pick up any slack you might have?"

"Well," Frank said, "there's always work to do. Lots of new construction popping up around town."

"I noticed an empty desk or two out front. Even Lizzie's. She still here?"

"No, she isn't. Shortly after you left, she had some date planned with a guy up in Kentucky, from what I heard. She wouldn't tell anyone his name. No one knew anything about the fella. We never saw her or heard from her after that evening, and when the authorities checked around, all her belongings had been stripped from her apartment. There were no clues as to her whereabouts. Like she'd disappeared overnight. Maybe she ran away with the guy. What happened to her is pure speculation at this point. Baffled everybody."

"Really?"

"And to top it all off, turns out she was embezzling from the bank."

"No! Lizzie?" Brody was shocked.

"Quite a bit too. Out of deference to her parents in Seattle, who still haven't heard a peep from her, the whole dishonorable affair was kept under wraps. Whether or not the guy she was going to meet had put her up to it is anybody's guess. Weird, huh? You think you know people …"

Brody shook his head in disbelief. "So …" He took another sip, savoring the aroma. The quality of the break room's coffee had always surpassed that of the available tables and chairs. "Think you might be able to use me?"

"Well, even shorthanded as I am, I'm a little out of sorts at the moment, as you can imagine."

"Sure."

Frank placed his chin on the tips of his fingers, elbows propped on the tabletop. "Tell you what," he finally said.

"What?"

"Let me run it up the flagpole to HR, see what they say. I'll give you a call as soon as I know something. Shouldn't take long. Sound good?"

That relieved Brody. "That'd be great, Frank. Ask 'em, and let me know."

"You said you'd accept part-time, right?"

"Yes, I would. Part-time—even if it's just temporary."

Frank dropped his chin. "Can't promise anything."

"No, I know you can't, but that'd be great. A big help."

Frank slid his less-than-sturdy chair out from underneath him and stood up, extending his hand. "Good then. I'll check on it and be in touch."

"Super. I really appreciate it, Frank." He shook Frank's hand.

"Well," he sighed, "I've got to head back out there. Long day ahead."

Brody smiled, a playful hint on his tongue. "If you need some help ..."

"Can't help with this, I'm afraid." He shrugged and shook his head. "You know, I've been in banking for many years, and this is a first for me. You read about it elsewhere but never think it'll happen at your bank. Helluva circumstance."

"I don't envy the rest of your morning; that's for sure."

"Neither do I," he said, placing his hand on Brody's back and ushering him out the break-room door. "Neither do I."

Teddy made it to the alley and to his and Lyle's car, which was backed into a driveway, shielded partly from Union Street by a row of hedges. He fumbled with the keys. "C'mon. *C'mon!*" He finally unlocked the door, jerked it open, and slid inside.

A cruiser passed slowly by and then continued down the street, away from Kline Alley, apparently having detected nothing out of the ordinary. Teddy waited a few seconds more to start the ignition, and the Olds sputtered noisily to life. He eased off the hardtop, crunching onto the gravel, and cautiously approached the end of the alley.

He stopped the car and got out. He walked slowly to the edge of the wooden fence on the corner of the last house on his right and peered around it. The coast was clear. He rushed back to the Olds. Gliding from the alley, he made the right onto Union, heading back in the direction of the store.

Just past Second Street, off to his right, he saw someone lying in the grass in front of a house with the sprinklers on. *Oh shit, that looks like Lyle!* He shoved the car into park and sprinted over. *It is him!* Lyle's left knee was raised, and he was breathing laboriously, gasping. Blood trickled from the corner of his mouth. Sopping wet from the sprinklers—which had since cycled through to drench another region—he was lying on soggy, red-tinged turf. Teddy's jacket was lying on the front walkway.

Teddy grabbed it and whipped it on; it was damp, not soaked. He dropped to his brother's side, cradling his head. "Oh Jeezus, bro. What the hell happened to you?" Teddy felt the pinkish puddle seeping into the knees of his denim trousers.

Lyle coughed, spitting blood. "Bastard at the store shot me! I was minding my own fucking business and—" He grabbed Teddy's lapel and twisted it tightly.

"All right. Let me help you to the car." Teddy tried hard not to panic but was not having success. "You're gonna be okay, little guy. I won't let anythin' happen to you; you know that. Have I ever let anythin' happen to you? Huh? Ever?"

"Too late, man."

"No. *No.* Nothin's gonna happen. Not on my watch!"

He assisted his brother to his feet and half-carried, half-dragged him over to the idling car. He opened the passenger-side door and made sure Lyle's dripping head cleared the upper doorframe as he set him down on the front seat, stuffing his legs inside. Teddy lifted his brother's jacket and twisted him slightly toward the driver's side of the car. Lyle was bleeding steadily from a bullet wound under his rib cage—precisely where Teddy had playfully slapped him a mere half hour before.

Amped out of his mind, he slammed Lyle's door, ran around the car, and jumped in. He took off down Union and made the left hook to return to Madison. There he turned right, heading away from all the commotion surrounding the bank.

He looked at Lyle. Lyle was not good; he was slumped over, and there was so much blood on him! Teddy pulled his only living relative's head back by his hair. "Stick with me, broha. Stay with me here!"

"Teddy?"

"What, man? What is it?"

"I need help."

"What?"

"Need a doctor. Hospital."

Teddy thought about hauling ass to the ER, but how long would they be kept there as Lyle was treated? How long would it take before the authorities pieced together that one of the robbers might have been shot somehow? Too risky.

"I'll take care of you, man. Haven't I always?"

Lyle produced a thick gurgle of a laugh.

Even in this most critical of situations, true to form, Teddy felt irked. "What? Haven't I?" But his ire was met by silence, as though Lyle was ignoring Teddy's growing panic and frustration. Then:

"Teddy?"

"Yeah, bro?"

"This is the last time, man," he rasped, the words bubbling forth.

Teddy shook his head. "What? What you talkin' 'bout?"

Lyle coughed again. A mouthful of blood emerged this time, a substantial portion splattering on the console and the rest dribbling down his chin. "I'm not gonna do this anymore. You're on your own."

"What? Don't you worry 'bout that right now. You hear me?"

"No, I mean it. This is really ... the last time. I want to be free."

"Yeah, yeah. Sure. Free." Teddy's tears came spontaneously, without warning. "Man, you stay with me! I'm gonna get you some help. I'll get you to Doc Petty's, back home. You just hang in there—don't you leave me!"

He drove the car up Madison and then onto US 41, heading north, heading home.

"... last time ... I'm ... leaving ..." Lyle slumped over again. "Tell me ... a ... joke ... one ... more ..."

Just then, in midsob, Teddy remembered. "Lyle? Lyle! Where's the money, Lyle?"

No response.

Teddy shook his brother, the wheel jerking in his hand. "Lyle! Lyle, where's the money, man? *Talk to me!*"

But Teddy sensed that his brother had already left him alone.

4

BRODY nervously waited on the leather couch in the lobby of the television station, hands clasped, thumbs twiddling nonstop. *Holy shit!* he thought. He felt as though he'd just cheated death somehow—a gun had been pointed to his head mere minutes before! He'd wanted to call Abby's school after the ordeal, to talk to her, hear the reassuring sweetness of her voice, yet such a notion was reserved for family emergencies only, and doing so might have alarmed her unnecessarily. So he was left to ruminate on the real possibility that he might have never seen his precious daughter again. *Thank you, God. Thank you. Thank. You.*

And while that morning could have proven to be his last, it was also yielding new promise, with not one but *two* new possible income streams. Yet the latter opportunity—at WCVL—had him in a quandary, for there was much to consider. *Okay—concentrate. Concentrate!*

Those who could communicate with the spirit world had been around for centuries, but frauds and charlatans had eroded mediumship's credibility throughout the years, creating more than a modicum of skepticism in the public eye. Though Brody had previously viewed television shows showcasing purported mediums, he had no direct evidence as to their legitimacy—or to the contrary. Of his, Brody was certain, yet this was brave new territory for him, for sure.

Taking his readings to the screen was a possibility that hadn't presented itself before, so he'd never truly considered it. Now it was staring him in the face. *What should I do?* Sessions had such an intimate, personal aspect to them; would making them so public seem like a violation of trust? After all, raw feelings exposed themselves when he channeled the spirits of departed loved ones. He had no idea what his clients' reactions to videotaping and broadcasting their sessions might be—it could go either way. But he had to at least hear Ms. Connors out, see if the idea she had in mind was favorable and in everyone's best interests.

A young blonde temp walked up to the couch and politely informed him, "Ms. Connors will see you now."

He followed her into a small conference room where a pretty redhead dressed in a turquoise business suit sat at a huge rectangular conference table speaking to a gentleman with a handlebar mustache and thick ebony eyeglasses. Behind the woman was a young girl, about Abby's age, dressed in a prep school uniform—crisp white cotton blouse with a plaid necktie and a matching, freshly pressed pleated skirt. The seated duo rose, and Jennifer Connors walked around the table to shake his hand. Brody caught a scent of her perfume, tantalizing and heady. Her shoulder-length auburn hair was pulled back into a tidy ponytail, held in place by a fashionable tortoiseshell clip. *Stunning* was the only thought Brody had of her bottomless green eyes that shimmered as she introduced herself. Her smile was equally as radiant.

"Hello, Mr. Whitaker. Jennifer Connors—we spoke over the phone. Thank you so much for coming." She shook his hand firmly. "This is Mr. Jack Walters, the owner of WCVL. We were just talking about how much we were looking forward to meeting you and talking with you today."

The gentleman remained standing where he was and waited for Brody to approach him. Brody reached out, and Mr. Walters shook his hand.

"How are you, Brody? Good to have you here at our little station." The charcoal curls on either side of his nostrils elevated with his ruddy cheeks when he greeted Brody.

"Good to be here, Mr. Walters, sir. I apologize for being a couple minutes late, but I was tangled up in a situation down at Planter's Bank."

"The one that was robbed a little while ago?" Jack asked. "We have a crew down there now."

"Yes, I'm still a bit shaken up by the whole thing."

"Understandably," Jack said. "Are you up to meeting right now? We can table this until later if you need some time."

"No, please—this might be exactly what I need to distract my nerves."

"All right, as you wish. Say, you wouldn't mind taping a short eyewitness account for us after we're through, would you? An exclusive?"

"Jack ..." Jennifer chided.

Brody chuckled. "If it'll help apprehend the criminals, I'd be glad to volunteer."

Jack gestured to an executive chair opposite him. "Thank you. My producer sometimes reminds me about my presumptuousness. Sorry."

"That's quite all right."

"Please, do sit down." Jack deflected Jennifer's stern expression with a return scowl.

As Brody took his seat, the schoolgirl carefully regarded him, and he noticed a rather large aperture in her neck. They exchanged winks, and she smiled.

Jack began their meeting. "Jennifer came to me a few months back and told me about you and what you do, Brody. I must tell you I personally am quite skeptical of mediums. It took me a while before I agreed to have Jennifer reach out to you about this project."

Brody glanced at Jennifer, staring briefly at her pale-pink lips and then at her emerald eyes, which returned his gaze. He felt a warm, tingling sensation invading his cheeks. It was an effort to steer his attention away from her. "Really? Why?"

"Well, we've all seen the major-network shows about others in your field and how they connect with those who have, uh, crossed over."

Jennifer picked up there. "I was suggesting to Jack that, because of the significant recent popularity of these types of shows, it might be worthwhile to try to establish a local version of one, involving people who might otherwise call on you for a private reading but instead phone in here to schedule a taping with you."

Brody was confused. "But if you're so skeptical, Mr. Walters, why would you commit the resources of your station to this type of experiment?"

"A fair question, Brody." He eased back in his chair, touching his fingertips together, silently passing the baton.

Jerry Gundersheimer

Jennifer took the cue. "Jack has told me that just because he doesn't necessarily believe speaking to the dead is possible, he doesn't want his own opinion to stand in the way of what could well become a popular segment on our *Daily Show—Live* broadcast." She smiled at him, her well-manicured hands folded on the table, her gold chain bracelet dangling delicately from her slender wrist. "We here at the station would like to remain, shall we say, a little more open-minded than our ... unconvinced owner."

"Well," Brody asked her, "what about you, Ms. Connors? Where do you stand?"

"Let's just say I've never personally witnessed a reading, but I'm ..." She paused, fishing for the right words.

"Open to the possibility?" Brody finished for her.

Jennifer locked onto his hazel eyes. "Why, yes. I was just thinking that. How did you know?"

He chuckled. "It's fairly typical. Nothing clairvoyant, I assure you. I hear that a lot." He looked at her and then at the schoolgirl. The girl nodded to him. He turned back to his hostess and informed her quietly, "Julie wishes to tell you something,"

That statement utterly caught her by surprise. "That was my daughter's name: Julie." She swallowed hard. "How? Where ...?"

"She's present with us now."

Jennifer and Jack quickly surveyed the room.

"Where is she?" she asked, still intently glancing around, unable to discern her daughter.

"She's here," Brody said softly. "She's right behind you."

Jennifer swung her chair around. She couldn't see anything or anyone there. Neither could Jack. Jennifer looked at Brody again and then at her boss, who arched his right eyebrow farther above its concomitant handlebar.

"Wh-what is she ... saying? How ...?"

"She's wearing a starched white blouse and a plaid skirt."

"That was her school uniform!"

"She's mentioning the number eight."

Jennifer raised her hand to her mouth in disbelief. "She was ... eight years old when she died." She began to tear up.

Jack passed her a box of tissues from the middle of the table, and Jennifer pulled one from the box. She dabbed the corners of her eyes.

Brody nodded. He waited briefly as the little girl pointed to the hole in her neck and placed her hand upon her chest. "She's pointing to her neck and chest. She passed away due to her lungs, didn't she?"

Jennifer stared at him. "She couldn't breathe well—she had a tube. Cystic fibrosis took her from me." Her eyes welled.

The spirit nodded her head and then shook it.

"She wants you to know she didn't suffer when she passed."

"Oh," Jennifer cried, "are you sure?"

"She told me that just now."

The little spirit mouthed something, and Brody repeated the communication. "She says she knows you stood beside her as she breathed her last. She also knows you have been burdened about whether or not she suffered, and she wants you to let go of that weight. She was not in pain—she slowly left the world of the living and drifted away, peacefully. You did everything you could to make her comfortable, and she's grateful for all the love and care you gave her throughout her illness. She is aware of all you sacrificed for her."

Jack had not taken his eyes off his producer and began to get weepy too.

"Ms. Connors, you should know that she's no longer suffering. Her lungs are clear now, and she is perfectly well and happy. She is at peace."

"How could you know this?"

"Her spirit told me. But she felt that *you* needed to know that. She wants you to know how proud she is of you for listening to her, for having the fortitude to heed her after she passed. Do you know what that means?"

"My God" was all she could reply. She blew her nose softly into the tissue and pulled out a few more, a fresh set of tears spilling over.

Brody reached out and took her hand. His touch seemed to steady her. He looked deep into her eyes. "When you come home from work sometimes, do you feel a brush of air and glance up, wondering if you've left your ceiling fan on?"

"Yes," Jennifer acknowledged, sounding astonished.

"Know that that is your daughter reaching out to you. Did you feel the slightest sensation on your cheek just now?"

"Yes."

"That was her kissing you."

Goose bumps visibly radiated down Jennifer's arm. "She kissed me?"

He nodded and smiled, releasing her hand. "Spirits have a way of letting us know they are near, if we're receptive to what they're attempting to communicate. She now wants you to know that when you put her bedroom in order and donated some of her things, she was pleased you held on to her Barbie collection."

Jennifer smiled.

"Especially the princess ones," he chuckled, prompting a staccato laugh from her as well.

"I was going to donate them, but something made me change my mind."

"She wants you to hold on to them, in case you might need them again."

Jennifer Connors wept.

Jack asked, "Is it true, Jen?"

Struggling to dry her eyes, she collected herself enough to face him, gently nodding. She sniffed and said, "Every … word."

◦◦◦

"Lyle, Lyle, crocodile! Bro, say something!" Teddy was frantic. "Lyle, don't you do this, man!"

He turned north onto US 41/79, heading toward the Red River and home. His brother was unresponsive. Teddy had no clue as to where the loot was. So what had it all been for? He wished he could go back a few hours earlier so Lyle could talk him out of the heist. He wished he was still in bed. He wished it was yesterday, last week, ten years earlier—any time frame but the present. *I want my bro back!*

"This is so fucked up!" He pounded the steering wheel and yelled at the top of his lungs. "Lyle, answer me, dammit!"

But Lyle didn't answer.

Clouds were rolling in as Teddy approached the Red River Bridge. All manner of thoughts added to his growing confusion. What the hell could he *do*? His brother was dead! Should he take his body home? Bury him? Could he risk the authorities uncovering Lyle's hidden corpse somehow? This was his brother! What? *What?*

He crossed the bridge and spotted a side road off to his right up ahead, and, without much consideration, he turned down the unpaved road. Stopping about a half mile from the highway, he shut the car down to gather his thoughts. Instead, the dam burst—he dropped his forehead to the leather steering grip and bawled, snot bubbling over the lip of his mustache. "Why? Why, little brother? This wasn't supposed to happen."

He summoned the courage to look through his veil of tears at Lyle again, whose head had now slumped over to rest upon the passenger door. Along with the dripping water from Lyle's clothes, a great deal of crimson angrily soiled the tan leather upholstery.

"Little bro. Little bro ..."

Teddy looked up through the fogged windshield and then smeared a small circle clear with the cuff of his jacket. Ahead of him was a dogleg to the left with a metal barricade protecting the turn. He thought he could spot the river on the far side of the rusted iron. He rumbled the car to life and proceeded slowly up the road. As he approached the curve, a red Challenger with a wide black racing stripe careened around the bend, nearly sideswiping the Olds. Teddy swerved to his right to avoid collision and then corrected, skidding to a halt. The driver of the other car thrust a single digit out the window as he flew past, greeting emphatically, "Fuck you, idiot!"

Teddy returned the salutation with similar enthusiasm. "Hey, fuck you too, a-hole!" In his rearview mirror he watched the Challenger, with a busted driver's-side taillight, knife through the dust in the distance.

He moved on and stopped the Olds by the rail. Seeing no one else in either direction, he creaked open his door and proceeded around to the passenger's side. He dragged Lyle out by the wrists, and his brother's bloodied shoes thudded sickeningly on the ground. Then he slid the body around the barricade and down through the weeds and muck, well out of view from the road, depositing Lyle flat on his back at the water's edge of an inlet of the river.

What should he do? He couldn't call anyone for advice or assistance. Their plan had called for leaving their phones at home, in case an alibi—supported by wireless GPS records—was necessary later on. Teddy knelt beside his brother, the soggy vegetation sopping again the knees of his jeans. He felt Lyle's neck for any sign of a pulse but couldn't find one. There was no rising or falling of Lyle's chest and no breathing sounds. Teddy held a hand over Lyle's mouth and nose and felt no breath. Shaking Lyle's shoulder induced no movement whatsoever. He could not bring himself to give his brother up fully to the stream, so he stood back and watched Lyle's right arm bob passively atop the lapping water.

"I'm sorry, bro," Teddy whimpered. "I don't know what else to do." With more reluctance than he had ever felt in his lifetime, he slogged back up to the car, walking backward mostly, hoping in vain to catch any twitch, any telltale sign of life left in his little brother.

He emerged from behind the guardrail and noticed the trail of blood on the ground. Grinding his boot back and forth, he mixed the blood with dust and gravel, eliminating it as best he could. Then he got back into the car. As he cranked the ignition, he glanced over once more to where his little brother typically rode. The only remnant of him ever being beside him in that car was a large stain—DNA evidence that would have to be painstakingly eliminated.

Teddy spun the Olds around and returned to the main road, sniffling and wiping his nose. He slowed briefly at the stop sign and then punched it north again—placing as much distance, as quickly as possible, between himself and the unbearable deed.

⌁

As the Olds sputtered and chugged to life, down by the bank of the river the backfire had its effects. In a finger of the tributary, a substantial gator was startled by the sound and lurched into the water. A wantonly transplanted denizen that had thrived for several seasons, it had begun as that proverbial trophy pet that eventually and inevitably outgrew its tank and thus its owner's wallet and welcome—a once-upon-a-time centerpiece that became instead a hastily, ignorantly discarded nuisance. Thrust into the river's ecosystem to survive, it now had become an unchallenged marauder.

Alerted by the noise and driven by the aroma of death, the huge reptile swam silently with legs hanging motionless, eyes and nostrils periscoping above the surface, tail propelling it below. Relentless, without a squandered twitch of muscle, it proceeded onward—floating destruction—honing in on the source of the odor enticing it from the bank.

⌁

Abruptly, Lyle's eyes opened wide, and he coughed, an acidic taste coating his mouth. Moisture—cold and numbing—penetrated the back of his clothing. He stared up at the trees and the sky, wondering where the fuck he was, and gasped, "Teddy?"

A ferocious jolt of excruciating pain pierced his right arm and shoulder like a bear trap.

"Aaaaagh!" Lyle's cry of agony drifted through the trees, stirring nearby nesting birds and sending them chattering and flapping to seek more-placid temporary roosts.

The gator—just under ten feet in length—chomped down on Lyle's arm until its teeth met bone. Then it took him, jerking him unforgivingly into the stream as he shrieked a final time in sobering, hysterical anguish. The turbid water suddenly choked off the sound as he disappeared below the surface. Man and beast twisted rapidly in a churning, spiraling tango of death as blood spun a murky shroud, blackening their turbulence.

The last thing Lyle sensed was the frigid river water closing over his head. Then his world went mercifully dark.

5

"How did you do that?" Jack sounded incredulous, fascinated.

Brody was accustomed to his question and the other standards that skeptics had for him. His own mother and father had had the same questions when they first became aware something was quite out of the ordinary with their little three-year-old boy.

Over a bowl of Cheerios one morning at breakfast, right in front of Walter and Jane Whitaker, Brody had nonchalantly broached the subject of the untimely death of his maternal grandmother, Lily—Gram-Gram, as he knew her. He astonished his parents by asking them if Gram-Gram had fallen down the stairs.

Walter lowered his newspaper to half-staff. "*Ahem.* Why do you ask us that, Son?"

Brody kept eating. "Gram-Gram told me."

His stunned parents collected themselves, and Jane asked softly, "When did Gram-Gram tell you that, honey?"

"Last night, when I was in bed. You were asleep. She said she tripped over the cat. She hurt herself real bad."

Lily—a frail, slender woman, with a prominent dowager's hump from severe osteoporosis—lived with them for quite a few years and had died after falling down the stairs. What caused her to tumble and break her neck was never fully ascertained. The popular assumption was that she'd had an extreme vascular accident. Jane had found her, unresponsive, on the runner after returning home one evening from her canasta group, the family calico, Evie, curled up on Lily's buttocks, its tail waving languidly, purring.

Brody's father squeaked, "How could he—?" Then, "Son, you say she spoke to you in your bedroom?"

"Oh, sure. My bedroom, lots of places. She's here right now."

"Wha—?" Jane looked around. "Where is she? Where is Gram-Gram?"

Brody giggled. "She's sitting right next to us, Mommy. Can't you see her?"

His parents glanced at the fourth seat at the table.

"No, honey, I can't." She pointed to the chair. "She's right there?"

He giggled again. "Yes, silly! Right there! You see her, don't you, Daddy?"

"In that chair?" Walter asked, pointing.

"Yes, Daddy. Right there."

His folks came to realize that his conversations with them about loved ones who had passed were not typical child-making-things-up situations. Dutifully, though, they had him medically evaluated. The tests revealed no signs of any organic causation for his "delusions" of deceased family members, much to his parents' relief. His doctor chalked it up to "an overactive childhood imagination." Slowly, as Brody grew and could better articulate to them what he was experiencing, his parents gained a greater sense of what their son was capable of. Of course, they'd had the same questions about his gift as anyone else might.

And Jack and Jennifer were no exceptions.

"It's quite natural, really," Brody told them. "I've had this ability since I was a toddler. It freaked my parents out, I assure you."

"Well," Jennifer chuckled, dabbing at the moisture underneath her nose once more, "it certainly had that effect on me. Was my daughter here with us the whole time?"

"Her spirit presented itself to me as soon as I walked in. She merely waited until it was needful to communicate."

Jack cleared his throat. "You mean she knew when the proper time would be to initiate 'contact'?"

Brody smiled. "Let's just say she was very respectful of the moment."

"Are they all like that?" Jennifer asked.

"Spirits? No, some are quite content to let me prompt them, but others, unfortunately, can be as blunt and obtrusive as an obnoxious stand-up comedian. And some can be downright mean."

"Really?" Jack asked, his curiosity obviously getting the better of him.

"Yes, and I never know quite when or where they'll present themselves. It isn't always when it's convenient for me or when a client demands it, and that makes things difficult to explain to someone who has hired me to channel someone so important to them. Please, don't get me wrong—it works out fine the vast majority of the time, as spirits are genuinely seeking that bridge from their world to ours in order to present themselves, to truly connect with those they've left behind. But there are occasions when they refuse to cooperate, and under those circumstances, I have no alternative but to refuse payment for my services."

Jack appeared concerned with that confession. "So there might be times when this won't work?"

"It's possible," Brody told him. "But not probable. It's only happened to me twice before. In both of those instances, there were individuals present—other than the one who requested my services—whom the spirit likely was refusing to connect with. Those spirits weren't receptive to appearing, and I can only surmise that there were ulterior motives for that being so."

"Like what?" Jack asked.

"Hard to say, really. But if a spirit chooses to remain unseen or unheard by someone in particular, there's a sound reason. If a spirit wants to be heard, it will find a way."

"Well, that does kind of worry me, Brody. We planned to funnel a fair percentage of the station's time and efforts into this project, right, Jen?" Jack dipped his head in Jennifer's direction.

Sensing some hesitancy on Jack's part and not wanting to jeopardize the opportunity, Brody said, "Let me see if I can explain this better. When spirits cross over, they leave behind the souls who have touched them—helped guide them—throughout the course of their lives. Those souls who have yet to cross over—and we *all* will—"

Jack grunted.

"—yearn to tie up loose ends, so to speak. There are those who are instrumental in molding and shaping each of us in the physical world. Many in the spirit world have a need to communicate that's just as strong as that of the people they've influenced and left behind in the physical world.

Sometimes stronger. The vast majority of those spirits desire to make certain that no one they've left behind is consumed by guilt or left ill at ease over unanswered questions. They simply can't rest in peace until that task has been accomplished. It's why they present themselves so emphatically, and it's why Julie reached out to you today, Ms. Connors. It's also why so many of us have seemingly unexplainable occurrences in our lives—which guide us in certain endeavors or make us choose certain paths, if we allow them to or, at the very least, are receptive to them."

"You mean *fate*, don't you?" Jack asked.

"It's what many of us would refer to as 'fate,' yes. Others use 'destiny,' even though the two are often used interchangeably. But our paths are actually predetermined before we're born into this world. It's really more a question of faith."

Jack shifted in his seat. "You mean we're all just put here on some conveyor belt and moved along to a designated drop-off point? There's nothing we can do about it? That sounds kind of mechanistic and rather fatalistic, doesn't it? Seems pointless to me."

Jennifer scolded, "Let him finish, Jack, please. Despite whatever you're thinking, there's no way he could have known those things about Julie. No way."

Brody continued, "It's really much more than that, Mr. Walters. It's difficult to explain in a short amount of time. Believe me, it's taken me all my years just to glean this much, and I'm still learning, each and every day. It's more like this: Each individual soul on earth is placed here to touch certain other souls. We touch each other's lives, and those encounters—some seemingly by chance, though that is never the case—redirect our souls on whatever path God, or whatever higher power you believe in, has chosen for us. It's our life's lessons that truly shape our souls, dictate their journeys, and prepare them for the afterlife."

"So instead, are you saying this is all just a cosmic pinball game?"

"No, it's far more complicated than that. It was confusing to have it explained to me. And that was by those who were experiencing it already."

"Who explained it to you?" Jack asked.

"My grandmother Lily, when I was three."

"How could she have known about all that?"

"Well, she passed away three years before I was born. It was her spirit that shared with me those first few inklings from which I gained such insight."

Jennifer and Jack looked at each other.

"Her spirit taught me the most about the other side. It was she who told me that if a spirit fails to show itself to a gifted one who summons it, there is a reason known only to the spirit and the one or ones who are requesting it to be called forward. In those two unsuccessful instances I mentioned previously, I didn't pry. I figured that the reasons were either too private or just weren't meant for me to know."

Jack shifted in his seat. "Are there any other constraints we should be aware of that might not allow for these readings to be successful?"

"The only other necessity is that a spirit must be present in the same astral plane as me."

"This is sounding more hocus-pocus to me. Jennifer, how do you feel about all this?"

The producer placed her palms down on the table and leaned forward in her seat. "Jack, just a moment ago, weren't you asking Brody how he managed to do what he does? Now he's attempting to give us the benefit of some of his insight, and you've turned the other cheek?"

Jack retreated from his line of questioning, and Brody continued, "What I meant is that the spirit being called upon must be in the near vicinity; it can't be beyond a certain radius or boundary. That area varies from case to case, and I've never quite been able to pin down its limits, but suffice it to say that there must be something available to enhance the possibility of its appearance. There must be an individual or object or location that the spirit has attached itself to. I refer to those individuals and objects as 'bridges' and those locations as 'touchpoints.'"

"Touchpoints?" Jack repeated.

"Yes, sir. If any of those criteria are fulfilled, then the session is highly likely to be a success. As I said, I am rarely unable to connect when everything falls into place and the client is receptive."

"Brody," Jennifer said, "I'm eager to pick your brain about all of this, but the bottom line for the station is, will this work on camera?"

Jack added, "Can we count on your readings to bear fruit?"

Brody stated without hesitation, "Yes. I believe they will. I believe the spirits we will seek will be eager to appear. As I've said, it is their chance to close those gaps left behind by their passing with those whom they cherished most. I have found that these spirits make themselves readily available and are often the most willing."

Jennifer stared at Jack.

Jack turned to Brody once more. "My mother."

"Yes?" Brody asked.

"My mother. She died when I was ten. Is she here? Is she in this 'astral plane'? I wish to speak with her."

Brody blushed and leaned forward, with each hand slightly cupped, thumbs up, saying ardently, "It doesn't work like that, Mr. Walters."

"What do you mean? I want to talk to her. Isn't she eager to talk to me?" He sounded rebuffed.

"But she hasn't stepped forward here. I cannot conjure up a spirit. It is up to them, not me, to decide if and when they'll appear. And …"

"And what?"

Brody then folded his hands in front of him. "Unfortunately, you are not quite what I'd call receptive, sir. Ms. Connors, on the other hand …"

Jack harrumphed. "I have some real doubts about this, Jen. But this is your show, your baby. This is your tail on the line."

Jennifer smiled at her boss. "I'm well aware of whose tail this project rides upon. So if you'll stop riding mine, I have to say that he's convinced me."

Brody politely whispered, "It wasn't me who convinced you. It was Julie."

Jack rose from the table. "All right, you two. Jen, you finalize the details with Mr. Whitaker. I want this to remain on a trial basis." He turned back to Brody. "You understand, of course?"

Brody nodded. "Of course I do. You'll have a change of heart, Mr. Walters. What you see will change it; I'm confident of that."

"It's not my heart that needs changing with respect to this project. It's my mind."

⌐⁄⌐

Brody penned his signature to a one-year contract, the terms of which were generous, including a guaranteed advance of $25,000, provided that the initial session felt genuine and was deemed "fruitful" by Jack. In addition, there would be a per-segment, weekly remuneration of $5,000 if the twice-weekly segments proved popular enough to eventually build an entire half-hour show around. If so, Brody would be eligible for any syndication royalties—icing on the cake.

It was a welcome offer, impossible to refuse.

⌐⁓⌐

Jennifer was eager to begin with the initial session, straightaway. Initiating the "Clarksville Medium" project had been her urgent priority for several weeks; she was raring to go. The *Daily Show—Live*'s share for its time slot had sagged in recent months, and she had been promoted to produce this show to boost the station's ratings. The half hour that started off Clarksville's day needed an infusion of novelty, something to galvanize the community's involvement with WCVL. Add to that the next sweeps week looming, and she wanted that locomotive of hers to chug along unimpeded, full steam ahead.

So she hurriedly cleared the tracks. The director had already been tapped for the project, and he spent time prepping Brody on the various camera angles he'd incorporate into the production. A camera crew had been placed on standby for this morning and were in the process of checking their gear. The necessary sound checks were conducted on the microphones before the crew was to head out. Jennifer asked that Brody not be coached in any way once he was on site—she wanted the sessions to be as raw as possible; he was not to alter his style or technique at all.

With this brainchild of hers, she'd settle for no less than the acme of Clarksville reality TV.

⌐⁓⌐

Brody already had a client in mind: Mrs. Ida Fleming, a pleasant woman who ran a local florist shop—one of the phone messages he'd listened to prior to entering the bank that morning. She'd heard about Brody through a friend from church and had phoned him to schedule a session for the following week, seeking some closure about a dearly departed loved one. He called her back while he was finishing his paperwork at the station, and she was more than willing to drop everything and claim her spot as his first on-air reading, several days earlier than expected. Everything was falling into place nicely, and quickly.

En route to Ida's place, Brody thought about the gauntlet Jack had thrown down. Convincing him of the authenticity of the inaugural session for WCVL was going to be a challenge Brody was all too familiar with—but one he'd been rehearsing for his entire life.

Unfortunately Jack's mother had been unavailable to Brody during the meeting, or the task would already be complete. However, the mention of Jack's loss of his mother when he was of such a tender age had brought back to Brody a recollection of his own family tragedy.

His thoughts drifted to years earlier—one Saturday morning when, as a six-year-old, he had lain watching an episode of *Lassie* on television with his dog, Ruffy, beside him on their beanbag chair. The Whitakers had gotten this playful and intelligent Pomeranian as a puppy and proudly taught him several tricks over the years: fetch, roll over, sit, beg, shake.

Brody liked to reenact scenes from the show with Ruffy, coaxing his pet to role-play as the mighty canine icon. Ruffy watched the screen and would alert when Lassie barked. It was as though, at times, the little dog on the beanbag was totally in tune with the überdog from TV Land.

This episode, one of Brody's favorites, found Timmy—played by the youthful Jon Provost—having fallen into an untended and uncovered well on the family's property. Lassie raced away, searching hither and yon for any Samaritan who would affirm her frantic barking by following her and rescuing the lad in peril.

So Brody had devised a game to play with his dog based on that episode. Whenever he wanted Ruffy to fetch something, especially from upstairs, he'd whisper in his dog's ear, "Timmy's in the well, Ruffy." Ruffy would then race up the stairs, barking at anyone available, and retrieve whatever object Brody had laid out for him in the room. It was this diminutive pooch's shining moment to emulate the great and powerful watchdog Lassie herself.

Today, though, Brody simply wanted to play a trick on his slumbering parents.

"Ruffy." Brody took hold of his best bud's snout and looked him between the eyes, their faces close enough that they could smell each other's morning breath. Ruffy licked Brody's nose. "No, boy. Pay attention." Ruffy obeyed, holding his tongue. "Ruffy, Timmy's in the well. Timmy's in the well, boy!"

Ruffy leaped off the beanbag with flair and hit the ground running.

In a moment, Brody heard his father's irritated voice moaning, "Brody! Are you watching *Lassie* again?"

Brody covered his mouth with his hand and snickered.

From upstairs, Walter commanded the dog, "Go!"

Ruffy scampered downstairs, back to the security of his laughing master. The four-legged hero jumped up and down in delight, landing once on Brody's face.

"Let Ruffy out, please, Brody!" Walter shouted downstairs.

"All right!" he promised. Then he hugged Ruffy. "I'll let you out." He padded to the door, but superdog had beaten him to it.

It was Brody's responsibility on those quiet weekend mornings to let Ruffy out to do his business. "Business," to Ruffy, equated to pooing and peeing and squirrel chasing and newspaper fetching, all compressed into a fifteen-minute, jam-packed odyssey. Brody opened the door for his little buddy. "Out you go!"

Ruffy excelled in barking squirrels up trees and trotting the newspaper up to the door in the mornings, as a postlude to his early-morning constitutionals on the front lawn. However, this morning, Brody watched from the doorway as one particularly pesky rodent decided to lead Ruffy on a wild squirrel chase across the street and through the neighbors' yards.

Brody waited patiently for his dog to return, but after twenty minutes of careful surveillance, Ruffy was nowhere to be found. Frantically, Brody ran out to the sidewalk and looked up the street in the direction the furry little rocket had launched, but to no avail—the pooch wasn't returning. Worried, he decided to wake his parents to let them know that Ruffy was missing.

He reentered the house and was mounting the stairs when he noticed the spirit of Gram-Gram above him, on the rise.

"Don't wake them. Let them sleep, Brody. Ruffy will be back soon." She shook a bony finger at him.

Her advice flew in the face of Brody's judgment, so he figured he'd ignore it. He climbed a few stairs more, and Gram-Gram drifted down swiftly to intercept him.

She was persistent in her request. "Please, Brody. Let them sleep. Do it for your Gram-Gram?"

He was determined, however, to recruit his parents in the search for his companion, so he closed his eyes and stepped upward, passing right through

Gram-Gram. A sudden chill penetrated him as he did so, vanishing as quickly as it came. He looked back in wonder and then invaded his parents' bedroom.

"Mommy! Daddy!"

His mother woke with a start. "What? What is it, honey?" She began pulling on her pale-blue bathrobe almost instinctively from the urgency in her son's call.

"It's Ruffy! I let him out to go to the bathroom, and he's not back yet! I can't find him! He's *always* back by now!"

Walter's muffled voice emerged from beneath the pillow propped over his head. "He'll be home, Son. Don't worry."

"But I *am* worried!" Brody was bawling, his balled fists grinding his eyes.

"There, there, dear." His mother reached for a tissue and gave it to him. "I'll go find him. He can't be far."

Brody blew his nose.

"Janie, don't go out. He'll be back—he always comes back," Walter groaned.

"Oh, I don't mind," she said soothingly. She slipped her fuzzy turquoise house shoes on and took Brody by the hand. "Let Daddy sleep. We'll find him."

They closed the door to the bedroom and headed downstairs.

In the living room, Gram-Gram was pacing nervously. When she saw the two of them coming into the room, she looked at her grandson, pleading, "No! Nooo! Don't let her leave, Brody!"

Brody regarded his grandmother insubordinately. Ruffy had to be found!

Jane went to the coat closet for something to cover her conspicuous bed head—the object of her search being her favorite woolen cap. She retreated to the powder room to tease her salt-and-pepper strands up underneath the edges of the hat and emerged with fresh, staunch purpose.

Gram-Gram barred her path, but Jane continued right through her, unknowingly.

"*Ooob.*" She shivered. "There's a draft right there. Remind me to tell your father about it, okay?"

"Brody," Gram-Gram begged, "you've got to stop her. Tell her not to go outside!"

"Why?" Brody asked.

Assuming his reply had been directed her way, his mother gently reminded him, "Brody, I've asked you not to question me when I ask you to do something, haven't I? Please do as I ask and remind me to tell your father about the draft, okay?"

"But ..." Brody was frustrated, caught in the cross fire.

"No buts, young man."

He surrendered in futility. "Yes, Mommy."

"That's my little man. Now, I'll be right back. I'll find Ruffy; don't you worry."

She grabbed her cigarettes and lighter from the end table by the sofa and dropped them into the pocket of her robe. Taking the leash hanging by the entrance, she attempted to open the door, but her mother's spirit was pressing it as tightly closed as she could. Lily tried valiantly, with all her spectral strength, to keep it from budging but proved no match for the power of one so vital, so alive. As Jane tugged harder, the door, and Gram-Gram, finally yielded.

"Have your father look at this door too. It's sticking." She felt for a place along the jamb where it might have been bearing but, to her puzzlement, could find no such obvious defect. "Hmm. Okay, I'll be right back." She stepped onto the porch and closed the door behind her. The door gave no resistance at all in resealing.

Gram-Gram wearily slumped into Walter's easy chair, exhausted and anxious. "She shouldn't have gone, Brody. Shouldn't have gone."

"Why not, Gram-Gram?"

But she just shook her head. That was all she said—all she *could* say to him. It would be years later that he understood why she couldn't say more.

Confused, Brody went to the front window, drew back the sheers, and stood watch over the front yard, peering in the direction in which his dog and his mother had both disappeared. For twenty minutes—an eternity to him—he waited. Finally, he spotted his mother walking up the far sidewalk with Ruffy secured, the little Pomeranian alternately strutting and sniffing the grass. Brody pumped his fists triumphantly. "Yay! She found him!"

"Brody, come away from the window, child," his grandma implored, motioning him to her with her spinster's hands.

"Why, Gram-Gram?"

"Just do as I say, Brody. Pretty please, with sugar on top?"

But Brody stubbornly watched—his disobedience fueled by curiosity, not defiance—as his mom halted directly in front of their neighbor's picket fence across the lane, cigarette between her lips. As she reached into her pocket and grabbed hold of her lighter, the squirrel that had previously tempted Ruffy decided to play cat-and-mouse once more with its canine stalker. It scrambled down the tree whence it had fled and sped right in front of the dog and across the street, erecting itself on its haunches on the opposite curb, tail twitching provocatively.

Jane bent slightly to shield the flame as she lit her cigarette, and Ruffy, sensing slack in the line, bolted. The leash yanked from her hand as Ruffy jumped from the grass to the asphalt. Jane's woolen cap tumbled as she ran over and stomped her foot down on the leash. It tautened and jerked the dog into an undignified somersault while the squirrel hopped away to seek another elevated bivouac.

Jane stepped into the street and picked up her little Pomeranian, hugging him to her chest and stroking his withers.

Brody watched her comfort the dog, and everything at that instant was perfection in his world. That was when the truck slammed into them from behind, catapulting his mother and hurling Ruffy into the air. The driver, who had been speeding through their sleepy residential neighborhood, heavily hung over from Friday night's revelries, jammed on his brakes, honking a tardy warning a split second before impact—much too late to alter the outcome.

Jane Whitaker would travel more than twenty-two feet in the air—according to later law enforcement measurements—coming to rest on the white dividing line in the street. Tiny Ruffy was located much farther away—on the grass of the neighbor's house at the base of the very tree from which the squirrel had originated its fateful torment. The squirrel's inquisitive rival shimmied down the same oak, sniffing the air around the lifeless dog, and then climbed back to its arboreal safety net.

Brody didn't cry out in horror; he stood transfixed, in shock. He stared at the scene of the accident as Walter, awakened by the sound of the intrusive horn, the skid, and what must have been an instinctual sense of something gone terribly wrong, rushed down to the living room.

"Brody? What happened?" he asked as he pulled on his robe, not bothering with tying it.

His son turned, ashen faced. Gram-Gram was sobbing in the La-Z-Boy.

"Son? Where's your mother?"

He stared at his father.

"Where's your mom, Son?" Walter grasped his boy by the shoulders, gently inducing the words from him. "Brody? Answer me, please."

"She ... got hit."

"What?" Walter bolted out the door. Panicked, he saw his wife's body crumpled in the street, barely covered by her robe. He raced to her, shouting out, "*Help!* Help me! Someone call an ambulance! Please!"

Brody temporarily anchored himself in the open doorway as his father knelt beside his mother, taking her in his arms, sobbing. Walter was dutifully attempting to reposition the torn garment around his wife's bloody torso and legs, hands shaking beyond control.

"Help! Call an ambulance!" Walter yelled again to anyone in earshot. He was holding his beloved, wailing, "Janie! Janie!"

As his father cried to his mother in tender persistence, Brody ventured timidly down to the end of the front walk, where he stopped and watched. In that precise instant, the only things he could perceive in the entire universe at large were his father in the middle of the street, clutching his mother, rocking back and forth on his knees, calling out her name over and over, and the spirit of his mother standing directly behind his father, her white-gloved hand perched lightly on his shoulder. She was there for a brief instant and then her form dispersed—fragment after fragment of her, carried away by the cool morning breeze.

6

TEDDY pushed the gas pedal to the floor and revved the Olds. Shaken and sick to his stomach, appalled at what had just transpired, he shook his head, trying desperately to combat the queasiness.

"Bro-man. Lyle. What the hell happened?" But true understanding escaped him. Struggling to concentrate, he turned only once to look at the maroon sheen on the upholstery, and then he drove on in stunned silence, Creedence Clearwater Revival's "Bad Moon Rising" blaring from the radio: *"I know the end is coming soon."*

Ahead of him a car was pulled over on the side of the road. As he approached, the color of the vehicle gave him pause to slow down—it was red, with a broken taillight and a black racing stripe! A Challenger!

He whispered in delight, "What the *fu-uck?*"

The occupant had left his door open and was standing among the weeds several yards from the highway, taking a whiz.

Well, how do you like that? Surprise, surprise!

Teddy accelerated to eighty, aiming for the open car door. He struck the door with his right fender, ripping it cleanly from the body of the vehicle and sending it careening onto the roadway ahead. It threw off a shower of sparks as it tumbled and scraped across the rough asphalt, clattering to a halt in the middle of the highway.

"I hear the voice of rage and ruin."

The figure in the grass wheeled around.

Teddy jammed on his brakes and skidded the car onto the shoulder, leaving the engine idling and John Fogerty singing. Teddy exited his vehicle with purpose and advanced on the Challenger.

"It's bound to take your life."

The driver of the Dodge ran up to his disfigured car. He bent over, inspecting where the door had previously been. "Are you crazy?" he shouted as he rose next to his mangled sports car.

"Yeah, maybe so," Teddy yelled back. "Didn't you see me back yonder? You damn near ran me off the road." He was laser focused on the burly man's eyes, anger bubbling inside him like a wellspring, rising to the surface. There was only he walking for revenge—there was no Lyle beside him now. No voice of reason. No buffer. No restrictions, no constraints.

The man took a step or two forward. He balled his fists, squinting. "Yeah, so? That makes this right, asshole?"

As the gap closed between them, Teddy reached behind his waist. "No, motherfucker," he flatly stated. "This does." He whipped his pistol around and shot five rapid rounds point-blank at the jackass.

The man flinched as he caught sight of the weapon. The split-second reaction was enough time for three of the slugs to find their target—in his chest, arm, and abdomen. He toppled backward, bloodied and lifeless before his head struck the pavement.

"There's a bad moon on the rise."

Teddy walked up to the dead man and stood over him. "Now you're the color of your pussy ride." He spat on the corpse and pointed his pistol at the dead man's forehead, firing twice more. Brains and blood erupted like pulp from an exploding watermelon.

"And *that's* because my brother would have told me no."

He replaced the warm Hardballer into his waistband. Slicking back his hair as he revolved and then grabbing both edges of his leather jacket chest-high, he strutted back to his car. He took a long stride or two and then chided, "Don't *ever* fuck with an Olds, a-hole."

He was fortunate there were no witnesses in sight along that stretch of road, not that it would have deterred him. As he reentered the car and tweaked the knob on the dashboard, Blue Öyster Cult's "Don't Fear the Reaper" intro riff was commencing.

Teddy banged rhythmically on the dash. "Need more cowbell!"

He laughed—Lyle would have appreciated that one! He closed his door and proceeded home again.

⌇

The television crew was setting up in the living room of Ida Fleming's modest home. The key grip and gaffer arranged and adjusted several HMI Fresnel lights, along with a couple of umbrella reflectors strategically placed around Brody and Mrs. Fleming. Everything was carefully readied to capture the first in the series of readings from the Clarksville Medium, Brody's newly assigned nickname, suggested by Jennifer. He was proud of the sound of it and was hopeful it would catch on.

Brody requested a brief isolation in which to meditate, clear his thoughts. Some mediums performed a sage cleansing or smudging ritual prior to connecting, in order to eliminate any negative energy from a room or house, an ancient practice of shamanic and Native American cultures, but Brody had yet to find doing so necessary.

He was nervous, not knowing what to expect. Of all the sessions he had conducted, in this one it was essential that the spirits cooperate. It would either herald the beginning of something life altering for him or turn out to be a gross waste of time for the television station. Which would it be?

He sat there on a cushion on the floor and cleared his worries away. Then he took one last deep, cleansing breath and rose.

He did not see Mrs. Fleming until they took their seats across from each other in her living room, separated by her coffee table—she on an expansive tufted couch and he on a floral-printed brocade chair. She'd revealed no details of her hopes to Brody beforehand and agreed right then and there to film cutaways with the producer after the initial experience with the medium was completed. With a soft face and a gentle smile and wearing a pale-pink blouse tied in a large bow at her neck and a straight khaki skirt, she sat upright, hands resting in her lap. She allowed the makeup personnel to finish touching up her powder and blush and to drape her jet-black single braid over her left shoulder. The key grip handed Brody a box of tissues, and Brody placed it on the table, nearby his client.

The sound engineer finished the microphone placements, conducted his sound checks, and gave the producer the signal to commence. The second assistant cameraman readied his camera while the director gave a countdown. "Three, two, one." The director pointed at Brody, and the session began.

"Mrs. Fleming, I'm Brody Whitaker."

"Hello." She smiled warmly.

"Hello. I'm here today to help answer some questions about your loved ones who have crossed over to the other side and who were near and dear to you. It is not important that you believe in whether or not they are here with us now, only that you are receptive to what they will say to you through me. It is my hope that you will leave this session with heaviness lifted from your heart and a strong sense of closure. Are you ready?" He looked directly into her amber-flecked eyes.

"Yes, yes I am, Mr. Whitaker. Please."

"Have we ever met before, Mrs. Fleming?"

"No, sir. Never."

"So I've had no acquaintance with you or knowledge of any of the spirits associated with you prior to this session, is that correct?"

"Yes, that is correct."

Brody swept all irrelevant thoughts away; his mental focus shifted to connecting with the other side, a skill that he had mastered over time. It came as effortlessly now to him as breathing. Whatever corner of his mind that drove that process, it was as though he could shift it into turbo at will, even with his eyes wide open.

It didn't take long before a male figure appeared to him just behind the couch over Ida's left shoulder. He was wearing a fishing vest speckled with lures and a tan hat with a wide 360-degree brim, itself replete with more tied flies hooked through a multicolored band. There were five large, diagonal slashes in the canvas of his vest. They were nearly parallel and ragged, some completely perforating the material.

"There is a male figure that's passed. Your husband."

"Oh," she gasped, not quite prepared for her roller-coaster ride to lurch forward so abruptly. She yanked a single tissue from the box and clasped it.

"Spirits sometimes present themselves to me in the way they appeared when they passed, as a way for me to ascertain certain circumstances surrounding their deaths. Oftentimes, they will then shape-shift to a form free of the physical infirmities that manifested when they were in the physical world. Their doing so allows me to allay the concerns of their loved ones as to how their eternal souls are resting. Your husband has come forward wearing a fishing vest and hat; he was on a fishing excursion when he crossed over."

"Yes." She choked back a sob. "Yes, he was. He was away in Alaska when he passed. He was fly-fishing with a dear friend, Jim. For salmon."

Brody nodded. "There are several large gashes through his vest. They are linked to his passing."

"Yes. He—he hooked a very large salmon, a Chinook. It was a real beauty, according to his friend. But they weren't the only ones after salmon that day."

"He says a bear attacked him."

"Yes, a big grizzly. Art and Jim didn't see it, because they were minding their own business, having the time of their lives. Art held up his fish to show Jim, and that's when the bear … It slashed him, stole the salmon, and disappeared into the woods by the shore. Jim dropped his rod and creel and waded against the current over to Art. By the time Jim reached him to try to help, Arthur was bleeding out. He got to Arthur just as he collapsed into the cold water, before the current would have swept him away. He dragged my husband's body back to shore. With such a massive wound, the authorities said that nothing could have saved him." She began to weep, attempting to cover her face with the tissue. "Just struck him down …" she sobbed. "He was only fishing …"

Arthur placed his hand gently on his wife's shoulder, and she looked up, glancing toward the spirit of her husband. She turned to Brody, confused.

"That was Arthur, Mrs. Fleming. He's standing right behind you. He just touched your shoulder."

She stared at Brody, the camera capturing her expression, a mixture of disbelief and awe. The cameraman and director exchanged a subtle nod of affirmation, smiling. That footage was golden!

"He's conveying the number sixty-three."

"That was how old Art was when this happened."

"Now he wants me to ask you about a blackberry."

"Oh my God," she said quietly. "Some of the only recordings I have left of his voice are his memos to me from his Blackberry. He would make entries of places we went together, things we did, and just random thoughts throughout the day—of me. They were like love letters. He left his phone back in his tent, and the authorities returned it to me. I play them over and over, listening to him speaking to me. It reminds me of him, keeps me nearer to his memory."

"He wants you to know he didn't suffer in Alaska; he believes you've been concerned over that."

"Yes," she admitted, "I have been. I mean, a bear *mauls* you. Don't you feel a lot of pain? Don't you hurt in some way as your life seeps from you?"

Brody left his chair and sat down beside the shaken woman. He took her hand in his. She immediately straightened in her seat, seeming more at ease, appearing revitalized.

He continued, "Mercifully, he felt no grave discomfort after the attack. It was because his last thoughts were of you—he wants you to know that. Arthur recalled your most recent anniversary trip to Venice and holding you in the gondola, the moonlight reflecting off the canal as the two of you floated along. He thought it fitting he was breathing his last upon the water, floating there. His final thought was when he met you in college, how you used to sleep over in his dorm room, against the rules, the both of you risking expulsion, as you would risk so many things to remain together through the years."

Her grip tightened.

"Ida?"

"Yes?"

"He wants me to tell you one last thing." Brody released her hand.

"Yes, what is it?"

Art led Brody silently once more.

"He wants me to tell you that some very hurtful things he did … well, he knows you kept silent about them all those years. He feels ashamed for his actions, and he wants you to know that you were always the love of his life. Arthur never told you he was sorry; he only tried to atone for those transgressions. He is grateful for your forgiveness, your loyalty to him and your love, and hopes he was able to repay you in kind, at least in part, for your devotion to him. It was the biggest regret of his life."

With tears in her eyes, Ida glanced away from the camera, trying to maintain her composure as best she could. Finally, resisting and caring no more, she collapsed into Brody's empathetic embrace, and he held her as she wept uncontrollably. When the floodgates had finally closed, she released herself and sat back on the sofa, sighing deeply.

Brody spoke softly and delicately to her. "I hope today provided some closure for you."

"Yes. Yes, it truly has."

"Good."

"Thank you so much."

"Thank you, Ida, for letting me speak to Arthur and, in turn, letting him speak to you today. Those who depart from us can only let us know in the most subtle of ways that they are still present in spirit, watching over us. Often it's through understated but observable occurrences: a light that inexplicably turns itself on, a keepsake that mysteriously turns up or moves, a gentle breeze or the sensation of a light touch, a stray animal that suddenly adopts us— these are all methods our loved ones use to remain connected to our lives in some small way. I am only a conduit through which they can communicate, in a semblance of their original fashion, once more."

"I understand."

"The love you and Arthur experienced is something to be cherished. Know that he remains with you in spirit—he is always close at hand, just as he was always close at heart."

She sniffed. "That's such a comfort, Mr. Whitaker; it really is. Knowing he's here now is such a gift. I can't tell you what this has meant to me."

He hugged her again. "And to me as well, Ida. I'm so sorry for your loss. I hope this has brought you peace."

"You have no idea," she told him with conviction.

With that, the lights extinguished, and the camera ceased recording. The crew began packing up. They patted each other on the back and thanked Brody for what would surely be an exceptional moment in broadcasting for the local affiliate. The cutaways captured in Ida's rose garden and edited into the main footage later, at the station, concluded with this memorable sound bite:

"At the very beginning, I was skeptical of this experience. I really didn't know what to expect. Would I hear from Arthur or not? How would I know if this person was actually communicating with him or if it was just a fabrication? Well, the bear attack was well documented. But there's no way he could have known about my keeping Art's Blackberry—that was the exact word I was waiting for, my trigger to really believe. There's no way he could've known that. Not even Jim knew about those messages that I listen to faithfully, every day. And he certainly had no inkling of Art's regretful behavior.

"I now believe Brody Whitaker is the real thing. He has convinced me beyond a shadow of a doubt that today I actually spoke with my departed husband, Arthur Fleming. This is a day I'll never forget."

⌇

Abigail Whitaker sat in her last class of the day—English. Her class had been assigned a book normally reserved for students a grade or two ahead of them, H.G. Wells's *The Invisible Man*, for Abby's teacher, Ginny Thompson, constantly implored her pupils to challenge their mental faculties. This particular tale appealed to Abby, for it dealt with certain themes to which she felt a kinship. She certainly wasn't invisible, but, like the novel's protagonist, Dr. Jack Griffin, she was experiencing some unique phenomena, the same her father had described as happening to him in his childhood.

"Abby," Mrs. Thompson, an energetic and youthful second-year instructor, said from the front of the classroom, "can you tell the class how Dr. Griffin actually made himself invisible?"

But Abby was glancing out the window, down to the street beyond the playground fence. *There he is again: that man!*

The man was sitting on a bench mostly just minding his own business, yet oddly, he was dressed in a full wetsuit, with a scuba tank, mask, and fins. Occasionally, he looked up at her classroom window, lifted his mask, and waved! As peculiar as this sight was across from a public school, not one passerby ever noticed him or cared, even those who randomly sat down next to him or, at times, directly upon him!

Abby had been witnessing this strange sight for several weeks, but the man had not been as noticeable as he was now. What began as distortions in the air over the bench—like heat waves off a scorching summer road—had taken shape over time. It started with a head, and then slowly the body parts each materialized, week after week, until finally, she'd witnessed a full form assembled, sitting there, waving to her!

"Abby? Are you daydreaming again?"

Red-faced, Abby redirected her thoughts to her teacher's original question.

"Well, my daddy explained it to me like this: Dr. Griffin knew all about how light is bent by certain things, like glass, when it passes through them. But it doesn't bend at all when it passes through air."

"Very good. Now, how did he make himself invisible to everyone? Did your father explain that to you?"

"Yes, ma'am. Since air doesn't bend or absorb light, Dr. Griffin invented some chemicals to make his body treat the light just like air does, and he became invisible." She folded her hands upon her notebook.

"That's right, Abby. That was a nice explanation."

"Mrs. Thompson, Mrs. Thompson?" A short, freckle-faced, towheaded boy was waving his hand.

"Yes, Lewis? What is it?"

"Umm, what does Abby mean by air not absorbing light?"

"Well ... Abby, you wish to try that one too?"

"Sure." Abby smiled. "Absorb, a-b-s-o-r-b. Lewis, you know that *absorb* means to take in or soak up something, like a sponge soaks up water or how our cereal gets soggy—by absorbing the milk. Air doesn't absorb any light at all—light passes right through it. That's why we don't see light passing through plain air during the daytime, we just see where it starts and where it strikes."

"Very good, Abby. Does that answer your question, Lewis?"

"Yes, ma'am. Thank you, Abby."

Abby gave him a minisalute.

"Mrs. Thompson?"

"Yes, Kanisha?"

A cute African American girl added, "I don't think Miranda absorbed all her chocolate milk at lunch. I saw her *un*absorb most of it in the hallway, and, like Abby said, I saw where it started from and where it hit. It was gross. The janitor, Mr. Mays—he cleaned it up. She was sent home."

Mrs. Thompson raised an eyebrow. "Oh, I see. Well, Kanisha, that's another good example. Thank you for bringing that to our attention."

Kanisha grinned and mimicked Abby's hand gesture of respect.

The school bell rang loudly in the hall outside the classroom door, and the teacher spoke quickly so her charges heard their next assignment before they all vamoosed. "Class, I want you to read the next chapter in the book by Friday. We'll have a quiz on Monday. Don't forget to turn in your homework, please, in the box on my desk. Have a super evening, and I'll see everyone tomorrow. Class dismissed."

A flurry of activity—shuffling of books into backpacks, chairs jostling, and jackets being zipped—began in the classroom as the students busied themselves in the preparations for departure.

"Oh, Abby?" Mrs. Thompson stood up.

"Yes, Mrs. Thompson?" Abby was just slinging her backpack over her shoulders.

"May I see you for a second?"

"Yes, ma'am." *Oh no. What have I done? Is she upset with me for daydreaming? Uh-oh!*

"What did you do?" whispered Abby's best friend, Maddie, who was standing beside the chair next to Abby.

"I don't know," Abby whispered back.

"Well, I'll be waiting in my mom's car downstairs, okay?"

"Okay."

"I hope it's nothin' bad."

"Me too." Abby adjusted her backpack, cinching the straps to balance the weight.

Maddie gave her one more look of concern before she exited the room, holding up crossed fingers behind her back for good luck.

Abby smiled at her friend's support and then trudged up to her teacher's desk. She placed her homework paper neatly in the tray. "Yes, ma'am?"

"Abby, you are a bright young woman, very intelligent for your age."

"Thank you, ma'am." She swallowed hard. *But ...*

"I think you are destined for greater accomplishments."

Abby relaxed; this sounded good, not bad!

"Since you were the winner of the Montgomery Central Middle School spelling bee last week, it is my privilege to tell you I will soon have your word lists for the county-wide spelling bee to be held in January."

Oooh, yes! "Yes, ma'am! I mean, thank you, ma'am. That's sooo exciting!"

Mrs. Thompson laughed. "You've earned it, Abby. You surpassed students who were even a grade higher than you. I should have the study materials and word lists to you sometime next week."

"Yes, Mrs. Thompson." Abby beamed.

"But you have to really concentrate on your studying. If you apply yourself as I believe you will, you could win the state-wide competition. Promise?"

"Yes, Mrs. Thompson! Yes, ma'am, I promise!"

"Now run along and tell your father. I know how proud he'll be of you."

"Yes, Mrs. Thompson. *Oh boy!*" She ran out the door and down the stairs. She couldn't wait to tell her daddy the news.

Sergeant David Jeffries's work on the robbery case was only beginning. His next destination was the Dollar General, for a conversation with Grady Minton, the owner and manager, and one of his employees who'd seen a stranger loitering behind the building. A neighbor across the street from the rear of the store had heard gunshots and called 911. The officer investigating the call had determined there might be some connection to the earlier bank robbery, so the sergeant had been entrusted with the department's follow-up.

David was all too familiar with the employee: Billy Coonrod, Grady's stock boy and a local jock who'd been a little too fresh with someone near and dear to David—his daughter, Kaylee. The incident had occurred the past Friday night after a high school football game, so the ill feelings hadn't diminished much. Kaylee was on a date with Billy and had come home visibly shaken, over an hour late, her blouse torn. Initially, she told her father that nothing had happened—she'd merely torn her clothing on a tree branch while walking home. But tree branches rarely tore three buttons off a brand-new top. And there was no rationale David could imagine that could justify Kaylee having to walk home alone in the middle of the night.

Finally, long after she supposedly had gone to bed, she knocked on her father's bedroom door and related the entire sordid episode to him. Billy, underage, had drunk a few beers and became belligerent, refusing to accept *no* as her answer to his request to round second base and continue on to third. So Kaylee had extricated herself forcibly from his clutches and climbed out of the car.

"Fine," Billy berated her, slamming the passenger door. "Walk home, then." There were two genuine problems with that directive: it was one o'clock in the morning, and they were a mile and a half from said destination. A real gentleman he'd turned out to be! It had certainly tainted David's opinion of the star athlete.

Most of the boys in school were circumspect when it came to Kaylee, knowing full well her dad was a police sergeant. Billy's father, however, was sheriff of Montgomery County and had a reputation for being somewhat lax when it came to his son, allowing Billy just enough rope to hang himself at times. Billy exploited the laxity in his reins to be a tad more unbridled than the average maverick, bolstered by the fact that, in addition to his old man being sheriff of the county, Billy was a gifted quarterback, with heavy Division I recruitment. Billy's tendency to overlook basic etiquette and chivalry failed to endear him to a good many of the morally correct young women in school.

David knew it wasn't the time to confront Sheriff Coonrod about his progeny's lascivious behavior. Hell, David hadn't detected even a whiff of an apology from either the sheriff or his wayward son. The fellow lawman's apparent aloofness over the matter suggested that he'd apparently turned a blind eye to his boy's plundering and blundering through yet another chapter in his saga of sowing wild oats. So David had done the only things he could do when his daughter had come to him: heard her out, hugged her, comforted her, and assured her that she had made every proper decision in the book, regarding one of *the* most difficult of adolescent circumstances. Her cell phone had died during the date, and, as a result, David had been unaware of the need to rescue her. His guilt was overwhelming; he was used to being his only child's knight in shining armor.

When he'd heard he would be interviewing the lothario who had abandoned his daughter to trek home in the wee small hours of the morning, he wasn't exactly conducive to the most professional train of thought. Reminding himself that he needed to shelve his emotions and stick to protocol, he walked into the store and asked the beehive-hairdoed cashier for the manager, flashing his shield. He waited next to cartons of Mountain Dew and stacks of Styrofoam coolers while Grady Minton was summoned.

"Howdy, Officer," Grady said as he approached. Grady was a heavyset man with an emphasized local drawl, halitosis, and body odor that correlated vaguely with the local dew point—the higher, the stronger. That day the dew point was fortunately rather low.

"Grady, how's business?"

"Pretty good—lots of dollars in gen'ral," he laughed.

The young quarterback sidled up behind his boss. Billy was a stud looker, but his horse sense sometimes took a backseat to his physical attributes.

"Hi, Sergeant Jeffries, sir. Listen, about last Friday night—"

David held up his hand to halt him. "Don't even go there, young man," he warned.

"But, sir, I wanted to—"

"I've got a gun, Billy. No jury would convict me." David made a slight move to unholster his weapon, and the quarterback turned tail and fled to the rear of the store.

"That wasn't necessary," Grady told him.

They stared hard at each other, and then they both laughed.

"But it was purty good, purty damn good," Grady said. "I gotta hand it to ya. I know he had that comin' to 'im, but believe it or not, from what he tol' me 'bout how he treated your daughter, I think he's feelin' purty remorseful 'bout it."

"Well, unfortunately, I'm not in much of a charitable mood today. I'll let him know I wasn't really going to shoot him, but first I want to ask you some questions about what happened here a little earlier today."

"Sure, sure."

He took out his recorder and readied it for capture. "Grady Minton, manager of Dollar General. Tuesday, 4:00 p.m. What can you tell me about the incident at the rear of the store that took place earlier today?"

"Well, this bein' a teacher in-service day at the high school an' all, there warn't any classes, so Billy was workin' a long shift today." He inched closer to the recorder. "Uh, that's Billy Coonrod, my stock boy. At 'bout quarter to ten this mornin', I had the young man takin' the empty boxes out to the trash like he always does, and a couple a minutes later, he come runnin' back in, all out of breath and ever'thang, tellin' me there was a vagrant with a gun out yonder, sittin' by one a our Dumpsters."

"Then what?"

"So I grabbed my shotgun from the office an' run out back. When I slammed the outside door open, I musta skeered 'im, 'cause he started hightailin' it towards Union. I called out a warnin' tellin' 'im to stop, that I was gonna call the *po*-leese. The guy flipped me off! Then he looked like he might've been reachin' fer a gun, so I fired a few rounds up in the air 'bove 'im just to skeer 'im."

"To scare him?" the sergeant repeated, translating for the sake of future dictation and reiterating for his own clarity in the line of questioning.

"Um-hmm."

"Uh-huh. And?"

"I think one mighta clipped 'im, 'cause he kinda stumbled toward the street."

"You shot him?"

"No! I shot *at* 'im. But I think I mighta nicked 'im, what with the way he stumbled. Hey," he whispered, "I gotta right to defend my store an' my employees, right?"

David sighed. "We've been through this before, Grady. You have a right if someone is in your store or on your property and threatening you or your employees directly with bodily harm." He recalled the incident a couple of years back in which Grady had shot and wounded a teenager rummaging through one of the Dollar General's Dumpsters. The teen's mother hadn't brought any charges, because the kid was found to be on a gang-related mission and accompanied by a large Bowie knife. Otherwise, the store owner could easily have been facing jail time.

Grady's beady eyes darted around nervously.

"All right," Officer Jeffries said. "Let's go talk to Billy."

They walked to the rear of the store and found Billy sitting on the cement incline near the garbage bin, biting his nails. He rose as they approached, spitting out the most recent crescent of fingernail. Sergeant Jeffries readied his recorder again.

"Billy Coonrod, Dollar General stock boy. Billy, tell me what you saw when you came out back of the store the first time this morning." He paused the recording and whispered, "And I'm not going to shoot you."

Looking relieved, Billy related his version. "Well, I pushed the cart out here to sling the garbage bags into the Dumpster, and I noticed this boot stickin' out from behind it on the ground over there," he said, pointing to the spot. "I thought someone had just left that old shoe over there, so I went to pick it up, but it was attached—to someone. Scared the *shit* outta—oh, sorry ..."

David held up his hand. "I'm familiar with the word, Billy. Go on."

"Well, it really scared me when I saw this scroungy-lookin' dude sittin' there with his back against the wall. I told him he couldn't hang here—he had to leave. That's when I noticed he had a gun inside his jacket. So I ran back inside to get Mr. Minton and told him what I'd seen."

"So, the two of you came back out here again?"

"Yeah. I mean, *yes*, sir."

Billy's politeness wasn't exactly warming David's icy cockles.

"Mr. Minton grabbed his shotgun and looked like he meant business."

"What do you mean 'looked like he meant business'?"

"Well, Mr. Minton doesn't like people hangin' out back here. He lets them know—"

"Tell Off'cer Jeffries what happened next, Billy," interrupted Grady. He widened his eyes slightly at the young man, who nervously shifted his balance.

Noting the exchange, David sighed. "What happened next, Billy?"

"Well, Mr. Minton saw the guy runnin' toward the street and warned him he was goin' to call the cops. Then he pointed his gun in the direction of the guy and fired some warnin' shots."

"He pointed his gun in the man's direction and then fired the shots?"

Grady stared hard at Billy, clenching his jaw.

"Y-yeah. He did, and I guess one of the bullets hit the guy, because he sort of stumbled, I guess."

"Did the man reach for his gun or appear threatening in any way?"

"I don't know, sir."

"What do you mean you don't know?"

Billy blushed slightly. "Well, I don't see real good far away."

"You ... don't see real well far away?"

"No, sir."

David thought about the logic for a second. "Well, how do you get the ball downfield to your receivers if you aren't able to see them accurately?"

Billy stammered, "My ... receivers make me look good, I guess. I get by with my eyesight on the field, but sometimes it's hard for me to see things that far, believe me."

Believe him? That was a tall order! "So you couldn't see if the man was reaching for his gun?"

"No, but it looked like he was." The young man sounded less and less convincing.

"So which is it, Billy? You couldn't see the guy, or he looked like he was reaching for his gun?"

"I couldn't see him real good, but he looked like he might've been reachin' for it. I don't know—it all happened so fast."

David could see he wasn't going to get much further with the two of them. It was pretty clear that this exchange had been rehearsed—Billy was covering for his employer, and the youth was not a convincing liar.

"That's all I need, Billy," he sighed. "Thanks for talking to me. Thanks, Grady. I'm gonna have a look around back here, okay?"

"Yeah, sure, sure," Grady said.

"Then I'll be back to talk with *you*, Grady."

Grady swallowed hard.

As David turned away from them, Grady grabbed Billy by the arm and dragged him inside, the heavy door shutting with a bang.

7

TEDDY slammed the front door and began pacing the living room. *What the hell?*

He reassessed his situation. They'd robbed a bank with nothing—*not a damn thing!*—to show for it. His brother had been gunned down, was dead. He'd left Lyle's body to rot by the side of the water. He'd shot and killed an asshole. *Well, at least that's one less a-hole!* So he'd committed a pair of felonies while sacrificing his best friend in the world, his only other living family member, his anchor to sanity.

He tugged at both sides of his hair and uttered animalistic grunts, stomping back and forth. Finally he came to rest at the mirror by the front door. An unrecognizable face stared back from the glass. It registered somewhere in his brain that that must be him, but his eyes went fuzzy, the reflection unclear.

He roundhoused his left fist and shattered the glass, the mirror frame tumbling to the floor. Littered shards surrounded his feet, and he crunched back a few steps. He kept retreating, into the kitchen, collapsing blindly into the chair his brother had occupied that same morning.

"Lyle, Lyle! What am I supposed to do now, bro-man?" Teddy rested his arm on top of the table, planted his face thereon, and let the dam burst. "Lyle. Why'd you leave me, man?"

He kicked the nearby wall; a partial black footprint then adorned the pale-blue drywall he indented from the impact. After a good long while, he sat back in the chair, slicking back his hair. He left his hands laced together behind his head, nervously tapping the toes of his worn calfskin Justins on the desiccated, peeling linoleum. His mind was starting to clear; the fog was lifting, gradually.

The car! What would he do about the car? The blood might be cleanable. It would take time and require some detailing, but that could be accomplished. Couldn't it? Although now there was front-end damage to boot—where he'd impacted the a-hole's car door. Nothing drastic, but it *was* obvious. Drivable, sure, but fixable? Not without insurance. Not without the cash.

The cash! The money! Where the fuck *is the money? What in the name of hell did Lyle do with it?* He had to go back to that damn Dollar General real soon, after the heat died down, to look for it.

But he couldn't take his car again; he'd have to take Lyle's. Too risky to be recognized in the car that had been cruising around town on the day of the heist. *Yeah, the El Camino!* He hadn't driven that baby in years—with Teddy's two DUIs, Lyle had forbidden it. *Well, Lyle ain't here no more, so Lyle can't care!*

He went to Lyle's bedroom and rummaged through his dresser drawers, finding the keys in the middle one, behind the Fruit of the Looms. Along with the trio of keys, a mint-green rabbit's foot was looped onto the lanyard. Teddy snorted at the good-luck charm. *Lotta good that fuckin' thing did!* But it did feel good to hold it—it was Lyle's.

His reflection in the mirror over the dresser appeared haggard; his face, worn. *Shit—the beard!* The beard must go.

He traipsed down the hall to the bathroom, took out a pair of manicure scissors, and began to snip away at the ragged whiskers. They tumbled into the sink, drifting down to arrange themselves in random, raveled clumps, a hairy metaphor for his life at present. After removing an inch or so from his chin, he next turned to one of the Bic disposables in the medicine cabinet and some Barbasol. He nicked himself only once in the entire process. He toweled away the tiny ooze of blood along with the remainder of the foam.

For the second time that afternoon, he barely recognized himself; it had been years since he'd seen his own jawline. *Pretty damn decent*, he thought. Then he laughed, and his critique performed an about-face. He had to find that money; he *had* to do something about those missing teeth!

As he changed his clothes, balling the present outfit on the chair in his bedroom, he decided to do the easy thing with the Olds—just get rid of it. It really boiled down to him being too lazy to attempt the purging of every iota of Lyle's DNA, and it was too awkward to have to explain all the new front-end damage, especially if law enforcement came poking around.

Carlos, from stir, had set up a chop shop outside of town. Teddy figured he'd donate it to the cause. Hell, this would be the tenth car he and his brother had brought Carlos this year, so Carlos would even award him shuttle service home! *Pretty good deal: get rid of the evidence, plus a free ride*, he thought as he headed back outside to divest himself of the damaged car.

⌐✗⌐

Sheriff Cletus Coonrod drove up on the scene just north of the river on US 48/79—Wilma Rudolph Road—and ground to a stop partially into the weeds, service lights flashing. He shifted uncomfortably in the seat, expelling some gas, compliments of the burritos he'd wolfed down a few hours earlier. He gave an immune sniff and vented his door, shifting his substantial physique to the lateral aspect of his seat and then dropping his left service boot down heavily onto the sunbaked shoulder of the road.

Surveying the scene, he sighed. Several deputies were either hunkered down around a body, poring over a red Challenger, or canvassing the crime scene. One was swinging a metal detector in wide arcs over the tips of the weeds.

The sigh signified lamentation over Cletus's own requisite movement rather than theirs; whatever shitstorm had been heaped up here, it was about as devastating as that which threatened the interior of his ride. He helped himself out of the car, reeling in his hat from the front seat and rounding off his recent crew cut with it.

Cletus had been a lawman for thirty-two years, originating his career with the Tennessee Highway Patrol. After two decades of law enforcement with the THP, at the behest of Clarksville's police chief he put in his bid for sheriff a dozen years back when the incumbent, Nash Jackson, had been indicted for bribery, grand theft of stolen property, and the tampering of evidence.

Sheriff Coonrod proudly surrounded himself with men of only the highest moral caliber, those who truly believed the badge actually spoke for something. Being their boss, their mentor, was a responsibility he took very seriously; it was a true labor of love for him. He taught them as much about every facet of law enforcement as he could—he considered every second a valuable teaching experience; no question was off limits in his classroom.

While Cletus took great satisfaction in his work, he took even more in his name, wearing it with as much tenacity and pride as his badge. Cletus had been his father's name and his father's father's as well—he came from a long line of "Cleti." With a moniker such as that, he'd taken a lot of ribbing in his youth and had needed to fend off insults and jabs referencing a certain extremely sensitive region of the female genitalia. One of his favorite records growing up had been "A Boy Named Sue" by Johnny Cash, for, much like the song's namesake, the scraps and scrapes he'd endured in his formative years had forged him into a tougher, more resilient man. Though strongly attached to the name, he decided to end the tradition—and thus the persecution—with his generation, bestowing an alternative first name on his grateful son, while shifting *Cletus* one position to the rear. William Cletus Coonrod—still had a good ring to it!

"What in the Sam Hill happened here?" the sheriff asked, walking up to his deputy Mike O'Reilly, who was squatting beside the victim. "Oh shit," Cletus said as the wounds became visible to him.

"Sure smells that way, Clete."

The sheriff grimaced at the one-liner. "Get it all out, O'Reilly." Cletus's fabled flatulence preceded him—trailed him too. It was the result of a prolific hemorrhoid procedure that had regrettably paralyzed half his sphincter.

"Seems you beat me to it, Sheriff."

"Good one, good one. Get on with it," he groused.

"Yeah, this poor bastard's brains are scattered all around here. That's his car door over yonder in the highway—we're getting ready to pull it off and reopen the lane. Wanted you to see it first."

"Okay, seen it. Pull it. Time of death?"

"Preliminary? I'd guess about an hour ago. Two, tops."

Cletus took off his hat and sanded his fingers across the grit of his flight deck, scratching the runway.

"I see several wounds—one exiting the arm there," O'Reilly said, pointing with his pencil eraser, "one abdominal, and of course the chart toppers."

"Motive?"

"Looks random to me. Small bag of weed with a couple a blunts in it stuffed under his seat but no weapon in the car, nothing. Road rage maybe."

Cletus shrugged his shoulders and sighed, adjusting his BVDs at his crotch. "Any chance this has to do with the bank robbery earlier in town?"

"Could be. Not out of the realm of possibility."

"Yeah, in today's wicked, twisted world, guess that's so. Weapon?"

"Tennyson found a .45-cal. full metal jacket over yonder stubbed into the ground. Searching for any other strays now. We'll comb 'er real good before the sun sets."

"Good work, Mikey. Good job."

"Thanks, Sheriff. We'll get everything there is to get here; don't worry."

Cletus patted him on the back. "I know you will, Mikey. Thorough. Do a thorough job. S'posed to rain heavy real soon. We don't want to lose anythin' we need here."

"We're good by nightfall."

"Good boy, good boy." Cletus started to turn but then added, "Hey."

"Yes, Sheriff?"

He held out his index finger. "Pull." He winked at his deputy, who raised a half smile, knowing better than to fall for *that* trick.

Then, dodging the splattering of blood and remnants of gray matter, Cletus sauntered toward the Challenger. Deputy Pfeiffer was lifting strips of fingerprint tape from the steering wheel.

"Barney, what've you found?"

"I'm recovering a few here and there."

"Get 'em all. Maybe we'll be lucky and they won't all be the driver's."

"You got it, Big Burrito."

"That's Big Burrito, *sir*, to you, Pfeiff."

Barney busied himself again, waving Cletus off over his shoulder.

The sheriff surveyed the work, pointing a beefy finger here or there and barking unnecessary directions, for his bustling worker bees were already performing the work to his satisfaction. Confident, he headed back to his car.

Something drew his attention, and he detoured over to the road to take a gander at a pair of skid marks a few yards behind his car. Wanting them documented, he stuck two fingers in his mouth and blew a shrill whistle. One of the other nearby deputies turned in the direction of the summons, and

Cletus waved him over with the same two fingers, pointing to the ground beside his feet. The dutiful deputy understood and undertook the edict.

Cletus moseyed on over and sat down in his front seat, sighing and farting once more. He left the door open long enough for the napalm to dissipate and render moot the need for the tiny spritzer bottle of new-car smell in his glove box.

~*~

David searched the area around the Dumpsters but found nothing out of the ordinary. He even hoisted himself up onto the lips of the bins to peek inside and rearrange the contents, but all he saw were some empty boxes and garbage-filled sacks. He started walking across the parking lot toward Union Street and, almost to the thoroughfare, noticed droplets of blood, fairly recent remnants. He followed the trail across the street and down the sidewalk. Somewhat orderly at first, the pattern became more haphazard as the trail continued, as though whoever was losing that blood was losing his or her battle. The spatters became larger and less spread apart and then diverted onto a front lawn, pooling into an impression impressive enough to be made only by someone prone, someone who had nearly given up the struggle to exist. There was enough blood there that the source couldn't have shed much more and survived.

The yard belonged a modest one-story with faded siding that resembled others lining the street. David walked up to the door and rapped loudly. After no reply, he tried the doorbell. An elderly man in a ribbed, dingy tank top peered through the textured glass panel above the peephole. An equally elderly voice, in a mild accent—European, of sorts—rasped, "Yes? Can I help you?"

David lifted his badge up so the man inside could see it. "Police, sir. May I ask you a few questions in connection with a bank robbery that occurred earlier today?"

"How do I know you're the police?"

Fair enough. "Good for you, sir. You shouldn't just look at someone's badge; it might not be authentic."

"10-4! I learned that on *Dragnet* years ago—Sergeant Joe Friday."

Smiling, David suggested, "If you want, you can call the police station and ask them if there's a Sergeant David Jeffries and describe what I look like. Ask them if he has bushy eyebrows."

"You don't have bushy eyebrows."

He laughed. "Thank you; you're too kind. Ask them anyway, and see if they don't think so."

"All right, wait right there."

The man left, and David chuckled. He knew the dispatchers would have fun with that. In a few minutes, the man came back and unlatched the door.

"She laughed at you. I told her she was rude. Don't worry; I got her name for you."

David's gaze zeroed in on the fellow's Brezhnev-like brows.

"Now these—these are bushy," the old fellow snickered. "My yard man keeps asking me to let him trim them!"

David certainly couldn't argue with him. It looked like two wooly worms had crawled up there and taken refuge above his expressive eyes. "Thank you for opening up. I'm Sergeant Jeffries."

"Well, you'd better be. That's who I inquired about. Can I see your badge, Officer? On *Dragnet*, they ask to see the badge."

"Certainly." David produced his shield again, appeasing the man.

The old gentleman scrutinized it. "Say, that's a beaut." He held out a spindly arm, unveiling curtains of substantial undergrowth. There was a large, flesh-colored Telfa pad adhered to his forearm. "Irv. Irv Crossman. Hey, haven't I seen you at temple?"

"Yes, I believe you have. May I ask you a question?"

"You just did."

David looked puzzled.

"Gotcha!" he chortled. "You asked me a question when you asked, 'May I ask you a question?'!"

David nodded, considering. "Yes, I guess I did."

"Gotcha, young man!"

This Irv's got some chutzpah! "Mr. Crossman—"

He held up a hand. "Irv. Please."

"Uh, Irv. Did you know that Planter's Bank was robbed this morning?"

"No! I have money at that bank. Did they steal all my money?"

"They stole *some* money, sir. But I assure you, your deposits are still safe and sound."

Irv drew a huge sigh of relief, coughing after the wheeze. "That's good, 'cause I gotta take care of Marie. That's my wife—Marie Crossman. We've been married seventy-six years. Seventy-six! She has cancer. Bladder cancer. It's spread to her liver now. And her lung. She's bedridden, on oxygen—her last days."

"I am so sorry to hear that."

He shrugged. "What can you do? You play the cards the man upstairs deals you, right? I'm here with her; I'll look after her. I've looked after her for seventy-three years."

David thought about the discrepancy with the number and then shrugged it off. "Yessir. Uh, Mr. Crossman—"

He held up his hand again. "Irv."

"Irv. Did you know that one of the perpetrators might have collapsed in your front yard, near death?"

"No! Well, my liability insurance is paid up, so I'm okay, right?"

"Sir, there's no liability. He wasn't dying because he fell over any hazards on your property—he was shot somewhere between the bank and here."

"Well, that's a relief. For me, not for him, that is. I mean, I'm retired, living on Social Security and a pension. It's not much but ..." He shrugged.

"Don't worry about that, sir."

"My pension? I gotta worry about my pension. You see my wife ..."

Despite his growing frustration over the pace of the conversation, David was nevertheless enjoying this fellow. Perhaps it was the sheer challenge in communicating with him. "No, sir. About the liability. There's no liability involved if a bank robber wounded during the act happens to fall onto your front lawn, weakened from loss of blood. None at all."

"Ohhh."

David soldiered on. "Irv, there's a lot of blood out there, and I wanted to make sure it wasn't you or the missus who might've tripped and fallen today."

"You mean Mrs. Crossman?"

"Yessir."

"No, Marie's bedridden. Didn't you hear me just say that? You say you're a sergeant?" he asked with a tinge of skepticism.

David blushed at his faux pas. "Yessir. I'm sorry; you did mention that. Well, it wasn't you then?"

"No, I'm not bedridden, Sergeant. I told you it was my wife. Get your facts straight, and we'll both be making headway."

Yes, we will, David thought, closing his eyes and rebooting his train of thought. "Let me try this again."

"Shoot." Irv laughed and coughed again. "Shoot! Get it?"

"That was a good one, Irv." He wagged his finger like a gun at the man, who raised his hands up in fake surrender, cackling. The sergeant withdrew his derringer digit. "So you didn't fall out there on your lawn today?"

"Nope. Wasn't me. I've been watching the National Geographic Channel all day. Did you know that there are some forty-six hundred species of cockroaches but only thirty are found in human habitats?"

"Wellll, no."

"I think I got the lion's share of those species right in my kitchen!"

"You don't say? Irv, respectfully, I'd like to press on."

"It's your dime."

"Uh, yes. So it isn't your blood out there on your front lawn?"

"Nope. I got all mine right here." He flexed his spaghetti arms.

"Well, did you hear or see anything suspicious?"

"Just those damn cock-a-roaches! Oh! Oh! And while I was watching the tube, Officer ... uh ... What did you say your name was?"

"Officer Jeffries. David Jeffries."

"Oh, yeah. I've seen you at temple, haven't I?"

No reason to deviate down that particular fork again, David figured. "Irv, you were saying that something happened while you were watching your show?"

"Yeah. I heard what sounded like firecrackers exploding down the street. I thought it was those delinquent Robinson boys again. They like to light 'em and stick 'em in people's mailboxes or trash cans, to scare us, you know? Ka-*boom*!"

David shook his head to try to clear the numbing. "Firecrackers, sir? Could they have been gunshots?"

"Yeah, they could've. I guess they could've. I hope those boys haven't graduated to firearms."

"Did you look outside to see if there was anything suspicious happening?"

"No, I was going to wait until the commercials."

"When the commercials came on, then did you look outside?"

"No. I guess I forgot. My mind isn't what it used to be." He glanced downward, embarrassed.

"Well, it's hard to remember everything these days, isn't it?"

"Oh, sure. Sure. Thanks for stopping by, Officer ... uh ..."

"Jeffries. Thanks for your time, Irv. Good day, sir."

"You too." Irv waved as he shut the door. David began to return the gesture but was cut off by the door slamming in his face.

⌐⁊ℓ⌐

As the front door slammed, Brody heard coming from the saltshaker by the stove, "Heeeeere comes Abby!" He picked up the saltshaker and smiled.

His wife's spirit was presaging its audience with him. Susan gradually appeared, sitting on the counter before him once more. "Hello, Giff," she said.

"Hello, Artie. How've you been?"

"Waiting for you both." She smiled. "You?"

"Long day but real good. Glad you came for a visit."

"You'll have to tell me all about your day later."

He so wanted to hug her, but the feeling was in vain; he had to be content to interact with her in the usual fashion.

"Daddy! Daddy?"

"Yes, princess?"

"Are you in the kitchen?"

"Sam-I-am!"

Abby ran into the kitchen, where her father, clad in a "KISS the Cook" apron—decorated with Gene Simmons wielding a spatula and protruding his colossal glossal muscle—was gripping his own spatula and standing in front of the open oven with his tongue similarly extended. He was holding her plate with a quilted oven mitt, about to transport a steaming hamburger patty to her bun.

"I've got something to *tell* youu," she singsongily baited him. Then she noticed him mimicking the image on his garment. "Ewww! Stick that back in your mouth!"

His imitation missing its mark, he retracted, as charged. "What is it, Queen Abbithea?" He plopped her burger onto its lettuce bed and blanketed it with its sesame-seeded coverlet.

"Guess what."

"Oh," Brody mused, setting her dinner on the table, "we're going to play *that* game? I love that game!" He scratched underneath his mouth with the corner of the warm spatula, leaving an oily smudge on his cleft chin. "Let me see. Your class is going on a field trip to Australia?"

She giggled. "Nope. Guess again!"

"You're running off to join the Bolshoi Ballet? Oh," he lamented, placing the back of his hand against his forehead, "I shall miss you so!"

"No, silly!"

"I'm all out, kiddo. What, what?"

She paused dramatically and then spilled the beans. "Mrs. Thompson said it's official! I'm in the county-wide spelling bee in January! I get my word lists next week!"

Pride saturated Brody, and he bear-hugged his daughter.

"Can't ... breathe ..." Abby teased.

"Don't ... care ..." Brody replied. He relaxed his death vise and held her at arm's length. "Really? Next week?"

"Yes! Isn't that cool?"

"Arctic!" He embraced his little girl again, kissing the top of her head and smelling her perspiration, sweet as nectar. "Well, guess what happened to me today."

"What, Daddy?"

He took off his apron and sat down beside his daughter. "Well, aside from witnessing an armed bank robbery and getting a part on a TV show, nothing much."

Abby gaped at him. "What? A TV show?"

He laughed. *Of course that's what she asks about!* "You mean you don't care I was almost killed in a robbery?"

A horrified look came over her. "Almost killed? You didn't say you were almost killed!"

She jumped up and hugged her father so tightly around his neck that he choked out, "Can't ... breathe ...!"

Abby smothered him with kisses. "Don't ... care ...!"

8

AFTER dinner, Abby excused herself to the small walnut desk in the hallway to work on her school assignments while Brody cleared the dishes. He set his cell phone on the counter and then retrieved the plates from the table and placed them in the sink. He decided to listen to some tunes while he worked.

"Will a little music bother you, honey?" he asked Abby. But she didn't answer; she was engrossed in her homework. So he leafed through his music library and came across a title that tickled him. He tapped his finger on the screen, and within seconds, the familiar rhythm began.

He picked up a dish towel and used it as a makeshift prop as his hips began to shimmy to the notes. He threw it over his shoulders like nunchakus and then stuck out his tailbone and took to sliding the towel back and forth across it as he shook that caboose!

He heard laughter behind him and glanced over his shoulder at his daughter cracking up. He slid over to her and grabbed her by her hand, and they began to flamenco to the song that all three of them—Susan, Abby, and Brody—used to dance to together. As father and daughter conga-lined around the table, shaking their hands with make-believe maracas and castanets and pointing their fingers in the air, they started laughing again. They collapsed on the floor in an out-of-breath heap as the music faded.

Brody caught his breath. "That was fun!"

"Yeah," Abby said. "We haven't done that in a long time!"

That brought a tear to Brody's eye.

"Daddy? Did I say something wrong?"

He clutched his daughter tightly. "No, baby. It's just that it made me remember Mommy; that's all."

"Me too. But why are you so sad?"

He sat up, propping himself against the warm oven. "Just missing her, I guess."

"Me too." She scooted over, sitting beside him. "But you get to talk to her, don't you?"

He smiled at her and ran his fingers through her hair. "Yep, I do. Sometimes I do."

"I wish I could."

They sat silently for several minutes, Brody at a loss for words.

Then Abby asked, "Why is that song so special to you?"

Brody grinned. "That's the first song I danced to with your mother."

Abby looked up at him, smiling. "Not like that, I hope!"

He laughed. "Well ..."

"Daddy, please tell me you didn't!"

"It was at a party in college, honey. It was after your mom and I had been dating for a couple of weeks. I thought things were going pretty smoothly between us, so I invited her to a party at my fraternity house. Neither of us had any idea what we would learn about each other that night."

"What? What?"

He looked down at Abby and chuckled. "Your mother was a very brave woman, Abs."

Susan had accepted Brody's invitation to the party at the Kappa Sigma house, indulged in one frozen margarita, and, after some fairly questionable dance moves by Brody and his brothers, accepted her Romeo's hand to venture outside to chat. They sat next to one another on a bench in the little courtyard, which was illuminated by strands of jalapeno-shaped lights haphazardly draped from the eaves.

"Did you have fun?" Brody asked her.

Her head resting lightly on his shoulder, she looked up at him, the waning moon reflected in her eyes. "The time of my life, thus far."

"Really?" That gratified him.

She laughed. "Except for that twirling thing you did where you ended up on your back between my legs. I don't believe I remember that particular series of dance moves in the Macarena."

"That's because they're original. I made them up tonight, just for you, Miss Tri Delt."

"For me?"

"Actually, Budweiser partnered with me on them," he confessed.

She cracked up. "Well, a toast then—to my tight blue jeans and to your beer goggles!" As her laughter subsided, she sighed contentedly, her gaze transfixed on the clouds sliding by in the chilly night's sky. He stared down at her flaxen curls, the color of moonbeams, sweeping back a trespassing tress that had interloped across her forehead. He kissed her there.

She eased herself closer to him. "There's no Budweiser up there," she giggled.

"Oh, I don't know—I tasted *some*thing."

"It's hairspray."

He spat in jest. Together they laughed, a wonderfully perfect synchrony.

"I'm really surprised your shoes stayed on, with that dance floor as tacky as it was!" she said.

"It's a unique combo of margarita mix, beer, and—you don't wanna know what else; trust me." He smiled.

"I'll take your word for it."

"It's fun, though; it's like dancing on flypaper! Not my worry, though—our pledges will have it spotless by morning." He paused, and the brief silence spawned a sudden worry over what she'd do if she only knew ... He chased it away by leaning down and kissing her warm, soft lips. Her tongue reached eagerly up to his.

As they finished their embrace, she sat upright. "That was nice," she said, leaning her hands shoulder-width apart on the front edge of the bench and swinging her legs alternately underneath.

"That was more than nice. That was heaven, Ms. Etheridge."

She smiled coyly. "So much better than our awkward first-kiss ordeal."

"Did you find that awkward? I didn't think that was awkward."

"As I was saying—"

He interrupted her again. "I hope that there will be many more—a far, far greater number."

She laughed. "I don't believe I've neglected you there. Just how many were you counting on, pray tell?"

"A multitude, perhaps?"

"Hmm. Perhaps," she allowed. "Wishful thinking, Mr. Whitaker—don't be presumptuous. There's all the time in the world for 'multitude.'"

All the time in the world … wishful thinking—amen! "Please, don't be so formal, Susan. We've enjoyed our fair share of smooches already. Brody's just fine."

"My, my, you *are* presumptuous! What else are you, Brody?"

What else? An involuntary shudder passed over him. "Sorry, sudden chill." He kissed the tip of her nose. "What do you mean?"

"Well, tell me more of what makes you tick. You hardly ever tell me about the pieces that make up you. If you could do anything on any given day, what would your first choice be? Who are your favorite musical artists? What's your favorite color? Dessert? What do you like to do in your spare time? Your *favorite* pastimes—that is, when you're not busy clearing out a dance floor?"

He laughed at her acute sense of humor—razor sharp yet not cutting. "The pieces of me? Hmm … what can I tell you? I'm a sucker for a good movie or a really tight football game. I like dogs, large or small—they're all cool with me; flannel shirts in the fall; a good long run on a crisp morning. I'm partial to the Stones, Zeppelin, the Who, the Eagles—almost any good classic rock. And I'm a Beach Boys fanatic …" He paused dreamily for a second or two. "No better vibrations."

Susan watched his mouth move as he spoke. "Wow. That's more than you've told me about yourself in the last month or so. Don't stop," she urged. "You're on a roll."

He picked up where he'd left off. "I'm a sucker for chocolate; I love a really good mousse—uh, the pudding variety, not the antlered kind."

"Whew!" She swiped her brow with the back of her slim hand, her nail glitter depositing golden stardust upon her milky skin.

"And, hmm—my favorite pastimes? I'm not sure you'd believe me if I told you that one."

"Oooh," she murmured. "A man of mystery?"

"No, it's not that. It's just that most people act sort of … put off when I tell them."

Her concern meter evidenced itself in her expression.

"I see that look on your face." He had just cast a hookless line, only a sinker on the end. He had to reel her back in.

"Is it drugs?"

"Nothing illegal, I assure you."

"Are you into porn or something?"

"No! Wellll …"

She bumped him in the shoulder. "Then what is it?"

"It's just that most people don't understand it when I tell them …"

"Tellll me!"

"Okay. All right. You promise you won't laugh?"

"You have three testicles? Tell me! I won't laugh; I promise." She crossed her heart and then her fingers and steeled herself for his confession.

"Five testicles, really."

She batted him on the arm. "Tell me, Brody Whitaker!"

"All right. I …"

She stared at him, waiting; he returned her stare, hesitating.

"I … talk … to … the dead." *There! I said it!* His lead weight had been lifted, only to sink once more, resting on the muddy bottom. "Those who have crossed over." He grimaced, closing one eye.

A snicker burst forth from Susan. "You what …?"

He pointed at her. "You see? You see? I *told* you you'd laugh at me, didn't I?"

"Well, technically it wasn't a laugh; it was—"

He held up his hands. "Doesn't matter, doesn't matter. Technical or not, you don't believe me."

"Should I?"

"Why on earth would I lie about that? Do you think I'd purposely try to break up this awesome time with an even more awesome girl here next to me?"

"Well, I wouldn't think … but *dead people?*"

"Those who have passed on. Relatives, friends. I've done it ever since I was a kid."

"Really?"

I'm losing her! Where was quicksand when you needed it? "Really!"

"Dead people?!"

"Dead people," he confirmed meekly.

"And I'm a ventriloquist!"

He took her hand, silently praying for damage control. "No, really, I can do it. I swear!"

She laughed. "No, silly! I believe you."

He raised his eyebrows. That response was totally unexpected—a first—and flustered him.

Susan chuckled. "I mean, who in his right mind would say that to a girl he ever wanted to see again? That is, unless you're trying to get rid of me or just not in your right mind."

"Yes, I am! I mean, no, I'm not! I mean …" He pulled her close and kissed her again, assuring her right before their mouths met, "Not a chance, Miss Tri Delt."

They kissed, and then she pulled away just enough so she could speak. "You mean, not a chance you're out of your mind?" she asked.

"No, not a chance I would ever want to get rid of you."

"Well, Brody Whitaker, I believe you—about that too. And guess what."

He looked into her intoxicatingly, insanely azure eyes again. "What?"

She smiled at him. "I really *am* a ventriloquist!"

⌒⋔⌒

The following evening at six thirty, he picked her up at her sorority house for a dinner date. At a local Italian restaurant, they dined on spaghetti and meatballs, with a fruity spumoni to top off the meal. Once back at the Delta Delta Delta house, she invited him to sit with her in the downstairs parlor. Her sorority sisters were in the adjoining room, assembled around a rerun of *Friends*, laughing hysterically.

"I have a surprise for you, Brody," she said to him, holding his hand.

"A surprise?"

"I'll be right back. Don't move."

"I won't even twitch."

She released his hand and ran to the stairs.

"Don't do it, Suze," Amy Crosswaite called from the TV room.

"Kiss of death," warned Tina Tyler.

Undeterred, Susan headed up the stairs and then returned with something behind her back.

Looking at her standing in the doorway, Brody felt a strong urge to bull-rush her and plant one on her mouth, but she looked so prim and pretty in the light of the entryway, in her gray skirt and patterned silk blouse, that he quelled the brashness.

"Well? What have we here?" he asked.

"Here," she began, "is ..." She produced a huge wood-and-feathers toucan from behind her back. It was impeccably detailed and obviously pricey—a professional-grade puppet. "Ta-*da*!"

Tina moaned. "She's gonna do it!"

"Zip it, Tina!" the toucan said with Susan's voice, its beak mouthing the syllables, one by one.

"Whoa!" Brody was impressed. "That's pretty dang good!"

The bird came closer to him and nuzzled its beak against his stubbled cheek. "You ain't seen nothin' yet, big boy!"

"How do you know that, Suze?" another sorority sister asked.

"That's enough, Veronica," Susan scolded over her shoulder.

Brody could see Susan's larynx subtly move when she threw her voice, but her lips were stationary. She was quite accomplished at this trick, and he was rightfully impressed.

Amy yelled, "He's not interested in that, Susan!"

Brody disagreed. "Yes, I am! Don't listen to them."

"Oh, I never listen to those birdbrains!" A very different sound—not Susan's true voice—now originated from the sassy bird, a kind of squawk in bass. Susan removed her hand from inside the rear of the bird, laughing.

"Please, don't stop," he pleaded.

"That's what she said!" Amy hooted.

Susan rolled her eyes. "That's *all* they think about!"

"I gathered that."

"But I'm not that kind of girl," she said with a Cheshire cat grin.

"Of course not."

She sat down with him.

Brody asked, "Hey, how long have you been doing that?"

"Well, I just came downstairs about two minutes ago ..."

He chuckled, and she nipped at his nose with the puppet's beak.

"No, really, how long have you been doing that? You're amazingly good at it."

She fake-fanned herself, prefacing her explanation like a southern belle. "Why, you flattuh me, Mistuh Whitakuh." She explained, "Well, I guess I was about twelve when I saw Wayland Flowers on TV with his alter ego, Madame. She was sooo hilarious!"

"I remember them. Really funny."

"Yeah," agreed the toucan. And then Susan laid it in her lap. "And I thought, wouldn't it be cool to be able to do that?"

"Hmm. Not your typical aspiration."

"Now, Brody Whitaker, is there anything about me yet that seems 'typical' to you?"

Abso-lutely not! He shook his head in negative affirmation.

She continued, "So I called my parents into the den, pointed to the television set, and told them, 'I want to do that.' Well, my parents didn't jump for joy, but they didn't slit their wrists either. So that Christmas I was presented with my very first dummy. They also gave me a book about ventriloquism and a video set teaching basic techniques."

"Was this toucan your first puppet?"

"Who, Beaky here?"

"Oh, Beaky?"

"Yes, I shortened it from Mr. Beakers."

"Good move."

Not missing a beat, she said, "I thought so. Him? No. He's actually my fifth!"

"Oh, really?"

"Oh, yes. First was a hobo named Joe, then a dachshund I called Schatzie. There was an iguana, Iggy—a sidekick to Beaky here—and most recently, I bought another one after I came to Vanderbilt. A talking banana."

"A banana?"

"Go get the banana," implored Becky Moore from the TV room.

"Not on your life!" Susan shouted back.

"Go get the ba-na-na!"

"That's enough, Becky!" She turned back to him. "The banana is the consensus favorite around here."

"Apparently. Should I be ... *jealous* of this banana?" Brody asked.

"Yes, you should!" another sister warned from the TV room.

Susan got up, walked over to the doorway, and leaned against the frame, her arm extended upward, flattened against the white fluting. She batted her lashes at Brody and chuckled. Then she whipped her head with purpose around the corner to propel a few choice words at her bosom buddies and casually returned, skipping over and swinging her skirt, to her date on the settee. "Let's just say Chiquita might get me in trouble tonight. So let's slowly ease into the banana."

"That is *sooo* what she said!" one of the sisters called.

"Ooh!" Annoyed, Susan barked, "Enough!" Laughing nervously, she said to Brody, "Well, you can imagine the banana jokes!"

"Yes." Conjuring up all sorts, Brody nodded. "I'm in a fraternity. Yes, I can."

She looked at him—the wind knocked from her sails, pouting. "You don't think less of me? You don't think this is all stupid, do you?"

He leaned over and whispered into her ear, "I talk to dead people. You think I think *this* is stupid?"

"Point taken. Well, at least my special talent is in the realm of believability." It was Brody's turn to be deflated.

Seeing the sudden slump in his shoulders and realizing the insensitivity of what she'd said, she corrected herself. "Oh, Brody, I'm so sorry." She took both his hands and clasped them to her chest. "I didn't mean that—I mean, *I* believe you! I know that at some point, you'll show me exactly how you do it!"

Expecting another snide comment from her sisters for that latter choice of phrasing, Susan glanced over toward the TV room. Instead of a verbal volley, a totem pole of feminine heads toppled from the side of the archway trim.

Susan's response had pleased Brody, however, and helped reinflate his ego. It also didn't hurt that his hands were nestled in a desirable location— and it had even been her idea!

She pressed on, as did he, his hands quite comfortable in their present resting place. "All I meant was that what I do is an art form; that's all. I hope I didn't hurt your feelings."

"Well, 'Artie,' I guess I'll forgive you. If yours is an art, mine's a gift."

"Okay, 'Giff.' It's a tie. Satisfied?"

He Eskimo-kissed her nose. "Satisfied, Artie."

And from that moment on, those nicknames, like the soles of his shoes on the dance floor of the frat house, stuck.

9

CARLOS Salazar's chop shop was off Hadensville Road, northeast of Guthrie, Kentucky, way out in the boonies. The maze of unpaved back roads that cut through the heavy woods took nearly twenty minutes to traverse. If the nuances of the intersections were unfamiliar to the traveler, Carlos's place would be near impossible to find—just the way he wanted it.

Due to the Oldsmobile's damage, Teddy waited until dark to make the trek in order to avoid unwanted attention. He pulled up to a heavily chained cattle fence with barbed wire binding it on either side. A diamond-shaped aluminum sign painted white was strapped to the entrance. The makeshift sign warned in red letters TRESSPASSERS WILL BE SHOT. Teddy speed-dialed Carlos's number and waited for the pickup on the other end. "Hey, *mi amigo*. I'm at the gate."

The line clicked dead. A few minutes later, a Jeep Cherokee with three heavily armed Hispanics skidded sideways to a stop on the other side of the barricade. The scar-faced driver stared in Teddy's direction while a brawny, bandannaed passenger with a toothpick in his mouth hopped out with his shotgun and unlocked the gate, kicking it hard toward the Olds with his worn leather boot. It swung with excess zeal and struck the passenger's-side fender, striking Teddy the wrong way.

He jammed on the horn. "Hey, *maricón*! That's my car!"

The man removed his toothpick and spat on the ground. "So what's one more dent, eh, gringo?" He laughed.

Teddy mocked him under his breath, bobbling his head, "So what's one more dent?" He tacked on a quiet expletive: "Shit."

The Mexican sauntered toward the car and peered inside. "Who the fuck are you?"

Remembering he no longer sported his trademark beard, Teddy said, "It's me, Teddy Trent."

The man was startled. "Shit, dude! I didn't even recognize you!" The Latino chilled and walked back to the Jeep, motioning Teddy to follow.

Several years before, in Whiteville Correctional, after Lyle had been awarded early release, Teddy had gotten into a fracas with a few Mexicans who didn't take kindly to Caucs. The tussle was over soup in the mess hall—soup that was in Teddy's bowl yet desired by another.

That "another" was Carlos, in the slammer for his fifth stint for banging cars. The avocation dated back to his teenage days with the Latin Kings, and he had been a master at it. He could jimmy in and boost most cars in a matter of seconds and then strip them down to untraceable shells. Caught in a shakedown outside of Springville one June, he was carted off to jail. Once inside the pen, he was proclaimed *khalifa*, or "king," and the title had followed him back to the streets. His minions guarded him, battled, plundered, and sacrificed themselves for him without a thought, without hesitation.

On the day of the fracas, Teddy had just dipped his spoon into his bowl when two muscle-bound Latinos sat down on either side of him, feigning indifference as they slurped their broth. After Teddy had taken a couple of spoonfuls, the men unceremoniously pinned down each of his wrists. One yanked his spoon from his grasp and flung it against the far wall of the mess hall.

Another goon approached, growling, "Señor Salazar is still hungry," and snatched away Teddy's soup bowl.

"Let him get his own then, *cabrón*."

With that remark, another beefy brute turned from the bench behind Teddy, sucker-punched him in the back, and then shoved his face roughly onto the table. Teddy struggled to resist, but the men were too strong. With the odds stacked against him—three against one—he submitted, biding his time.

Seething, Teddy played possum long enough that the bookends loosened their holds. Twisting his deceptively powerful arms, he freed himself, swinging around and right-hooking the sucker puncher. Before the others could subdue him, he scurried under the table and crawled through to the other side, racing over to the diminutive Salazar. Though short in stature, the pudgy kingpin stood his ground, perhaps with the self-assurance of adequate protection close at hand. It wasn't close enough, however. Teddy grabbed him by the collar and threw him backward onto the floor.

One of the bodyguards rushed to Salazar's aid, attempting to apprehend Teddy, but Teddy swiftly kicked the unfortunate oaf's kneecap into dislocation and tripped him up, sending him sprawling to his back. The bodyguard's head struck hard on the cement floor, dazing him. Salazar watched with smug security as Teddy faced down the other henchman. Teddy balled his fists, baring his freshly inked knuckles, the tattooed slogans inches from the goon's eyes.

"Look hard, *maricón*. Tell me what you see."

"I see me wasting you, *gilipollas*."

"Then look harder."

The enforcer followed his opponent's brandished fists—the indigo letters circling in front of his face.

"What do you see now, motherfucker?" He extended one fist nearer to the Mexican's face. "This is your destiny." He brought up his other hand. "This is your absolution. Which do you want? Call it, *pendejo*."

"Fuck you!" the bodyguard yelled, lunging at Teddy, swinging hard at him.

Teddy deftly ducked. With his left, he "absolved" Salazar's man with a hard jab to his ribs, buckling him. Then he staggered the man with a swift uppercut to the jaw. He was about to finish the guy off with a punch aimed directly into his nose when he was grabbed roughly from behind. The guards had arrived and quickly extinguished the melee with force in numbers.

Teddy struggled back and was billy-clubbed behind his knees. Buckling, he glared at Salazar, who winked at him! *What the fuck*, thought Teddy, kneeling there, restrained by the guards. *Is Carlos jackin' with me?*

But Salazar had a newfound respect for Teddy after their altercation. Arrogance and bravado backed up by brute force was a potent triad in the slam, and the mandate quickly spread that Teddy was not to be messed with. Teddy became better acquainted with the king of the Mexican Mafia, eventually earning fledgling member-at-large status by helping patrol the yards and keeping Carlos's enemies at bay. He'd burned his white supremacist bridges in the process, but he was content to reap the benefits that might result later rather than sooner from his newfound loyalty.

The two inmates had kept tabs on each other—literally, using cars as currency. Teddy and Lyle would bring stolen vehicles from time to time into Salazar's new garage, and for every ten cars the brothers tallied, they'd receive a rebuilt and revamped one in return to either keep or sell. Teddy had found himself presently in need of his freebie, something less attention-grabbing than his damaged Oldsmobile.

He followed the Cherokee down the bumpy road a fair distance until the small caravan came to the clearing housing Salazar's chop shop and domicile, side by side. As Teddy pulled up to park in a precise spot, he could see the familiar twin rows of pit bulls, restrained, insomuch as their lengthy, sturdy chains allowed, just out of reach of one another. It was this part of the trip to Carlos's hideaway that had always frightened Lyle, for there was a bite-free zone of only four feet or so between the rows. Since Carlos's armed bodyguards were posted on either side of shoulder-high electrified fences bordering the posts, it was the only clear path to the chop shop; one false step could mean contact with the unforgiving teeth of one of those dangerous canines. And, while the dogs were inches out of reach of each other on both sides of the path, they could drag a careless person to a spot where two sets of biting jaws could simultaneously rend that unfortunate individual to shreds in a matter of minutes.

The nearest pair of dogs barked and lunged at Teddy as he got out of his car, slobbering foam and straining their tethers, taxing them continuously for any trace of flaw. He walked a true line directly between the rows, marked by small stones recognizable only to those who knew of them, respecting the dogs' rotating boundaries as he maneuvered his way through the gauntlet of snapping jowls to the expansive garage.

Two men rapidly approached him as he cleared the obstacle, and to one, Teddy handed over his keys. They continued right past him, the dogs snapping at them as well, collecting his car and driving it through to the garage as Teddy angled left toward Salazar's office—a small room in the building's rear corner, closest to the escape route of the surrounding thicket. He looked up to the video camera capturing his approach and waved.

Teddy could see and hear the frenzy of activity from within the open bays: welders arcing, torches cutting, air guns issuing loud bursts, metal clanging against metal, chains rattling. The smell of fresh paint hung in the air. Men were talking, arguing, and swearing, alternating between Spanish and broken English. All routine noises from a day's—and night's—work.

He was buzzed into the office. The temperature dropped a cool ten degrees courtesy of the bank of fans diminishing the heat originated by the hustle-bustle on the opposite side of the office's adjoining wall. A ceiling fan coupled with a dilapidated window unit humming obtrusively also contributed to the downright refreshing feel in there.

"Carlos, how you doin', dawg?" He walked over to the desk to shake Salazar's portly paw, attached to a log of an arm.

Carlos stared at a vastly different-looking Teddy. "Man," he laughed. "Dude, you look like Brad Pitt!"

Appreciative, Teddy smiled.

"With baaad teeth, man!"

Teddy withdrew his hand. Then he laughed and approached Carlos, and they hugged. Teddy's wingspan barely encircled the Mexican's exaggerated torso. "How you been, dawg?"

The khalifa bragged, "Business been good, almost too good, amigo."

"Whaddayu mean?"

"Some new heat on the street. We been burnin' through a lot of wheels, man. Some fingers are pointin', eyes lookin' around. We gotta be careful about buckin' the odds for a while. Whatchu bring me tonight?"

"I brung you my old Oldsmobile, man. It's yours. Do whatever you want to it—I need it dismembered."

"No worries." Salazar sat on the corner of his desk, reached for the Sauza 901 bottle resting on his blotter, and offered it to Teddy. "Dismembering's what we do here!"

Teddy accepted the bottle and swigged the liquor hard. It was a quenching burn going down. "You always got the good stuff, Carlos."

"Nothing but the best for you, ey?" He smiled, hoisting his thick black mustache to half-mast on either side. "How you been, bro?"

"Good, man. Good."

"Where's that brother of yours this fine evening?"

Teddy flashed back to the roadside where he'd dragged Lyle's body from view. He took another gulp of tequila and then coughed. "Couldn't make it tonight. Got held up."

"Thass cool. No prob. Let me show you what I got. This makes ten, so your punch card's filled. You get to supersize it tonight!" He made a stroking gesture at his crotch, laughing, his gold grills gleaming from the ceiling fan lights.

Teddy tried to hand back the bottle, but Carlos refused it. "No, man, you look like you could use it." He put his hand on his fellow felon's shoulder. "C'mon, let's go out into the shop."

As they entered the main area, the decibel level vaulted louder. The random air gun bursts silenced certain of their syllables like audio strobes, so sentences needed repeating from time to time—apropos for habitual hoodlums: repeated sentences.

They walked over to the remnants of Teddy's car, pushing aside the electrical cords dangling from mechanics' lights hooked onto ceiling struts like massive incandescent microphones. The doors of his vehicle were already detached, the wheels removed, the cockpit gutted. These men were quick, thorough.

Carlos circled around the pulled seats and whistled upon seeing the bloodstains. "Man, that's gonna be hard to get out, dude. That's really sunk down into that leather."

"But that's not a problem, right?" Teddy yelled in Carlos's ear.

The Mexican laughed heartily. "Hell no, amigo! Blood? No sweat, no tears 'round here! My boys'll have those seats looking as bare as a showroom virgin's vajayjay in about an hour! Bald and swee-*eet*!" He kissed his fingers. "M-*mmmn*!" He let out a short laugh, clapping Teddy on the back. "Trust me!" Carlos walked around the opposite side, terminating his inspection. "Okay, cool. Let me show you what I got, mi amigo."

"You got plates too, right?"

From a nearby revolving rack of labeled vertical slots, Carlos slid out several license plates and handed them over. "Cali-fornicate. In-Diana—where I'd be if I wasn't here. And oh, here we are—home base, Kentucky and Tennessee. Collect 'em, trade 'em with your friends!"

Teddy took the last two pairs of stolen plates and tucked them inside his jacket, zipping them secure. He and Carlos moved on, passing right by the two goons who'd pinned Teddy's arms down in the pen. They inquisitively looked the gaunt visitor over and then laughed when they suddenly placed him.

Teddy bobbed his fists, flashing his calling cards. One of the musclemen tapped the outstretched fists in eeny-meeny-miny-moe fashion before he feigned jabbing at them. He and Teddy weaved, avoiding each other's swings.

"Still got it, amigo," the taller one said.

"You're my destiny!" sighed the other, hands clasped over his heart. "Dang, man—you look like a freakin' movie star."

Teddy laughed, "Don't you friggin' forget it!"

"Except for the teeth, man!"

Teddy snapped his jaws shut. *Gotta get these friggin' teeth fixed!*

Carlos interrupted the reunion lovefest. "All right, Teddy Bear. I have four or five fine rides to choose from."

At the far end of the garage, somewhat clear of the cacophony, Teddy surveyed the selections, all road ready. The assortment included a maroon Caddy, a piss-yellow Passat, a couple of Buicks, and a white Chevrolet City Express panel van. Like a moth drawn to a flame, Teddy beelined it to that van. He opened the front door, checking out the interior, and then ran his hand over the polished chrome rims. He turned around and held out his arms like Noah christening his ark.

Carlos laughed, slapping his knee. "You are *so* easy! I knew you wouldn't want the Seville. You're predictable as hell! Here, let me show you what we've done to it."

He walked Teddy around the vehicle, bragging about how they'd amped up the horses—if he ever needed the extra kick—tightened the steering, put in a new sound system and modified heavy steel front and rear bumpers, and added air struts. They walked to the rear of the van.

"Now, check this out," said Carlos.

Teddy stuck his head into the back of the van.

"Reinforced steel cage right behind the driver's seat. Can haul dogs, or other species, if you choose. No latch on the inside; can only be opened from the outside."

True, Teddy found no inside release of any kind. He smiled.

"You want us to give it a dope exterior for you? Any business you looking for?"

"Nah, just leave it a blank canvas for me. Cool."

"Yeah. You change your mind, though, let me know—I got me some of the best airbrush and graphic artists in four states, man!"

"Hey, let's go back to the office and get the keys."

Carlos dangled them like a carrot from his outstretched finger; it was the only set he'd brought along. "You are *waay* too predictable, amigo!"

~~

"Did you apologize, Son?" Cletus looked over from the doorway to his son lying on the bed, his laptop open and resting on his chest.

Billy closed the computer and sat up. "I tried, Pop. A couple a times. But he wasn't real open to it."

"No?"

"He threatened to shoot me."

Cletus chuckled; that was just like Jeffries.

Billy hung his head.

"Seriously, though," Cletus admonished, "what you did was totally outta line, you know that?"

"Well, I—"

Cletus raised a hand, stopping him. "On so many levels, William. Haven't I taught you better'n that? Drinkin' and drivin'? And worse, you made her walk home in the middle of the night! How'd you like it if she'd done that to you? What if somethin' had happened to that young lady?"

"You've tried to teach me better; that's for certain. I'm stubborn, though, like you. Set in my ways."

That's true, Cletus had to admit. The stubborn part, anyway. "Listen, you're still too young to be set in your ways. You got plenty of time for that cement head of your'n to set up yet. Have you *ever* seen me treat a woman like that?"

"No, sir."

"Your momma?"

"No, sir. Never."

"And you never will neither."

"Yes, sir."

"Good enough. Well, you sit in here and contemplate how you're goin' to apologize to Kaylee too. I'll talk to Sergeant Jeffries soon, see if things can be straightened out. I want you to strongly consider never treating *any* woman that way again, y'hear? I know you know what 'strongly consider' means."

"Yeah, Pop, I do. I'm sorry."

"I believe you, Son, but I ain't the ones you gotta make restitution to, understand?"

"Yes, sir. I copy."

"All right. You're a good boy, Billy. Just gotta make sure the decisions you make are the right ones. Try to consider the consequences when you make 'em—the ramifications. Think about your reputation; your reputation's everythin'. Sometimes tryin' to undo a wrong is much tougher'n creatin' one."

"You're right, Pop. I'll give it some real thought. Promise."

"All right." He paused and then added, "And no more beer. Unless you wanna spend a night in jail. Do *not* test me on that."

"Yessir."

Cletus backed out of the room and shut the door. As it closed, he saw his wife, Doris, standing down the hallway—high school sweethearts they'd been. She had her robe and reading glasses on and curlers in her hair, and she was still pretty as a picture to him. She'd been listening to the conversation, all of it, and smiled her approval at her husband of twenty-three years.

He winked at Doris Coonrod and chased her into their bedroom.

～❦～

Brody pulled the paisley comforter up to Abby's neck and leaned over, bussing her lightly on the forehead. "I'm so proud of you, sweetie. That's a huge deal—the spelling bee."

"Thanks, Daddy."

"Your mom told me she's very proud of you too."

Abby's eyes misted, and she smiled. "Is she? Did she really say that to you?"

"Most certainly, princess."

"Is she here now?"

Brody glanced around to be certain. "Nope. But this is our private time—yours and mine. Mommy kissed you good night when you were brushing your teeth."

"I thought that was her, but it just felt like my hair tickling my face."

"That's what it feels like sometimes, but that was her."

Abby was pleased with that. "Daddy?"

"What is it, pumpkin?"

"I saw something today. Well, it wasn't just today. It's happened a couple of times since the school year started."

"What do you mean, Abs? What have you seen?"

"Just a man. Sometimes I look down outside of our classroom window, and he's just sitting on the bench across from our playground."

"A man? Just sitting there on the bench?"

"Yes, and every so often he looks up at me and waves."

As any responsible parent would, Brody had concern over this. "Have you told anyone in the principal's office about this man? How about Ms. Thompson?"

"No, not really—it's a little bit peculiar."

Brody furrowed his brow. "What do you mean?"

"Well, he sorta just sits there, and he's wearing ..." She hesitated.

"What is he wearing, Abs?" *A trench coat?*

"A ... well, it looks kind of like a ... wetsuit. A scuba diver's wetsuit."

"A scuba diver?"

"You know, a frogman. He has a mask on and a snorkel and some swim fins—the whole deal!"

"And he's just sitting there on that bench? Across the street from the playground at school?"

"Yep. Smiling and waving. And you know what else?"

"You mean there's more?"

"Yes! Sometimes ... sometimes someone else ... someone just walks by and wants to sit down on that bench right where he is. They'll sit down, and they'll go *plop*—right through him! Like he's not even sitting there at all!"

Can this be ...? Whoa—take this slow. Do not *jump to conclusions here.* "Then what does he do?" he asked.

"He either stays hidden by the person who sat down on top of him or slides over. And when he slides, it looks like he's coming right out from that other person, like he was inside of them or something!"

He stood up and backed away from his daughter.

"Daddy? Daddy, what is it?"

He began pacing, mumbling to himself.

"Daddy, did I say something wrong?"

He rushed to her. "Oh, no, baby. No, no. I think I know who it is that you're seeing."

"You do? Who?"

"Has this happened before? Have you seen anything or anyone else like this?"

"No. Who is it?"

"You can't think of any other time this has happened to you?"

"No, Daddy, I can't. Who, who, who?" She sounded like an inquisitive owlet.

"Abby, unless I'm mistaken, I think you're seeing your great-grandfather, Grampa Eddie."

"Who's that?"

Abby sat up and raised her knees, the comforter sliding to her waist. Brody sat down next to her and stroked her hair. "If it is him, that's really incredible. Let me tell you what I know about him; it's not very much, because I never knew him and I'm actually not that familiar with his spirit. According to Gram-Gram, Grampa Eddie was a navy frogman during World War II. He died trying to disentangle a submarine named the *Nautilus* from a cargo net attached to several sea mines."

"*Nautilus?* Like Captain Nemo's submarine?"

"Yes, the same name. After he released the net from the sub, one of the mines exploded. He drowned. He was a real hero. Gave up his life to save all those sailors."

"Wow."

"Yes—wow! This is incredible! You know what this means? I mean, I thought it might be possible ... Abby, the same things that began with me at an early age are happening to you right now!"

"I see dead people?"

"You can channel lost loved ones!" he exclaimed, sounding as if he'd just won the lottery. "How does that feel?"

"It's kinda scary," she answered, "kinda creepy."

"It'll seem like that at first, but I promise you, it'll get to where it's more and more routine. I'll teach you how to do it better and better. We'll work on it together, okay?"

"Yeah?"

"Yeah," Brody replied. *How fun will it be to help her with this?*

Abby lay down in her bed again. She seemed to be considering what her father had just told her, trying to process everything for the first time. It was daunting. Looking up at him, she asked, "Hey, Daddy?"

"What, pumpkin?"

"When will I be able to see Mommy?"

"Well ..." *Ooh, that's a toughie; how can I put this?* "When I started seeing those who had crossed over to the other side—"

"You mean dead people?"

"Uh, yes. But there are plenty of other ways to refer to them to make people feel more comfortable with what we do." *We? How cool is that?* "So try to think of other ways you might want to express that. Listen to how I put it sometimes. But to answer your question, I started out seeing one spirit at first. Then, over time, I was able to see others who had passed. And one thing I learned was that you won't be able to see any spirit until they are ready for you to see them."

"What do you mean? Isn't Mommy ready to see me?"

He smiled at her. "Honey, this will be hard to understand, but it's not that Mommy wants to stay unseen by you. Quite the opposite—she can't wait for you to see her. It's just that it takes time for those who've crossed over to be able to present themselves in spirit form to someone whose gift is at such a tender stage, like yours is now. When I was a toddler, it took me many months before I actually spoke with Gram-Gram's spirit. She first had to establish that connection to me with the tiniest of encounters, like bumping an out-of-reach teething biscuit to me or saving me from tumbling over my crib rail the night I first tried to climb out. As my abilities strengthened, it took fewer and fewer of those telltale signs for a spiritual bond—or a bridge, as I call it—to be made. Now I can create those connections—summon a spirit—by merely focusing my concentration really hard. It's a gift that took me years to become good at, and I'm *still* working on it, refining it, trying new techniques, and such. You'll get there too."

"I will?"

"Yes, honey."

"So you can call on any spirit you want to, no matter when or where?"

"Well, it's not as simple as I made it sound just now. As I said before, a spirit has to be willing to step forward. I can concentrate all I want to, but if a spirit doesn't wish to communicate with me, that's their choosing, not mine. And it has to be within a touchpoint too; it can't be in any old random place."

"A touchpoint? What's a touchpoint?" Abby asked.

Brody chuckled to himself. The term, which he had actually coined, was so commonplace to him that it hadn't dawned on him that Abby had never heard of it. An idea came to his mind. "Think of it like a dot-to-dot drawing."

"I used to love doing dot-to-dots!"

"I know! Well, think of each dot as one of the places you go, or have been to, in your life. It can be someplace as everyday as the bathroom or school; a place you visit only once a week, like when we go to Walmart; or even a once-in-a-lifetime place."

"Like when we went to Disney World with Mommy?"

He smiled at her. "Exactly. Think of each of those places on your personal map as representing the dots on your puzzle page. Once you've connected those dots, they form a familiar pattern, right?"

She nodded.

"They're no longer random, meaningless points. Similarly, the places you go form the pattern of your life, a spiritual road map of sorts. Each one of those places becomes a destination where those spirits who have attached themselves to you can be called upon. Those places are interconnected touchpoints, and they're in addition to that spirit's personal road map— whatever touchpoints the spirit experienced when he or she was part of the physical world, the world of the living."

"What does it mean when a spirit 'attaches' itself to me? Is that good or bad?"

Brody was enjoying these questions of hers and having to explain these things to Abby, who had never seemed too curious about these things before. "It has to do with those bridges I mentioned. There are certain souls who are as important to us in our lives as they also were, I believe, to others in past lives. Each soul has a purpose either in this, the physical world—whether it's to be present along with us on our journeys, directly impacting the world around us in some form or fashion—or from the spiritual realm, to simply guide us from the other side. We all have a select few of the latter, those spirit souls, to influence us. Those souls help mold us in certain ways—often subtly but sometimes in very dramatic fashion, like causing us to make a choice that could alter our day or even our entire destiny. The more-subtle impacts can seem like pure chance—certain things that we can't explain—but they're actually far from random."

She raised an eyebrow and frowned at Brody, arms akimbo. "Like when I'm positive I've turned out the fishbowl light for Pinky and Goldie before school, but I come into the room and it's on?"

He chuckled. "I see your point—sorry I've accused you. Yes, like your goldfish's light. That could have been a sign from Grampa Eddie or Mommy or some other spirit adding to their bridge. It's those things that—when you notice them, *really* notice them—indicate that a spirit is trying to attach itself to you. Those instances then become the building blocks for the eventual connection with that spirit. They all add up and make the process go that much quicker. Those telltale signs are the only ones that are available to those who don't share our gift. Without the ability you and I possess, they have to be content experiencing only those seemingly coincidental building blocks; they cannot make the final, real connections we can. Even so, it's only if they *want* to see the signs that they will see them; if their minds remain closed to the possibility, they'll simply ignore what the spirit world presents to them, believing the signals to be nothing more than meaningless happenstances, never to acknowledge the awesome meanings behind each and every one."

"Signals like Mommy wiping my tears or kissing me on the cheek?"

"*Excellent* examples, Abs! After all the necessary blocks have been laid and the bridge has been fully established and the actual connection to the spirit is in place, then that spirit is what I call 'attached.' It can be encountered at any of your touchpoints. And when you get to the stage I'm at, you'll be able to summon any spirit at any of its touchpoints, as long as it is willing to present itself to you. Is this making sense at all?"

She nodded in an uncertain fashion. "I think so."

"But remember, like bridges manufactured in real life, spiritual connections cannot be built overnight. It takes time. It takes many building blocks to accomplish those first few bridges, especially when your command over your gift isn't as well established. You can't rush that process; you can't *make* that happen. But it will. Promise. The connections will get easier with time and require fewer and fewer building blocks. They will happen faster and faster with each new spirit. Each bridge you establish strengthens your gift. In time, you'll reach the point I have when those blocks won't always even be necessary."

"That explains why I couldn't see all of Grampa Eddie at first, only his head."

"That's right. It takes time for apparitions to appear fully to you, especially your first few. Just like with Mommy. That's why she hasn't shown herself to you—she can't. But she's laying the groundwork to be able to. Bit by bit. You're just not ready yet. You're getting there, though. You've made a connection with Grampa Eddie already. Your first one! I'm very proud of you!"

"Thanks," she said with a chuckle, "I think."

He laughed. "I know; I've been there too. Just try to be receptive to the smallest of signs Mommy presents to you. They might be all the steel and stone that's needed. It's coming. Soon, baby, soon." He caressed her hair. "There, does that help?"

"I ... think so, Daddy. You're saying I've got to let it happen on her terms, not mine?"

She is so *smart!* "Yes, that's *exactly* what I meant."

Abby nodded. "I wish it didn't have to be that way."

Brody reached out and erased her fresh tear before it strayed too far from the corner of her left eye. "I know. Now listen ..."

"Yes?"

He helped her relinquish her seated position, returning her once more to the comfort of her pillow. "As far as telling anyone about this, my advice is to keep it to yourself."

"Why?" she asked.

"Well, I learned the hard way that most people won't understand. Whether they know you or not, they'll think you're off your rocker if you tell them about this ability. Others may try to take advantage of you—make you do things with your ability you might not want to. I wouldn't say anything even to your closest friends about this right now. Again, I've learned this the hard way; I don't want the same things to happen to you if they can be avoided. It'll make things a lot easier."

"So even though I might want to tell somebody, I should keep it a secret, or I might find myself in trouble. Trouble I never saw coming."

"Yes, that's right. Brilliant! Of course—you're *my* daughter!" He tickled her, and she giggled. He added, "I wish I would have had someone offer me that guidance early on. I would've saved myself a ton of embarrassment." He kissed her forehead again. He wished he could watch over her at all times, protect her—even from herself now.

"Well, I'll tell you one thing, Daddy."

"Yes, my queen?"

"I can't wait until Mommy can talk to me."

She surrendered to the nighttime, closing her eyes. He leaned over and gave her a bonus good-night kiss, sorting out her slightly matted tresses.

Brody rose and turned out her room light, angling her door to allow in, at most, a sliver of the hallway glow, and whispered, "Me too, baby. Me too."

On his way back to the house, Teddy decided to make a pit stop at Corn Silk Liquors on US 79 to pick up some grub and another twelve-pack. The local package store and sports bar was a large wooden A-frame with tables along two walls and a few big screens hanging in strategic locations for patrons to catch the latest pro competitions.

Teddy walked in, placed an order at the bar for some pulled pork sliders, and headed to the john, needing to empty his bladder in preparation for a refill. He unzipped early as he approached the urinal and placed his arm against the wall above to steady himself, for his head was swimming from the tequila. As his bladder drained, he let out a lengthy sigh of contentment.

The door swung open behind him, and a large fellow, reeking like an ashtray, with a full brown beard, assumed a stance adjacent to Teddy for the same calling.

As Teddy was nearing completion of his golden draining, he heard the guy beside him hawk a rather prolific loogie into his urinal. He eyed the hawker. *Shit! Of all the dumb luck: Big Jim!*

He'd never expected to encounter Big Jim here! It wasn't Big Jim's natural habitat—there was no illicit gambling. Teddy said a silent prayer that he wouldn't be made and shook his sausage, stuffing it back into its cotton casing. He turned his back to Big Jim and zipped up.

As Teddy stepped toward the door, Big Jim said, "Ain't ya gonna flush?"

Teddy paused in his tracks.

Big Jim snorted up a repeater. Then he cleared his throat and said, "I said, 'Ain't ya gonna flush'?"

Teddy cracked the door open to leave.

Big Jim spat out one more substantial phlegm ball and then ordered, "Hey, man. Flush the goddamn urinal!"

Inching slowly backward, Teddy reached his hand blindly behind him, palm purposely facing Big Jim, hiding the distinctive tattoo. The man grabbed Teddy's wrist and placed his palm on the cold handle, never looking directly at the owner.

"No one's gonna flush the damn thing for you."

Jim released his hold, and Teddy pushed down on the polished lever. Water swished his urine away. "Sorry," he growled, disguising his voice. He opened the door a little wider and slithered into the main room, closing it with a huge sigh of relief—of a vastly different variety. Halfway to the exit, Teddy glanced behind him and caught Big Jim emerging from the gents' room. With horribly rotten timing, the bartender called out, "Hey, Teddy! Teddy Trent! Your sliders are ready to go, brother!"

Without hesitation, abandoning his pulled pork, Teddy bolted. As he fled the premises, he heard the bartender call, "Hey, Jimbo, tell Teddy ..." The door closed behind Teddy, causing the bartender's words to fade out.

Teddy rounded the corner to the street side, heading quickly to the outskirts of the lot. When he was just inches from his van and escape, Big Jim called out after him, "Hey, *hey!*"

Teddy stopped dead in his tracks. He wheeled around, his back against his van, and displayed his gap-toothed grin, which had been provided courtesy of that very same behemoth and his pair of jackals running him down a couple of weeks earlier.

"Yo, Big Jim," he chuckled nervously. "Didn't know you were in there, man. How're—"

"Where's my two-and-a-half deuces, Teddy?"

"Well, it's funny you—"

Jim grabbed him by his collar, lifting him into the air. "Ain't nothin' funny about it! Don't fuck with me, Trent—or you'll lose more than just your measly teeth tonight."

Teddy's boots were dangling. "Put me down, Jimbo, and I'll tell you."

Jim lowered him to the ground but held firm to Teddy's sturdy collar and shook him. "I mean it, Trent. Where's the dough you owe?"

"I'm gettin' paid this week. I'll have it for you by the weekend; I swear!"

Jim released his grasp, taking a deliberate step backward. "You know I know how to find you, fuckface."

"Why do you have to call me shit like that, man?"

Jim, glaring down at Teddy's face, advanced upon him. The sudden, deliberate move, along with the foul smell of this snorting bull's stale beer breath, was intimidating, as it was meant to be. Wild hairs emerged from Big Jim's nostrils, merging themselves with those of his flourishing mustache, the snot from some recent respiratory malady crusting there. The night air was chilling rapidly, crafting vapor from Big Jim's exhalations that echoed the fog filling Teddy's head, the fog that was threatening to cloud his better judgment.

He imagined himself stomping down hard on his foe's toes, and when Big Jim bent over to clutch at the acute pain, Teddy'd drop his elbow hard on Big Jim's back, felling him. A gun butt to the skunk ape's chin would send him flipping over, flopping around like a crappie about to be filleted. Then he'd stand over his tormentor, wielding his fists. "This one's your destiny; this one's your absolution," he'd taunt. "What's your pleasure?"

Instead, with his gun stowed out of reach in the console of his van, he defaulted to "I'll have it by the weekend. I swear!"

Big Jim glared at him. "You damn well better, Trent, or that lame-ass brother of yours' ass is grass. You catch my drift?"

In more ways than one ... "Yeah, I gotcha. Don't you worry, man."

"It ain't *me* who's gotta be worried, Trent." He swung his fist toward Teddy, who nimbly tilted his head. Jim's fist settled into the side of the panel van. A four-inch-wide dent was now Teddy's newest battle scar.

"That's your brother's face if you don't deliver. Remember," he warned, pointing two fingers at his eyes and then at Teddy, "I got eyes, Teddy. I got eyes. I'm watchin' you. *Comprende?*"

Teddy nodded submissively.

Big Jim lowered himself to Teddy's eye level and snarled, "Now get the *fuck* outta here!"

His nemesis guffawing behind him, Teddy scrambled into the van and gunned it out of the parking lot, swerving onto the highway. Glancing in his rearview, he noticed Jim dusting his hands together with the vigor of wiping off something vile. The huge man shuffled into the glow of a parking lot light and ignited a smoke, his back to the road.

Teddy spun the van around and headed back, jumping the curb into the parking lot, shooting toward Big Jim's back. The big man twirled around and was hurled into the air by the tremendous impact of Teddy's reinforced front grill. Jim's flight ended a row of cars away, his bulk heaving down onto the roof of a Honda Civic, caving it from the impact.

Teddy idled the engine and got out, keeping his high beams trained on the figure draped over the import like a deer in season. The limp, unconscious head was dangling upside down, flopped over where the passenger window used to be, much like Teddy's weathered speed bag suspended from the ceiling of his garage. He balled his fists. "You got eyes, huh? Eyes? Let's see ..."

Jim's face became his punching bag. Once—*destiny!* Twice—*absolution!* The first blow missed its mark, busting the big man's nose but calibrating Teddy for the remainder of the flurry. *Destiny! Absolution! Destiny! Absolution!* Again and again he pummeled Big Jim's eyes until they ruptured into a bloody stream. "Let's see who's got eyes now, fuckface!"

The ruby orbs on Teddy's grinning golden skull ring became smeared with more scarlet—the ungiving metal peening Big Jim's bony orbits. Vitreous humor oozed out of the deflated and fractured sockets, mixing with blood into a pinkish gel that crawled down the side of the Civic.

Shuffling back to the Chevrolet van, shaking off some of the slime and wiping off the rest on his shirttail, Teddy surveyed the vehicle's damage: dented front end, cracked headlight—that was all. *Huh. How 'bout that? Carlos can fix that shit easy.*

He spat into his hands, removed the rest of what he could of Big Jim's goo onto his jeans, and climbed back inside. As he cruised down the road a piece, his choppy panting slowed pace until the precise instant his cell phone went off, scaring him half to death. Laughing at his own jitteriness, he slid the lock off the phone call and held the device to his ear.

"Teddy?"

"Yeah, man."

"How are you doing tonight?" asked the voice.

"Okay. Just stopped for a piss and ran into an old friend. What's up? Why you callin' me?"

"You got the money?"

"What?" Teddy had heard the question; he was merely stalling, strategizing.

"You got the money, Teddy?" the voice repeated, agitated.

The money being referenced wasn't that which Big Jim had demanded; it was the loot from the bank heist. "Well, no, not exactly."

Agitation turned into aggravation. "What do you mean, 'not exactly'?"

"Lyle hid it."

"He hid it? Where?"

"I don't know."

Aggravation became aggression. "You don't—well *ask* him, *idiot!*"

Irked, Teddy held the phone out in front of him, glaring at the screen. The name and number of the caller showed as UNKNOWN. He pressed the phone back to his twelve o'clock shadow. "I can't."

"What do you mean? Isn't he there with you?"

"Uh, no—he's with my pa."

"Well, where's your pa, Teddy?"

"With the angels, man."

"What?"

"Lyle's *dead*, man!" Teddy yelled at the phone.

Silence. Then the voice calmly asked, "Dead?"

"Yes." Teddy began to weep.

Maybe he expected an ounce of sympathy from the other end of the line. Instead, all he received was a quiet, controlled monotone. "Did he tell you where the money's hidden?"

"No, man," Teddy cried. "He got ripped up before he could tell me."

Silence. "So ... let me get this straight. You have no idea where the money is?"

"No, man, I swear."

"Are you shitting me, Teddy? Do you *have* the cash you heisted? Or are you holding out on me?"

Teddy hit a pothole in the road and dropped the phone into his lap. Fumbling it back to his ear, he growled, "I lost my *brother*, motherfucker!"

Sounding neither impressed nor sympathetic, the caller said, "Let's get one thing straight, Teddy."

"Yeah?"

"I don't give a flying *fuck* about your scumbag brother." There was a pregnant pause. Then, "You find that money, you got it?"

"Yeah, and how am I gonna *do* that? The only person who knew where the hell it is was Lyle, and he ain't exactly able to clue me in anymore!"

Sarcasm dripped through the phone. "Then let me enlighten you in words you'll understand: it ain't my problem."

"What?" Teddy jammed on his brakes and skidded over onto the shoulder. "Now you listen to me! That was my brother, you—"

"No! You listen to *me*, you ignominious moron. You find that money! I don't care how, but you find it. No excuses, do you hear? Does that pinheaded, half-wit brain of yours follow what I'm trying to get across? If you don't come up with that cash by the end of the weekend—"

What is it about the weekend? Who died and left this weekend the deadline for every fuckin' thing? Well, Big Jim's dead, but ...

"—shit is going to rain down on your ass like a spring shower, like tripe strewn to the ground from a gutted pig. Either of those images stick? They should. You'll be stuck just like that pig. And this time, it won't be just your teeth you'll be missing."

"Well, how am I gonna—"

"Not my problem, Teddy. When I tell the boss in Chi-Town who fucked this up, whose balls do you think he'll want mounted to his mantle? Not mine. *Your* sorry-ass cojones."

Teddy was partial to his balls—he was very attached to them and preferred it to remain that way. "I'll find it," he conceded.

"You'd better. You find that money, or you're a dead man, Teddy. Plain and simple. You won't be able to hide from him. He'll separate you from more than just your teeth or your testicles—he'll have your head. That is truth in its purest form. I don't know how to make myself clearer, do you?"

Silence.

"I thought not. Good. By Monday then."

The call disconnected. Teddy sat there and looked out the windshield. That was some real serious shit just heaped onto his plate. Should he drive over to Clarksville in the middle of the night and search around the Dollar General? Hell, he had until Monday—plenty of time. He could go tomorrow. No telling about the weather, though. *S'posed to rain like a sonuvabitch throughout the weekend.* He weighed the alternatives and opted for heading back to the house, cracking open a couple of cold ones, having a smoke, getting a good night's sleep, and heading out in the morning to search for the dough. Even though doing so was placing his cojones in greater jeopardy.

As his family jewels shrunk to the safety of loftier heights, in the high beams up ahead and on the glass, he could already see it was beginning to drizzle.

Sitting on her bed in her pink pajamas, listening to P!nk on her portable speakers, Kaylee Jeffries was brushing her long hair when David knocked on her door.

"Come in," she called out. A pretty teenager with chestnut hair and smoky eyes, she had inherited just the right amount of her father's genes to endow that beautiful Brooke Shields quality to her brow line. She poked her remote in the direction of the sound system, pausing the song as her father poked his head into the room.

"Hey, Kay. You A-OK?"

She smiled. "Yeah, I'm better. Just another day in paradise," she kidded him.

"Know what you mean, jelly bean. Can I come in?"

"Always." She beckoned to him.

He closed the door behind him, standing just inside the room. "You speak to Billy at all?"

She shook her head. "Nope. You?"

"As a matter of fact, I did. Sort of."

She put her brush down beside her on the turned-down blanket. She asked him, winking, "What do you mean, 'jelly bean'?"

"All right, I get it; I hear ya. Point taken. What I meant was I had to question him at the store."

"Why? Was he in some other kind of trouble?"

"No," chuckled David. "Nothing like that. He saw a guy behind the store who might be connected to the bank robbery today."

"I heard about that robbery. I was wondering if you were investigating that."

"Yep, they put me on it." He came over and sat down on the side of her bed, looking across at her. "Anyway, I went by the Dollar General and spoke with him."

"What did he say? Was the guy he saw someone who might help you solve it?"

"Hard to tell if that guy was involved."

"Oh. Well, did he say anything else?" She picked up the brush again and began stroking her hair.

"Well ..." Her dad seemed kind of stuck.

"What?" She dipped her chin. "Was he an ass again?"

"No, he wasn't."

She frowned. "So what happened?"

"He was sort of apologetic about the whole thing."

She immediately brightened, placing the brush on her nightstand. "He apologized?"

"Well, he started to."

She slumped.

"He tried. I kind of cut him off—"

"Oh no. What did you do?" she scolded.

He clenched his teeth, baring them. "I ... sort of ... threatened to ... shoot him."

She broke out into a belly laugh. "You did not!"

He raised his right hand. "Guilty."

She cracked up again and then reached across the bed and hugged her father. "Dad, that is *so* hilarious!" It took her a moment to catch her breath. Then she looked at her father and smiled at him with unflinching esteem. "Thank you for sticking up for me."

David's eyes watered. "Sure, sweetie," he choked.

She scooched back toward the head of the bed, crossing her legs. "Was he really sorry?"

"I don't know," he chuckled, forcing the lump down his throat with a swallow. "I didn't really give him a chance to say. But if I was a betting man—which I'm not, by the way—I'd say he was trying to tell me something. I wasn't real receptive to the message, though. I thought it might make him think harder next time about what he put you through."

She smiled at him again. "You're pretty cool, Dad. I'm lucky to have a dad like you."

"Well, I'm even luckier to have a daughter like you, Kay-Kay." He blew her a kiss and bade her good night.

"Good night, Dad." Kaylee switched off her bed lamp, eased down onto the cushy pillow, crossed her wrists over her forehead, and stared up at the ceiling, its textures illuminated dimly by the LEDs from her computer. She sighed.

Maybe he *was* sorry.

Maybe he really *did* care.

She sighed again and closed her eyes.

Maybe there *was* hope, after all.

That was the best news she had heard all day.

⸻

Brody came downstairs and went into the kitchen. Lacing his fingers around his warm mug of coffee and partaking a quick savor, he considered Abby's revelation. *Wow! What a bombshell!*

She was embarking on a magical, mysterious tour—a journey full of discovery and adventure around each bend and yet full of danger too, especially if not taken seriously and with the utmost discretion. It was his duty to instill whatever precautions were necessary—a huge undertaking, for certain, and an even greater responsibility. Were they both truly ready to handle all of that?

Coffee mug in hand, he walked into the living room. As he sat down in his favorite chair, a brown leather recliner, he looked around at his long-gone loved ones gathered there to end the day with him.

His dream team was at hand: Susan sat across the modest living room on the sofa, with Gram-Gram Lily beside her, both smiling. Walter was on the brick hearth, puffing on his pipe, next to the love seat, where Jane sat. Even Ruffy was present and accounted for, lying on an oval braided throw rug in front of the fireplace, his head resting on his front paws.

That reminded Brody—his feet were freezing! He wiggled his toes. He could sure use his slippers. On several occasions, he'd tried sending his spirit dog after his night shoes, but the errand was never carried out successfully; he always ended up heading upstairs to fetch them himself. He decided to try it again, though, and called out, "Ruffy!"

Ruffy sprang to attention, tongue flicking.

"Ruffy! Go get my slippers, boy!"

The tiny spirit took a seat on his haunches, the usual prelude to their exercise in futility.

Brody smiled and shifted his attention away from Ruffy for the time being. He peered over his mug, through the steam, unsure of where to begin his discussion with the others.

As spirits—and Brody was keenly aware of this—his departed loved ones had made themselves available because *they* wanted to, not just because he had summoned them. Spirits routinely made their presence known to the living in their times of need, doubt, trouble, or insecurity, though generally they remained silent yet ubiquitous—content to monitor rather than intrude.

In fact, direct interference sometimes carried with it a high price—possible loss of any further contact with that particular individual whom they'd attached themselves to, depending on the extent of the intercession. Saving the life of a living individual—cheating death—that act would permanently break the connection between that living soul and the dead. So warnings or modest assistances were far more commonplace than actual psychic-physical interceding.

This wealth of knowledge had been imparted to Brody both directly and indirectly through his conversations and encounters. Gram-Gram had provided young Brody the lion's share of his knowledge about spiritual warnings. And warn spirits did—while understandably, with what was at stake should they choose to alter the fate of the living, most opted to remain relatively detached from attempting to influence any ultimate outcomes.

That latter aspect was largely reserved only for the most powerful of spirits anyway, usually those associated with a substantial energy force, either of a positive or a negative nature, according to Gram-Gram. Those spirits— those foolhardy enough to risk the loss of a handsome sum of their spectral energy—had power to burn, so to speak, while still maintaining their ability to inhabit the other side. Those spirits were capable of sapping enough energy from living souls to recharge or supercharge their otherworldly dynamos.

The number of twists and turns a soul took along its path while alive— whether right or wrong—had a cumulative effect, determining in large part how the spirit presented in its afterlife. The majority of spirits were imbued with positive energy. The more altruistic and self-sacrificing a soul's antecedent accomplishments were, the more positive its subsequent existence, and vice versa. That polar opposite—evil spirits—were almost universally miserable souls, having spent their time in the physical world littering their pathways with misdeeds and missteps, dooming themselves in the process to their ill-fated afterlife. Others in that same category might have been recipients of relentless undesirable consequences—often victims of violent, unspeakable crimes. As a result, only vengeance could guide their eternal souls. For true evil existed not only in the physical world but also on the other side. When attached to a living soul or existing at a certain touchpoint, manifestations of spirits comprised of negative forces ran the gamut: mischievous, malicious, downright menacing, and, in extreme cases, malevolent. Luckily, those threatening apparitions were much fewer and farther between, and Brody had encountered only one thus far—when he'd been a college coed.

Brody was having a hard time articulating what he wanted to say to his gathered departed loved ones. Susan seemed to sense this and jumped in for him. "She's quite excited about witnessing her first, isn't she?"

Brody lowered his coffee cup onto the end table beside him. "Yes, she is. At least I think so."

"It was Edward," stated Lily.

"Yes. It was, wasn't it?" Brody said.

Walter removed his pipe, blowing ethereal smoke. "What are you thinking, Son? You okay with Eddie coming forward to Abby?"

"I always thought that if it ever happened, it would be you, Susan."

"Edward had one heckuva start on me, you know," she said.

"He always was bullheaded," Lily explained with a smile.

"Well, I just spoke to Abby about keeping this whole thing private, but that's hard to do when her grampa Eddie shows himself in such a public place. Can you ask him about that?" Brody asked.

Lily sighed. "I'll try, but it rarely matters anymore; he still flits about to the beat of a different drummer."

"I'd appreciate it."

"You seem troubled, Son." Walter took another puff on his pipe. Of Brody's parents, his father had always been the better judge of what Brody was thinking and feeling. "What's got you so uptight this evening?"

"Mixed emotions, really. I'm excited as hell, obviously—"

"'Hell,' Son?"

Brody chuckled. "You know what I mean. But as fired up as I am about this—"

"There's that reference again ..."

Jane gave Walter a brusque tap on his arm. "Let our son finish, you old coot!"

"I have some real concerns as well," Brody finished.

"What are they, sweetie?" Lily asked.

He sighed and took a sip of coffee. "I discovered this gift at an age far earlier than Abby and recall how awe-inspiring it seemed to me. But that sense of wonderment quickly became tempered with, at times, a twinge of regret."

"Regret? What do you mean, Giff?" Susan asked.

"Well, I remember schoolmates and grown-ups alike hearing about my ability and then *expecting* things of me. Some wanted information from family or friends who had passed, but I didn't want to provide it, because I thought that once I'd confirmed to them what I was capable of—that it was legitimate, real—they wouldn't stop hounding me. I tried to explain that to Abby tonight, to stop her from letting the cat out of the bag tomorrow and getting herself caught in the middle of a snowballing situation she might not be able to control or escape from right now without being ostracized. At this stage in her gift, it could easily become too much for her to handle at one time, overwhelming her before she ever gave her ability a chance to unfold.

"I remember I felt kind of invincible at first, like some childhood fantasy. I saw myself as some sort of new superhero! But in reality, there were so many negative consequences. Shunned or derided by most kids my age because they thought I was a weirdo or some sort of monster, I was pushed around, bullied, made fun of. I had deluded myself into imagining that making my ability public would bring nothing but positives. Instead, I became a pariah—a loner forced into near seclusion, like Quasimodo. I learned what it was like to be a misfit. I don't want that for Abby."

"How do you know it would turn out that way? Maybe it would be a whole different ball game for her," Susan said. "After all, she has you there for guidance and support if things go awry."

"Yes, that's true, but is it all really worth the risk?" asked Brody. "If it went sour, she could end up regretting or, even worse, hating her gift, maybe for the rest of her life. Who knows what would happen then? She can't just turn it off, you know."

Jane took a drag of her eternal Salem menthol. "But you had friends, honey. I saw when you had sleepover guests."

"One guest, Mom—Tommy Jennings. And did he ever come back for an encore after hearing my solo conversation with you in the middle of that night?"

"I don't reckon he ever did."

"And do you remember any other friends of mine prior to my junior year?"

She thought about it. "Well, now that you mention it ..."

"I rest my case. My point is, Abby has a bunch of friends—her fellow troop members, her classmates. She's a popular little girl, and I don't want that boat rocked, or it'll rock her world. It will stunt her true personality, which is pretty fabulous right now."

Susan smiled at him. "I couldn't agree with you more on that—she's a special girl, Giff."

He nodded. Feeling a chill around his ankles, Brody looked over at Ruffy, who was still sitting on his haunches, panting obediently, tail wagging, awaiting further instruction. Brody gave it another shot. "Timmy's in the well, boy; Timmy's in the well! Go get my slippers, boy! Fetch!"

Ruffy let out several yips, turning in tight circles as though chasing his tail—a pointless exercise for his breed. Then he bolted to the stairs.

Brody chuckled. He knew Ruffy wouldn't really be able to fetch the slippers; they were much too weighty for his compact spirit buddy to transport any great distance on his own. Still, it was a kick to send him on those missions, and Ruffy seemed to enjoy the challenge.

Lily said, "Listen, I don't pretend to know everything you went through or what you're experiencing presently, sweetie. But I do know this: without you and your gift, all the people that you've helped over the years wouldn't have received those blessings you've given them—the relief they'd sought for so long, all those questions they had that would have forever stayed unanswered. Think of all the good you do, what you've done for folks. Yes, it took time to get to that point, but hasn't it been worth everything?"

She continued, "I remember the day Janie died. You knew I was trying to tell you something important. But were you just too young to comprehend the meaning behind my premonition, or did you simply mistrust the spirit world at that point? In that moment, did you follow your heart or your head? That would be a tall order for anyone to figure out, at *any* age, let alone a child. Don't you agree?"

Brody nodded in agreement as Lily finished her thought.

"Think of all those times in your life you've called out for our help and our guidance. Have we ever let you down when you needed us most?"

"Never. I see what you're saying," Brody said. "What you've said is extremely important. But, first and foremost, this all *has* to be on her terms, not mine. Just hers. I can't let what *I* want influence what is in her best interests—eager as I am for her to become proficient with her gift."

"That's the way it should be, Son," Walter said.

"You've just got to be careful to take things slow with her," Susan said. "Teach her well. Counsel her about the pitfalls she may encounter—they're as vital for her to experience as the triumphs in this."

"But some of those she'll have to experience personally, just like you did, Brody," Walter added. "You mustn't shield her completely because of your concerns. If you do, she'll never learn from those trials and grow in her ability. She'll never know the wonders you've known."

"Yes, you're right. All of you."

Brody knew that these spirits that were so special to him were correct more times than not; those on the other side possessed a divine knowledge—a genuine gift!

At the sound of something slapping the foyer, Brody arose. He walked to a spot just beneath the upstairs balcony and found his slippers, delivered as if manna from the heavens. *Whoa! That's never happened before!* Ruffy had never been able to move an object as heavy as a leather house shoe! Moving an object about was a moderate effort even for a human's spirit—gargantuan to a Pomeranian's—and required otherworldly energy and focus to achieve. *Man*, he thought, *what a day of firsts!* "C'mere, boy! C'mere!" He slipped his slippers on and stood at the foot of the stairs.

Ruffy bounced down to the bottom stairstep and put his front spectral paws up on Brody's thigh, panting from the extraordinary adventure.

Knowing he couldn't actually pet the spirit dog, Brody rewarded him instead with praise. "Good boy, Ruffy! Good boy! Amazing! You da man!"

Ruffy barked; the sound was much lower and louder than normal.

"Hey, where'd that come from, boy?"

Ruffy had channeled his own inner Lassie.

Abby hoped she'd made it back undetected to her bed; she'd been listening in, up on the landing—something she'd never done before during one of her father's late-night get-togethers with family spirits. A few minutes prior, she was rousted out of shallow slumber by her daddy calling out, "Ruffy!" She slid out from under her covers and, under cover of darkness, tiptoed quietly out to the railing to catch whatever she could of his conversation below.

She knew he had those meetings; she would sometimes catch bits and pieces of him chatting to her mommy or Gram-Gram or others downstairs after she'd brushed her teeth, but whenever she interrupted and inquired about whom he was speaking to, he simply told her, "Please go nighty-night now."

Tonight, straining to hear his words, she'd had a hard time ascertaining the gist of the subject matter. She caught bits and pieces here and there and finally deduced that the discussion was about her and what she and her father had spoken about before he turned off her lights.

Her father, at certain points in the conversation, sounded just as pessimistic about the entire situation as he sounded optimistic in others. It was hard to make heads or tails out of it. One moment he seemed ecstatic for her; the next he couldn't have come across as more worried, concerned. Which was it?

And what was that stuff about being a misfit? *Misfit? I don't want to be a misfit!* She'd seen the Disney movie *The Hunchback of Notre Dame* and recalled how Quasi had been mistreated, misunderstood. *I don't want to lose my friends—no way!*

And then those slippers! What on earth was up with them? Right after her daddy had asked for someone's help with someone named Timmy, who was somehow in a well, of all places, she'd felt a sudden chill as she'd knelt on the carpet. That was weird. But what happened next was even weirder!

She'd heard a soft scuffing sound from down the hallway, and when she turned her head to see what it was, one of her father's slippers was dangling over the edge of the balcony. Then the other slowly, jerkily inched across the carpet toward her! The incredible sight startled a stifled cry from her. The second house shoe crept eerily closer, eventually assuming an approximately parallel position adjacent to the first. Wide-eyed, she watched as they dove, one after the other, over the cliff's edge, hurtling to the wood floor below!

At the sound of them striking below, she had frantically hustled back to her bedroom and into bed, wondering, *Did he hear me?*

But that was just one of many thoughts swirling around in her mind. *What was he talking about? Who was he talking to? What did I just see? Those slippers! What do I say to him in the morning? What do I do?*

As she struggled to organize those thoughts into a legitimate plan, she strategized herself finally, wearily, into a deep sleep.

10

At seven o'clock the next morning, Brody was in the midst of fixing breakfast for Abby. Clouds would be rolling in again in a few hours, with more local showers and thunderstorms expected on and off over the next several days.

In the wee small hours, Brody had lain awake, listening to the rain drumming on the roof, the thunder and lightning skirting town, wondering how he might revisit the subject of Abby remaining mum. It was a sensitive topic for sure, and he thought about leaving things be but decided otherwise. If it meant sparing her from potential grief, he had to do it.

Abby stepped into the kitchen, yawning and dropping her backpack onto the chair beside hers.

"Sleep well, princess?"

Apparently too weary to quibble over her royalty rank, she stretched and sat down to her instant oatmeal and grapefruit. "Yes. How about you, Daddy?"

"Like a rock," he fibbed. "The rain helped."

"Helped me too. I slept like a baby as soon as you turned out my light," she said, powering into her oatmeal. "*Mmm.* Brown sugar and cinnamon— my fave."

"Yup. Just for you, princess. We only deal in faves here at Chez Whitaker's." He sat down next to Abby, trying to figure out an icebreaker to their vital conversation.

She interceded. "What's your favorite kinda oatmeal, Daddy?"

He scratched his head, pondering. "I don't know. Cream of coconut and squid, I guess. I'd say it's right on up there."

She wrinkled her nose. "Ewww! Is that in the box?"

"I'm not sure. I'll check, but I think the good folks at Quaker took that one out of the variety pack. Waay too popular."

"Who would *buy* that?"

"Oh, Samoans and Greeks, I imagine."

She dug further into her bowl. "Well, *I* sure wouldn't. *Ewww!*"

Brody tickled her armpit. "Gotcha!"

Bits of oatmeal flicked onto the plastic tablecloth from her spoon as she flinched from the tickle, giggling. "I knew you were joking, Daddy. They don't put *squid* in oatmeal."

"Since when?"

"Since forever, silly!" The last spoonful found its way to her mouth, and she gulped down a few ounces of her milk, neatly disposing of the telltale ivory mustache with her napkin. "Daddy?"

"Yes, pumpkin?"

"I'd like to talk with you about something."

"Sure thing. What is it?"

"It's what we were talking about before I went to sleep last night."

Uh-oh—what's the upshot gonna be? "What, Abs?"

"It's about the talking to dea—I mean, to those who've crossed over."

She remembered my advice on that. Good girl! "Well, I wanted to talk to you about that same thing before you left for school this morning."

"Okay, you first."

He tickled her again. "Nope. You brought it up. Tell me what's on your mind, pigeon."

"So ... I've been thinking."

Brody sniffed the air. "Yes, I smell the wood burning ..."

"Daddy," she pouted, "I'm being serious here."

He dropped his flattened hand down across his face, "erasing" the smile behind it. "Sorry—serious face on here."

She flashed a mildly exasperated expression at him; he crossed his heart with his index finger.

"As I was saying, I've given this a lot of thought, and I've decided to sorta keep things to myself right now."

What? "Really? That's what you've decided?"

"Yes, I suppose." She folded her arms on the table and half-scowled as if participating in serious negotiations. "It might seem a little weird to my friends and the other kids at school if they know about my ability. I'm not sure if I'm really ready to spring that on the world just yet. Some of the attention might turn out to be bad attention, I think."

"Wow, you thought that up all by yourself?"

"Kinda. Yes, sir."

I'm soo off the hook! "That's pretty grown-up, Abby. I was actually going to say the same thing to you this morning. You literally took the words right out of my mouth."

"I know—uh, I mean, I know I sounded pretty gung ho about it last night, but I feel like it's probably for the best. At least until I can get a real handle on things, don't you think?"

"Oh, yes, I wholeheartedly agree! That's very mature of you, Abby. I wish I'd made that same decision when I was your age."

"I bet you do, Daddy." She smooched him on his stubbled cheek. "I bet you do."

⌐⫟⌐

At a quarter after nine, the phone rang, and Brody answered, "Hello?"

"Brody?"

"Frank? How are you today?"

"Good, good. You?"

"I had a great breakfast with a great girl—couldn't have started out the day any better."

"Oh, really? Are you dating someone?"

He chuckled. "No, Frank. I meant Abby."

"Oh, right, of course. How asinine of me. How is Miss Abby?"

"She's going through some slightly atypical growing pains right now."

"Well, wait until she becomes a full-fledged teenager and the PMS starts!"

Brody chuckled. "Sometimes I think we're already there. Or maybe it's just a convenient excuse on my part."

"Oh no, my friend, you wait. You know I had two daughters myself."

"Didn't your wife have something to do with that?"

"Funny. You're a fun-*ny* man, Whitaker. And she's my *ex*-wife too, you recall. I meant that there'll be times you'll expect your teen's head to spin and for her to spew green pea soup at you. She'll speak in tongues—it's the only legitimate explanation for it. I kid you not. You wait!"

"Uh, Frank? That's real enlightening and all, but was there another reason you called this morning?"

Frank laughed. "I'm sorry. Just waxing nostalgic, I guess. Oh, that's another thing—the waxings ..."

"Okay, if you set out to scare the dickens out of me, you've succeeded."

"Well, put your dickens back where it belongs."

Brody sighed. It was this aspect of Frank—his lame, and often inappropriate, sense of humor—that Brody was not keen on; it was funny for all of a few brief snippets. "So what's really on your mind, Frank? Have you heard anything?"

"As a matter of fact, I have." He paused.

"Yes? And?"

"And they're ... gonna-take-a-pass-right-now, Brody." Frank had paused for effect and then rapid-fired the bullet point as if doing so would lessen its impact. It hadn't; it had still wounded Brody's ego, even though the position was no longer vital to his welfare. He thought his reputation for going the extra mile in his previous tenure at the bank might've carried more weight. Apparently, he was wrong.

Frank explained, "You see, the bank's been losing money, roughly five thousand a month or so for the past year. Can't figure out where the problems are, but corporate has been up my ass and sideways about it. Hard to tell if it's our loan portfolio or if it has anything to do with that controversy surrounding Lizzie. So we're now in a hiring freeze, division-wide—may even be looking at some salary and staffing cuts. They told me to check back with them in a few months and then they'd reevaluate the situation."

"Oh. I see."

"Sorry."

"No, no," Brody said, scooping his pride up off the floor and pocketing it once again. "I appreciate your asking about it for me. I really do."

"I wish there was something ... Hey, you'll be all right, won't you?"

"Oh yeah, yeah. Fine." Brody cleared his throat.

"Well, that's good."

"Actually, things took a turn for the better for me yesterday, late afternoon."

"Hallelujah! Oh man, I wish I could say the same."

"Why? What's the matter?" asked Brody.

"Well, it's looking more and more like we'll never see any of that money again."

"Really? Are the authorities pretty pessimistic?"

"Let's just say that others involved in the investigation—the higher-ups—are. They say it's like looking for a needle in a haystack. And add to that the damn FDIC breathing down our necks before we even unlocked the doors today … whoo-ee! I've got to answer umpteen questions and fill out literally reams of paperwork. You wouldn't want to be around here this week anyway; trust me."

"Yeah, I'm sure. Sounds like you've got your work cut out for you."

"Yes, well, we'll keep the faith, though. You never know. If they can find those crooks before they spend it … Anything can happen; never give up, I say."

"True."

"When life gives you lemons—"

"—you make lemonade," Brody finished.

"Hell no, Whitaker! Seriously? When life gives you lemons, it basically *sucks*!"

"Ha, ha, Frank. Good one. I've gotta remember that."

"Yep, words to live by. Listen, tell that little sweetheart of yours hello for me."

"Sure. She has a Girl Scout meeting this afternoon again. It's a short one—"

"Not your dickens again."

"No, Frank—the meeting." He shook his head again. "They're supposed to get their cookies today."

"Sweeet!"

Ignoring the pun, Brody asked, "Hey, can I put you down for some?"

"Yeah, seriously, put me down for a case of the Lemonades. I feel one coming on, Brody."

Teddy was jostled rudely out of sound sleep by someone banging loudly on his front door. He rolled over quickly and snatched his gun from atop the nightstand before hustling to the hallway. Groggy and naked, he leaned out the bedroom doorway and glanced toward the front of the house as the pounding repeated.

Because broken glass—from the mirror he'd smashed the day before—still littered the foyer, he clumsily stepped into his boots, trying to tug them on while clenching the gun, expecting the door to suddenly implode any second. "Who's there?" he yelled.

"It's the Big Bad Wolf, Teddy Bear! Ah-*oooh*!" the man at the door called in a high-pitched voice.

Teddy recognized the voice, even in soprano, as belonging to Big Jim's right-hand man Slots. *Shit!* "Just wait, Slots! I'm openin' the door!"

"Three seconds," Tommy, Big Jim's other right-hand man, warned him. "You got exactly three seconds, shithole!"

They took up the countdown in tandem. "Threee ..."

Teddy finished yanking on his boots and took the safety off the gun.

"Twooo ..."

They were going to get in anyway—no sense in having them bust down the door. Teddy crossed to it, threw open the lock in one swift, circular flip, and then backed quickly down the hallway as they reached "One!"

As Teddy ducked around the corner into his bedroom, the door flew open, and he heard movement inside, the crunching of glass shards.

Slots chided, "Bad boy, Teddy Bear. Not much of a booby trap! Big Jim's not gonna see eye to eye on this. In fact, you pretty much took care of him *ever* seeing eye to eye with anyone, or anything, again."

"Yeah," Tommy said. "He's in intensive care right now, but he said that was too good a place for you. He said he wants you to come visit him real soon—in a body bag!" He laughed maniacally.

Shit! Teddy thought. *I thought I finished off the bastard. Just my luck. Fuck! I'm dead meat now. Well, we'll see ...*

"Ya know," mocked Slots, "the morgue's a lot cheaper than a semiprivate room, 'specially if you ain't got Blue Cross, Teddy."

Teddy swung through the doorway and took aim at Tommy. Two quick pops took him down—one shot hitting him in the neck; the other, the groin. Teddy flashed across the hall amid Slots's return fire and into the den.

"How's it hangin', Teddy? Pretty tight by the looks of things," Slots chortled.

"You're dead! You're screwed, man! Throw out your gun, and I'll take you to see Big Jim. Keep your weapon, and it's only your balls I'll be bringin' 'im!"

Not much of a choice. Teddy would take the odds once more with his nads. He tensed up as Slots pivoted around the corner, meeting Teddy standing there, aiming his Hardballer right between Slots's petrified eyes. "Idiot move," snarled Teddy, his shots sounding before Slots could squeeze off a round.

Slots's body crumpled backward, his fall interrupted courtesy of the hardwood coffee table, which took a generous gouge out of the back of his head before allowing him to slump to the floor.

Teddy moved to the front door, stepping over the bodies, and pushed it closed without hurry or worry. It was at times like these that he was grateful to his pa for placing their humble abode on an expanse of several acres that the family had acquired generations back—it meant no neighbors in earshot.

Sitting down on the flat, rectangular arm of the Naugahyde sofa, he gently laid his gun down onto the cushion. *Fuckin' idiots*, he thought, looking down at the stiffs. *Bargin' in like elephants at a shootin' gallery. Jerk-offs!* Now, where was his cell phone?

He went to his nightstand and found it lying beside the previous night's empties and the keys to the van. *Shit, the van!* He speed-dialed Carlos. "Yo, bro."

Carlos's accent was loud and proud. "Yo, man. Wazzup?"

"I need your help, bro."

"Whatchu need, amigo?"

"I hit some roadkill last night on my way home. The front end of the van is a little bent out of shape."

"Nooo! Teddy! Already? Well, was it the four-legged variety or the two-legged variety?"

"It don't matter—it ain't walkin' no more."

Carlos laughed. "You're a barrelful of monkeys, dude! All right, as long as it ain't *you* bent out of shape."

"Yeah, I'm fine. Listen—I got somethin' I need disposed of, and I need a wipe-down too."

"Yeah? You don't ask for much, do you?"

Teddy laughed. "Nah."

"Like that bank bitch and her apartment?"

"Yeah, somethin' like that. Somethin'-somethin', really."

"*Two* somethin's? You're a busy beaver too, ey, buddy? Hey, here's a joke for ya: Why is Teddy Trent like a jukebox full of old Top 100s?"

Teddy shook his head. "I dunno, why?"

"'Cause the hits just keep a comin', man!"

Teddy chuckled proudly. "Ha! Yeah, good one. I like that. Yeah." He chuckled again. "So, Carlos, can you handle that for me?"

"Y'know, my dogs is hungry as shit. Y'know how expensive food is for all those mangy mutts? You'll be helping me out with a little Kibbles 'n Bits for 'em. I'll toss in a free front-end alignment for that, Teddy Bear."

"Cool. Real cool, Carlos."

"I'll send a couple of boys around. An eye for an eye, ey?"

"Yeah," Teddy chuckled, "you could say that, amigo. You sure as shit could say that."

⌁

Irv Crossman entered his wife's bedroom, having showered and shaved for the first time in two days. The National Geographic Channel was promoting a new *Creatures of the Amazon* special to be featured later that afternoon. To Marie's brunch tray of cream of wheat, buttered pumpernickel toast, and V8, he had added a romantic touch—a single primrose sprig from the garden out back erected in a slender bud vase. The vase was balanced precariously on the wicker tray and wobbled as he walked, yet it remained upright, steadfast.

"Here's your brunch, *bubalah*," he sweetly greeted her.

Marie rested quietly, her eyes closed, her withered, seraphic face framed on her pillow by her coarse sterling hair, its once-enviable luster now gone.

He shuffled to her bedside, setting the tray on the hospital-grade overbed table. Her chemo bag was half-empty. That was fine, for the hospice nurse wasn't going to be more than twenty minutes late, or so she had said on the phone. He tapped the suspended latex-free bag for good measure and adjusted the drip valve. It would take another couple of hours for the slow IV to complete—plenty of time for the help to arrive.

Due to her apnea, Marie usually slept partially upright at a twenty-degree slant. Irv checked her oxygen tank to see how heavy it felt and looked at the gauge. The numbers were too fine for him to read, but the tank felt unusually light. He took out his glasses from their vinyl case in his pants pocket, rubbed them on his shirtsleeve, and put them on.

The gauge appeared to show an empty tank. *Empty? How could that be? Could've sworn it was half-full last night. Or was that yesterday afternoon? Or the night before?* Panicked, Irv couldn't recall exactly when he'd last read the tank.

It was then that he noticed no vapor accumulating in her oxygen mask, no rise and fall of her chest. He checked her wrist—no pulse!

Whimpering, he bent over and kissed his wife on the forehead. There was no warmth. *At least her eyes are closed.*

Mr. Crossman sank down onto the chair beside the railing of her bed, his hands dangling in his lap. All the cherished memories of his beloved wife flooded him as he stared over at her. From the time they first met in the death camp to her final days in that bed, they were as one. He raised one to his face and began to cry, restrained at first but unbridled in the end.

Like the flower he had carried in, his love for her had remained forever steadfast.

And after what seemed like seventy-three years—or had it been seventy-six?—but was a mere twenty-seven minutes, he slowly reached for the push-button phone to make final arrangements for his dear departed Mrs. Marie Crossman.

⌒✺⌒

Kaylee closed her locker and spun the combination dial. She placed her heavy trig book under her arm and turned to head to class.

There was Billy, rooted in the middle of the hallway, a boulder parting raging rapids, the other students streaming around him on both sides. He blushed and approached, the hollow he'd created drawing to a close in the sea of schoolmates behind him. "Hi," he said sheepishly.

"Hi."

He fell silently into step with her. After a few footfalls, they began simultaneously:

"What do you—"

"Kay—"

"What?" She stopped by the corner of the hallway down which she had to veer for her next class and propped her shoulder against the off-white tiled wall.

He fumbled with his words, embarrassingly tongue-tied, a circumstance not totally lost on such a perceptive young woman. It was a welcome vulnerability, something she'd not seen heretofore in this cocky boy, a hint of disarming charm.

"I just … well, I … Look—what I did to you last Friday night was wrong."

She wasn't about to let him off the hook—he needed to squirm a bit. "Ya think?"

"Yes, it was real wrong, and I just wanted to tell you how sorry I am."

"You are?" His charm was indeed disarming her.

He whispered, lest any faculty overhear him, "Yeah, I was drunk. But that's no excuse for actin' like an ass, and that's what I did, and you deserve way better than that. You're a great girl, and I didn't treat you with proper respect, and I bet I blew any chance of ever seein' you again. And did I say I was sorry?"

She straightened, her body language more open. "Yes, you did. But you're wrong."

"Wrong? No, I screwed up big time."

"Oh, no, you're not wrong about that, Billy. You definitely screwed up big time the other night."

He was puzzled. "Then what was I wrong about?"

"You're wrong about that bet—about blowing any further chance with me."

The dim bulb brightened. "What? Really? You mean that, Kaylee?"

She smiled at him and nodded. "Yeah, I do. I was hoping you felt that way and *really* hoping you'd apologize. I gotta admit, you came through just now. Everyone deserves another chance."

"And I meant it too, Kaylee," he said with sincerity. "You're gonna see a different Coonrod from now on."

She laughed. "I'm kind of partial to the original Coonrod—last Friday's brain fart excepted. Don't know if the world can handle a new-and-improved version, but we'll see."

"All right, I deserved that. Hey? How about a movie or dinner or somethin' tonight?"

"Sure. Sounds nice."

"Which do you want?"

"Yes." She smiled and slid around the corner to her class.

He called out after her, "I'll pick you up at six!"

She just kept walking, her avocado-colored culottes sashaying away. She smiled as, behind her, she heard an exultant "Yesss!"

11

OKAY. *he's there again! Sitting on that bench!* Abby tried to ignore the apparition, but he was extremely persistent; he kept waving at her.

When recess came and the children stampeded from building to turf, Abby bypassed the slides and swings and jogged over to the aluminum barricade surrounding the playground. She grasped the silvery diamonds and pressed her face close to the fence.

The frogman on the bench across the street rose and entered the thoroughfare. Abby flinched and almost called out as a passing motorist bore down upon the fellow flopping his flippers toward her. But the car passed harmlessly through the frogman, or vice versa—the two intersectees both emerging utterly unblemished.

The scuba man came right up to the fence and stared down at her, his mask semifogged. He removed the snorkel from his mouth and pulled the mask up to rest on the crown of his charcoal-colored neoprene onesie. Abby gazed into the most ocean-green eyes she'd ever seen.

"Hello, sweetness," the man said. "Finally we meet!"

She hesitated. "Hello."

"Do you know who I am, Abby?"

So he does *know my name!* "Are you my great-grampa Eddie?"

"Right as rain. Just call me Gramps. It's easier. Your father tell you about me?"

She nodded, relieved enough to continue the conversation with someone who had been a complete and total stranger a few seconds ago. "Well, he told me all he could. He doesn't really remember that much about you, mostly what Gram-Gram told him." Abby desired further corroboration about the frogman's identity in order to satisfy her curiosity. "How did you die—I mean, pass away?"

"Well, I was killed by an underwater mine while trying to rescue a submarine full of sailors."

"Just out of curiosity, what was the name of that submarine?"

Eddie laughed, his eyes twinkling. "I know what you're doing, young lady. You're testing me, aren't you? I think you know the name of that sub—the *Nautilus*. I was present when your father told you that."

Embarrassed, she admitted, "Yes, he did tell me that. You were there?"

"Yes, but I left Pinky and Goldie's light alone. I just wanted to listen."

"So it *was* you turning on their light!"

"Sure as the sun rises. I've been signaling to you for some time."

"Well, I'm sorry I didn't believe you were who you are. This is all new to me and very confusing. I wanted to make sure this was really real; I had to know for sure you were who you're supposed to be."

"That's because you're an intelligent, cautious young lady; that's all. I'd have expected no less from my great-granddaughter! And I can promise you, I'm who I'm supposed to be!"

Her spirits buoyed up, she smiled. "Really? You're my great-grampa?"

"Certain as summertime. Ask me anything you want to."

"Okay. Tell me the rest of the story of what happened with the *Nautilus*, please."

"I was working with three other navy divers trying to remove a cargo net entwined in the sub's propellers. Several hundred men were inside that sub. They were all counting on us because we had been trained for just that kind of situation. We were their only hope of survival. Those mines were suspended all around, so we had to be mighty careful. The slightest wrong move could've detonated one. Do you know what *detonate* means?"

"Sure," she told him. "Detonate—d-e-t-o-n-a-t-e. To cause to *kaboom!*" She circled her hands in mock explosion. "Detonate."

"Very good! Very smart, Miss Abigail."

"I'm going to be in the county spelling bee soon!"

"Well, you sound like you're pretty well ready for it, if you ask me. Yes, you do. True as tomorrow."

"Well, not quite yet. I've got to do a whole lot more studying for it. But please, tell me more about the rescue. Then what happened, Gramps?"

"Oh, I like the sound of that! No one's called me that in such a long time."

"So you've never met my daddy before?"

He cocked his masked head. "Well, the last I tried to visit with him, he was just a wee fella. He couldn't really talk then. So we haven't seen each other in many, many years."

"Oh." She thought a moment, looking up into those bottle-green eyes. How they shined! "How come so long? I mean, didn't you want him to see you?"

"Oh, honey, your father had so many spirits stepping forward, from family and elsewhere—he didn't need me. I didn't wish to overload him. I was fine with watching. Gram-Gram, my wife, was his main influence, and when his father passed, it was your grampa Walter's turn to guide your daddy. And Walter was a very positive force in your daddy's life. So ..." He shrugged his shoulders.

"Then why did *you* present yourself to *me*?"

"I could tell you were ready. You have his gift—spirits can sense that. We are drawn toward people with that unique power because most of us want to be seen or heard from again. I wanted to see my great-granddaughter, be the first spirit she encountered. So I sorta crowded others out of the way to be your first. Kind of selfish of me, I guess. But I began connecting with you years ago. I've actually waited for you right over there on that bench for the past couple of months!"

"No, really?"

"Cross my heart and hope to die! Well, I guess that doesn't apply to me anymore." He smiled. "I've also sent you other signals around the house, like the goldfish's light."

"I kept wondering about that darn light. My dad was getting frustrated with me over it; he thought it was me forgetting to turn it off."

"Well, that was me. I'm glad you noticed it. Every time you did, it brought us closer to this—meeting face-to-face."

"I'm just glad it *was* you! What else? What other signs were from you? I've seen things, felt things. Which were from you?"

"Well, I wiggled your spoon once on the table when you ate your Jell-O."

"That was you too?"

He smiled. "Yep."

"I looked all around trying to figure out who was playing a trick on me!"

"Me!"

"I thought I might've imagined it or something! That was sneaky!"

"And that was me moving the letters around in your alphabet soup to spell *hello*."

"Nooo ...! Gramps! That freaked me out!"

"I'm sorry if I spooked you. Oh, what a choice of words, huh?"

Abby giggled. His eyes twinkled, literally, which amazed her.

"I was just having a little fun, sweetness. We spirits sometimes get our jollies causing a bit of mischief! And Lily always said I marched to a different drummer. So I've sat here too, just like at home, waiting for the time when you'd see me. Say, I haven't caused you any trouble by being here, have I?"

She smiled. "Nah. I'm glad you're here. I gotta say, though, this is strange, different—kinda scary, sorta."

"It must be at first. I've got to admit, though, that I have no idea what you must be feeling or how your dad must have felt when he discovered this gift the two of you share."

"I'm not very good at it yet," Abby said quietly, glancing downward.

"Oh, but here we are!"

"Yes, we are, aren't we?" She raised her chin again and smiled.

"The first is always your hardest; they'll become easier for you."

"I hope so," she said dreamily.

"Your mother's spirit will be next."

Abby brightened. "Really?"

"I would bet on it. She's right on my heels with all the signs she's giving you. I'd say another week or two. It'll happen."

"Oh, yay!" She clapped her hands. "Gramps, please tell me the rest of your story."

"Oh, yes. Well, the other divers and I finished untangling the net, releasing it to sink. We didn't know that down below us there were more sea mines. When the net drifted onto their detonating spikes, they exploded! *Boooom!*" He circled his hands as Abby had. "The shock waves underneath the water were huge!"

Abby watched in amazement as Gramps's form rippled back and forth as though acted upon by some gigantic concussive force.

"The force of the first one tossed me against the hull of the *Nautilus*, knocking me unconscious. It stunned my buddies too, and by the time they reacted and began searching for me, I had drifted too far down into blacker water. Since they never found me, everyone knew I had drowned. I was awarded a Purple Heart and a Medal of Honor posthumously."

"Does that mean after you died?"

He stooped down to her eye level. "Why, yes! My, you're a smart one! Well, that's my story. Now you know even more about me than your daddy does. How 'bout that?"

"I can't wait to tell him we talked!" She beamed, grasping the fence and hopping up and down several times.

"That's wonderful, Abigail. I'm so glad we had this chance to get acquainted."

"Me too, Gramps."

"My, what lovely angels' kisses you have sprinkled there!" he said, pointing to the perky freckles dotting the bridge of her nose.

She giggled. "That's what Daddy says my mommy called them!"

"Well, it's my firm belief that only angels have angels' kisses. On everyone else, they're called freckles. So they make you all the more special, little angel. Oh, it certainly was worth the wait to get to talk with you! Thank you for coming to this fence to see me today. We've got to go now, dear."

"Aww, do you have to?"

"Well, actually ..." He raised his snorkel and pointed it at the school. The class bell suddenly rang, startling Abby and indicating the end of recess. "You do!"

"Oh! I guess I do! Well, I loved talking to you, Gramps! Bye!"

"Bye, my dear." He drifted backward, away from the fence, vanishing as another car sped into him.

She watched his spirit disappear as the vehicle passed through him, as though he somehow vanished into the car, and waved again. "Bye!" She turned to her right and saw Maddie staring at her as though she had the plague. "H-hi, Maddie." Abby felt queasy and clammy at the same time, like she was dropping down a steep roller-coaster incline.

"You ... were talking to someone named Gramps?"

Embarrassed, she fired back, "So?" Her legs felt wobbly.

"Abs, there was no one there."

Abby stared back, unable to muster any words; she felt confused.

"You were talking to the street, Abby. To thin air. Are you okay?"

Abby gulped, staring back at her best friend in the entire world. Abby's feet felt riveted to the ground, yet she wanted with every fiber to flee.

An idea suddenly broke through. She laughed tentatively at Maddie and said, "Gotcha!"

Maddie shook her head and then pointed a finger at Abby. "You! You ... you *knew* I was standing there the whole time, didn't you?"

It worked! "Well, of course, silly! What'd you think?" She circled her finger beside her temple, lolling her tongue, googly-eyed.

They both laughed.

"That was a good one, Abs!"

"Yeah, I gotcha good, huh?"

"Oh, yeah! You really had me fooled!"

After a few seconds more of controlled, contrived laughter, Abby shouted, "Race ya!"

She scampered from the fence and ran back into school as fast as her racing heart, without a backward glance.

_ﻌﻌ_

"Brody?"

It was Jennifer Connors on the phone, a pleasant surprise. Brody welcomed the sound of her voice. "Well hello, Ms. Connors."

"Please, call me Jen. Everyone does."

He blushed, for no conceivable reason. "Sure, sure. Sorry."

"No apology necessary. Listen, I just looked over the tape from yesterday. In all my years of broadcasting, I haven't been this excited about airing a piece. Ever. I really mean that."

"You really mean that?" He felt his cheeks warming from the flush. *Doof! She just said that!*

She laughed. "Yes, I do."

"Uh, that's good, Jen." *Think of something to save face!* "I'd ... like to hear more about it. Should I come down to the station? I mean, a little later, perhaps?"

"Tell you what—I have a better idea. Why don't I tell you a little more about it over dinner? How would that be?"

He felt uncannily awkward, having been out of the social scene for so long. He was woefully, inadequately prepared for her offer—being a ladies' man required a strict regimen and dedicated practice, of which he had neither. His palms were even sweaty! "Dinner? Tonight?"

"Yes, would that work for you? We can talk about the session then."

Brody couldn't think of any other plans he had. "Let me work on a sitter, and I'll let you back." He cleared his throat. "I mean … I'll get back to you." He thudded his forehead with the heel of his palm. "Is that all right?"

"Sure."

Brody thought he could detect a hint of a smile in the tone of her voice. Was she enjoying twisting him in the wind? Or was he doing a good job of hari-kari all by himself?

She added, "I completely understand. I'll be here at the station until close to six. I can meet you at the Blackhorse Pub on Franklin around … six thirty, if that works for you."

"The Blackhorse?"

"Yes. Sound good to you?"

"Good? Great! Let me work on it. If you don't hear back from me otherwise, I'll be here—I mean, I'll meet you there, at six thirty."

"Perfect. Hope to see you then," she replied. "Bye."

"Good-bye," he said, hanging up the phone—and his "man card."

He was full of nervous excitement, for the first time in a very long while. As he sauntered to the living room entrance, he stopped in his tracks as a jarring thought occurred to him. *Oh my gosh!*

"Susan?" He glanced around, calling her name a couple of times. Had his wife's spirit witnessed his conversation with Jen? Why did he feel such abrupt impropriety? He hadn't experienced such guilt since his mother caught him polishing off half a package of Chips Ahoy before dinner. He furtively glanced around but could not detect Susan's presence.

Why would Susan care? Why wouldn't she? Brody took a few deep breaths, calming himself, allowing the absurdity in his mind-set to wane.

Whew! All right. Now, where to start? Oh, yes! He had to call Lizbeth

Stewart, Abby's sitter, and see if she was available that evening. After that, his main concerns would boil down to how to reclaim some semblance of his old swagger in the remaining three hours and where to locate that last shred of his dignity.

⟶∦⟵

Carlos's men arrived at Teddy's house midafternoon. In a matter of seconds, they rolled the bodies up in the very rug upon which they'd fallen and toted them out to a van with Reynolds Carpet Cleaning in red letters on the sides. Most of the crew piled into the carpet van; a lone straggler took Teddy's new vehicle and backed it out, following the others to the road.

Once the day's carnage had been carted off and the living room purged, eliminating all vestiges of struggle, Teddy swept up the glass from the broken mirror. Then he took the empty frame down from the wall and put it out beside the trash can.

Back inside his pristine living room, he dialed Carlos's number and waited for him to answer. *C'mon, c'mon, Carlos—answer the fuckin' phone.*

"Hey, Teddy Bear. How's it hangin', amigo?"

"Someone else asked me that very same question earlier today."

"Yeah, who?"

"Not sure if it was Kibbles or Bits."

Carlos lost it in a fit of laughter. Finding it contagious, Teddy began to convulse as well, draping backward over the arm of the couch and lying there hooting.

"Hoo, man, my sides hurt," Carlos told him. "I haven't laughed like that in weeks, man. Kibbles or Bits—"

They both started guffawing again.

"All right, all right." Carlos was winded. "Listen, amigo ... no worries ... we'll get the front end cleaned and ... fixed up again for you in no time."

"Hey, Carlos?"

"Yeah, amigo?"

"I owe you, man."

He laughed again. "Yeah, you do, man! Hey, we'll work it out in trade. Don't worry; we'll think of something to square ourselves."

"Cool, Carlos."

"Later, gator."

Teddy hung up. Those last words made him reminisce about how he used to call his brother "Lyle, Lyle, crocodile." Sentimentality threatened on the near horizon but was not embraced in Teddy's forecast that day.

A telephone message from dispatch caught David's eye. It was placed on the corner of his office desk, tucked underneath a photo of his wife, Ruth, and Kaylee, precisely angled for easiest view. In block letters, it read, "SHERIFF COONROD CALLED. PLEASE CONTACT HIM AT EARLIEST POSSIBLE CONVENIENCE."

He debated strongly whether or not to subject himself to that particular machismo—or masochism—at that time, for his temper was likely to be tested, and his blood pressure needed no extra stimulus.

Tap, tap, tap—David struck a rhythm on the wood with the crease of the folded pink paper. *What can Cletus want?* Finally, curiosity trumped procrastination. He dialed the number.

"Sheriff's office," the switchboard operator said.

"Sheriff Coonrod, please."

"I'm sorry," the woman politely apologized. "The sheriff is out on a call right now. May I take a message?"

"This is Sergeant Jeffries at Third Precinct returning his call."

"Just a moment, Sergeant Jeffries; he wanted us to patch you through."

"Thanks." He waited, drumming his fingers and then kicking his heels up onto the edge of his desk, next to the photo. He bent forward and picked it up, staring at the two most precious women in his life—in the world.

The sheriff's voice boomed, "David?"

"Hey, Clete. You called earlier?"

"Yeah. What do you boys know 'bout a homicide just north of the Red River late yesterday afternoon? Fella in a red Challenger gunned down. No apparent cause. Someone just had a hankerin' for cold-blooded murder, near as we can figure. You think it might have anythin' to do with your 211 yesterday a.m.?"

"Don't know, Clete. Those two guys almost made a clean getaway, but I think one of 'em was clipped pretty bad by a local businessman while fleeing the scene."

"That right?"

"Near as I can tell at this point. There's evidence of a fair amount of blood in a neighbor's yard down the block from the store. The fellow that lives there is a real character." David chuckled. "Any help you could be to me in that robbery, I'll return the favor if we hear anything about your 187."

"Well, we did the best we could gatherin' all the details before the sun finished cooperatin'. Now the rain's washed any lingerin' evidence away."

"Know what you mean." Out of habit, he almost instinctively added "jelly bean" but stifled the urge in the nick of time.

"I might swing by and take a look at that lawn."

"You're welcome to our samples."

"Thanks. I'll keep that in mind. May take you up on that. Hey, David, listen. One more thing."

"Yes?"

"Uh ... about Billy and the other night."

The precise topic David didn't wish to entertain and the actual intent, he figured, of the call. "Clete, listen, you don't have to—"

The sheriff interrupted him. "I didn't tell my boy that what he did to Kaylee was in any way, shape, or form how to treat a lady. He knows, or shoulda known, better'n that. It's not what I've tried to instill in him."

David listened, somewhat dubious.

The sheriff continued, "I had a long talk with the boy last night about it, and he was pretty damn remorseful for his inappropriate behavior. He told me you were pretty hard on him when he tried to apologize."

"Yeah, listen, about that ... I—"

"No, now you listen."

Okay, here it comes ...

"I'm glad you didn't let him off the hook for it. I appreciate the way you handled the situation. It was a lesson that needed to be drilled into that thick skull of his. I've been tryin' to get that message across by myself, but apparently it carries more weight when it also comes from elsewhere. Know what I mean?"

David knew full well how hard it was to get teens to listen to their folks once in a while. "I get ya, Clete. I wish I could say Kaylee minds me every time, but I'd be lying if I did. They all have their moments, don't they?"

"Yep," he laughed. "Some more'n others. Unfortunately, thick skulls are a Coonrod trait," he admitted.

Surprised, pleasantly, by Cletus's response, David replied, "Well, I have to say that I'm glad you feel that way, Clete."

"Shore as shit do, David. Hell, if she'd been my daughter, I'da done the same damn thing," he chuckled. "Listen, Billy called me a little while ago and told me he apologized at length to Kaylee at school today. Thought you oughta know."

"Oh, really?" David suddenly questioned whether or not he might've been too hard on the boy. "Well, that's good. I hadn't heard."

"Yeah, he told me that she made him squirm a bit too."

David grinned. *That's my girl!*

"Yeah," Cletus continued, "she's a chip off the ol' block, Jeffries. She's a good girl."

Proudly, he stated, "Yes, she is."

"You and Ruthie've done real fine by her."

"Appreciate it." Feeling a tad remorseful, he added, "Hey, maybe I misjudged your son a bit."

"Well, I warned him he needs to get his act cleaned up, and pronto. You keep your eye on him. Make sure he flies straight, doesn't do anythin' else he's likely to regret when it comes to your daughter. If he does, I want to know. You tell him we're both on the same page about this, okay?"

"I will the next time I see him, Sheriff."

"Well, that'd be tonight."

⁓

With her first three fingers pressed against her right temple, Abby recited, "... make the world a better place, and be a sister to every Girl Scout."

All seventeen young women in Junior Troop 645 dropped their hands to their sides and took their seats in the school cafeteria.

"Very *nice*, ladies. Well done!" said Brenda Culligan. She was a pert, curvy thirty-six-year-old woman who favored her umber hair in a ponytail for the sheer ease of arranging it. The style worked well for an outdoorsy Tennessee gal like herself and meshed well with that particular gaggle of preteens. As their troop leader the past few years, she was duly pleased with her scouts.

Raising her hand, she gave the quiet sign, and the girls responded by giving her their undivided attention. "When the hand goes up, the mouth goes shut," she preached. "Remember, ladies, it's important to give me your attention, so you won't miss any important announcements or instructions."

"Yes, Mrs. Culligan," they responded in unison.

She beamed. "Now, girls, this is a short meeting; I know we met yesterday afternoon for our regular one. I thought our cookies would be in by then, but they arrived this morning instead. I wanted to give you all a head start in your sales efforts, so we'll be handing them out to you now. Everyone is responsible for six cases individually to start with. Plus we will be gathering at Walmart at nine o'clock Saturday morning to sell, sell, *sell*! So tell your parents that we will be there until early afternoon and that they'll need to provide you with lunches or else bring them by for you. Remember—all the profits we make are to be used for our activities, and we've got some real doozies planned, so let's make an all-out effort to sell, sell, *sell*!"

Abby nudged Maddie and whispered, "That's funny how she always says that."

Maddie muttered out the side of her mouth, "You should *live* with her!"

A diminutive girl with braided pigtails named Dotty Trumball raised her hand. "Um, Mrs. Culligan?"

Brenda pointed three fingers toward Dotty. "Yes, Dotty. You have a question?"

"Yes, ma'am," she said as she rose. "Do we need to wear our uniforms this Saturday?"

Brenda clasped her hands together. "That's a *very* good question, Dotty. No, we won't need to wear our uniforms this Saturday. Wear your normal play clothes if you'd like. We'll have our banners hung up at the table and elsewhere there, so everyone will know we're representing Troop 645! Okay?"

"Yes, Mrs. Culligan," they responded in sync.

"Any other questions, ladies?"

Not a one.

"All right then, gather with your mommies, and let's get these boxes loaded up, shall we?"

The scouts spent the next half hour divvying up and securing their precious caches before disembarking. Inside the Culligan van, strapped in beside each other, Abby and Maddie chatted during the drive.

"Hey, Abs? You were being honest with me out on the playground today, weren't you?"

"What do you mean, Maddie?"

Maddie squirmed against the seat belt to face Abby. "I mean, you were really just having fun with me about your gramps? You knew I was there all along, right?"

Abby asked with mild unease, "What do *you* think, Maddie?"

"I think," she said, "you *were* just playing around with me. Right?"

"Just being me," Abby truthfully told her friend.

"Thought so."

"Yep, that's me: Abs the Magnificent!" Changing the subject quickly, she called to their chauffeur, "Mrs. Culligan?"

"Yes, dear?"

"If my daddy can't take me on Saturday, can you? Please?"

"Why, sure, dear. You know we'll pick you up. Now don't wait until Saturday to start selling your cookies, though."

The girls giggled, knowing what was coming next, and chimed in as well. "Sell, sell, *sell*!"

They laughed together, and Brenda repositioned her rearview mirror to briefly view their cherubic faces.

As they turned into her driveway, Abby noticed her sitter's silver Mustang parked in front of the house. *Hmm. I wonder why Lizbeth's here?* She jumped out of the van with her schoolbooks and, dodging the puddles, went to get her father to fetch her cookies while repeating in her thoughts Mrs. Culligan's mantra: *Sell, sell, sell, sell,* sell*!*

12

BILLY stood on the porch, nervously clutching a small bouquet. As David opened the door, Billy thrust the mixed flowers at him.

"These better not be for me," he warned the young man.

The blooms were summarily retracted. "No, I was just kiddin', sir."

"You mean you didn't bring me flowers?"

Billy blushed. "No, sir. They're for Kaylee. I was just—"

"Come on in, Billy. I was kidding you."

"Ohh ..." Billy thrust his chin upward in recognition. "Good one, sir." He timidly crossed the threshold, and David closed the door behind them.

"Ruth'll tell Kaylee you're here." David nodded to his wife, who was looking over her shoulder at the two of them in the doorway. She rose and went upstairs.

"Sit down, sit down." David sat on the couch and motioned to his recliner.

"Thank you, Sergeant Jeffries."

David leaned forward and placed his elbows on his thighs, hands laced together. "Please, no need to be so formal. You can call me *Mr.* Jeffries."

Billy smiled. "You're playin' with me again, aren't you?"

"Yeah, just can't totally shake it yet."

"Well," he said with a grin, "at least you don't have your gun on you."

David whispered, pointing, "It's in the next room."

Billy grinned. "I deserve that," he said, which encouraged forgiveness in David's eyes.

They sat and talked—genuinely talked. David accepted Billy's sincere apology for how he handled things with Kaylee the other night and listened to his promise to never treat her with disrespect again. In response, he told Billy that everyone deserves a second chance—and that his gun wasn't loaded anyway.

◦※◦

Kaylee was upstairs applying one final dab of deodorant beneath her blouse and a finishing layer of gloss. Approving of herself in the mirror, she opened the bedroom door and almost bumped smack-dab into her mother.

She smiled at her mom. Ruth took her by the hand, led her to the threshold of the stairs, and lightly kissed her daughter on the cheek. She then rubbed off the remnants of lipstick with gentle fingertips.

Midway down the staircase, Ruth gave a heralding flourish. Kaylee followed, dropping both men's jaws.

◦※◦

The Blackhorse Pub had been a mainstay of downtown Clarksville since 1992, when Travis McGee handcrafted his first pale ale. Since then, Clarksville's original microbrewery had produced some delectable spirits, and Brody had hoisted many a pint there.

He pulled into one of the parking slots near the front of the restaurant and headed inside, where the aromas of good food and better beer filled the air. He spied Jennifer holding a table and waved to her.

As he sat down, Jennifer gave him her hand, and he shook it briefly, placing his other hand over their intertwined pair. "Sorry I'm a little late. Final details with the sitter and all."

She held up her half-empty mug. "This is only my fourth." She winked.

She looked fantastic. She was wearing a fuzzy, off-the-shoulder peach top, the neckline of which was tantalizingly low enough to tickle the fancy but not be considered tawdry. And her aroma surpassed that of the food by a landslide! She was mesmerizing, and he was helplessly lost in the trance. "Your fourth? Really?"

"No," she laughed. "It's really my first. *And* my last. I've been nursing this one, waiting for you."

"I'm so sorry to have kept you."

"Me? A kept woman? Ha!" She tossed her hair in mock melodrama. "No, I've really only been here about fifteen minutes. It's a nice wait in here; I never mind it."

"Well, thanks, Jen. I appreciate it. I'm really glad you invited me. And I have to tell you how nice you look in your civvies and how *wonderful* you smell!"

Jennifer grinned as their waiter sidled up to the table and asked, "Hello, my name is Ben. May I interest you in one of our craft beers, sir?"

"Yes, you may. Very crafty of you, Ben. What are you drinking, Jen?"

Jen was in midgulp. She placed her mug on the table and blotted her upper lip with her napkin. Deepening her voice, she said, "I don't always drink beer, but when I do, I drink the Vanilla Cream Ale, my number one choice. Stay thirsty, my friends."

Both the waiter and Brody smiled, appreciating her effervescence.

"I believe I'll have the same, Ben. Another for you, Jen?"

"No thanks. Really, one's my limit. I will take an iced tea, though."

"Very good, folks. I'll get those for you right away." The waiter departed for the beverages.

Jen had both hands wrapped around her mug and was staring at Brody. He returned her gaze, and they sat, locked onto each other for several unawkward moments, allowing the world to just continue around them. It was only when Ben returned with their libations that Brody broke their shared silence.

He picked up his mug and said, "A toast."

Jen raised hers in response. "A toast."

"To fine spirits," he proclaimed.

"And good beer!" added Jen.

They laughed, clinked their glasses together, and drank.

⁓⁓⁓

A short distance away, over on Madison Street, Billy was holding the chair in which Kaylee was about to sit down. He had chosen Michael's Pizza, another

Clarksville staple ever since Mike Jackson had founded the first back in 1985. Over the years the pizzeria had sired several others around the area, and all were favorite hangouts of the teenage crowd.

Kaylee was impressed with the gentlemanly way Billy was treating her—opening the car door and then the restaurant door, shielding her from the cold drizzle with his jacket, and even pulling out her chair. So far, he was pushing all the correct buttons. Maybe it was time for her to push a few of his. "I love the pizza here," she said.

"Yeah, it's pretty good. Me and the guys hang here a lot. What's your favorite kind?"

"I like the Hawaiian pizza—you know, with Canadian bacon and pineapple on top. You?"

"Me? Oh, I'm not partial. I like almost all of 'em. But I've never tried the Hawaiian. Hey, I'm sorry about the movie tonight. It's just that we have a long practice tomorrow, and I've still got homework I gotta do before I hit the sack."

Kaylee smiled, leaning forward. "Oh, don't worry—I've got stuff I need to do too. This is nice; this is great. Thanks for taking me."

"Well, thanks for taking me—back, that is. That tells me a lot, Kaylee."

"This is telling me a lot about you too." She repeated, "This is nice."

They ordered their pizza—Hawaiian—and sodas. As they carried on their conversation at that table for the next couple of hours, one thing was for sure: there were no more reservations.

Brody chowed down on his Cajun pasta while Jennifer enjoyed her pork chops. She inquired about how he had met his late wife, and he abridged the lengthy story.

"May I ask you how she passed?" Jennifer took a sip of water.

"Of course. It was rather sudden. We got the diagnosis of her pancreatic cancer when Abby was five. Susan left the physical world four months later."

"Oh my. That *was* sudden. I'm so sorry."

He drew his lips tight and nodded. "Thanks."

"You and Abby took it hard, didn't you?"

"Yeah, we did. We did." He took a gulp from his beer, as if to wash the bitter feelings away.

"I'm sorry. I didn't mean to get too personal."

He shook his head slightly, misty-eyed. "It's okay, Jen. I need to talk about it more. It's cathartic in a way that only opening up about it can be. It's difficult to hold those emotions inside for so long."

"I know what you mean. Very few people can understand what you're going through when something like that happens, right? Listen, let's change the subject."

He dabbed his eyes with his napkin and then wiped his mouth. "It's all right, really. Ask any questions you want."

"Okay," she mindfully began, "if you say so. Tell me, was Susan having any symptoms?"

"Lack of appetite, listlessness, weight loss. Oh, and abdominal pain—it started disrupting her sleep, keeping her up most of the night. She wasn't as worried about it as I was."

"What did you do?"

"I convinced her to consult a GI doc. He was immediately concerned and ordered some tests."

"What kinds of tests?" she asked.

"A CT scan, then a needle biopsy. We didn't get the results right away."

Jen rested her chin atop her clasped hands, elbows on the tablecloth. "That wait must have been horrendous."

Brody bit his lip, nodding. "Yeah. It was agonizing, all right." He had to stop speaking for a second or two to collect himself. Then he sighed. "We, uh ..." He cleared his throat, hesitating. "We got a phone call from the doctor's office at, uh, one of ... one of Abby's ... dance recitals."

"No. Oh my God, Brody."

"Yeah." He continued to nod, feeling the swelling in his Adam's apple, forcing himself to curb his emotions and concentrate on his train of thought. "Do you have any idea how difficult it was to sit there the rest of that recital, knowing we had to see the doctor again the very next day for those test results?"

She shook her head.

"That was tough."

"I'll bet."

"So the next day, we were sitting in Dr. Fielding's office, holding hands, waiting for him to come in—wanting to know yet dreading it at the same time.

The world was spinning normally up to that point. When he sat down and told us the news, all time stopped for me. I don't remember anything much after those two words: pancreatic cancer. They might as well have been *death* and *sentence*." He paused and then humphed. "Susan took it much better than I did, or at least she held up better in that office than me."

"I can't imagine ... You both must miss her a great deal, don't you?" she asked.

He nodded again.

"Can I ask you something else?"

He took a deep breath, attempting to wipe clear his mental slate.

She cocked her head. "You said a moment ago to ask you anything."

"And I meant it."

"Okay." She appeared reticent with her next question. "Do you ever talk to her spirit?"

He smiled.

She quickly added, "You don't have to answer that. I might have overstepped my bounds."

"No, it's fine. I'm enjoying our conversation and the open and honest exchange. I do talk to her." He'd been apprehensive about discussing that very thing with her, expecting responses ranging from misunderstanding to intense jealousy, so her expression of wonderment was a welcome sign. "Quite often, actually."

"That's so wonderful. That must be so cool!"

With her positivity and receptiveness, he was instantly at ease. "It is," he agreed. "I'm not sure how I could have handled things without having been allowed that gift."

"It's tough, all right." She nodded, pursing her lips slightly.

Brody could see that Jen was reflecting about her daughter.

She smiled again, her curiosity increasing, and asked, "Was it right away? I mean, after her death, when was it that she first appeared to you?"

"I tried to channel Susan almost immediately after she left the physical world, but after she breathed her last, her spirit hovered over her bed only for an instant before it vanished. It was the following day that I first connected to her at some length on the other side."

"Wow. That soon?" Jennifer shook her head, lowering her voice and leaning in. "I'm sorry. These are very personal questions I keep asking. But this is so fascinating to me!"

"It's fine. Channeling is so second nature to me now, and I don't mind sharing this at all with you. I actually was trying to think of how to tackle this very subject with you and couldn't come up with a way that would sound adroit or clever, so this definitely satisfies the both of us." He smiled. "Getting back to your question, I learned a long time ago that there is an interval of time after a person leaves the physical world in which their soul cannot be summoned. It's been described to me as a sort of processing period, and it varies from soul to soul. Some can be brief; others can be quite lengthy. I haven't been able to ascertain the variables that govern that process quite yet, but there seems to be some correlation with the strength of the bond between the two souls and the length of time they shared together in the physical world."

"Really?"

"That's as near as I can ascertain from my own experiences and from what various spirits have informed me over the years. Susan explained the processing bit to me best, by comparing it to a trip we took to Disney World about six months before her diagnosis."

"Disney World?"

"Yes."

"You mean with rides and things?"

He chuckled. "With *lines* to get on those rides. Some take an hour's wait or more for the most popular ones, but some folks have these passes to get to the front of the line and get on those rides much quicker. Like that analogy, some souls are ushered through that initial phase sooner. By who or what or even where or how that occurs is what I'm still not sure of, even though I've heard descriptions of what happened to certain spirits, at least as much as they can recall. As for Susan, it took almost twenty-four hours before she appeared to me again."

"I can't imagine what that must be like for you, to still be able to communicate with someone you loved so much who's no longer there physically. It's mind-blowing. I've got to say, I'm jealous of that!"

That was a jealousy he could handle! He took another bite of food and washed it down. "Now, please, my story has been monopolizing our entire evening so far. Tell me about you."

She took another forkful of chop. "What would you like to know?"

"Tell me about Mr. Connors."

"Well …" She took a sip of iced tea and sat back, sighing. "There never really was a Mr. Connors."

Brody tripped over his tongue. "Gee … I'm … I didn't …"

She waved him off. "Nothing you could ever have known. The only good thing that came out of that particular high school romance was Julie—my inspiration. She battled her illness with such courage. She was my role model; she helped me become a better me."

"I saw in your expression a moment ago how tough that must've been for you." He gazed sympathetically at her and then, after a second or two, spooled up some more pasta with sausage and tucked it in. He licked his lips and chased it down with his ale.

In the pause, she laid her silverware down on her plate. Then she folded her hands together. "There were late nights she called to me from her bedroom, early mornings spent together in the ER, breathing treatments, chest thumpings, crying jags. You name it—we went through it. But we *got* through it. My rock and me. My precious ray of hope. When I bottomed out, her composure—in the most trying of circumstances—helped pick me up again. She chose to be steadfast—to help me get through *my* days, not to get her through hers. I didn't realize why she was so damn tenacious, why she hung on for dear life for so long. It dawned on me only after she'd passed: she did it for me. She was always fearful I wasn't strong enough to carry on without her, and there were days I believed that myself. That's how unselfish she was, down to her last desperate breath."

"Wow. Beautiful, Jen. What a tribute."

"Yeah …" She tried hard to swallow one of the last sips of her brew. "We both know *tough*, don't we, Brody?"

He could see she was struggling to hold it together. He reached out and placed his hand on her arm. "Are you okay, Jen?"

She looked down at his hand—appearing to feel better almost instantly from his touch—and blurted out a chuckle to avert an emotional deluge. "See, I know exactly how you feel. It helps for *me* to talk about it too. Like you, I've been holding it all inside for so long. As long as I can remember. I haven't had anyone else I could talk to—*really* talk to—about all this."

That surprised Brody, for she was such a lovely woman. She certainly came across as poised and articulate, someone driven by success, not self-pity. How could there *not* have been others, men specifically, wanting her to confide in them? He gave her arm a reassuring squeeze and then reluctantly retracted his hand. "What helped get you through the days after she passed?"

Jennifer angled her mug and peered at the last few ounces of alcohol remaining. Then she tilted it toward him. "This," she said, her lower lip quivering. "I took to *this*, Brody. I took to it heavily and wholly, and it damn near killed me. It almost cost me my job, my reputation, my respectability, my *life*. It was my crutch—a brutal, *hateful* one."

Brody sat back, intent on hearing more. "Please, go on," he urged.

She set her jaw. "My light had been taken from me, stolen. Forget all the philosophic rigmarole—my life was darkness distilled. I know you've seen how black, how empty it can be, having lost your wife."

"Yes, I definitely can relate."

"I looked to something—anything—to fill that void. I started depending on something I'd never had an interest in before—alcohol. I drank on occasion at first, hiding it at work, feeling like a criminal but not caring. Soon I was hitting it pretty heavily at night—beer, hard liquor, you name it."

"Jen, you don't have to—"

"No," she said, pleading, "I want to. I *need* to. Please?"

He nodded.

She pressed on, "I wasn't myself. Jack began to take notice. He was worried about me—he's such a sweetheart to have held such faith in me. Well, one night when my self-destruct mode was in full swing, I poured the last few drops of Wild Turkey into a glass and sat there listening to the deafening silence, staring at the ever-changing reflections on the disintegrating ice, feeling like my life was dissolving bit by bit all around me—just like those damn ice cubes. You know how that feels, Brody? When everything around you seems like it's melting away? Or like you're in some sort of vacuum? When all the sensation, all your meaning, is sucked out of existence and drawn into the black hole of y-o-u?"

"Yes. Yes, I do."

"I was lost in that utter stillness, and then I thought I heard a voice, searching faintly, plaintively, from somewhere distant. One word: *Mommy?* It was Julie! I looked up from that glass of poison in my hand, glanced around, and saw nothing, gaffing it off as a hallucination—a drunkard's delusion. So I raised my glass once more to sip, and there the voice came again! Only nearer, and this time it said, 'Mommy, don't—I need you.'

"I set the glass down and checked every inch of that room for whoever was toying with me—for that's what it had to be. I was certain I'd heard it that time! Not satisfied after verifying that the living room was vacant, except for me, I searched every crevice of that house, even her bedroom—a room I'd avoided as much as possible after the day she died. No one. Not a soul—or so I thought."

She set her mug down; Brody watched her keenly. She cleared her throat and went all in. "I sat back down in my comfortable chair, uncomfortable with what I'd heard. I reached for my highball again instinctively—in hindsight that's a scary thought in and of itself. I tried to raise it, but something heavy weighed on my wrist, keeping me from lifting it! I didn't know what in heaven's name it was, but it was *there*, counteracting my efforts. I was so scared that I released my grip on the glass. I wondered if I had released my grip on sanity as well. Then Julie repeated, 'No, Mommy, please don't. I need you!'

"It sent chills up my spine. I pushed myself back from that chair, away from that glass of whiskey ..." Her voice trailed off.

He yearned to hear more. "Yes? Then what, Jen?"

"Then it came to me." She looked him square in the eyes. "I knew my little girl was there, somewhere, somehow, and she was telling me what I had failed to tell myself—what I was too damn *cowardly* to say to myself: 'Get your shit together!' So I did what I had to do: I emptied out every drop of booze I had in the house and have rarely looked at alcohol since."

Brody glanced at her near-empty mug. "Really?"

She saw where his gaze rested and where his mind was going and laughed tearfully. "Yes, I promise you. No more two-or-three-cocktail evenings to unwind. When friends drink wine, I enjoy water with lemon. I hardly ever drink a brew here, except for once in a blue moon." She smiled, tipping her mug toward him. "And I heard we were having one of those lunar events this evening, so ..."

He laughed.

"Brody, I swear, my little girl spoke to me loud and clear. The one thing I was proudest of, my greatest achievement, had nothing to do with my career. It was that if Julie ever needed me, for anything, even to wipe her runny nose, I was *always* there for her. She was calling to me from somewhere, letting me know she still needed me—to be there for her still. For us both. She was returning the favor—watching over me, caring for me! And she literally saved my life—the ultimate affirmation of her love. I'd be cheapening that, rendering it baseless, all for naught, if I failed in her one request of me. That's something I'm *never* going to come close to screwing up again."

⌒⁂⌒

"Say," Billy said after a swig of Dr Pepper, "me and a couple of the guys from the team are headin' up to Bell Witch Cave this weekend, if you want to come along. As my date, that is." He blushed.

Kaylee frowned. "That creepy old place? Why would you want to go up there? I hear it's haunted."

"Nah, that's just legend. Besides, me and the guys'll be right there. I wouldn't let anythin' happen to you."

The warmth she felt inside from that statement made her smile. "Well, I'll think about it."

"And no beer—I promise. My dad threatened me with a Scared Straight kinda deal if I crossed that line again. Besides, there are way more important things to me now than stupid ol' brew." He reached out for her hand, and she gave it to him.

They eyeballed each other.

Kaylee used her other hand to pick up her glass. "I thought about it. I'm in!"

"That's my girl!" Billy blurted out.

She made no move to correct his statement. She liked the sound of it; it was growing on her. Kaylee smiled and changed the subject. "Hey, are you nervous about the Rossview game on Friday?"

"Nah, not really. I usually put myself mentally through the paces a few hours before game time, as I'm suitin' up. And Coach has us pretty well prepared by Wednesday. We know what he wants us to do. We just gotta go out and execute the plan."

"Well, I admire how prepared you are."

He smiled. "This game's a little more special, though," he confided.

"Oh really? Why?"

"Coach told me there're gonna be some scouts attendin' this one—from Vandy, Tennessee, Austin Peay, even a guy from Bama."

"No!" she shot back.

"Yeah. They penciled in this game to see if I might be worth takin' a longer look at, maybe for a scholarship or somethin'."

"Really? That is *so* cool!" she exclaimed.

"Yeah, I'm pretty pumped."

"I should think so! That's awesome, Billy!"

Their pizza arrived. Billy grabbed Kaylee's plate, served her a slice, and handed the plate back to her. The cheese stretched taut from the mother ship to its triangular offshoot. He snapped the mooring line and licked his fingers.

"Yeah, the scouts are important and all ..." He sounded unconvinced.

"What? What is it? Don't you want them there?" She was a bit bewildered.

He put a slice on his plate and took a bite, tasting a new combination of flavors. "Yeah, of course I do ... I mean ..."

"What is it then?" she asked, concerned.

"Well, I'm glad they're comin' ..."

"But?"

"Well ... *you're* gonna to be there, right?"

She jumped up and ran around the table and hugged his neck. "I wouldn't miss it for the world," she whispered in his ear.

～

"Whew," exhaled Brody. "That was ... something. I know that was hard for you."

She paused and then asked, "Do you believe in angels, Brody?"

"I believe there are certain spirits sent here to watch over us, guide us, at times protect us—sometimes from ourselves. Guardian angels, if you will."

She nodded. "Amen. One was sent to me to make me take a good hard look at what I was doing to myself, to break that evil spell." She reiterated, "I believe I owe my life to my little girl's spirit. If that's not a guardian angel, she's as damn close to one as I'll ever have." She sipped her water and smiled. "Do you know how many guys I've been honest with about that? Gotten even halfway through it with?"

"No. I'm curious, though. How many?"

Jennifer cocked her head. "Oh, about three. Maybe four. There have been others that I didn't share even the least bit of that very private information with—I could tell right away they weren't worth baring my soul to." She paused, easing back in her chair. "Do you know, out of all those men, how many ever asked me out again?"

Brody smiled. "I can only imagine."

She held up her hand, circling her thumb and fingers together. "Zero. Zilch. Nada. I thought that with you, it might be different. I didn't expect it—that's a limb I've climbed out on far too many times only to have it fail to bear the weight of my story, dashing my hopes in the process. I was just optimistic that, of all people, you would know, you'd understand, what I'd been through and realize that I wasn't in *The Twilight Zone* when I told you all of that just now."

Yes, I can understand. You bet I can. Deeply touched, he said, "You know I can relate. We've both been there, Jen. After Susan passed, I went through much the same thing. But it was Abby who helped me, much as your little girl pulled you from the brink. We are kindred spirits, you and I."

She sat looking at him, her eyes filled with gratitude.

"It should also give you comfort to know," he said, "that her spirit is still with you, watching over you."

She dabbed the corners of her eyes with her napkin. Her voice wavered as she spoke. "You have no idea how you made my day yesterday. No idea. That was the greatest gift you gave me and *so* unexpected; that's why I began to bawl like a baby—I'm sorry."

"No apologies for that—ever, you hear?"

"You have a true power to heal, Brody. You really do. When you touched my arm a moment ago, I felt stronger, like I could continue to confide in you, no matter what."

"Well, it can be quite healing." He chuckled. "Certainly very revealing."

"You restore *faith*. It's amazing—freaking amazing."

He smiled. "Say," he said, "that reminds me. Tell me about the finished session. How does it look?"

She smiled and cleared her throat. "It's freaking ... *amazing*."

13

"GOOOOOD morning, Clarksville! This is the *Daily Show—Live*, and I'm your host, Holly Nichols. It's time to jump-start your day!"

Brody sat down to view the show, TiVoing it for Abby to watch later. That fine morning, the hostess, an attractively fit African American, had donned a multicolored, patterned jumpsuit with a matching scarf wrapped around her updo. Judging by her kinetic perkiness, she must've partaken of her morning coffee—something Brody was in the midst of enjoying.

She pointed her finger toward the viewing audience. "We have a lot of exciting things to talk about, like the upcoming Craft Day downtown. And we have a brand-new spot today on the show—a little later, one lucky viewer will have a reading with our own Clarksville Medium, Brody Whitaker. You don't want to miss that! So keep it tuned to the *Daily Show—Live!*"

"Now, ladies," Holly read from the teleprompter, "how many of you have been struggling, trying to shed those extra ten or fifteen pounds? Do you require Spanx in order to squeeze into your leotard? Is your muffin top trying to take over, or do you just need a minimakeover? Well, we're going to show you how to resculpt those love handles with a new set of exercises, right after these words from our sponsors. Our resident guru, Joaquin Amendola,"—the shot cut away to a smiling Hispanic bodybuilder in a muscle shirt waving at the camera—"from Weight a Minute gym has created this winning routine *just* for *us*. So don't—go—*away!*"

As the show segued into a Dannon commercial, Brody rose to head to the bathroom. Same vice as Holly, apparently—a little too much coffee!

⌒*⌒*⌒

Lucy Smalls rapped on Mr. McGuire's door. "Mr. McGuire! Mr. McGuire!"

Frank opened his office door. "Yes, Lucy? What is it?" The head teller sounded frantic.

She grabbed his arm—quite uncharacteristic of her—and beseeched him to follow. "You gotta see this!"

"What?"

"In the break room! Right now!"

All right, what now? Someone's birthday slip my mind?

"Hurry!"

Frank entered the break room. It was as though the entire bank was sequestered there, and all eyes were tuned to the television set above the far cabinets. A path was made for Mr. McGuire to slip through, and he peered intently up at the screen, trying to ascertain what all the hubbub was about.

"... a big grizzly. Art and Jim didn't see it, because they were minding their own business, having the time of their lives. Art held up his fish to show Jim, and that's when the bear ..." a woman on the screen was saying.

"What is this? What's going on here? Why is everyone watching this?" Frank asked.

"Sssh!"

"Watch!"

"You'll see."

"Just keep watching, Mr. McGuire."

So watch he did.

"Just struck him down ..." the woman sobbed. "He was only fishing ..."

Something caused the woman to react, to glance over her shoulder—something invisible to the viewers—and then suddenly, Brody appeared on-screen.

"That was Arthur, Mrs. Fleming. He's standing right behind you. He just touched your shoulder," Brody told the woman.

Frank was now transfixed. He slowly lowered himself into a chair slid conveniently beneath him, and he watched the entire segment.

Toward the end, Brody hugged the woman and said, "And to me as well, Ida. I'm so sorry for your loss. I hope this has brought you peace."

"You have no idea," she told him.

Frank was astounded. Neither he nor Brody's coworkers had ever seen firsthand what he was capable of doing. He turned to Lucy, and they stared at each other in awe of what they'd just seen. Then they watched the tail end of the segment.

The woman on-screen was finishing up a final monologue. "… I now believe Brody Whitaker is the real thing. He has convinced me beyond a shadow of a doubt that today I actually spoke with my departed husband, Arthur Fleming. This is a day I'll never forget."

Silence filled the break room.

"Hi!" Holly was back on camera. "I hope you enjoyed that, folks, and thank you, Brody Whitaker for that wonderful, moving experience. If you'd like Brody to channel a loved one as he did for Ida, call the station at the number on the screen and ask for the Clarksville Medium hotline. Some lucky viewers just might have their session make it on the air here at WCVL!

"And in case you didn't catch this story, we will repeat it in its entirety on both the six and ten o'clock newscasts! So tell everyone you know to tune in and watch the Clarksville Medium on WCVL—don't miss it!

"This has been Holly Nichols. I'll see you again tomorrow morning, Clarksville! Remember, there's no excuse for a bad day—a good day depends"— she pointed to the camera—"on you! From all of us here on the *Daily Show—Live*, bye-bye!"

The break room slowly began to clear as folks came to the realization they needed to engage their respective posts and initiate the business of the day. Not so Frank McGuire, however—he continued to sit there, still amazed, staring at the screen, his mind having completely tuned out the subsequent batch of commercials.

The control room at the television station was about the expanse of a three-car garage. One wall housed a mosaic of monitors, each flashing snippets in various stages of production. The middle of the room was devoted to the editing and control boards, and on the other side of that was a glass partition separating off the switchboard room, overseen by Irene, a spritely Vietnamese woman who had come to the United States because of Mike Argent. Mike—an award-winning senior editor WCVL was fortunate as Hades to have on staff—had wooed and proposed to Irene online. Several years, a wedding, and several children later, once all three young'uns were finally enrolled in school, Irene ironically was recruited to replace an operator who'd needed to step down in order to devote herself to her firstborn.

To Irene's back, along the wall, was a mirror spanning the full length of the room. Each lit-up phone line was reflected in this mirror and thus visible to those in the control booth. It was a tall order to maintain thirty incoming phone lines, and Irene prided herself for owning the station record of personally directing seventeen of them simultaneously.

Jennifer sat atop one of the control room's consoles. She and Mike were eyeing each other as the Clarksville Medium segment came to a close. Mike sat back and placed his arms behind his head, elbows jutting arrogantly upward. Jennifer looked at the mirror through the glass partition. The phone bank was unlit.

"Have we misjudged our story?" she asked Mike.

He calmly said, "Wait for it … wait for it …"

They waited for it. Nothing thus far. Jennifer was getting antsy, fidgeting.

Jack entered the room. "Any response?" He went and stood at his producer's side, staring along with her at the reflection in the adjoining room, as though the two of them might somehow will the lines to light up.

"Watch, Jack. Watch," Mike insisted. "If you build it, they will come."

The trio watched; no one appeared to be coming.

"You're about to see history in the making at WCVL," Mike bragged.

Suddenly, as if on command, a single line flashed and then sustained, representing a response. Irene calmly picked up the line.

Jennifer looked at Jack, wringing her hands, holding her breath.

Another light! The producer rose, facing the reflection. Another! And another caller! The phone lines suddenly went ballistic, a hodgepodge of flickering lights against the far wall, each new one a glowing indication of higher ratings in store for the station.

Jack grasped Jennifer's arm, shook her hand, and then hugged her. Then they threw caution to the wind, hooking arms and pogoing in blatant, gleeful revelry. Mike was right—they had a bona fide hit!

The editor was tickled by the display of his superiors, still linked but now circling as they hopped, giddy as schoolchildren on a playground. He kicked back; it was totally ordained as far as he was concerned. "Told you so," he yawned, then he stretched out his award-winning, trademark grin. Mike held the intercom line out to Jennifer and proclaimed, "Better call up front. In a moment, Irene's either going to break her own record, or she's going to need reinforcements."

✳

The half-empty Miller Lite can finally slid free from Teddy's limp fingers and dropped to the floor, its contents dribbling into a stale amber puddle. The clatter startled him awake, and he shot up on the couch, believing the sound to have come once more from the front door.

"What the ...?" he croaked, still groggy. Although the spilled beer was an annoyance, mercifully no one was busting down the door. He pressed the butt of his right wrist onto his temple and rubbed it counter-clockwise. *Oh, my head—that buzzing!* Wait—it wasn't his head; it was his cell phone vibrating on the coffee table. He grabbed it and looked at the screen. UNKNOWN again? *Fuck! What now?*

He answered, and the voice asked, "Teddy?"

He ran his roughened fingers through his hair and then clenched some of the greasy strands. "Yeah?"

"Any luck yet?"

"Any lu—? You mean with the money?"

"Yes, the money. What did you think I meant?"

Trying to clear his hungover head, he said, "What—what time is it?"

"Are you speaking into your phone?"

"Of course I'm speaking into my phone."

"Well look at the screen! It says the time, doesn't it?"

Well, so it did. Teddy looked at it. "Man, it's only fuckin' eleven thirty."

"By noon today, how many people will have come and gone through the parking lot where your brother was hiding, idiot? Are you going to allow someone to stumble across that money by accident, or are you going to get your bony ass over there and look for it?"

"Shit, man ..."

"What do you think, Teddy?"

He wrung his hair between his fingers again, tighter this time. "Yeah, all right. I'll get dressed and get over there."

"Goood idea, Teddy!"

Angered, he spat, "Why you gotta be so fuckin' condescending, man?"

"Condescending? Four syllables—impressive! I had no idea any four-syllable words were ensconced in your vo-cab-u-lar-y. But, in answer to your question, someone has to do the thinking for you, Teddy, since you can't seem to do it yourself!"

Ooh, my head! That hurts! He kicked the coffee table, bruising the arch of his foot. *Shit fire!* "Okay! I'll get over there."

"Another salient suggestion."

He shook his head. *Ensconced? Salient?* "Hey, man ..."

Exasperated, the voice moaned, "What, Teddy? What is it? What could it possibly be now?"

He violently flipped a middle finger at his phone—daring to do so only because the voice on the other end was blind to the insult. He asked quietly, hesitantly, hoping the voice might also fail to discern what he was about to say, "What if I can't find it?"

Pause. "I could have sworn you just meekly asked, 'What if I can't find it?' I couldn't have heard that correctly, could I?"

Like a child in trouble, Teddy squeaked, "Yes."

"I thought we went through that little scenario last night, didn't we?"

"Yeah, but," he whimpered, "what if it's gone, man?"

"Again: your problem. You could have gone back there to look for it last night but opted for home instead, to get your buzz on. Damn shame. I hope that when I hear from you this afternoon, you'll have better news for me." The voice began to sing: "*A snip-snip here and a snip-snip there ...*"

The tune Teddy recognized immediately—it was from *The Wizard of Oz*, when the Cowardly Lion was getting a clipping in the Emerald City. Teddy covered his crotch with his hand.

The voice continued, "If you value your scrotum, you will. Besides, I'd hate to have to incur another round of long-distance charges to Chicago. *And a couple of la-di-da's ...*"

Teddy cringed. *Fu-uck!* "All right! I'm headin' over there in a matter of minutes."

"Best idea you've never had, Teddy."

Screw you, man!

"Oh, and Teddy?"

What the hell now? "Yeah?"

This time the voice took on an a capella operatic persona, belting out in tenor: *"Don't get a speeeding ticket!"*

Teddy held the phone up before clenched jaw and bared teeth and emphatically jammed the off button, several times.

⌁

Brody entered the station and had Jennifer paged. He had barely sat down and settled in before she rounded the corner and motioned for him to come with her. They went into the same meeting room where they'd met a couple of days prior, only this time it was just the two of them sitting on either side of one of the table's corners.

"Well," Brody asked, "how'd it go this morning?"

Jen smiled at him. "Good to see you too, Brody."

He felt the blood rushing to his cheeks. "You enjoy doing that, don't you?"

"Making you blush?"

He nodded.

"It's not that much of a challenge really," she laughed. "And yes, I do enjoy it."

"It's good to see you too, Jen. I just keep shooting myself in the foot, don't I?"

She nodded. "Um-hmm. But it's a charming trait."

"I really had a nice time at dinner last night."

"I did too, Brody. I'm just giving you a hard time."

"You're … pretty good at that too."

She laughed again. "Again, just *not* that challenging! But fun—*really* fun! Listen, about this morning"—she leaned toward him—"it was off the charts."

"Really?" *Cool!*

"I can't remember our phone lines ever exploding like that before; I really can't. We had to put three people on them. It was like a solar flare had erupted inside that switchboard room—I kid you not!"

"Yeah?"

"Yeah." She reached for his hand, and he gladly gave it to her; the warmth of her touch was reassuring, pleasant.

Pleased, he gushed, "After watching the session this morning, I couldn't be more excited about the next one!"

"Great! I'm glad to hear that because ..."

"Yes?"

"Because ... we've tentatively scheduled another reading for tomorrow morning."

"You have?"

"Yes. It'll be at a downtown hardware shop."

"Really?"

"Does that work for you, schedule-wise?"

"Well, yes, it should. Abby'll be in school."

"Super! We'll get all the details confirmed and have the equipment and personnel on standby. We'll leave at ten. So can you be here by nine thirty?"

He nodded. "Sure. That sounds cool."

That prompted another laugh from her reddish-orange lips. "I'd be inclined to agree with 'cool,'" she said. "You're a pretty 'cool' guy, Brody Whitaker."

"Well, thank you, Jen. Coming from you, that's a real compliment."

She clasped his hand more snugly, and he returned the squeeze, their gazes locked together with electric magnetism.

14

THE El Camino was tight, really tight. Lemon yellow and lovingly maintained, it was totally original; 1978 G-body—a real head turner. Lyle had been extremely obsessive with his one prized possession, keeping it under tight lock and key. So even though Teddy had been itching for so long to get his hands on its leather-wrapped steering wheel again, if only for a joyride, he'd ignored his primal urge to hijack it.

But Lyle won't mind anymore! The thought both saddened him and, in this case, gladdened him. He felt a guilt-ridden euphoria as he sat down on that buttery-soft, kid-glove upholstery and turned the key. The purring of the engine banished all lingering doubts and twinges of guilt. He backed the car out, pulled the garage door down, and then revved out to the highway.

Even with the torrential rain pouring down, the drive to Clarksville was emancipating in a number of ways: Teddy was out of his damn house again— always a welcome change of scene. He was king of the road, cruising in a dream car. And he was on his way to hopefully find that money, get himself off the hook, and set himself up in style for a while with his half. His *half*— that was the only silver lining he could think of with regard to his brother's death—*More money for me! Oh, and once again drivin' these bitchin' wheels!*

He turned the radio on, cranking it up so he could hear the music over the deluge. Concomitant rain sounded from the stereo! Thunder … then ride cymbals … a bass line … a little free-form keyboard. *Ahhh! The Doors, man!*

"Riders on the Storm"—how cool is that? He drove down US 79, tapping his thumbs on the sides of the steering wheel to the beat of the song.

Not far from the spot where he'd popped that a-hole the other day, he began to sing along: *"There's a killer on the road."*

He hummed a line or two and then continued the vocals: *"If ya give this man a ride, sweet family will die, killer on the road, yeah."*

As he approached the Red River, the instrumental bridge coincided precisely with the physical bridge he was about to traverse. Nearly hydroplaning once on a treacherous patch of water in the middle of the span, he swerved and regained control, intoning, "Whoa, big fella," as he patted the top of the dash.

It was a brief slippage, and it slid quite nicely into the second keyboard run. Teddy finger-played it down the length of the dashboard and smiled as the thunderheads rolled in once more, this salvo emerging from the rear speakers.

Woo-hoo!

What a thrill ride!

"Hi, Daddy!" Abby said as she jumped into the Honda and slung her backpack onto the rear seat, drying herself off with the fresh towel conveniently supplied courtesy of her faithful driver. "So what did you do today? Oh! Hey! How was the show this morning?"

"I TiVoed it for you. I want you to give me your feedback."

"Yeah! Let's hurry home—I want to see it."

"Well," he said, "we have an errand to run first, remember?"

She crinkled her brow. "What errand?"

"Remember? We're running by the bank to sell Mr. McGuire a case of cookies."

"Oh, yeah, I forgot!"

"Senior moment, huh?"

She smacked him playfully on the arm.

"Hey! I'm driving here," he said, teasing her.

"That's debatable!"

He gave her a smidge of a noogie. "Keep it up—it'll be cold porridge for supper!"

"Not again," she moaned.

Brody grinned; he lived for their mutual teasing. "What's wrong with porridge?"

"I kinda had my heart set on more coconut-and-squid oatmeal!"

They laughed as they drove on through the rain.

~~~

Brody, toting his dripping umbrella and a large cardboard box embellished with plenty of fresh, moist polka dots, traversed the bank lobby with Abby in tow.

Frank met them outside his office and gestured with his finger. "Let's head to the break room, shall we?"

They followed Frank, who held the door open for them.

"Set it over there on the counter, please, Brody."

Brody obliged. "There you go. One case of the Lemonades."

"Perfect," Frank said. "Just what the doctor ordered." He looked at Abby. "My, what a pretty young lady you are, Miss Whitaker! I haven't seen you in ages! You're looking more and more like your mother each day." He offered his hand to her.

She took hold of it and then released it, shying away, cowering behind her father. Brody tried to nudge her out from behind him, but she wouldn't budge.

"Did I say something wrong, Miss Whitaker?" Frank asked.

A solitary, empty Styrofoam cup on the counter behind Frank suddenly spun, as if caught in turbulence, and then tipped over on its side and rolled to the floor. Brody saw it; he wondered if Abby had noticed it too. When it hit the linoleum with a soft smack, Frank turned and went to pick it up.

"Hey, now," Brody whispered, bending down to Abby, "are you okay? Don't be shy—these are your cookies, honey; you have to be the one to sell them."

She looked up at her dad, clinging to him. It was a behavior totally uncharacteristic of her; normally Abby was very self-assured, not the least bit timid.

Frank threw the cup away and returned to them, saying sweetly, "Miss Whitaker? How many boxes have you sold so far this campaign?"

Softly she said, "These are my first."

"Well," he said gaily, "I'm honored to be your number one customer. Thank you so much for trusting me in such a way."

A wan smile washed over her. "Sure, Mr. McGuire. Thank you, sir." She began easing out from behind her tall shelter.

"My pleasure, Miss Abigail."

"You can call me Abby," she ventured.

"Well, thank you! That's the nicest thing anyone's said to me all day!" He leaned over to Brody, muttering, "I'm telling you, that's the truth!"

Overhearing him, Abby snickered.

"There! See? I knew you could laugh!"

She was becoming less apprehensive, but his daughter's unexpected unease still concerned Brody.

Frank removed a folded piece of paper from his shirt pocket and handed it to Abby. "Here you are, sweetie."

"What's this, sir?" she asked.

"I took the liberty of acquiring a list for you."

She began to unfold the ruled yellow paper. "A list of what?"

"Orders from other employees here at the bank, my dear. I believe there are quite a few Girl Scout–cookie lovers in our fine establishment. Those little treats are quite popular, you know."

"Yes, sir, they are." She looked the list over and exclaimed, "Daddy, there are orders here for over thirty more boxes!"

Brody squeezed Abby's shoulder and then shook Frank's hand. "That was a really nice gesture, Frank. Thank you so much."

"It was the least I could do for you Whitakers." He saluted Abby. "All of us at Planter's Bank and Trust are glad to do our part for the cause." He bowed, extending his arm as though greeting royalty.

She smiled and told Mr. McGuire, "I'm selling more this weekend at Walmart, if you want to come by and get some more."

"Oh my lands! When?"

"On Saturday, if the rain lets up."

"Well!" He clapped his hands together. "I might just do that! Hopefully, the weather will cooperate, and I shall need more cookies. It's my firm belief that you can never have too many, can you?"

"No, sir," she chuckled.

"Now, how much do I owe you?"

Abby thought briefly, the mental math coming quickly, with little effort for her. "That's forty-two dollars, sir."

"You figured all that out inside your head? Well, we might be able to use you down here at the bank, young lady!"

She glanced up at her father. Brody smiled his approval, putting his arm around her shoulder and patting it gently.

"Tell you what," Frank said. "Let's make it an even fifty, shall we?"

Abby nodded, pleased.

Frank continued, "Let's go back to my office, and I'll get you your check, young lady."

"Yes, sir."

After securing payment for the case of Lemonades, father and daughter returned to the car. Abby strapped herself in and turned away from Brody, ashamed.

Brody turned on the ignition and set the heating vents. "Honey?"

She began to whimper.

Brody's heart melted. He touched her gently on the shoulder. "Hey. *Hey.* What's wrong, pigeon?"

She turned farther away.

"Abs, what's troubling you, baby?"

No response, just soft crying.

"What happened in there? Was it what he said about you and Mommy?"

She shook her head no.

"What is it then? Is there something you want to tell me?" All manner of explanations flashed through his mind: *Did the babysitter get upset with her last night? Someone giving her a hard time at school about her newfound ability? What can it be?*

"I don't know, Daddy," Abby said, finally looking at him, her eyes filled with tears and confusion.

Brody squeezed her hand, his concern heightened. Whatever it was troubling his little girl, he believed that she was telling him the truth.

⌒⋎⌒

It was a little before two when Teddy parked the car on Union Street, catty-corner from the rear parking lot of the Dollar General. The rain had abated

⌒ 168 ⌒

somewhat, and he got out and crossed the street, glancing around to try to spot any hiding place wherein Lyle would have tucked, tossed, or dropped the money.

He peeked into sewer holes along the street, around the cement foundations of streetlight and parking lot stanchions, and even around parked cars, just in case. The goal was to leave no stone unturned between the store and where he'd found his brother bleeding to death down the street.

His search took him to the twin trash receptacles along the back wall of the Dollar General. Getting down on his belly, he peered underneath one and then the other. *Nothing.* He checked around them completely. Not a sign. Staring at them, he knew he had to get his hands dirty; the task would not be complete without him Dumpster diving and sifting through all that freakin' garbage.

⸙

Because of the heavy rainstorms, Coach Pirelli canceled the team's extended practice. Instead, they all retired to the gymnasium to walk through their game plan, and then Coach dismissed them early. With the remainder of the day off, Billy decided to swing by the store for his paycheck to have some extra cash for his date with Kaylee after the game the following night.

Walking in, he greeted the skyscraper-coiffed cashier, "Hey, Bev. He have the checks?"

Beverly Greenwood scanned another item and, woman of many words that she was, grumbled without glancing up, "His office."

Billy parted the swinging doors to the stockroom. Grady's office was off to one side, and Billy knocked on the door, taking a peek through the small square Plexiglas. There was Grady's balding head, bobbing as he spoke to someone on the phone. Upon Billy's knock, Grady waved him inside, hung up the phone, and slid his top desk drawer open. "Hey, Billy. Lookin' fer yer check?"

"Sure am, Mr. Minton. Need it for tomorrow night."

"Got 'nother date? With Kaylee?"

"Yes, sir."

Grady pointed his sausage finger at the young man as he plucked out the proper envelope with his other meat hook. "You treat 'er like a lady now, Billy."

Billy laughed. "I've learned my lesson, Mr. Minton. And I don't want any more guns pointin' my way anytime soon!"

His boss chuckled. "Well, I'm just glad you an' the sergeant are on better terms."

"It's a work in progress, sir. But at least I'm bein' allowed a second chance."

"Not to be squandered. You don't always git do-overs in life, young man; they're skeerce as hen's teeth. Make the best o' that opportun'ty. Here ya go," Grady said, dismounting from his soapbox and forking over Billy's wages.

"Thanks. Gotta run and cash this before the drive-throughs close. See ya Saturday!"

"Hey, Billy," he called after the stock boy.

Billy retraced his steps, sticking his head back inside. "Yes, sir?"

"Would you mind takin' that one load by the back door out fer me?"

"I've really gotta hurry, sir."

"You kin cash it tomorruh. Give ya an extra hour o' overtime ..."

That was incentive enough. "You bet. Sure!"

He closed the door and strode to the trash cart. Whistling the school fight song, he grabbed hold of the front rung on the cart and opened the rear door. Rolling it down the ramp, he noticed the Dumpster closest to him was wiggling— something was rustling around inside. *Damn raccoons! Musta gotten in through the side.* He picked up a small two-by-four lying next to the bin and lifted the top, preparing to scare the shit outta the varmints and chase them away.

Instead, a man popped up, scaring the crap out of Billy. Billy jumped back as both men sputtered simultaneously, "What the—?"

The man scrambled out of the trash bin, soiled and stained, and brushed himself off.

Billy shuddered. "Hey, man, I don't want any trouble."

"Sure don't look like it," the man snarled, pointing to the board Billy held.

Billy carefully dropped the two-by-four, retreating a few slow, cautious steps.

"You the one who shot my brother?" the man demanded.

"Wha—no, mister. I didn't shoot anybody." *That vagrant—he must be this dude's brother!*

The man whipped out his Hardballer from his rear waistband and pointed it straight at Billy, who raised his hands in front of his chest.

"Hey, mister, I swear, I never—"

"Where's the money?"

"What?"

"The money! The money my brother had on him before you shot him, a-hole!"

"Mister, I didn't shoot anyone, and I don't know anythin' 'bout any money! I swear!"

The man waved the pistol in Billy's face. "I ain't gonna ask you again, shit-for-brains—where's the fuckin' money?"

Billy backed several more paces to the rear, the man matching him step for step.

Just then, a car across the street backfired, and, in a knee-jerk reaction, the man spun his head toward the sound, tensing his trigger finger. Sickening, searing heat exploded on the left side of Billy's face as something foreign pierced his skin. Billy tried to raise his hand to the wound but fainted backward onto the loading ramp, striking his head.

❦

Grady heard a loud bang from outside. *What's that boy up to now?* He left his office and proceeded to the back door. It was wide open; he hurriedly trotted to it.

Dang it, Billy, there's coons out there! I told you about leavin'— His mind went blank as he saw Billy lying there, blood oozing from his head. At first Grady thought the lad had merely fallen, but when he tugged at Billy's arm, he got no response. "Billy? Billy! You all right?"

There was no movement from Coach P's star athlete.

Grady raced back inside, and through the parted stockroom doors shouted as loud as he could up to the front, *"Bev! Bev!"*

"Yessir?" she called back, nudging up her bejeweled cat-eye glasses.

"Call 911. Billy's had an accident on the loadin' dock! *Now!*"

"Yessir!"

He rushed back to the rear of the store and waddled down the dock ramp. It was then that he saw the entire picture. There was a great deal of blood—a *whole* lot. The faint rain was randomly thinning the crimson slick here and there.

"Billy! Billy!"

Still no movement, no sound.

Hell's bells! Where's the damn paramedics? Suddenly remembering his cell phone was in his pocket, he shakily located the number to the sheriff's station and tamped a bloody fingerprint onto the screen.

15

DAVID reached for the phone on his desk. Dispatch had just informed him of an emergency call coming in from the sheriff. "Clete? That you? How's it going?"

"Headin' to the hospital right now, David. Billy's been shot." The sheriff was audibly upset.

The sergeant bolted upright in his seat. "What? Shot?"

"Yeah, back of the Dollar General. Store owner has no idea what happened."

Sure, I'll bet he doesn't! "That was Billy? I got a call from dispatch that there'd been another shot fired in that neighborhood. I was just getting ready to head over there. I had no idea your son was involved. What happened?"

"Don't know any of the particulars yet. He's over at Gateway," Cletus said. "I'm almost there now. Doris is on her way. Just wanted to let you know."

"Clete, that's horrible. Is he okay?"

"Don't know. They're not sure yet."

"Are *you* okay?"

"If what they think is true, prob'ly just a flesh wound. Then I'll be okay. Won't know for sure till I get there."

"I'll be over there as soon as I can."

"David? Listen."

"Yeah, Clete? What is it?"

"You'd be doing me a helluva favor if you could first run by, like you were plannin' to, and question the owner, see what he knows 'bout alla this. Could you do that for me?"

David nodded. "Yeah, of course. I'll swing by and see what I can find out. Then we'll be there."

"We?"

"Yeah. Me and Kaylee."

"Thanks, David. That means a lot to me, and it'll mean a lot to Billy too."

"You're welcome. Go to your boy. See you soon." Shaken, David hung up the phone, grabbed his jacket, and hurried out of the building.

⁓⁓

"I tell you, Sergeant, I was in my office, heerd a loud noise, went outside 'cause I thought Billy might've had an accident, an' he was lyin' there, bleedin', unconscious."

David wasn't positive he was getting the truth, but there was no reason to doubt Grady's story. The slug had been easy to find and dig out of the rear wall—he'd send that on to ballistics for the specifics.

"Is Billy gonna be okay? Have you heard anythin'?"

David regarded the owner—Grady had genuine concern for his employees; that much was evident. "I heard from his father, who was on his way to the hospital. Preliminary word is that Billy's going to be fine."

Grady let out a huge sigh, apparently quite relieved.

David told him, "I don't know anything more than that. I'm on my way to my daughter's school to pick her up from choir rehearsal and take her with me to the hospital. She was pretty shaken up by the news when I called her a little while ago."

Grady nodded.

"Are you sure," David asked once more, "that you didn't see anyone suspicious at all hanging around your store? Anyone who might've done this?"

"Nope. I swar."

"Okay. Listen, I appreciate it, and if I hear anything more about Billy, I'll pass it along to you or have someone update you." He placed his hand on the worried man's shoulder.

"Thanks, Sergeant."

The rain picked up once more as David left. As he turned onto Union, he checked to his right and noticed several black cars parked in front of Mr. Crossman's house. A sinking feeling rose from the pit of his stomach as he drove away.

❦

David's daughter pulled her umbrella closed and got into the car.

"How was rehearsal, Kay-Kay?"

"Great," Kaylee said. "We're just getting familiar with the holiday stuff. The harmonies will be super fun." Her tone turned serious. "Have you heard anything else, Dad?"

"No, honey. I haven't." David pulled away from the curb, staring grimly straight ahead.

"What's wrong? Are you thinking about Billy?"

He snapped to, shaking his head. "No, I'm sorry. I just saw something that made me sort of sad as I was leaving the Dollar General."

"What?"

"Someone I know—his wife, actually—must've passed away. There were a couple of cars outside his house."

"Oh, that's so sad. What a day, huh?"

"Yeah, what a day."

"I hate these gray days."

He smiled at her and sighed. "Me too."

They drove on for a while, the drumming windshield wipers keeping time for them, diverting the tempo of their thoughts. After a few minutes, Kaylee asked, "Who was it, Dad?"

"Who was what?"

"Who was it that passed away?"

"Oh. The wife of a really sweet old man I questioned the day of the robbery. He goes to our temple."

"Who?"

"Irv something or other. I can't recall his last name."

"It's not Mr. Crossman, is it?"

He tapped the console. "Yeah, that's it. Irv Crossman. You know him?"

"Know him? He taught me Sunday school for three years!"

"No."

"Yes! He's sooo sweet. You know he's a Holocaust survivor, right?"

"No, really? I didn't know that."

"Yeah, Auschwitz, from what I heard. Look at his left forearm if you ever get the chance—that's where his number is. He keeps it covered up most of the time when he's at temple, even puts a Band-Aid over it when he can, but he showed it to the class once when he lectured to us about the war."

"Yeah, come to think of it, he was wearing a bandage on his left forearm when I questioned him the other day. Huh."

"And he knew Simon Wiesenthal personally. Someone in my class said he might have even been at the Nuremberg trials."

"Seriously? That's amazing. Sounds like you know more about him than I do."

"Yeah, he's a big deal, but you'd never know it, because he hardly ever talks about any of that stuff. He likes to keep it to himself. Doesn't want the notoriety that comes with it. Pretty humble guy for what he's been through."

"Wow. I never realized. I've passed him countless times and had no idea."

"Yeah, that's how he wants it, though. You said it was his wife who died?"

"Yes. At least I assume she passed. He said she was gravely ill, and there were cars out front, so ..."

"Aww. She was so active with B'nai B'rith at temple. Sometimes she helped Mr. Crossman with our lessons and our crafts too. I loved her! They were so cute together! They had quite a story, those two. He told us a little about how they met in the camps and how they both survived and became inseparable after they were liberated. That's so sad about her passing."

"Yes, it is. That's what was on my mind just now. And Billy too," he added. "Listen, Kay—he's going to be all right."

"Yeah, I feel better about it now than when you first called me," she said, sounding as if she was trying to convince herself. "We've just started getting to know each other better ..."

He glanced over at his daughter. "You really like this boy, don't you?"

"Yeah. At least I think so. We had a really good time last night. Aaand— drum roll, please." She provided her own accompanying percussion on the center console. "He drove me all the way home!"

They chuckled.

"He probably won't get to play tomorrow night, though, right?" she asked him.

"Oh, I really doubt it, honey. Why?"

"It's just that he was so excited. He said some college scouts were supposed to be there to watch him play. Who knows what might've happened?"

"Well, don't you worry," David reassured her. "If they want to see him that badly, Billy'll get another shot."

"Ooh, Dad." Kaylee winced. "Poor choice of words."

With a pained expression, David drew the connection. "You're right. Sorry—that was purely unintentional."

"Yeah, I know," she half-whispered, "but be careful when we get there."

"Point taken, Kay-Kay. Point taken."

They were just a few blocks away when Kaylee asked, "Hey, Dad?"

"Yes?"

"Did you see Mr. Crossman outside or anything?"

"No, I don't think so. Why?"

"Well, I just thought—hoped—he might've seen something, maybe the person who did this to Billy."

Eureka! This precious child! "You know, that's brilliant!" he exclaimed as they pulled into the parking lot of the hospital. "I may go talk to Mr. Crossman again tomorrow. I'll check in with him and ask him just that. Great— no, *awesome*—idea!"

She exhaled on her knuckles and then haughtily rubbed them against her upper chest, bragging with a sigh and a dose of playful sarcasm, "That's why I get paid the big bucks!"

⁓

Teddy was almost home when his phone alerted him again to an incoming unknown caller. *Oh God! That friggin' a-hole again!* "Hellooo," he answered mawkishly.

"Tell me you found it," the voice intoned.

Teddy gritted his teeth. "No," he said through the clench. "I did not. I was interrupted."

Heavy sigh. "Teddy, Teddy. Tsk-tsk-tsk. What are we going to do?"

Well, I'm at a loss!

"So—you have no idea?" asked the voice.

"Well ..." Teddy stalled for time.

"I do. Watch the news on WCVL."

"What?"

"Are you deaf?"

"Man, why you gotta—"

"Good! You're not! Now hear this, you grungy weevil: there is another way to locate that money. Watch the fucking news. Tune in to the Clarksville channel. There'll be a guy on there who can help us locate the money. I'll call you afterward, at six thirty. Now repeat what I just said, so I know it didn't go in one ear and pass through thin air before exiting out the other."

What a shithead! Seething, Teddy repeated the demand verbatim.

"Good. Make sure your phone is powered, or I will personally drive over there and strangle you with the charging cord."

"Nice talkin' to you too, man."

"I do not find your vain attempts at humor funny, Teddy. I do not find you interesting or intelligent or capable of much lately, but I do know how to fucking *find* you. If you hold your life in high regard, if you'd prefer to keep your balls dangling between your scrawny, redneck legs, you watch the news and then answer your goddamn phone! I will expect you to tell me how to find that money when next we speak. Understand?"

Mercifully, before Teddy could spit out, "Yeah, dickhead," the call disconnected, which probably, at least for the afternoon, spared him his giblets.

≈

David and Kaylee went up to the elderly volunteer nested behind the hospital's information desk.

"May I help you?" she asked, her rosy cheeks rounding out her cheery face.

David produced his badge. "We're looking for Billy Coonrod's room."

Kaylee's grip tightened like a constrictor around his arm.

"Visitors' waiting room—around the corner and through the double doors, Officer. Press the large button, and they'll open the doors for you. I'll call back there and let them know you're coming."

"Thanks." He nodded at her.

Kaylee's grasp shifted to her father's belt loop. They were buzzed through as promised.

As they walked down the long hallway, Kaylee peeked into all the open doors as she and her father passed them. Sensing Kaylee's unease over the sights and sounds of the hospital equipment, David took her hand and squeezed it as they neared the waiting room.

It was easy to spot Doris Coonrod through the open doorway. She was standing with a handkerchief in her hand and talking to someone to her right, a member of the clergy. Fearing the worst, David pulled Kaylee close to his side, should she need extra support.

Doris's voice became audible as they approached. "Thank you for being here, Father Jacobs. We so appreciate you looking in on us and Billy."

"Certainly, Doris." The reverend clasped her hand. "Anything I can do, just ask," he said, retreating to an enclave of occupied seats against the opposite side of the room.

Doris greeted the two new visitors. "Thank you both so much for coming."

Kaylee hugged Doris's ample waist, and Doris wrapped her arm around Kaylee, squeezing her tightly.

"You're welcome, Mrs. Coonrod."

"Ruthie would have been here too, but she's away taking care of her mother," explained David.

"I know she would. I understand. Thank you both so much."

"How is he?" Kaylee asked.

With a steam kettle's release of pent-up energy, Doris exhaled and said, "The doctor says he was *extremely* lucky. But the bullet did pierce his left cheek."

Kaylee raised her hands to cover her mouth.

Doris continued, "Although it was a flesh wound, it bled profusely. It just missed his facial nerve, we were told. Worst-case scenario is that he might smile a little crookedly, and even then perhaps only temporarily." She gamely managed her own smile and then seemed troubled over something unspoken.

Cletus entered the room from the hallway, a cardboard carrier of coffee cups in his huge mitts. He set them down on a table next to his wife and gave her a bear hug. As he released her, he held out his hand to David. "Thanks for bein' here. And thank you too, young lady," he said to Kaylee, embracing her.

"Doris was filling us in," David said.

Cletus grabbed a cup of joe and handed it to his wife, who clutched it, warming her hands with it before sipping. He raised another up to David. "Coffee?"

"I'm good, but thanks."

Cletus took off the lid, blew on the beverage, and sipped from the lip of the cup. "You find out anythin' from the store manager?"

"No, he said he didn't see a thing, and I think he was being straight with me. I found the slug; sending it through ballistics. The local witnesses have all been canvassed, but there's a long shot I might be able to jar one's recollection, get a few more details. I'll check that out tomorrow, if you'd like."

"Thanks. I appreciate it more than you know."

He clasped David's shoulder. What Cletus probably considered to be a light squeeze felt to David as though Cletus's thumb was embedding itself halfway to China. David masked the discomfort in his shoulder blade admirably, slumping only slightly on that side and smiling.

"Yeah, he took a hit there, but he's a tough nut, like his old man," Cletus chuckled.

"Is he really going to be all right?" asked Kaylee.

The sheriff smiled at her. "We're hopeful. There's no perm'nent damage from the gunshot, but he took a real lickin' on the concrete ramp behind the store when he fell. It knocked him unconscious, and he hasn't come to yet. His doctor says the CT scan revealed a large subdural hematoma, which, as I understood him, means there's some bleedin' on his brain."

Kaylee gasped. "Oh no!"

David placed his hands on her shoulders, pulling her close.

"He's in a mild coma right now. The doctors expect him to come out of it once they're able to drain the blood and relieve the pressure within that thick skull of his." He smiled at Kaylee, trying to help her relax. "They've got him ready for surgery right now, and they expect him to be in there a couple of hours."

David eyed Doris; she looked pale. "Would you care to sit down, Doris?" he asked her.

"No, I'm okay. Really. Thanks. The coffee's helping."

"Well, we'll stay through the surgery, of course."

"No, you go on home," Cletus said. "No need for y'all to be waitin' up here too. We'll let you know what's goin' on with him as soon as we find out anythin'."

Kaylee walked straight up to him and politely said, "Please, sir. We're staying here."

He hugged Kaylee again and laughed. "Stay here with us then, Miss Jeffries. He's lucky to have you puttin' up with him; that's for sure!"

✒

Teddy turned the sound on the television down in anticipation of the call. What he'd just seen on the six o'clock news was first-class *bizarro*—way out there. And the dude, the *dude*—he looked familiar, but Teddy just couldn't place him.

His phone rang on schedule. "Yeah," he answered and took a slurp of Miller.

"What'd you think?"

"What'd I think?"

Silence.

"I'll tell you what I thought," Teddy said.

Silence. Finally, "Well?"

"I thought the Dalmatian puppies at the firehouse were real cute."

Heavy sigh.

"All right, all *right*! You're talkin' about the guy who reads minds, yeah?"

Another sigh. "He doesn't read minds, Teddy. Did you even watch the footage?"

"Yes."

"Did you see what that man did, what he's capable of doing?"

"Yes."

"What did he do?"

"He talked to that old bag's husband—that's what he did."

"Point of fact, he spoke to that sweet woman's *dead* husband."

"Yeah, yeah. That's what I said."

"No, you—oh, why do I even bother?" Pause. "Can *you* do that, Teddy?"

"Do what?"

"Talk to the dead? Your brother? Would you ask him right now to please tell you where the money is?"

"You know damn good and well I can't do that, any more than you or the man in the moon can."

"No, you can't, I can't, and the man in the moon can't; but *that guy* can."

"Yeah?"

"So what do you think we should do, Teddy?"

"Call the TV station and schedule a fuckin' powwow with the dude? I don't know!"

"No, Teddy. Think, *think*! For once in your life, use what's between your two ears—that pitiful excuse for a brain. Please. I know you can figure this one out if you try."

"So what then? If I'm so stupid, do you think he's gonna just agree to meet me, to come over and sit down and share some peanut butter sandwiches and Oreo cookies? Maybe he'd like to play Parcheesi, and if I win, he'll try to conjure up my dead brother or somethin'?"

"No, I doubt he would agree to any of that."

"So what then, man? What are we gonna do? If you're so smart, how do we get him to cooperate? Huh?"

"Teddy, you're a man of limited imagination, but one thing you do possess is the simple power to *persuade*. We *can* get this man to help us converse with Lyle in the afterlife and maybe, just maybe, get your departed brother to inform us where the money is."

"How, man? Like I walk up to him and say, 'Hey, Mr. Clarksville Medium, can you help me talk to my dead bro so I can find the money he stashed from our bank robbery Tuesday?' Like he's gonna just bend over and help us? Get real!"

"Bend? Perhaps. But break? Absolutely. There is another way, Teddy. A way to make him break."

"What did you say?"

Sigh. "Remind me to get your earwax evacuated, and soon. I said there is another way to assure us of his compliance."

"Tell me what *that* is," he said snarkily.

And the voice proceeded to do so.

"Hey, man."

"Teddy! Amigo! We got your van fixed up, good as new."

"Yeah? Cool, man. Hey, Carlos?"

"*Sí?*"

"El Coronel. I might have somethin' for him."

"Oh yeah?"

"Yeah. How soon could he make it up here for a package?"

"He could be here in one, two days tops, if he wanted to."

"Call him, Carlos; he'll want to. Is he still payin' the usual?"

"Twenty Gs? Far as I know. What should I tell him about this package?"

"Tell him he's gonna like it. That's all he needs to know. And now I know what I want painted on my van. Can it be done by tomorrow night?"

"Piece of cake, amigo. Piece of cake."

"I may need your help in picking up this package."

"Sure, and we'll split the finder's fee, so we'll be square for all the extra work I done for you."

"Cool, man. Cool."

"Good, Teddy. Now, tell me about this package …"

16

Brody fiddled with Abby's bangs—much like he used to do with her mother's—and looked down at her bright blue eyes. She held her comforter in her hands, raised all the way to her chin.

"Sweetie, you want to talk to me about what happened this afternoon?"

She swung her eyes away in the direction of her two goldfish in the bowl on the dresser and said, "It's kinda embarrassing, Daddy."

"Hey," he said soothingly, "when haven't we been able to tell each other anything?"

She thought about it. "Never, I guess."

"You guess?" He placed his hand on the comforter near her knee and began creeping it, tarantula-like, up her torso.

As the spider hand was about to pounce on her face, she giggled. "Okay—*never!*"

"That's right," he said, swatting his flesh-and-bone arachnid away. "So why start now? Say, it didn't have anything to do with me going out last night, did it?"

"No."

"What then? What's troubling you?" Leaning over, he lovingly coaxed, "You know, it might help if you and I talked about it." He smiled.

With some determination on her part, she allowed, "Okay."

"Good. Shoot."

"Well, I saw Grampa Eddie at school again."

"Oh?"

"Yes." She twisted the comforter in her hands. "Only this time I actually spoke to him, through the fence on the playground."

He raised his eyebrows, sitting up slightly. "Whoa. Really?"

"Uh-huh."

"That's *something*, Abby. Well, what did he say?"

"Well, first of all, he said he likes to be called Gramps."

"I didn't know that." He nodded.

"Yeah. And I asked him to tell me how he die—I mean, passed on—"

"Good girl."

"—to see if he would tell me the same things you did the other night. Sorta testing him, I guess."

"And?"

"What you told me was all true."

"Really? Wow!"

"He's really pretty cool, Daddy."

"I'll bet he is. He must be."

"Like you."

That far-from-faint praise fanned the embers of Brody's heart. "I'd love to talk with him someday."

"I think he'd like that too. He said he wanted to be the first spirit I connected with."

"I see."

"He also said it *was* him turning on the light by my goldfish bowl! See, it wasn't me. I told you."

"I stand—no, sit—corrected," Brody apologized. "So what else happened? How did the rest of the conversation go?"

"I know we talked last night about my keeping this ability private right now, and I found out how hard that's going to be, especially when it happens at school! Maddie was standing there, watching me talk to him, and I didn't even know it—it was really weird."

Uh-oh. This must be the real reason. "You mean she saw you speaking to him?"

"Yes."

"And as far as Maddie was concerned, he wasn't there, right?"

She nodded. "She thought I was spazzing out or something."

"Yeah. Been there, Abs. I understand. So tell me what happened next. How'd you handle it?"

"I told her I was only goofing around with her, trying to trick her."

"You did? And she bought it?"

"Yeppers. Even when she asked me about it again on the ride home."

He nodded his approval. "Good job, Abby. You know how I feel about telling the truth, but that's one circumstance where you're gonna have to fudge a little bit in order to keep your gift a secret. You handled that really well."

"Yeah, I guess I did. It all worked out," she said with a yawn and a gigantic stretch. Then, settling back down, she continued, "This time, anyway. She's easy, though, Daddy—she's my best friend." She curled into the fetal position, facing her father. She traced her finger randomly over his knee and asked, "What if it's someone else next time? Someone who doesn't know me as well? What will *they* say? And who will they say it to?" Without raising her chin, she looked up at him. "I'm kinda worried about that."

He nodded again, caressing her forehead. "Yeah. I can empathize. Do you know what that word means?"

She smiled. "Empathize, e-m-p-a-t-h-i-z-e, I think."

"Perfect."

"Doesn't that mean to feel the same way someone else feels about what they're feeling about?"

"Yes," he chuckled. "Excellent. I couldn't have put it better, princess."

"So you sorta know how I feel because you went through the same things when you were my age?"

"Well, that's all correct except for one tiny detail. I was even younger! Imagine how much harder it was for me to make decisions as wisely as you did today."

"Did I make a good decision, Daddy?"

"You made a *great* decision—*fantabulistic!*"

That seemed to gratify her. She thought for a moment. "Yeah, it must've been hard for you when you were so little, huh?"

"You betcha it was. Listen, Abs?"

"Yes, Daddy?"

"I got to thinking today, even before whatever happened with you at the bank—"

"I saw something else, Daddy," she interrupted.

He raised an eyebrow. "You did? What?"

"At the bank, behind Mr. McGuire. I saw a cup spinning around, and then it fell off the counter."

"I saw that too. But I didn't know if you'd seen it or not."

"Yes, sir, I did. That wasn't what bothered me, though."

"What was it then, pigeon?"

"It was like when I saw Gramps's spirit trying to appear those first few times. It looked like wavy lines where a face might be. It was right behind Mr. McGuire. You didn't see that?"

"No, honey, I didn't." But Brody could recall similar episodes from when he'd been first developing his own gift. Spirits would fade partially in and then out, as though he wasn't yet capable enough to complete the bridge or as though they were trying to seek him but weren't quite strong enough to fully connect. The phenomenon was akin to a flickering lightbulb. "Was it like going in and out of focus to you?"

"Yes. That's what I saw."

"Could you see anything else that might have resembled a spirit?"

"Not really. It only happened once or twice—really, really fast—when Mr. McGuire first saw me and I started talking to him. And then I shook his hand, and it was so *cold*!"

"Cold? What do you mean?" That was something he'd never encountered before—at least not with a living soul.

"It was like the temperature of hamburger meat you'd pick up in the supermarket. You know, the refrigerated section?"

"Really?"

"Yes, why was that, Daddy?"

Brody was stumped. "I have no idea," he said, shaking his head. "Really." The only thing remotely similar he could think of was how a spirit from the other side felt when it contacted him physically, either by direct touch or by passing through him. But that certainly hadn't been the case at the bank. And he had shaken Frank's hand too. It hadn't felt at all cold to the touch to him. All of a sudden there was something inexplicable that he couldn't help his daughter with.

"It scared me," Abby said, "and I was embarrassed."

"I was wondering why you were hiding behind me."

"I didn't know how to explain it! I'm sorry!"

Her eyes watered; Brody could see the shame returning. As it engulfed her face, he leaned down and kissed a tear from her cheek. "Abby, there's *nothing* to apologize for, baby. I wish I knew why his hand felt like that to you, though." *Hmm ...*

"You mean you don't know?"

"I wish I did, Abs."

With that, her vexation surfaced. "Why can you do this so well, and I can't? I'm your daughter! I should be able to do it! Right? Why can't I? Why can't I even see Mommy or Gram-Gram?"

"But you saw Gramps. Even *I* can't do that! And you experienced a couple of other things at the bank that I didn't."

She sniffled. "I guess that's true."

"Well, sure it is. And you know what else?"

"What?"

"What you experienced today at school happened to me too, years ago. It all just takes time to sort out. As difficult as it may become at times, you've got to be patient. Remember, it doesn't all happen at once. Okay?"

She rolled away from him, just as she had in the car.

"What is it, Abs?"

Her shoulders heaved as she began to sob. "I don't even know if I want this! What I felt with Mr. McGuire was freaky! I'm a *freakazoid*! It's like someone flipped a switch on and I can't stop it now!" The tears gushed.

Brody lay down beside her and hugged her. "Honey, *honey*."

He held her until the well began to run dry. She turned back to face the ceiling, calming herself, and told him, "When I watched what you did today on the show, how you helped that nice lady feel so much better, I wanted to be just like you—to be able to do that for people too. I want so much to be able to handle what's happening to me, Daddy, but at the same time, I'm scared. Really scared."

How he felt for her! He looked over at Pinky and Goldie—at the signal light from Gramps—and an idea popped into his head. "Hey, Abs?"

"Yes?"

"Remember I said just a moment ago that I can empathize with you?"

"Yes."

"Well, it's because I went through almost all the same ups and downs that you're going through. I can teach you what to expect and how to deal with them—just as they happened to me."

She turned her gaze up to him. "Yeah?"

After all, these experiences are going *to happen, like it or not; she'd better know how to deal with them, handle them. And who better to teach her? But what about that handshake?* "Yeah." He tweaked her nose. "You betcha. You know, for years and years not even by age ten—I didn't have the benefit of anyone who could help me sort all this out, but you do. Would you like that? You want me to help you? It could make things *so* much easier."

"Oh yes, I would! I'd like that—a lot! It would help me feel so much better about things."

"Then we can start tomorrow, after school, if you want."

She clutched her comforter again—in comfort, this time. "Thank you, Daddy. I *do* want to. Very much."

"Then we shall, Princess Abbithea." Brody leaned over and kissed several of the freckles on her forehead. He tucked her bedclothes in around her and crossed to her door. He lingered there, watching his daughter close her eyes and yawn once again. "Good night, my princess."

Then, as he was about to shut the door, from the twilight came, *"Queen."*

That's my girl! He smiled.

～

Carlos's call to El Coronel was brief, as usual.

"El Coronel, there is a package for you here."

"How much, C-zar?"

"Twenty."

"Up or down?"

"Down, amigo."

"I will send my courier by Saturday evening."

C-zar—the nickname given to Carlos Salazar by El Colonel—grinned and hung up his telephone, puffing on a contraband Coronas Especiales cigar. He downed a shot of mezcal and left the office to check on the status of Teddy's paint job out in the shop. Teddy's bill was about to be paid.

⌇

"Willy," El Coronel droned.

Immediately, a tall, wiry, peculiar-looking man strode into the room and assumed his place by El Coronel's side. Willy's pale skin and alabaster hair were typical of an albino. His haircut resembled an inferior rendition of a Beatle mop top, a subpar Andy Warhol.

"Willy, you're going to Nashville. The arrangements have been made with the Lear. You will leave right away. C-zar's men will pick you up at the tarmac."

Dressed in an ebony footman's jacket and white Victorian dress shirt with a high-stand collar, Wilhelm Haimann was majordomo to the estate, as well as El Coronel's point man—an accomplished killer. If his weapons skills were challenged, his catlike reflexes and strength were sufficient to snap a neck as easily as most could a twig. Willy was more old-school when it came to altercations, preferring methodical hand-to-hand combat over the more rapid ballistic resolution.

"Up or down?" asked the butler.

The code for the gender of the package was simple: How did they pee? Standing up or sitting down?

"Down, C-zar says."

Willy's thin, rosy lips curled upward.

⌇

Jennifer turned off the television in her den, having watched the segment for the third time that day. Earlier, when she and Jack had been watching the playback at the station, Irene had informed them of a couple of stray calls from viewers demanding that the station issue a retraction for airing what they considered to be a fraud, endorsed by WCVL. She was going to discuss those calls with Brody in the near future and see how he wished to address them. But she and even skeptic Jack were ecstatic about the finished product. She was looking forward to the next reading in the morning. *Full steam ahead!*

She was also starting to feel kind of tingly whenever she thought about Brody, a sensation that had been unfamiliar to her for quite some time. When he'd walked into the Blackhorse Pub, his smart sense of style pleased her—long-sleeved shirt, untucked, nice casual slacks, and trendy leather loafers. An etched metallic cross hung around his neck, dangling down to the leading edge of some sexy chest hair—not a forest, rather like an inviting meadow. The aroma of his cologne was very masculine as well. With his tousled tan hair—carefree yet tame—he was like a hunk from one of those cologne ads sailing through a sheltered harbor, his rugged hands expertly guiding the ship's wheel. And that dimple on his chin—it had been pretty damn irresistible!

Doggone it, she thought, jumping back to the present, *this day demands a celebration!* She needed to break out the good stuff; she'd earned the reverie. Her cravings were driving her crazy, and there was only one way they could be quenched.

She moseyed into the kitchen and opened up the cabinet above her head and next to her Vent-A-Hood. There were several bottles of liquor sequestered inside: Wild Turkey, Bacardi, Gordon's, Crown Royal, Stolichnaya.

Jennifer reached up to the shelf ...

～※～

With the news finally over, Brody switched off the set. He was heady from the rush of his on-screen accomplishment, yet his excitement was tempered by his anxiety about what his daughter was going through.

Brody was walking a very fine line himself, a tightrope—one end anchored to the normalcy of private life, the other tugging from the tenuous tether of fame. He was itching with anticipation yet wrestling with much trepidation over the prospect of becoming a public icon. If successful, it could mean financial peace of mind for him and Abby, but fame might come hand in hand with a breach of a more sacred security—their privacy. Was fame worth the possible sacrifice? Only time would tell.

～※～

Jennifer grabbed the chocolate sprinkles from the shelf just below the liquor bottles. Then she got out a small bowl and a spoon and opened the freezer.

Ah! Here it is—that badass Ben & Jerry's chocolate-and-hazelnut ice cream with fudge chips. Decadent! Ooh-la-la!

Forgoing the bowl at first, Jen dipped the spoon right in and began slowly, sensuously licking off the sweet, creamy concoction. *Mmmm-mmm! Just rewards! Yeah, bay-bee!*

She scooped some more into a bowl and topped it off with some chocolate jimmies. Then she skipped back to her bedroom, where Chaka Khan's "I'm Every Woman" blared from her wireless speaker, and began dancing around, the spoon doubling as her microphone. Finally, she sprang backward onto the mattress, the covers billowing beneath her. Her derriere bounced once across the silk linens, up to the head of the bed, her back coming to rest—with flair—against the propped-up pillows. She indulged in another heaping spoonful, tugging the frozen treat off between her lips in four separate, sensationally satisfying portions.

Perfect end to a perfect day.

⌒⋎⌒

Brody sighed and picked up a scrapbook—the uppermost of a short stack next to him on the end table. On the oversize, paisley-covered front of the book, situated diagonally, were the appliquéd letters THE WHITAKERS. Beneath the letters was a picture of Brody, Abby, and Susan standing in front of the huge Spaceship Earth globe, the iconic entrance to EPCOT Center. Abby had her Mickey Mouse ears on, standing atop a three-foot-high landscaped wall beside them, her arms outstretched, expressing fully, in grandiose depiction, her Magic Kingdom conquest.

He opened the volume and began leafing through it. There were photos of him and Susan in college, including two photos taken at the entrance marker to the Bell Witch Cave attraction. He'd coaxed her into a spur-of the-moment day excursion there. He recalled how nervous she'd been when they had finally reached their destination and how freaked out they both were after the visit. They had always wondered about those mysterious amorphous black smudges that appeared a few inches above the sign in the developed photographs—just over her left shoulder in one photo, just over his right in another.

⌒⋎⌒

On a sunny October Saturday, a few weeks after Brody and Susan first began dating, Brody called her up and asked, "Hey, up for a road trip?" So stoked was he about the possibilities of the day that he performed a comical jig while talking. He pranced around as though playing hopscotch on steroids.

"Oh," she lamented, "I've got a midterm this Wednesday. I'm sorry."

"Well, I'm sorry too. It would've been fu-unn!" He was breathing heavily from all the gyrating around. "I can tell you're curious. Looking for an excuse to blow off studying?"

"All right. Whadja have in mind?"

"Trip to Adams."

"Adams? Why Adams?"

"You know why. Think ..."

"I haven't a clue."

"Think!" He knew it would come to her, and it did.

"The *cave*?"

"Yeah! Now wanna go?"

"Oh, you betcha! Just let me fix my hair and get decent looking and—"

"Susan, really?"

"Well, I just wanted to—"

"How can you improve on perfection?"

"Oh my gosh, Brody Whitaker! I hope you haven't used those lines before, young man."

"Been savin' 'em. Waitin' fer the right time."

She laughed at his backwoods impression. "Oh, now I *really* want to go!"

He had moved on to a different groove, pushing his hand out in front of him and thrusting his backside. "Yeah, girlfriend," he chuckled. "Be there in about twenty to pick you up." He began circling his hips, free hand on his belly, eyes closed. "Uh-*huh*, uh-*huh*!"

"Brody? Why are you breathing so heavily?"

He ceased his boogying, panting. "Nothing. No reason."

She chuckled. "You're doing your dance thing again, aren't you?"

"Busted—dang! How long have we been together now?"

When he pulled up to her sorority house, she was sitting on the front steps, with her hair tied back in a pixieish ponytail and a Vanderbilt Commodores jacket tucked under her arm. She looked adorable!

They headed north, through the picturesque rolling hills of north-central Tennessee.

"So," Susan asked him, "what brought this on? Your term paper? Or are you reliving prior conquests?"

"I've never taken a date up there—you're my first," he said, sounding a bit overly guilty of his innocence. "Yes, the term paper did give me the idea. Have you ever been?"

"No, but I've always wanted to!"

"Then I'm honored to be your virgin Bell Witch experience! I actually haven't been there since middle school, and it'll be fun to see it with you."

They drove north of Springfield on I-65 and at Mount Denson turned east onto Highway 11/41 heading into Adams. Their objective wasn't hard to spot with its white clapboard sign:

Historic BELL WITCH CAVE, Inc.
May, September, October, Weekend Only
June, July, August, 6 Days A Week
Hours 10:00 A.M. *to* 5:00 P.M.
Closed on Tuesday

Tuesday? Huh. What's so special about Tuesday? thought Brody.

Following the red arrow at the bottom of the sign, he turned off Keysburg Road to his right, heading into the entrance driveway.

"I'm a little nervous," admitted Susan.

He looked over at her; she was serious. "Are you really?"

She nodded.

He immediately pulled the car over. "Hey, we don't have to do this. We can turn around and go back."

"But we've driven all this way, and you want to see it."

"No, I wanted to see it *with you*. If it's not what you want to do—if you're nervous—we don't have to. Your call, baby," he said earnestly, laying his hand upon her knee.

Her courage seemed to gather. She smiled at him. "No, I'm fine," she replied.

"Okay, but if you change your mind, you just tell me."

She kissed him. "Let's do this! Mush, Magoo!"

"Okay. But first ..." He beckoned her out of the car and over to the sign. He took his Kodak FunSaver camera from his jacket pocket and snapped a quick pic of Susan leaning against the sign. They reversed positions, and she shot one of him holding out his arms in proclamation of the marker. Susan laughed, her unease far less evident.

They drove down to the visitors' cabin, where they found out the next tour would be embarking soon. Brody paid their admission, and they waited with the rest of the impromptu platoon before being herded outside by the guides, Midge and Pete Benson, a middle-aged couple who had inherited the property through Midge's side of the family.

The Bensons piped their narrations of the legend of Kate Batts—the Bell Witch—over loudspeakers linked between twin custom trams. Brody and Susan, bouncing gently along in the cart, listened attentively as Pete began the tale.

"Good day, folks. Any child brought up in Tennessee schools is familiar with one of America's most famous and endurin' ghost stories, the legend of our own Bell Witch.

"In the early 1800s, a farmer by the name of John Bell moved his wife and children from North Carolina to settle on a three-hundred-and-twenty-acre farm situated here, in northern Robertson County, right along the banks of the Red River. It didn't take very long for the Bell family to become fairly prosp'rous, with John turnin' himself into a gen-u-wine land baron, even earnin' the coveted position of deacon in the nearby Red River Baptist Church."

Brody and Susan glanced at each other and smiled. He took her hand in his.

"Accordin' to the legend, one of his neighbors, Kate Batts, entered into a land agreement with Mr. Bell, but he swindled her outta her purchase. Now, Kate was somethin' of a notoriety in these parts too, though of a very different sort. It was believed she dabbled in witchcraft or black arts of some variety. She was largely shunned by the locals, and folks were afraid of what might befall 'em if they ever looked crosswise at her. No one wanted to get on Kate Batts's bad side. She never did forgive John Bell for what he did to her, and she carried the grievance to her deathbed, whereupon she swore vengeance on John Bell and all his heirs. She vowed that they would forever be haunted by her spirit, thus earnin' her the name the Bell Witch!"

As the cart bounced along, so did the story.

"Late summer 1817, extraordinary things began to happen in and around the Bell house: farm animals strangely frightened; weird gnawin' sounds, like rats chewin' on bedposts; loud thumpin's comin' from inside the house; chains a-draggin' down the hallways; chokin' and a-gulpin' noises—all servin' to terrify the bejeebers out of 'em all! These things were also experienced by a neighbor couple, Mr. and Mrs. James Johnson, whom the Bells had offered a night's stay to. After puttin' up with these infernal occurrences for nigh a year, it was suggested that word about these otherworldy circumstances be spread far and wide in an effort to locate someone who could purge their home.

"The Bells soon found their man, or so they thought—a Dr. Sol-o-mon Mize. He swore he possessed the elixirs that could render the invisible visible, so the witch could *finally* be seen and cast out. As he mixed together his potion, the spirit eerily informed him that he was lackin' a few key ingredients. He was plum scared senseless when his body was raised above the floor and doused with the od'rous mixture. He fled from the residence, stinkin' to high heaven. The Bell Witch then added injury to insult by spookin' his horse, which threw him to the mud as it bolted off into the night. Poor ol' Dr. Mize followed that e-quine, never to return."

"Sir?" Susan raised her hand.

Pete glanced in his rearview mirror, releasing the microphone button. "Yes, miss? You have a question?"

"Yes. Did you say that the witch picked the doctor up? I mean, actually lifted him off the floor?"

"Yes, ma'am. Accordin' to eyewitness accounts, that is what happened. Scared him half to death! Did that answer your question, ma'am?"

"Yes, sir." She added under her breath to Brody, "Unfortunately." She shivered again, zipping her jacket up to just below her neck, and held on to Brody's hand ever more tightly.

"The next volunteer to attempt heroism over hoodoo was a certain Revolution'ry War gen'ral named Andrew Jackson—*the* Andrew Jackson— who'd heard about the odd events from a couple of his infantrymen, John Jr. and Drury Bell, John Sr.'s sons. In return for their service, he vowed to help 'em eradicate the witch. Ridin' into Robertson County, accompanied by several soldiers and a renowned witch-layer—that's a professional slayer of such entities—his carriage wheels suddenly locked up for no apparent reason as the fellas made their way toward the Bell estate. Not one man could free those frozen wheels until a certain spirit made her presence known. The witch called out her identity to the men, and the wheels miraculously unlocked! She merely wanted those men to acknowledge who they were a-dealin' with, and then—and *only* then—did she graciously allow 'em to continue their passage.

"Once inside the Bells' home, the team gathered 'round a large wooden dinin' table. The witch-layer produced a pistol from his jacket and boasted that the single silver bullet chambered in his gun could destroy the Bell Witch. Behind him, an amused voice said, 'Oh, really?' He swung his pistol 'round, but nobody was there! 'You think that puny thing will kill me?' He shakin'ly pointed the gun 'round the room. 'I'm right in front of you,' the witch challenged. He aimed the gun directly at the man seated across from him—the man who was to become the seventh president of the United States! 'Shoot if you're so inclined,' she provoked. He pulled the trigger—*right at Andrew Jackson*. But the gun mysteriously failed to fire! The witch snatched it from his grip and hurled it across the room. Then she levitated the witch-layer to the ceiling and dropped him hard to the wooden floor."

Susan didn't wait for him to call on her. "Uh, sir? Has the witch flung anyone around recently?"

Pete chuckled. "It's legend, my dear; that's all. This is what's been passed down through the years."

Brody nestled himself closer to his girlfriend and patted her arm as they continued to bump down the drive.

Undeterred, the tour guide continued, "'Let me remove this fraud from your presence, Gen'ral,' the spirit declared. 'Who am I to argue with the Bell Witch?' Jackson agreed, and the witch tossed the charlatan outdoors. The followin' mornin', the milit'ry officer departed from the Bell house, expressin' a pref'rence to clash with the entirety of the British army rather than to further invoke the ire of that one omnipotent and vengeful spirit!"

The passenger cart ground to a halt, and Pete asked everyone to step off and follow. The two small groups headed down a rocky path, a wooden handrail on their right and a curved stone outcropping on their left, about waist-high, that forced the path to bend to the right and back again. Then another stretch of railing led down to the entrance of Bell Witch Cave. A series of four or five wooden steps dropped down to their left, to the cave's entrance, where the group gathered along a much shorter, weathered wooden rail. There, flashlights were doled out.

Midge took the helm at this juncture. "Now Pete has already told you a lot about our Bell Witch, but that's not all there is to this story. As we move into the cave, I'll be telling you more of the legend, and we'll both be pointing out some of the unusual landmarks found in this fascinating geological formation. The cave is actually part of a bluff that overlooks the Red River. Although this normally is considered a dry cave, when heavy rains move through, it houses a stream that flows out from the mouth—one of the cave's paradoxes—and over that cliff," she said, pointing in the direction of the rushing water that could be faintly heard beyond the rocks, "and on down to the river. It's too treacherous inside when there's stormy weather, so we close the whole place down until it's safe to reenter the cave."

Everyone funneled into the trapezoidal mouth of the cave, the roof barely above Brody's six-foot height. He had to duck slightly at times to avoid scraping his head on the uneven rock. Susan's arm was intertwined with his, and her opposite hand gripped his forearm. Her eyes flashed around as she guardedly stepped onward. As they steadily descended, Brody kept checking her for telltale signs of claustrophobia.

Midge continued the story. "Over the next several years, the witch tormented John Bell's children—his daughter, Betty, in particular. At first, she endured only minor displays of supernatural aggression—hair pullings, pinchings, scratchings. But over time it escalated into near torture—beatings, painful pin piercings. Betty was to marry a young man named Joshua Gardner, but the prospective groom eventually broke off their engagement, citing the gleefully relentless nature with which the witch had persecuted his prospective fiancée."

They moved down the irregular passageway, Pete pointing out several offshoots and other routes too confining to be explored by amateurs. Midge mentioned that professional spelunkers estimated the cave system to extend some fifteen miles deep.

A little farther along, she took up the tale again. "John Bell also was far from immune to the witch's aggressions. His throat swelled up inexplicably from neither allergy nor illness, and he developed occasional stabbing pains. He was convinced that jagged pieces of wood were pushing deeper and deeper down his esophagus. As a result, he began to manifest facial tics, jerks, and twitches, and he refused all food, slowly wasting away. In 1820, John Bell died. It was believed that somehow, someway, the witch poisoned him in the end. A vial of unidentifiable black liquid was found mysteriously beside his bedside. According to the legend, the witch's spirit conceitedly boasted of her hand in his untimely and painful demise.

"This cave was said to be inhabited thereafter by the spirit of Betty Bell, whose death followed her father's by a few years. Some say that Kate had decided to carry on Betty's torment in here as well. Many locals claim that the witch has never left this farm at all, as the strange circumstances in and around the house, the barn, and this cavern have persisted, from time to time, ever since her death."

Brody whispered once more in Susan's ear, "Are you okay?"

She looked up at him and nodded. "Much better, thanks. This is kind of fascinating. I can see why you're writing your term paper about this."

"Yeah." He nodded. "I'm getting more ideas by the minute. I'm glad we came."

"Now that we're in here, this is really pretty cool!"

They continued along the narrowing passage. Pete turned around and, treading backward, said, "We're about to enter the main room, folks. Everyone come on in, but watch the slight step down."

The main room of the cavern was much more spacious, a bit less than half the size of a football field, with several ledges scattered about. Flowstone—a reddish-orange composition of iron oxide and other minerals—dotted the walls, creating illusions of oozing, liquid lava spills that were in reality as solid as the surrounding rock. Numerous limestone stalactites were also distributed across the ceiling.

Once everyone had gathered inside the room, Midge said, "The portion of this cave open to tourists is about five hundred feet long. There is another passageway back yonder, and another cavern is through there. In just a few minutes we'll let y'all explore that one too."

Pete interjected, "Bill Eden, Midge's uncle, who was the guide here a couple of years back, told us of many strange happenin's and even encounters with shadowy figures here inside the cave. We've seen visitors whose flashlights would suddenly extinguish—and not because the batteries were dead—and whose video cameras would suddenly stop workin'. Some skeptics have actually been restrained by unseen forces, and even strong servicemen who scoffed at the presence of the witch have almost had the life squeezed out of them by something inside this cave. Whatever resides here, it doesn't pay to be a nonbeliever, we've learned. Better to remain on its good side; the spirit of Bell Witch Cave can be pretty vindictive."

"Now that's a bit much, isn't it?" Susan whispered to Brody.

"*Ssh*. I'd take that to heart, babe—you heard what they said."

"Yeah, well, I was pretty worried at first, but that is just a little too over the top for me. I might just have an idea of my own." She smiled wryly, newly emboldened.

"What do you mean?"

"Watch. In a minute or two I might try something."

"Susan ..."

The guides moved over to one of the walls, training their flashlights upon it. "Come closer, everyone. Come and take a look at our Bell Witch."

The visitors crowded near.

"What do you see?" asked Pete as he pointed to the upper wall.

The guides' lights were trained on some rock striations that combined to create the image of an old woman's profile. The visage was complete—a pointed nose, forehead, eye, mouth, and chin. A kerchief covered her hair, and she even appeared to be wearing a shawl. It was a strikingly realistic, natural portrait in stone, hard to pass off as mere random patternization.

"This here's our Bell Witch herself. It's almost as though she's branded her face into this wall, marking her territory, so to speak. How 'bout that, folks?"

"Interesting," whispered Susan.

"Yeah, pretty wild, huh?" Brody smiled at her.

Her eyes sparkled back. Brody sensed the gears were turning inside that pretty head of hers. *What's she up to?* he wondered. He decided to take a photo of the stone face. Brody tried pushing the shutter down several times, but it seemed locked. "That's strange ..."

"What?" Susan asked.

"The camera's not working. It won't snap a picture."

"Maybe it's used up," she said.

"No, it's brand new. I bought it on the way over to get you. Let me see your light." He shined the flashlight on the back of the camera, looking for the number of exposures remaining: 33. "I've only taken three pictures so far." He tried it again with the same result. He swiped his thumb across the advance wheel, thinking perhaps it wasn't clicked into place. But it was. *Weird coincidence*, he thought, shaking his head and shoving the apparently defective device back into his jacket pocket. *I'm damn sure gonna get my money back for this faulty piece of—*

"Let's move into the other tunnel," Midge said, ushering the tourists farther into the cave. "Now back here …"

"Miiidge … Miiidge Bennnson …" The name penetrated the cavern in a low, vibrating moan.

Everybody halted, Susan and Brody apart from the others by several yards.

The call came again, this time with greater volume and inflection. "Miiiidge … Bennnsonnn!"

Brody turned and looked at Susan, who was grinning at him, lips a hairbreadth apart. *Oh no, Susan! Really?*

Her larynx subtly undulated as the voice came again. "You brought these people here, Miiiidge Bennnnsonnn. Whyyyy?"

Midge abruptly pivoted around, horrified at the macabre voice emanating from who knew where, the sound echoing hollowly off the walls. "Uh, folks … I think we ought to leave now," she suggested.

Even Pete heeded her advice. He guided the visitors, overseeing their impatient exits, each hastily queuing into the tunnel.

All except for Brody and Susan. They lingered by the wall, snickering.

"I can't believe you did that!" Brody was doubling over.

"Neither can I," moaned the voice.

Brody slapped his knees, trying to curtail his whooping. Susan grabbed his arm. Still much amused, he glanced over at her. She was saucer-eyed and slack-jawed.

"Okay, you can stop now," he said, finally catching his breath.

But she stood, fixating here and there, her mouth agape.

"Susan? Susan?"

She finally spoke, her voice wavering. "That last 'Neither can I'—I didn't say that! That wasn't *me*!" She looked at him.

"Look, it was really funny. But now—"

"Brody!" she half-whispered, sounding dead serious, commanding his attention. "Listen to me! I *swear* that wasn't me!"

"What?" Now *he* was nervous.

"Honest!"

"Then who was it?" He began looking over both shoulders.

"Or *what* was it?"

They turned to the wall, and Brody shined his flashlight up at the humanlike striations. Suddenly and without warning, what had been a two-dimensional rendition of the Bell Witch sprang like a jack-in the-box out from the wall in full relief, halting several yards in front of them. The spirit slithered her pale, craggy face back and forth, pivoting on an impossible stalk. Her deep-set eyes were black as coal, and the teeth in her snarling mouth were decayed, rotten. The face jerked from side to side, encroaching down upon Susan, stopping just shy of her.

The witch glared at them, vapor wafting from her nostrils, her lips drawn back in an evil grin. "So—you doubt my power?" she hissed.

Susan shook her head. "N-no, ma'am," she stammered.

"You're not the only one who can throw a voice, insolent girl. Would you like me to prove *that* to you?"

Brody stepped between the angry spirit and his girlfriend. "Please, she meant no harm."

The face reared up and cast a downward gaze over the frightened pair. "Chivalry can get you killed, medium!" The behemoth swayed downward again, the witch's eyes as empty as the pitch-blackness of midnight. Her mouth stretched open wide enough to swallow both coeds as she gutturally chastised Brody and Susan, their clothes and hair rippling from the brute force of the witch's stale-smelling admonition: "Learn this lesson well, impetuous meddlers: *Leave!* And *never* return here! Or you will rue the day that you challenge me a second time!"

Brody snatched Susan's hand, and they fled the cavern, racing up the long tunnel as deafening laughter reverberated through the corridor behind them.

They burst from the cave, she stumbling once while climbing up the steps and he catching her. Holding hands, their adrenaline pumping as fast as their legs, they sprinted up the path, past the carts into which the others were still cramming. The terrified duo ran all the way back to Brody's car, which he spun toward the entrance, skidding in the direction of the interstate.

Only after they had put several miles between themselves and Bell Witch Cave did they begin to relax and catch their breath, their panic diminishing with the increasing distance.

Brody was the first to exclaim, "Oh. My. God!"

"Oh my! What *happened* in there?"

"I think we saw the witch!"

"No!"

"Yes!"

"Oh—my—*God*!"

"I *know*!"

They hit the interstate, and Brody pointed the car in the direction of Nashville.

"Hey, Suze?"

"Yeah?" she said, still somewhat breathless, speechless.

"That was *too* cool!"

"Wasn't it?" She rested her head back, closing her eyes. "It scared the *shit* out of me, though!"

"Me too. Effin' *bizarre*!"

"How'd that thing, whatever it was, know you were a medium?" she asked.

"Well, it's a spirit, much like any other."

"Well, I hope *that's* not true—that there's too many more like her! That whole encounter was *weird*!"

"Hey," he said, removing the disposable camera from his jacket pocket and offering it to her. "See if you can get a picture of the scenery over there with it while I'm driving."

Susan took the camera and pointed it out her window at the beautiful rolling hills. It clicked the first time she tried it. And the second and the third.

"Effin' bizarre," he repeated.

They drove on for a while, and then, out of the blue, Brody said, "Artie, I have a favor to ask."

"Yeah?"

"Yeah."

"Okay. What?" she asked, aiming the camera at him and snapping a photo.

He glanced over at her, solemn as can be. "Teach me how to do that."

Snap! "What, take your picture?"

"No, stop," he said. "What you did in that cave."

Snap!

⌇

The lamp beside Brody's chair dimmed, and a hollow voice came from the flickering LED bulb.

"Gifff … Gifff …" Susan was having fun with him.

He decided to spar with her. He threw his voice into the fireplace and intoned, "Arrrtie … Arrrtie … is that you, Arrrtie …?"

His departed wife appeared right beside him, sitting on the arm of his chair, laughing. "How are you, Giff?"

"Oh, man. Highs and lows today; a real roller coaster."

"It's the ride of life," she chuckled.

"Is that akin to the 'Circle of Life'?"

"Down, Simba." She smirked.

"Hey, did you listen in on Abby a little while ago?"

Susan nodded, her shoulder-length blonde hair bouncing right along with her chin. "I was outside the door. What are you going to say to her?"

"I don't know. Not sure where to start. I told her I'd teach her some dos and don'ts of channeling. But how? Any suggestions?"

"Well, for one thing, she's got to be made to feel comfortable with her ability, like she's not a freak of nature."

"Yeah, but how?" He crossed his arms, rested his chin on the crook of his palm, and tapped his finger against the tip of his nose. "*I* wasn't comfortable with it for a long time. And I had quite a head start compared to her."

"You'll think of something. I have faith in you, Brody Whitaker. Always did."

That was true. Through thick and thin, he had always been there for her to lean on, just as she had been for him. "Thanks, Susan. This is a tough one."

"So what did we do in the tough ones?"

"Punt?"

Laughing, she said, "No, silly—that was our alma mater! You and I always went for the first down, stretched for the chains. Even on fourth and long, we never gave up, not when we knew we had the greatest weapon on the playing field at our disposal—*each other*. In the vast maelstrom of the divine human tempest, our love was the eye of the storm, the calm in the raging sea. We could count on being each other's anchor. Who's your anchor now, my dear?"

"Abs," he said unequivocally.

"Yes, and you, hers."

"She misses you so much," he said.

"I know she does."

"When can you show yourself to her? It would help her so much to see you, talk to you. She pines for that."

"Soon. It's happening. She's receptive to my touches, my telltales. I'm fairly certain my attachment to her will be complete in the near future."

That eased his mind a great deal.

She snickered. "Someone beat me to it!"

"Well, Gramps *did* have a head start on you, Artie."

Susan nodded and returned to the original subject. "Abby needs to learn to gather herself by herself first, to channel her own emotions and be fully ready to receive me. You know how important patience is in her calling out to those whom she wishes to see. Teach her that, Giff. Start there. Make sure she knows that we will all be there with her in time—the coming months, years."

Susan was right of course; it wasn't her time just yet. It had been Edward's time, and that was why he'd appeared to Abby. His spirit had been around her long before Susan passed, so perhaps that was the reason his attachment was stronger. All those reasons were known only to the spirit world. But Susan's advice was both insightful and inspirational. His path was becoming clearer.

"I see you've been practicing your ventriloquism," she said.

"Yes, I have. I've gotten quite good at it."

"You know, that's another skill you can teach her, just as I taught you."

"I've thought about that. But she hasn't really shown too much of an interest in it, so I tabled the idea."

She nodded. "Agreed—if the desire's there, I'm sure she'll let you know. Tell me, do you ever use your ventriloquism when you channel?"

Brody hadn't yet, though he confessed that he'd been tempted to on more than one occasion, for the added flair. He found he could utter what a spirit was communicating in nearly the precise tone of the departed, but he'd decided against doing so. His clients might feel uneasy with the heightened drama—thus adversely affecting their referrals. It was best not to challenge that. Plus, it was too much like a parlor trick and felt borderline immoral to him, so the right time had yet to present itself for that particular demonstration.

"Try me," she said.

"What?"

"Try *me*. Now. Go on."

"Susan—you?" *Maybe. Maybe this is a good time to test it*, he thought.

"Yes, me. Try it. See how you do." Those were Susan's words, yet they came not out of her but from Brody's mouth—he gave them real voice.

Brody proceeded to throw Susan's voice around the room. "Good, good," the table lamp seemed to say. The next words came from the direction of the television: "Oh, now you're just showing off!" The throw rug in front of the hearth appeared to respond, "No, really!" Brody then projected Susan's voice from the grandfather clock: "All right, I'm beginning to wish I hadn't suggested this!" A figurine on the étagère seemingly concluded the exercise: "Now this is *really* enough!"

Brody and Susan laughed.

"Verrry impressive," she complimented him.

"I've been playing around with it."

"That was *quite* convincing," she told him.

"Thanks," he said proudly. He paused for a second or two and then asked, "Hey, Artie?"

"Yessir?"

"What do you think about her?" He knew that she'd know to whom he was referring.

"I think you two are a cute couple."

"Really?"

"She's a really nice woman, and she seems to have taken a real liking to you, judging from the way she's opened up to you."

"You think?"

"Why, Romeo? What's there *not* to like? You won my heart with your dimple and your sticky shoes!" She smiled.

He returned the grin. "I did, didn't I?" Though compelled to initiate his next topic of conversation, he nevertheless felt the reins of better judgement tugging him back. Should he or shouldn't he? It seemed the right time and Susan sure seemed in the right spirit. He went for it: "You know, I had this strange sense that you were present when I was talking to her on the phone yesterday."

"That was private, between you and her. I won't be present where I'm not wanted."

"You're always wanted where I'm concerned."

"No, my love. That isn't true. I'm not always wanted where you are. I needn't be hovering over you, making you worry about what you're saying or doing when it comes to matters of the heart. You had *my* heart once; you need to capture another's, if it's what you or Abby deserves," Susan said to him sincerely. "You know how I feel about you dating. If she's the right one for you, then you go for it. If she isn't, you search again. You find your happiness, Brody."

He stared at her, misty-eyed.

She shrugged. "I'm nice to look at, sure."

He laughed and then said, "Well, it's just important to me that you—"

"Hold it right there, buster. You don't need my endorsement for the woman in your life. It *isn't* important what I think of her, only what you or Abby might. If I sensed there was a danger to you in any way, either emotionally or physically, I'd watch it play out until I felt a need to step in. If you don't hear from me on the subject, then consider no news to be good news, and that'll be that, okay?"

He nodded. "Okay."

"Talking to the departed isn't how you should occupy the majority of your time, dear man. Other than your line of work, that is. You're in the world of the living. You're still our daughter's world. Make those two worlds coincide, sync. Live your lives to the fullest, *live them*, but—most importantly—find what gives each of you center. You owe it to yourself and to Abby to explore those feelings your heart tells you to. That's the only way I want it, the only way it should be, Giff."

Brody nodded more enthusiastically. "All right." He took her words to heart, telling her, "Thanks, Susan. I needed that."

"And for heaven's sake, don't you dare let *me* come between you and her, got it?"

"Got it." He laughed again.

She blew him a kiss, and then she was gone.

17

EVERYTHING was in place at Parker's Hardware. Brody leaned against the outside wall of the store, underneath its blue-and-white-striped awning, watching the showers continue to fall. The water, inches deep, rushed in rivulets along the length of the sidewalks, attempting diversion into the nearest swollen storm drain. To park along those streets sans galoshes, try to ford from car to curb, and remain moisture-free below the shins was a near impossibility.

The street was nearly devoid of customers. The precipitation was taking its toll on local commerce, the inclement weather making matters worse for merchants trying to also weather the present taxing economic downturn. At least the torrent was forecast to abate overnight, and the waters would, hopefully, soon recede.

Brody preferred having isolation from his client during the studio's prepping. This way, in case there was any doubt over the session's legitimacy, there would be no covert or overt telegraphing of details beforehand, either material or trivial. In fact, the message on WCVL's switchboard requested that callers keep the particulars surrounding their story as bare bones as they could; the fewer details, the better, so as to avoid any bias on the part of those who were tasked with selecting the next reading, as well as any chance of Brody familiarizing himself with any tidbit of data about those who were to be channeled.

In the past eighteen hours, hundreds of requests had poured in through the switchboard—far outnumbering any detractors. There'd been so many calls the selection committee hadn't even had the chance to sift through them all, but it had narrowed down the search for the next session's subject to two callers: Sid "Pinky" Yosten, the manager of the hardware store, and elderly Holocaust survivor Irving Crossman, whose dearly departed had just recently passed. Pinky got the nod first, due to the greater duration of time transpired since his loved one's passing, while Mr. Crossman was slated for the following week, after his faith-based bereavement was completed—a nice antithesis to Pinky's extended period of mourning. Variety would be the spice of life of the Clarksville Medium series.

Brody looked through the iron bars reinforcing the glass door to Parker's, where the crew was finalizing the setup for the session. Connor Tidwell, the director, was finally motioning for Brody to head inside; they were ready to begin.

It was decided that Pinky—a nickname derived from a run-in he'd had with a table saw at home that had severed the most diminutive digit on his right hand at its second joint—should remain standing behind the hardware counter, if able, throughout the session, in order to convey the desired ambience to the piece. By showing more local venues in the segments, places frequented by Clarksville residents, Jennifer felt that the videos might breed familiarity and thus be more likely to potentiate a steadier flow of interest, and therefore drive ratings higher.

Connor counted them down. "Three, two, one ..."

The cameras rolled.

"This is Brody Whitaker, the Clarksville Medium. I'm speaking downtown today with Pinky Yosten, manager of Parker's Hardware."

Pinky waved to the camera.

"Mr. Yosten, we've never met before we began filming today, right?"

"Correct."

"So I've had no prior association with you or knowledge of any individuals pertaining to you?"

"Not as far as I know. No."

"You've given no details to anyone at station WCVL, other than your name and the approximate length of time since your loved one has passed, true?"

"True."

dark hair in a bun, appeared behind Pinky and cradled the two smaller spirits in her arms. She had a radiant smile, full of love and adoration.

"There is a female figure who has stepped forward," Brody said. "She has the girls in her arms."

Pinky sobbed.

The figure said something to Brody. "She's trying to tell me a name—Ursula."

"Yes."

"Your wife."

"Yes."

"She's telling me that the ultimate sacrifice was made for your daughters."

"I'm sorry, I'm sorry," he cried.

The crew was trying hard not to be swept up in the emotional riptide, but it proved too strong—the muffled whimpers and sniffles only intensified the pathos around the hardware counter.

"Remember—no need for apologies," Brody softly reminded him. He reached out and placed his hand on the man's shoulder. Within seconds Pinky had caught his breath and regained some composure, as though Brody's arm supported him, gave him the strength to carry on. He wiped his nose and blew it again, dropping the wadded towel into a trash can beneath the cash register.

"Thank you." Pinky exhaled.

Brody said, "Ursula tells me that she had a very difficult pregnancy, with fatal consequences for her."

Pinky nodded. "She was on bed rest from about six months on. By that time, we already knew from the ultrasounds about the special situation with our twins. When she was eight months along, there were complications, so she had to deliver prematurely. The doctors did a C-section, and when they took the babies, Ursula hemorrhaged. They gave her multiple transfusions, but we lost her on the delivery table." He shook his head slowly, the words having great difficulty emerging. "Three weeks before I lost both my daughters, I lost my partner, my best friend. Ursula battled hard, but she could not overcome the massive blood loss from her complicated early delivery."

"I'm so sorry, Pinky," Brody said. Here was a man who had lost everything near and dear to him during what should have been such an auspicious, joyous occasion.

Pinky lifted his head and looked Brody in the eyes. "I believe she had a higher purpose—that she went before them so she could make the preparations to receive our daughters into heaven."

"You were very close to the mark with that sentiment."

He took up another shop cloth and dabbed his eyes. "I never thought I was kissing Ursula for the last time when they wheeled her in, kissing my love *good-bye*."

"She wants you to know that she knows you were there for her at the very end. She knows how much it devastated you when you were told how she had passed. She also knows how you agonized over your decision with your daughters and wants you to know that she would have made the exact same choice."

"Really? She said that?"

"Yes, sir, she did."

"Oh, it means the world to me to hear that."

Brody gave him a moment and then said, "Pinky, Ursula wants me to tell you that the girls love the unicorns and the rainbow."

"Herregud. Herregud," he uttered in his native tongue. "I painted two unicorns prancing underneath a rainbow on the nursery wall opposite their cribs. There were always two cribs; never did we expect to lose either or both of our little angels. How could you know that too?"

Brody smiled. "I couldn't, of course. It was Ursula's spirit who told me—who is communicating with you right here, right now, through me."

Pinky shook his head in disbelief. "Amazing," he said. "Unbelievable."

The twins held their hands over their hearts and then out to Pinky.

"Pinky, finally, I want to tell you that your daughters both just indicated to me that their love for you is eternal. They, above all others, understand the choice you had to make, and they respect it."

He slumped behind the counter, trying to remain on his feet the best he could. "Herregud," he whispered again. "Oh my God."

The camera zoomed in to make certain the manager's emotions could be easily seen.

Brody finished the spirits' message. "They know there were extreme risks involved. It is important in your healing process to understand that Katrina forgives you—"

"Ohhh ..."

"—and is happy to be joined, in a different way, a much more positive way, with her sister and her mother once again. They are all content and no longer in pain and totally, *completely* whole."

"I …" Pinky trailed off, unable to complete his reply.

"Sid, it is my hope that their spirits have shown you today that you did not fail your wife or daughters at all. You were brave and loyal in your duty to each of them. They want nothing but your happiness and unburdening of every ounce of guilt you've been carrying around since that terrible tragedy."

"Ohhh," he reiterated, shaking his head slowly.

A few minutes later, after Brody had shaken Pinky's hand and hugged him, Brody excused himself and stepped outside to deeply breathe in the fresh, moist air. The coolness of the breeze was a welcome relief. The rain had subsided for a while, and the barometric pressure had changed; he felt a much-needed decompression from deep within. He backed up, kicked his right foot up against the brick, leaned his shoulders back, exhaled, and let the sturdy wall support the weight of his heavy heart. That poor, poor gentleman—his life certainly hadn't been all rainbows and unicorns. All that time, carrying around all that guilt. *What an impossible choice he'd had to face!* At least Brody felt a modicum of redemption for finally absolving Sid's pain and remorse.

Brody knew firsthand how much a father was devoted to his daughters—it didn't matter if it spanned their first thirty breaths of life or their final thirty years. Did the intensity of that feeling ever waver or diminish? He thought hard about the limits he would go to for his little girl, drawing a blank when he tried to imagine whatever they could be.

After the session at Pinky's Hardware, the final cutaway was filmed. Pinky said to the camera, "I don't know what to say. It was like he was there in that hospital waiting room with me, yet he wasn't. He knew about my wife's death and about our sweet little twins, who fought as gamely as their mother did. I don't know how he does it, but what a gift I was given today! I can finally move forward now. All the guilt I've been carrying around for the last seventeen years is gone. Like that!" He snapped his fingers. "I'm so grateful to've had that opportunity today; it changed my life. I am a believer in Brody."

"Whoa, sweeet," Teddy said, looking at the reworked, freshly painted Chevrolet service van.

"That what you wanted?" Carlos flashed his handlebar-raising grin.

"That'll work just fine. Do I owe you, man?"

Carlos chuckled. "Like I told you: if we deliver the package tomorrow as planned and I get my broker's commission, we're all square again." He clapped Teddy on the back.

"No problemo. Is El Coronel comin' for sure?"

"He's sending his courier by late tomorrow evening."

"Cool." Teddy jumped into the cab and fired up the engine. "I'll meet you at the designated time in the morning."

He motored toward the bay door, his arm extended out the window, slapping his palm several times against the door panel. *"Shitchyeah!"*

Carlos shouted after him, hands cupped to his mouth, *"Hey, amigo! Don't you dare dent anything else!"*

The van disappeared into the rain.

⁓

Doris was slumped in her chair, her head on Cletus's shoulder, his leather work jacket draped over her as a makeshift blanket. Kaylee and David had returned home in the early-morning hours, against her wishes, for Kaylee had two upcoming midterm exams in trig and AP history to study for, and she needed to get some rest. David promised her they would both return to check up on Billy later that afternoon.

Local neurosurgeon Dr. Arnold Sullivan entered the room. A fairly recent addition to the medical staff, he'd relocated to Clarksville following his residency at Bellevue. "Sheriff? Mrs. Coonrod?" the doctor said.

Clearing his cobwebs, Cletus opened his eyes. Seeing the doctor standing before them, he gently nudged his wife. "Doris. Doris. The doctor's here. Wake up, honey."

"Oh," she said, sitting up and straightening her outfit. "How is he, Doctor? Did everything go well?"

"Yes, I'm sorry we got started at such a late hour. There were problems getting the OR set up. The good news: I don't believe there'll be any lasting complications for Billy."

The sheriff and his wife hugged; there was light instantly at the end of the tunnel.

"The hemorrhage fortunately was highly focal and easily accessible. We were able to relieve it without a hitch. There was a certain amount of cerebral edema, though—swelling of the brain. It means he'll be unconscious for a while."

"How long?" She sniffed.

"He'll be okay, though, right?" Cletus asked.

"Can we see him, Doctor?" Doris asked.

Dr. Sullivan smiled and tried to field all their questions. "You can see him now; he just won't be able to respond. He's resting comfortably in the ICU. I don't expect he'll be unresponsive for too long. The swelling should subside in a matter of hours. After that, we should see him coming around fairly quickly. He's a game one, that son of yours—"

The Coonrods both managed a smile, and Cletus took Doris's hand in his.

"—so I expect a full and complete recovery." The doctor turned and motioned them to follow him. "C'mon, I'll take you up there. Now don't be alarmed—we've got him on a ventilator, but that's only temporary, until he regains consciousness. I think we're out of the woods, but the next twenty-four hours will tell us a whole lot more."

"We can't thank you enough, Dr. Sullivan," Cletus said. He helped his wife to her feet, and they followed the doctor to the elevator and to their son.

〜〰〜

David found himself once more on Irv Crossman's doorstep. He rang the bell and waited. After a brief interval, he tried again. There were sounds of movement from within, and soon he saw Irv's demonstrative eyebrows dusting off the glass.

"Yes, can I help you? If you're selling something—"

David held up his badge so Irv could view it. "It's me, Irv—David Jeffries."

"Sergeant? That you?"

"In the flesh."

To David's stark amazement, Irv immediately unlocked and accommodatingly opened the door.

"Hello, Irv."

"Sergeant, it's good to see you again." Irv stood there in plaid shorts and a wrinkled white linen shirt, unbuttoned and with its sleeves rolled up, worn over a ribbed cotton Hanes tank. "What brings you out here once more?" he asked as he scratched his belly through his tank top.

"Well, before I get to that, I have to ask, did I see that Marie passed?"

The elderly man hung his already slumping shoulders. "Yes, she did. Two days ago."

"I'm so sorry to hear that."

He nodded. "Thank you, thank you. Oh!" He pawed the air. "Where are my manners? Would you like to come in?"

Another surprise! "Well, sure. That'd be nice. Thank you."

David followed the feeble fellow, who shuffled about as fast as Tim Conway did on *The Carol Burnett Show*. Patiently, David trailed Irv past Marie's empty bedroom, spotting the hospital bed where she must have spent her final days. Around the corner was a modest living room, where Irv shakily waved David to the couch as he methodically deposited his *toches* onto a lift recliner, conveniently waiting in its up position. He pressed a button on the corded controller, and the chair whirred slowly downward, its occupant adjusting his legs now and then to accommodate the persistent, gentle descent.

"Coffee?" Irv asked.

David held up his hand. "I'm good."

"That's the impression I had of you the last time. Coffee?"

"Uh, no thank you." David noticed that the tattooed number Kaylee had told him about was uncovered on Irv's left arm—B2267.

"You're welcome, Officer."

"Please, if I can call you Irv, you can call me David. Deal?"

"*Deal or No Deal?*" He cackled. "Aw, that Howie Mandel … 'Open the case!'" Irv drifted momentarily, his train of thought clearly detouring from the present set of tracks.

"Irv?"

He snapped out of his fugue. "Yes? What?"

"I was saying that I was sorry to hear about Marie. My daughter was telling me yesterday how involved she was at temple, especially with the youth."

"Oh, yeah, yeah. My bubalah loved those kiddoes. *Loved* 'em!" He rocked slowly in his chair.

"Well, please accept our condolences."

"Thanks." He raised his arms, elbows bent, palms upward, as if surrendering. "What can you do? Huh? When it's your time, it's your time."

"That's very true, sir."

"But Marie, she had a good life, a long life. And she had me!" He gave a dry chuckle that wheezed into a cough.

"Yes, she did, Irv. She was lucky to have you."

He collected himself from his coughing spell. "Well, I hope so. I mean, she never really *told* me that. I kind of took it for granted, because she wasn't very forthcoming with her sentiments toward me—never was. She was a shy girl, Officer—er, David. An evening primrose. As beautiful as those roses I planted in our garden out back in her honor, twenty years ago. Or was it twenty-five? *Pfhht!*" He gave a brief Bronx cheer. "I would have given anything for her to have said 'I love you, Irv' once more before she passed, but by the time I brought in her breakfast, she had already breathed her last." He went misty-eyed, lost in a daydream. "I love you … It was eons ago. So," he said, coming back to the present once more, "you know what I did?"

"What?"

"I was watching the television—"

No!

"—and that *Daily Show—Live* was on. There was a fella on there who talks to the dead."

"Yes, I saw that too. I actually met that guy the other day."

"Did you? Well, I hope to meet him too. I called in to the television station and asked for one of his readings! I so want to talk with my bubalah again, to hear those words I long to hear. Maybe she'll say them to me. I can't remember the last time I heard those words from her …" He pondered once more. "I think it was before Israel was declared a state!" He laughed again, "Ha!" and then hacked. He exclaimed hoarsely, "Good one, huh?"

David laughed. Was it out of politeness or pleasure? The distinction was becoming fuzzier as his fondness for this affable fellow grew.

"You young 'uns think you've got the market cornered when it comes to funny business! Well, we had some great ones in our time: Gleason, Skelton, Lucy, Hope, Abbott and that Costello kid, those Marx Brothers. Ha! Now *that* was comedy!"

"What about Seinfeld?" David asked, offering a more contemporary Jewish example.

"Who?"

"Seinfeld—Jerry Seinfeld."

"Does he go to our temple?"

David was about to clarify things for Irv but then changed horses in midstream, abandoning that exercise in futility. "Irv?"

"Yes?"

"Late yesterday afternoon—you didn't hear or see anything unusual, did you?"

"Like the baboon special? I recorded that one on my VHS machine."

He smiled. *Do they still* make *VHS tapes?* "No, nothing on Discovery. Like ... outside. Anywhere up or down the street?"

"Oh! Oh!" He pointed a bony finger approximately in David's direction. "I was going to call you! I was going to call." His exuberance shifted to mild embarrassment at the admission. "But then I got sidetracked." He said softly, "I get sidetracked very easily these days." That statement caused him to tear up, and he looked slightly away from David, murmuring, "Marie, Marie. Your oxygen ..." He looked once again at David, wiping his nose with the back of his hand. "I do; I get sidetracked." He sniffled.

"Me too, Irv. We all do. Too much crap to try to remember these days."

"Yes." He cleared his throat. "We're all full of crap. Where was I?" He cleared his throat again. "Oh, yes—*yesterday.* Well, the folks from Gilbert Funeral came yesterday. Finally! You know I called those meshuggeners right after she died? It took them twenty-four hours to get over here to pick her up! A *full day*! My bubalah was just lying there, decaying, rotting in her bed—God bless her soul," he said glancing upward, "while they figured out when they could schedule a pickup! They're not UPS; they're supposed to be a mortuary!" He scratched his head and then his belly once more. "At least, I *think* I called them right away. Oh well. Yes ... getting back—I was standing outside as their hearse finally drove up, and I heard a loud *bang!* like a firecracker from one of those pesky Robinson kids down the block again. But it was just that old jalopy the funeral home had sent. Backfiring! *Ha!* Scared the shit—oh, pardon my French, Officer—"

David raised his hand, conveying his acquiescence.

"—right outta me! Er, figuratively speaking. Figuratively speaking, you understand."

"I was hopeful. Go on."

"I thought nothing more of it until a bright-yellow hot rod peeled out"—he slid one hand rapidly over the other, palms together—"from the parking lot down the street."

"The Dollar General?"

"Oh," he said, waving his right hand, "I never watched that show."

"What show?"

"That *Dukes of Hazzard* show. Wasn't that what they called their hot rod?"

"No, sir, that would be the General Lee. I was talking about the store down the street, the Dollar General."

"Oh! *Hee, hee!*" He put a hand over his mouth and pointed at David with his other index finger. "You're right. Yes, it was coming out of the parking lot at General Dollar—"

David's eyes ventured heavenward.

"—and it hauled ass down the street!"

"Irv, you said it was yellow?"

"Yeah, bright yellow. Like a lemon or a daffodil or one of those little birds."

"Canary?"

"Can we what?"

David suddenly felt as if he were the straight man to *this* Lou Costello. "Irv, did you get a look at the make or model of the car?"

"Well, I was too far away to see if a model was driving it, but I wish I'd—"

"No, Irv. Sorry to interrupt, but what *kind* of car was it? Could you tell?"

"Well, of course I could tell you—if I had been closer, but ..."

This line of questioning is crumbling quickly ... I'm losing him!

Suddenly, something seemed to cross Irv's mind—a feat unto itself. "Oh, I know! What was that car from that Clint Eastwood movie? I just saw that one on TNT."

David shook his head; he needed an extra clue.

Irv was gesturing as if in a battle of charades. "Yeah, you know—the angry vet, the oriental kid next door ..."

It came to David suddenly. "*Gran Torino?*" He felt as if he'd just correctly answered Final Jeopardy.

"Yeah, that's what it was, a yellow El Camino."

"Uh, which one was it, Irv? A Gran Torino or an El Camino?"

"It was the Camino kind. Not the Torino."

"Are you sure?"

"As sure as I'll ever be," Irv said, a befuddled yet smug expression on his face.

"You didn't by any chance see the license number on that car, did you?"

"No, Sergeant, I told you, I was ..."

David chimed in with Irv on the last part: *"... too far away!"*

18

JENNIFER and Mike reviewed the footage from the morning, satisfied they had cooked up another tantalizing taste of what their viewing audience was hungry for.

Jennifer left the control room and hurried around the corner and down the hallway to her office. Breathless, she called Brody. "Hi."

"Hi, Jen. How are you?"

"Couldn't be more pleased. I think this segment is every bit as good as the first. Maybe better."

"That's good news."

She frowned. "You don't sound too thrilled."

"This one kind of hit me harder than most. I gotta tell you—this was a difficult one."

"Why? What happened?"

"You remember the story you told me about your daughter and everything you did for her?"

"Sure."

"Well, you saw what this guy went through—much the same experience as yours in the precious few days he was blessed with his daughters. His grief was perhaps as intense, as profound, as yours, though not nearly as lengthy. Does that make sense?"

"Sort of ..." She couldn't see where he was taking her with his thought process. The segment certainly was tragic, but she failed to see how Pinky's story could really compare to the stretch of her ordeal with Julie's illness. There was no way, she thought, that Brody could possibly know about everything she went through. Oh wait, she realized, perhaps he could! After all, he did have access to Julie's experiences.

"I'm sorry, Jen. I may be way off base here. I've never stood in your shoes, but I walked in his this morning, and those were shoes I hope are never mine to wear. I can't imagine anything of that magnitude befalling Abby or what I would do. Does that make more sense?"

"Now *that* is something I can surely relate to."

"Yes, I imagine you can. Say ..."

"Yes?"

"Why don't we talk about it some more over dinner tonight?"

"Brody, I'd love to, but I already made plans with a girlfriend tonight. How about tomorrow night instead?"

"Sounds good."

"Perfect. I'll look forward to it."

"So will I."

⌒⁎⌒

Arranging her snack of Cheetos and lemonade, Abby sat down on the living room floor in front of the coffee table, crossing her legs underneath her.

Brody sat on the couch, opposite her. "All right, ready to start?"

"Yup," she said, taking a Cheeto and nibbling it to a nub and then popping the last tidbit into her mouth. She took a sip of lemonade. "Ready when you are."

"First of all, did anything happen at school today that we need to talk about?"

"Nope. It really made me feel better talking to you about things last night, so I decided that if there was anything that I couldn't figure out today or that made me feel uncomfortable, I was going to ask you for help with it."

Brody beamed. "And I will always gladly give my help to you and talk to you about whatever's troubling you. Anytime. Seriously."

She nodded and grabbed another cheesy puff. "I gotcha. Thanks."

"Good. I was thinking about where to begin, and—"

Shortly after five, Jennifer called Brody and said, "Listen, my friend crapped out on me, and I mean that literally. Looks like food poisoning from lunch."

"Oh, that's pretty shitty, Jen ... Now *that* was too easy!"

She rewarded him with laughter. "Okay, okay. I was wondering if you'd maybe like to come over for dinner instead, if you don't have anything else going on. Do you think you could get your sitter on such late notice?"

He tried not to trip over his words. "That's a really nice invite, Jen. I'd love that. Let me call Lizbeth. There's a big high school football game tonight, and I'm not sure if she's going to want to miss it. Can I call you right back?"

"Sure. Let me know."

"I'll call her now. Bye!"

They hung up, and Brody dialed Lizbeth.

His sitter picked up after a couple of rings. "Hello."

"Lizbeth, hi. This is Mr. Whitaker."

"Hi, Mr. Whitaker, what's up?"

"Listen, I could sure use you again, to sit tonight. I know you were just here and that there's a game, but I *will* attempt a bribe. It's important."

"I accept bribes." She laughed. "I'm listening, sir. Go on. What did you have in mind?"

"Well ... how about free movie passes for you and a friend?"

"How about two friends?"

"Two friends?"

"And money for snacks?"

She drove a hard bargain. Brody cratered. "Sure. I'll throw that in too. What do you say?"

"Well, it *is* short notice. Would you consider time and a half?"

What? Time and a half?!

Lizbeth said, "It's a big game tonight. It's for the district lead."

Brody would usually have rifled through his monthly budget in his head, but the advance from the station had thankfully rendered that necessity moot. "All right. You got it."

"Great! You've got a deal, Mr. Whitaker. What time do you need me?"

"Well, how about ... an hour from now?"

"Sure, I can be there by then."

"Good! Thanks. Oh, and Lizbeth?"

"Yes, sir?"

He chuckled. "You should think about becoming a lawyer or something, the way you negotiate! All right, see you in a bit, then."

⁓𝓎𝓀⁓

Lizbeth Cooper hung up her phone. Maybe Mr. Whitaker was on to something—maybe she should consider law school. She smiled. Score one for her—she'd just as soon skip that silly ol' game anyway. She *hated* football!

⁓𝓎𝓀⁓

At exactly 5:53 that evening, Billy's eyes flashed open, and he struggled in panic against the endotracheal tube. The attending nurse called for assistance in restraining the young man to prevent him from self-extubation. Once that had been accomplished, she called Dr. Sullivan to inform him his patient had awakened and to obtain an order to wean Billy off the ventilator. Then she called in a message for the respiratory therapist to facilitate and oversee the process. The charge nurse then left to alert the sheriff and his wife of the favorable development.

⁓𝓎𝓀⁓

Earlier, David had telephoned Cletus about what he'd learned from Irv Crossman. The sheriff, in turn, had relayed the information to his deputies and charged them with finding out who, given a hundred-mile radius of Clarksville, owned that yellow El Camino.

Cletus was surprised at how well his wife had been holding up, although his own state of mind was fraught from the continued stress of waiting, just waiting. He had been pacing back and forth, heading to the bathroom almost every half hour; the worrying was wreaking havoc on his digestive system, as if another excuse was needed!

When the nurse came in and told them that Billy had regained consciousness, the Coonrods rushed upstairs and waited impatiently outside his door, for they had to allow the respiratory therapist to perform the necessary tests on their son and pull his tube. Only after their son was stable were they allowed into his room.

⁓ 227 ⁓

Doris rushed to their son's side, grabbed Billy's hand, and clasped it to her generous bosom. Sheriff Coonrod went to the opposite side of Billy's bed. He stroked his son's hair and gazed down at him.

Billy opened his eyes again, blinking a few times before slowly focusing on his parents' faces.

"Hey," said Cletus. "How you doin', Son?"

"Pretty good," he rasped.

"Rest, baby," Doris told him. "Don't strain your voice."

"I'm okay," he croaked. "Dad?"

"Yes, Son?"

"Call Kaylee for me."

Cletus made the call on his son's phone and set it down again on the bed. He and his wife stood vigil by their boy's side, smiling at each other and at Billy and thanking the man upstairs.

19

"I HOPE you're hungry," Jen said as she opened the door. She looked ravishing. Her hair was pulled back and draped sexily over her left shoulder.

"Famished," Brody assured, stepping inside her home.

Jennifer resided in a subdivision of Clarksville named Plantation Estates, not far from Fort Campbell Military Base. Her two-story house was a combination of gray stucco and garnet brick, with a front-entry two-car garage, a large multilevel deck out back, and an abundantly landscaped yard with well-tended flower beds encircling well-manicured trees and shrubs.

"Let me take your coat," she told him, slipping it off his shoulders and depositing it in a small closet adjoining the marble-tiled foyer.

"This is a nice place you have here, Jen," he said, glancing around at the intricacies of the moldings and angled juxtapositions of her ceilings. The fixtures were ornate without being ostentatious, very tasteful. "Did you build this to spec, or did you purchase from a previous owner?"

"All me," she said proudly. "Everything you see in here I selected and designed."

He followed her down the hallway, past a large gilded mirror, and to the living area. "You did a really lovely job. I admire your taste."

"Thanks." She glanced over her shoulder and smiled. "Come in, come in." She showed him into the great room with its vaulted ceilings, bare beams, and large stone fireplace.

"Now this—this is homey," he said. "Impressive."

She motioned for him to sit on one of the two love seats. "Drink?"

"Sure, what are you having?"

"Oh," she said with a smile, "I'm just having some iced tea. But I have water, Coke, ginger ale, coffee. Nothing hard. Sorry."

"I'll have some tea as well, thanks. Sounds great."

"Make yourself comfortable. I'll be right back." She went around the corner to the kitchen.

Brody heard the clink of ice cubes and called out, "Do you need any help?"

"Nope!"

He rose anyway and went to the kitchen and was impressed all over again. It was spacious and open, with custom antique-washed, walnut-finished cabinets. A large island garnered the central focus, with a rectangular copper rack suspended above, replete with a chef's array of accoutrements. Whoever had equipped this kitchen was indeed a culinary gourmet—and whatever was simmering in the pans on the stove smelled *heavenly*!

"Here you go," she said, handing him his tea.

"Thanks."

"A toast," Jen said.

They raised their glasses.

"To what?" Brody asked.

"To another successful episode of the Clarksville Medium."

"Hear, hear."

They clinked their glasses, and each took a sip, Brody staring into her eyes. He yearned to take her in his arms, but she might find that move too presumptuous, he figured. So he opted to bypass it for the moment, optimistic that the opportunity would later present itself. The way she looked, though— he didn't know how much longer he could resist. Although exhilarating, it felt awkward being in an intimate setting with another woman again. It was so difficult to recognize the signals after such a lengthy hiatus from the dating pool. *Well, it's either sink or swim tonight!*

He sniffed the air again. "What is that smell? It's amazing!"

"It's Gucci."

Brody blushed. He'd meant the meal!

"No, silly.," she chuckled. "I knew you meant what was on the stove. I was just having fun!"

With that, he threw resistance to the wind, crossed to her, took her in his embrace, and kissed her. Her lack of willpower rivaled his—she coiled one arm around his neck and the other around the small of his back, her lips opening, her breath entering his mouth. As she pressed her body longingly into his, Brody's eager tongue found hers, cool from the iced tea. They held each other for several sensual minutes.

As they separated, he held her face and looked deep into her amorous eyes. "Well?"

She allowed her chin to rest without opposition in his tender cradle and said breathlessly, impishly, "Scampi … I hope you like shrimp."

⁓∕∕⁓

"There's one more stop I gotta make," David said to his daughter. "You go on up. Tell Sheriff Coonrod I'll be back soon."

"Sure, Dad." Kaylee leaned over and gave her dad a peck on the cheek.

"Sorry you had to miss the game," he said.

Kaylee shrugged. "Wouldn't have it any other way." She got out of the car and waved. "Bye!"

David waved back and watched as the lobby doors slid together behind her. He pulled away and drove to his destination, Gilbert Funeral Home. Entering the building, he was greeted by a dapper aide dressed head to toe in black, a white carnation boutonniere affixed to his left lapel.

"Are you here for the remembrance of Mrs. Crossman?"

"Yes," David replied, "I am."

The aide ushered him into the chapel, adorned this evening with the Star of David. In the front of the modest auditorium was a closed casket. David recognized several people from his congregation milling about. He saw many unfamiliar faces as well—apparently Marie had known a lot of folks outside the temple. He signed the guest registry and walked up the center aisle. Over to David's right, in the front row of seats, Irv had his head bowed in prayer, his white satin yarmulke perched atop his sparse silvery hair. His eyes were closed, and his lips moved silently as David approached. The sergeant respectfully and quietly sat down beside him.

When Irv opened his eyes and saw David, he threw his arms around the police officer and hugged him fervently. "Thank you for coming. Thank you, Sergeant Jeffries. Uh, I mean, David."

"You're so welcome, Irv," he said, returning the squeeze.

"I'm very pleased that you came. You didn't have to, but you did—for Marie. That means a great deal to me."

David smiled at him, glancing around. "There sure are a lot of people here tonight. It's good to know Marie was so well admired, isn't it?"

"She touched a lot of people—some of them twice!" he cracked. He pointed to his left temple and then at David. "Gotta laugh, else I'd cry," he sighed.

"Irv, you're a rascal. Tonight you do whatever you think Marie would want you to."

"We bury her tomorrow. Then I'll sit shiva. I wanted a week, but she demanded I grieve no more than three days. How about that? Seventy-five years together—"

David smiled at the ever-changing number.

"—and all she deserves is three days? If it was up to me, it'd be seven!"

"I'll try to pay you a shiva call next week."

"Sergeant, I know how busy you are. You have gone above and beyond for someone who only met me a day or two ago, and I am grateful to you for the kindness that you've shown. If you can come by, come by; you're more than welcome in my home. You're here now, and that's substantial in my book. Besides, I have family coming in. Did I tell you my grandson Aaron is coming all the way from Israel?"

"No," David said. "That's wonderful that you have family willing to travel so far to be with you to remember Marie."

"He's a good boy, that Aaron. He was in the IDF, special forces unit. Branch called the Sayeret Matkal."

"Really?"

"Yes." He cupped his hand to David's ear and whispered, "That's between you and me, okay? You're in law enforcement, so I know you know the meaning of secrecy for security's sake."

"Okay," David whispered back, nodding.

Irv sat back, continuing quietly, "He's doing his own thing right now. Still works with me sometimes ..."

David cocked his head. *With him?* His curiosity over that last remark was tempered by the knowledge that Irv's nearly hundred-year-old mental faculties were not quite up to snuff.

Irv sighed contentedly, plowing on, "Look at all these people! One of Marie's last wishes was that there be some sort of way for her Gentile acquaintances to come and pay their respects. So I put together a little tribute in her memory."

As a slide show homage of Irv's bubalah's numerous watershed moments and milestones commenced, David put his arm around Irv's shoulder, and they sat back, the younger man supporting the elder, together shedding a little water of their own while viewing the lovely, sentimental memorial.

Kaylee exited the elevator and approached the nurses' station.

"Kaylee, honey?" Doris called from down the hallway, waving Kaylee over.

Kaylee headed toward Mrs. Coonrod, bypassing the counter.

Doris gave her the update: "They just moved Billy to a private room about a half hour ago. He's conscious and off the ventilator, thank God, and is steadily improving. They're keeping him through the weekend for observation, but if all goes well, it looks like he'll be able to come home on Monday. His doctor said that with plenty of rest, and if everything checks out, he should be able to return to school sometime late next week."

"What a relief! May I see him? Is that all right?"

"Well, it better be—he's only been asking for you ever since he woke up!" She led Kaylee into the room.

Billy was halfway upright in the bed, eyes closed. The monitors attached to his fingers and forearm intermittently beeped and hummed his vital signs. Numbed and sobered by the appearance of all that necessary equipment, Kaylee walked over to his bedside and took his hand. Doris and Cletus retreated quietly from the room, leaving the young couple alone.

Billy opened his eyes a crack, saw her, and smiled, gripping her hand tightly. "Hey, Kay. Glad you're here." His voice was still thin and raspy. "Thanks for coming."

"I came as fast as I could."

"You're missing the game, though."

into expeditiously. Billy had also been able to provide his father a detailed description of the shooter.

David, in turn, was using that info to piece together any possible connection between Billy's assailant and the pair who'd robbed the bank.

"I took the liberty of arranging something for you," David said to Billy. "There were a lot of people who drove here to see you tonight, so I pulled some strings and …" He bowed and directed their attention to the doorway.

Coach Pirelli poked his head into the room. "Hey, champ!"

"Coach!" Billy propped himself more upright. "How was the game?"

"I'll let them tell you."

"Them? Them who?"

"Hey, Billy!" Luke Ryan, one of Billy's receivers appeared in the doorway. "You good, hoss?"

Billy looked completely blown away. "Luke! Yeah! We win?"

"Thirty-eight to eighteen—*plucked* those buzzards, buddy!" He disappeared from the doorway, and the next teammate assumed the position.

"Tim! Hey, dude," Billy called hoarsely.

"Hey, Billy boy. You get better now, y'hear? We need our hurricane at full force."

Then another and another new face appeared as every player on varsity filed past his room, one by one.

"Yo, Billy! Get well, bro!"

"Thanks for takin' care of him, Kaylee!"

"Get well, Billy Bob!"

"Quit tryin' to miss practice, lightweight!"

"Quinton!" Billy exclaimed. "Man, whatchu doin'? You guys got dates waitin' for you!"

His left tackle smiled. "They're waitin', man. All our dates are waitin'. There's plenty of time for that. There's more important things in life than pizza, isn't that what Coach taught us? We're here for you, bro. You know there was a whole candlelight thingy for you at halftime? Players from both teams met in the middle of the field and prayed for you, dude! Both stands lit up. We sent you some pictures. Check your phone!" Quinton grinned again, waving to the one whose back he protected both on and off the field, and to Kaylee as well. Then his face yielded to the next.

"Miss ya, man."

"Ain't no bullet never gonna stop *you*, Billy!"

Billy flashed the thumbs-up.

Each player filed by and then looped around along the opposite wall of the hallway, back to the stairs, and down to the lobby, where they were all reconvening. The giant assembly line of gridiron brethren snaked the entire three floors of the stairwell.

As the last of the players spoke to Billy and departed for the rendezvous point, Coach Pirelli reappeared in the doorway.

"Eighteen? How'd they score eighteen, Coach?" Billy asked him.

"Six field goals, son. The defense never let those Hawks inside our twenty. Your team dedicated this win to you. They made it happen."

"Man, that's cool. That is *so* cool, Coach. Hey? What about those scouts?"

"Don't you worry about them. I called them earlier today, and they all wanted to reschedule, given the circumstances. They still want a look at you."

Billy sank back onto his pillow, looking relieved beyond measure.

"See, I told you that an hour ago," Kaylee said, winking at her dad.

"Yeah," Billy answered, "you did, Kay."

The coach continued, "We've got them on alert for each of our last two home games, including the first of them two weeks from tonight. I'll e-mail them all back before then, if your doctors clear you to play. And there's also the play-offs, so don't you let that put a damper on your weekend!"

Cletus shook the coach's hand. "Thanks, Coach Pirelli. You don't realize what this has meant to my son."

"That's who and what we are. We're a team, Mr. Coonrod. When one of our men is down, we rise to the occasion. I'm an ex-marine—it's the only way I know."

"Wouldn't know you were a marine by your lightweight practices," razzed Billy.

Coach pointed his finger at the bedbound boy. "Ohhh, you wait, Coonrod. You *wait*! You'll be suiting up again soon. You *will* regret that. No free passes on *my* team, especially the QB!" He laughed heartily. Then he said his good-byes and headed for the stairs.

Kaylee took Billy's hand again. "Pretty cool, huh?"

"Yeah—cool, all right," he said. He glanced at the others in the room in rapid succession and added, unabashedly, "But I'm lookin' right at *pretty*."

Kaylee blushed.

Cletus elbowed David in the ribs and whispered, "I taught him that too!" Doris rolled her eyes, expressing wry endearment.

"I have something else to show you all." David stepped forward, rubbing his freshly tender side and producing his iPhone. "I shot this downstairs—"

"Hey, you said no guns!" Billy exclaimed.

"As I was saying, this was *taken* downstairs. I wanted to share it with all of you."

He placed the phone on Billy's lap, and they all hunkered around the miniature screen to watch the video of the scene David had happened upon.

Coach Pirelli stood in the middle of his players, who were all kneeling in an immense circle around him. He spoke to them animatedly. "Our leader, one of our warriors, is lying up there! He couldn't be with us in the flesh, but he was damn sure with us in spirit tonight, right?"

The whole team raised their fists in unison. "Oo-rah!"

Coach went on, "Let's say a prayer for the recovery of our fallen comrade, our warrior brother."

The players all bowed their heads, each placing a hand on the shoulder of the teammate in front of him—a reverently unified huddle. Following the prayer, the group rose en masse and began filing inside.

And the video was over.

20

DOTTY Trumball was getting her breakfast. Her parents were sound asleep, so she would have to see herself out of their double-wide and walk all four blocks to Walmart unaccompanied. Typical. She was used to it.

In the pantry, she found a box of stale Corn Pops. A paper bowl would suffice for her, a plastic spoon and generic paper towel rounding out her place setting. The box's top was already open—her own pops must have helped himself to a late-night snack. She unfurled the thick silver wrap and dug out a few clumps of yellow deliciousness, dumping them into her cellulose china.

She pulled a large jug of milk out from behind twin cartons of Busch in the fridge. She checked the sell-by date on the plastic neck: a week ago yesterday. *Hmm.* She pulled the red cap off the top and took a whiff, wincing. Oh well, it wasn't *too* bad, and she needed something to moisten those clumps, so into the bowl it went, a few pungent drops splattering onto the plastic place mat. She tore off another paper towel and mopped up the spill, knowing full well what corporal punishment would befall her should she fail to do so. She tossed the damp towel into the Hefty bag on the floor next to the screen door and pulled the ruby drawstrings taut. She sat down and dug in.

The cereal tasted a tiny bit sour, but it was passable; she'd had far worse. She finished the last cereal conglomerate and drank the remainder of the now ochre-colored liquid from her bowl. As she uncinched the rubbish sack and shoved the bowl and spoon into it, a hefty cockroach clambered over the relaxed plastic sphincter, fell on its back to the floor, wriggle-righted itself, and then skittered under the molding. Dotty recoiled, shocked at the sight of the nasty insect, as afraid of it as it was of her.

It was a good thing she didn't need to wear her uniform, for it was smothered in a weeks-old heap of laundry by the couch, surrounded by scattered rodent droppings, awaiting a latent trek to the Wash-'N-Dry. But spare change had already been earmarked for higher priorities—in other words, twelve-packs for the next binge—than clean clothes.

Quietly, she opened the unlocked door to the trailer and walked down the makeshift, wobbly cinderblock steps. Skipping along the sidewalk, she burped. It was not a friendly burp at all, and she hesitated in midskip, balancing her weight on her right leg, her other knee slightly raised, gauging her faint queasiness. Sensing nothing more ominous, she resumed her jaunt to Walmart and to the rest of her troop members.

Brody was in the process of clearing the remnants of Abby's meal—a cinnamon Pop-Tart, some scrambled eggs with cheese, and a small glass of Tropicana OJ.

Brenda had already picked Abby up for the morning's sale. Brody knew that when Abby was among her fellow scouts, she preferred it if he didn't hover around. It tended to embarrass her. More and more lately—at least when Abby was surrounded by her friends—she was definitely asserting her tweenage independence. It was why she preferred to have Maddie's mom drive her to scouting events rather than Brody, and while he applauded her independent nature, it secretly saddened him as well. His little girl was growing up! And, he felt, growing away … another reason why he was pleased about her newfound ability: it might help strengthen their bond again.

As he rinsed off Abby's plate, he couldn't help but wonder why Frank's touch had felt so cold to his daughter at the bank the other day. When a spirit was in very close proximity, Brody typically felt an otherworldly chill. Whenever he cooked a meal on the gas range with Susan's spirit beside him, her mere presence greatly mitigated the heat from the appliance. And when a spirit made physical contact with him, or vice versa, the apparition definitely felt cold to the touch. It was an oddity he'd long since grown accustomed to. But Frank was still alive; Brody drew a blank as to why Frank's odd handshake could've felt so cold to Abby—he'd never encountered that before—unless the spirit she had seen behind Frank was somehow involved. It certainly was a topic for future discussions with her.

Brody's phone suddenly rang; it was Jennifer. "Good morning," he said.

"You too! I was just calling to see if we were still on for lunch."

"Of course. A nice meal and some good company would be a pleasure. Hey, Jen, I just wanted to tell you that I really enjoyed the meal and our time together yesterday evening."

"Likewise."

He dove in, wholeheartedly headfirst. "You're a wonderful woman, and I'm very glad we're getting better acquainted."

"Me too, Brody. You're a helluva guy." She added softly, "I'm enjoying myself with a man for the first time in forever."

"Me too, Jen."

"Not with a man, I hope!" She laughed.

"No," he chuckled. "I meant with you. It's been a long time for me too. I'm looking forward to seeing you again."

"Well, how about today?"

He said without hesitation, "How *about* today." Then he added, "Tell you what—I'm going to swing by the Walmart where Abby's troop is selling their cookies and just check up on things. I have a few items to pick up there anyway. Then I'll meet you at the sandwich shop around eleven thirty. Okay? I know that sounds a tad overprotective."

She chuckled. "You know I understand the 'tad overprotective' thing. I'll get myself ready, and I'll see you there for lunch."

"You're on," he told her.

～※～

"All right, ladies." Brenda assembled her little ducklings and called for their attention. "Thanks, everyone, for coming out today. It looks like the weather is cooperating with us, and the rain is hopefully holding off for the better part of the day, so we can ..." She cupped her left hand to her ear.

"Sell, sell, *sell!*" the girls replied in unison.

"Music, sweet music to my ears, ladies! Yes!" She applauded them. "Now we have twenty cases to sell today. That's a *lot* of cookies, but we have a lot of great salesladies here too, so let's set up and get crackin'!"

The girls hung banners on the concrete with care as visions of dollar bills danced through Brenda's head. They pulled several of the cardboard cartons open and precisely stacked individual cookie boxes six high across the front of the table. Then the eager scouts each took a package or two and, following strict troop protocol, found their buddy and positioned themselves two by two at designated locations, busily soliciting patrons entering and exiting, and polling them about their particular favorites. With their technique honed to perfection, their sales grew steadily, as did the money in the cashbox, minute by minute.

⌒⁂⌒

After an hour or so, close by the entrance to the store where the girls were selling their cookies, a van joined the other vehicles angled in the parking lot row. On the side, the van was adorned with West End Baptist in a multicolored arch; underneath the rainbow of letters was a jumbo violet cross.

Inside the van, two figures eyed the little girls. Dangling from the ignition, attached to a lanyard, was a mint-green rabbit's foot.

"Which one is she, amigo?"

"Dunno. I'm told she's got blonde hair and her name's Abby."

"Well?"

"That's all I know. If no one calls her by name or we can't figure out which one she is, I'm supposed to get some video of 'em on my phone and send it to a guy I know who's gonna single her out."

"Cool, cool."

⌒⁂⌒

Brody pulled into a parking spot, got out of his car, and approached Brenda and the girls. He spotted his daughter and Maddie selling a box of cookies to a store patron. He waved to Abby, but she was busy making the sale, or at least feigning ignorance of her father's impromptu appearance. Brody chuckled to himself.

"Hello, Brody," Brenda greeted him.

"Hi, Brenda."

"Thanks for having one of our best salesladies up and ready today!"

He laughed. "You're welcome. I'd hang out here with you for a while, but I've got to go home with you-know-who." He thumbed toward his daughter, who was already closing another sale with Maddie.

Brenda laughed. "I know, I know. Listen, whatever you'd like. You won't be stepping on *my* toes."

"Appreciate it. I'll just run inside for a couple of things. You can still bring her home for me, right?"

She nodded. "Be glad to."

"About what time will you be closing down shop?"

"Oh, shortly after lunch. Probably around two," Brenda said.

He thanked her again and then snuck up behind Abby. He tickled her on both sides of her rib cage.

She jumped and then turned around. "Daaaddy!"

"Sorry, pigeon! I just couldn't resist."

"I'm in the middle of a sale!" She nodded her head in the direction of a kind-looking elderly woman. The woman had her hand in her purse and was smiling at the sweet situation.

With hands up and palms facing forward, Brody backed off, whispering to his daughter, "Sorry!"

Abby shook her head in mock exasperation, glancing at Maddie, who grinned at her.

"I've got to pick up some more squid oatmeal and a couple other things, anyway," he joked. "I'll just head inside now ..."

She raised her eyes to the heavens. "Love you, Daddy," she said with a sigh.

"You too, pumpkin. See ya later, alligator!"

As he turned to head inside, he saw Abby shake her head again, which made him grin from ear to ear.

⌒⁓

When Brody stepped back outside, he made it a point to smooch Abby—despite her exaggerated irritation—on the forehead, before walking triumphantly back to his car. He got in and lingered, watching the storefront for a moment longer. Then he checked his watch—the time was eleven fifteen. He started the car and backed out of his space, paying more attention to Abby than to how far in reverse he was traveling, nearly backing into a white van behind him.

Whew! That was close! He swung the Accord past the storefront, waving at the busy scouts and their watchful leader once more. At least Brenda waved back to him.

He pulled out of the parking lot and headed to meet his lunch date.

⌁

"Did ya see?" Teddy asked Carlos. "The one he kissed. That's her!" He was pointing directly at Abby. "That's who we need, dude. There's our little package."

"You sure?" Carlos was sitting in the driver's seat of Teddy's new van.

Teddy had already explained his reason for targeting that little girl—he needed Brody's help in squaring a debt, and kidnapping the girl would create the motivation for his cooperation. Not that it mattered to Carlos which one they were snatching or why; the reward was the same for any of them. What El Coronel would do with her—that was his business.

"Yeah. It's gotta be. That was the guy on TV, for sure. Mofo looks so familiar to me, but I just can't think of where else I seen him before, other than on the tube. Can't believe he almost backed into us! Jerk-off!"

"Yeah. So … when we wanna do this, amigo?"

"Soon. Gotta be patient. Let's wait until that leader bitch is distracted. Then we'll make our move."

⌁

Brody was having lunch with Jen at a restaurant aptly named Wicked Good Sandwiches, noshing on a Reuben. "Glad this worked out," he said, licking his fingers.

"Me too. You sure everything's okay at the sale?"

"Brenda looked like she had everything well in hand—as well as anybody could have those little bundles of energy under control," he chuckled. "It's like that commercial where the frantic cowpokes are trying to herd all those riled-up cats! Brenda really does watch 'em like a hawk, though."

"Well, I'm glad this worked out." She picked up her turkey-mushroom melt.

He wiped the corner of his mouth and placed his hand around his beverage. "Me too. You're a great gal, Jennifer."

"And you're a great guy for putting up with me and my stories. Oh, and for springing for lunch!"

"Who said anything about springing for lunch?" He smiled.

She wrapped one hand around her drink cup and then circled her other hand, palm down, over the lid, intoning with a gypsy's accent, rolling her *r*'s, "I see it een your future ..."

"Okay, you win!" He then wiped his hands and reached for her left one. "About putting up with you: it's pretty easy. Well worth the effort."

She beamed at him, nodding in affirmation, and then cocked her head. "Effort? You mean buying lunch?"

"*Especially* lunch."

✴

Dotty approached Brenda, looking a bit green around the gills. "Mrs. Culligan?"

"What is it, Dotty?" Brenda asked her. "Are you okay, honey?"

Dotty's hands overlaid her midsection. "I think so, Mrs. Culligan. My tummy's kinda acting goofy. I think I'm just hungry; that's all."

"Well," Brenda said soothingly, "let's see what we can do." This wasn't the first time that Dotty had complained of something. She received little to no companionship at home and therefore sought it everywhere. Her pleadings and posturings were generally designed to get attention. But just as little Dotty's forlorn plea was fairly typical, equally so was Brenda's granting her the benefit of the doubt. Flagging down a nearby cart boy, Brenda handed him a five and asked him to please go inside and purchase her a box of Saltines.

Delighted to help, the young man dutifully carried out the favor, returning with the carton and her change. Brenda peeled open a sleeve, offering some crackers to Dotty. "Would you like a couple of these, sweetie? They might settle your tummy down."

Dotty took a small sampling and devoured a half dozen or so, eagerly at first and then slowing the pace on the remaining few.

Brenda smiled and patted Dotty on the head. She picked out a bottle of water from the cooler beneath the table. "Here you go, sweetie; drink this. Let's see if that helps."

Abby shook her head and bent over the large box she had been filling. It was then that she was suddenly jerked up; the cookie boxes she'd held tumbled to the ground. She twisted around and saw that it was the winking man.

"Hey!" she cried out.

He was taking her! With one arm wrapped tightly around her waist, he clapped his free hand over her mouth, cutting her off midshout: "Hey, mist—"

He hoisted her to the rear of a white van, the door of which was closed.

"What the fuck?" the man holding her said. He released his hand from her mouth to open the rear door again, which allowed her the opportunity to scream. He quickly clamped down on her mouth once more, silencing her cry for help. Just then Abby saw Grampa Eddie—in full scuba gear—kicking the door to the van closed with his flippered foot. "Fuckin' wind!" the man holding her cursed, catching the rear door from closing with his elbow and throwing it open again.

Maddie screamed out as the man tossed Abby into the barren rear of the van and slammed the door shut in her face. Abby scrambled to the door but couldn't locate any handle whatsoever, frantically canvassing the entire surface of the smooth metal with her hands, finding no purchase. She screamed, "Help!" and beat on the doors, the muffled sounds inaudible amid the din of the bustling storefront. She crawled quickly to the front and beat on the cage, testing its strength.

Suddenly, she tumbled like a rag doll to the rear of the van again as it lurched forward. She tried to right herself but was tossed backward, striking her head against the metal door, knocking her out cold.

Brenda was holding Dotty's hair back for her as the child tossed up her crackers, along with her sour breakfast, in a series of wrenching spasms.

Brenda turned when she heard what sounded like a pair of screams behind her. A white van was rushing away, rudely ignoring the scattering pedestrians in the crosswalk. A loud bang sounded, and she and several nearby folks reflexively cringed and crouched. She looked over at the girls and saw Maddie but couldn't pick out Abby. The blood rushed from her cheeks, and her own tidal wave of nausea headed ashore as terror seized her. "Dotty, something's not right. I'll be right back, honey," she blurted out, her scout's unfortunate purging not concluded. She ran over to the table. "Maddie? What's wrong? Where is Abby?"

Maddie's eyes narrowed, and she whimpered softly, "I-I don't know, Mommy. She was right there." She pointed to where Abby had been packing. "But I don't see her anymore. A man was winking at us."

"A man? What man? Where is he? Where is *Abby*?"

"I don't know," her whimpering daughter repeated.

Brenda rushed over to the edge of the parking lot, panic-stricken, scanning about and shouting, "Abby? Abby Whitaker!" She turned upon Maddie. "What did you mean when you said you don't know? What happened? She was right there with you, wasn't she? You were supposed to be *with* her!"

Maddie began to cry. "I was. I *was* with her! We were all packing up the cookies, and—"

Brenda was visibly shaken now, her temper flaring at her child's horrendous breach of Troop 645's inviolable buddy system. "Madrigale June, I told you not to let her leave your sight!"

"Yes. No! She was standing right there. I didn't leave her, I promise! She was right there! We were teasing about his missing teeth, and I turned around to get a box, and when I turned back, she'd disappeared around the corner of the building. I couldn't tell why she'd disappeared so fast—I thought that something was very wrong, like that man took her, so I screamed!"

"The man took her?!"

"I think so, Mommy. I don't know! I thought I saw him grab her and put her into that van. It all happened so fast." The next words out of her daughter's mouth chilled Troop Leader Brenda Culligan to the bone: "But she's gone."

Brenda screamed, "Help! *Help*, somebody!" She shrieked at the top of her lungs, *"Call the police!"* Without hesitation, she whipped out her own phone from her purse and frantically dialed 911. She related to the operator what she feared had just transpired. The operator wanted so many details, more than Brenda had any idea about. Time was of the essence, so Brenda barked out a few choice words to the woman and ordered her to get the authorities there *now*. Then she hung up and dialed Brody.

As she waited for his response, her gaze shifted to the ground. She slid her foot off of a crushed box of Thin Mint cookies—a chocolate tire-tread pattern thinned sheer to asphalt as it trailed away.

21

LUNCH was going smoothly when Susan's spirit appeared behind Jennifer's right side, startling Brody. Susan shook her head, mouthed to him, "Go!" and then faded from view.

A bolus of bread snagged in his throat, gagging him.

"Brody, are you all right?" Jen asked.

He was ashen faced.

"You look like you've seen a—"

The obvious absurdity of what she was saying must have struck her, for she stopped in midsentence and glanced behind herself.

At the same time, Brody's cell phone rang, and, in light of what he'd just seen, he checked the call. It was Brenda's number! "Hold on one sec, Jen," he said hoarsely, clearing his throat a time or two. "Let me get this, okay?"

She nodded.

"Hello? Yes?" He coughed. "Brenda?" He pushed himself away from the table, feeling as though he suddenly required more room. A pang of dread stirred in his stomach. "Brenda, what is it?"

"Brody!" Brenda shouted on the other end of the line. "She's gone!"

Jen placed her sandwich on the table. "Brody? What's wrong?"

He held up an index finger. "Brenda, calm down! What do you mean 'she's *gone*'?! Where is she?"

Jennifer gasped.

Brenda's distraught voice was barely coherent. "I-I don't know! She was right here, and then she wasn't. Maddie was right with her!"

Brody sputtered, "Brenda—please, calm down! Tell me what happened!"

"Brody, I've called 911. The police are on their way. But I don't know what else to do ... I—"

"All right, Brenda. I'm coming. You stay there with the police. I'll be there in ten, fifteen minutes, tops." He hung up the phone, hand trembling, and looked at Jennifer in disbelief. "Damn it! Damn it!" he cursed.

"Brody, is there anything I—"

"I gotta go, Jen. I'm sorry."

"Should I follow you?" She rose from her seat.

"No!" He was frantic and unintentionally terse with her. "I'm sorry. I'm very sorry. I'm not upset with you. Listen, I gotta—"

"Go," she told him.

He turned and hoofed it out the restaurant, an electronic peal from the front door chime blandly marking his exit. *Damn it! Shit!* he cursed as the door swung shut behind him.

⌒✐⌒

Todd County sheriff's deputy Landon Popplewell's transmitter crackled. "Unit 73, Unit 73, check out a possible suspect at 311 Downer Lane. Subject may have been involved in a 211 on Tuesday in Clarksville. Suspect considered armed and dangerous; proceed with caution. Evaluate and report, Unit 73. Over."

Landon picked up the transceiver. "Unit 73 responding. 10-4."

Shit, what now? He knew the occupants at that address all too well. He polished off his Polish sausage dog, swung his car around, and headed to the aforementioned residence.

⌒✐⌒

Carlos made his way to an unoccupied corner on the upper level of a nearby parking garage. He parked, and he and Teddy stepped out. They hadn't heard a peep from their package.

Teddy surveyed the artwork on the side of the van. Carefully, he lifted the edge of the oversize magnetic panel and peeled it away, unveiling a different company name and logo, airbrushed by Carlos's artists directly onto the exterior: PETER'S PETS AND MORE. The logo boasted a tongue-lolling, tail-wagging pooch. He circled around to the other side and repeated the transformation. He then stuffed the magnets inside the van on the passenger's floorboard.

Carlos meanwhile was affixing a different set of plates, held strategically in place by magnetized wafers resembling screwheads, to the front and rear of the vehicle. Once the alterations were finalized, they met behind the van.

Teddy high-fived his Hispanic counterpart. "Your artists kicked ass!"

"Damn fine artwork, if you ask me. I told you—best around! No job too big or too small."

"And the package is secure. Call El Coronel; let him know."

"No need. His courier is already halfway here by now."

"Ten Gs each, man!"

They exchanged skin again.

"Meet you back at the shop with the package, amigo," Carlos said.

"Yeah. Gotta make a quick pit stop at *mi casa* first, though."

Carlos strode to his Escalade and hurried away.

Teddy was still heady from the rush as he climbed back into the van, exited the garage with his precious cargo, and motored home to retrieve the few things he'd packed earlier. Once he had his share of the heist money, plus his procurement fee for the kid, things would be *waay* different. But first, he'd have to make himself scarce.

The message about a possible 207 at the Walmart reached David around twelve forty-five. He arrived at the scene within fifteen minutes. The last kidnapping he had been called in on had taken place a little over six years prior—an estranged husband had beaten his ex-wife near senseless and then stolen their child and fled. It had taken nearly eleven months for David to track him down. A tip from an astute Amber Alert recipient had helped him finally zero in on the kidnapper up north at a Cleveland motel. Mercifully, the child had not been harmed, and with the FBI's assistance, she had been reunited with her mother days later. A rare outcome for a case that cold, for with child abductions, time was of the essence—every second proved critical in yielding success; every wasted hour served only to whittle away the odds of ever locating the victim alive.

He walked over to the entrance of the superstore, where other officers were already questioning folks about what had gone down minutes before.

"What have you got for me, McGready?" David asked.

Officer Jeff McGready, a twelve-year patrolman, had been first on the scene. Several other police officers were presently scouring the parking area, gathering clues, and searching for other potential witnesses.

"Definitely a 207, Sarge. The scout leader, a Brenda Culligan, says the victim, one Abby Whitaker, was last seen packing up cookies at the end of their sale. The Culligan woman turned her back to escort a sick child over yonder to the trash can, and then she heard a couple of screams—her own daughter's and the abductee's—yet thought it could've been the sound of tires, which were peeling out at the same time."

"What do we know about that vehicle?"

"She noticed it heading away—a white service van. According to eyewitnesses, a Chevy van. Had a rainbow painted on the side."

"Plate numbers?"

"I interviewed a young couple that was almost mowed down by the van while taking their groceries out. The man ran after the vehicle and was fired at—a single bullet from the passenger. Luckily the guy ducked when he saw the gun. The shot missed him and took out the side window of a Tahoe right over there." He gestured toward a nearby row of cars, the SUV with a shattered window being the closest. "He and his wife both caught a brief look at the passenger—the man whom the little Girl Scout says snatched the girl. Gave me a description of him. Scoutmaster's daughter did too; they match up. The couple who was shot at also said the rainbow on the exterior of the van was comprised of the words *West End Baptist*. There was a violet crucifix underneath the letters. They got the plate numbers too."

"'West End Baptist'? Doesn't sound familiar. Ever heard of it?"

"Already checked. No such church. Least not from anywhere around these parts. We're running the name and the plates through the database to see if either's a hit."

"Bogus, more than likely."

"Probably, Sarge. But we'll run 'em through nonetheless. And ..." the patrolman paused.

"Yes?"

"The tires crushed a box of cookies. There are tread marks leading away from the scene, made out of chocolate. We're photographing those and sending them in too."

"Where's the slug?"

"It's lodged in the passenger door of the Tahoe. We left it in place for you. Want to take a look?"

"Yeah, let me see if I can dig it out."

"We'll send it through ballistics then."

"Perfect." The sergeant nodded and then shook his head in a mixture of incredulity and disgust over the dire circumstances. "What did the couple say the guy looked like?"

"Stringy, dark hair, shoulder length. Wearing a dark leather jacket. Bastard even spit at them."

"Did the scout leader's daughter add anything to the description?"

"Said he smiled and winked at them."

"Yeah?"

"The guy was missing a few teeth."

A few teeth? Shit! What if …? "Do we know anything more about the abductee?" David asked.

"Yeah. Abby Whitaker is …" Jeff flipped through his notes. "… Ten years old, daughter to a Mr. Brody Whitaker."

Brody Whitaker? The other eyewitness at the bank? The same fellow that was on WCVL? That was a strange coincidence. Or was it? What about Billy's wounding? Was there a connection between all these events somehow? "McGready, when we pull that slug, let's check it against the one I recovered from the rear of the Dollar General, see if they match up. I want to find out if this abduction is somehow related to that Coonrod boy's shooting."

"Sure, Sarge. For sure. Listen, I'd already put out an APB on the van, soon as I got the description."

"Good, let me know if a sighting comes through. Let's get the Amber Alert out too, with a description of the girl."

"Yessir. Right away. The scout leader has some pictures on her phone of the victim with the Culligan girl. We'll have a headshot we can distribute."

"I'll talk to the scout leader."

"She's pretty shaken up," Jeff warned.

"Well, maybe she oughta be," David said crossly. He was curious to know how a Girl Scout could be abducted in broad daylight from a bustling parking lot right under the nose of the person charged with watching over her.

～*v*～

Brody whipped his car into the Walmart parking lot. He came to an abrupt stop just outside a cordoned-off area and exited his car. As he rushed up to the group gathered by the table, someone grabbed the crook of his arm from behind, halting him.

A uniformed officer informed him, "Excuse me, sir, you were speeding almost the whole way here."

Unaware he'd been followed, he resisted the officer's grip. "I had no idea you were behind me, Officer. Please, my daughter's been abducted!"

A plainclothesman stepped forward. "It's fine, Glenn. I've got this; I need this man right now."

The officer backed off. "Sure thing, Sarge."

"Hey, Glenn, while you're here, could you help Jeff over there talk to those other witnesses, see if they can add to anything?"

"Yeah, sure, Sergeant." He stepped aside and made his way over to his fellow officers already working the rows of cars.

Brody angrily approached Brenda. "Brenda, what the hell—"

The sergeant hooked him by the arm and steered him aside. "Hey, you're the guy from the bank the other day, aren't you?"

"Yes, Officer …" he began, annoyed.

"Jeffries. David Jeffries. You're also the guy I saw on TV recently—was it yesterday?"

"Yes. Can you tell me—"

"I'll tell you what I know. Only be easy on the gal over there—Brenda, right? I came down pretty hard on her already; no need for you to. Instead, be the hero here; let me play the jerk."

Brody could tell that David was attempting to soothe him, but he was not very receptive to it at the moment. "Go on, Sergeant."

"A white van pulled up to the stand a short while ago—couldn't have been more than thirty minutes—and your daughter—"

"Abby. Abby's her name."

"Yes. And Abby was snatched by someone. The troop leader there had a sick kid she was attending to. She told her daughter to be vigilant of Abby—"

"Well, it doesn't look like *that* happened."

The sergeant looked him in the eyes. "Listen, I know you're upset; you have every right to be. I've got a daughter myself, so I know how you feel—"

"Really?" Brody asked indignantly. "All due respect, Sergeant, but was your daughter abducted in broad daylight while selling Girl Scout cookies?"

Brenda, apparently overhearing the conversation, stared at the ground in shame.

The sergeant paraphrased what he'd said. "I meant that, as the father of a daughter, I know how much we worry about them, even if it's only to cross the street to get to the playground. That's all. No, my daughter was not abducted, but she *was* abandoned, made to walk home—about a mile and a half—in the dead of night last weekend, so I can kind of relate. Now, let's move on to what happened here so we can set about finding Abby, shall we?"

Brody simmered down to a more productive level of composure. "Okay, Sergeant. Forgive me; I'm tense."

"Perfectly understandable, Mr. Whitaker."

"All right. Tell me the rest of what you know, please."

He nodded. "Brenda here had to take a sick child over to that trash can to throw up. She was only steps away from that table; she never left the immediate vicinity. When she heard screams, she turned around, and your daughter and the van in question were gone. She immediately called 911 and then you. Her daughter got a look at the guy we think is responsible, and another couple backed up the description. We've issued an APB on the van, so law enforcement officers have their eyes peeled for it. We're also issuing an Amber Alert on your daughter."

An Amber Alert! Brody felt lightheaded; this was all too surreal.

"Mr. Whitaker?"

Brody leaned against the wall of the store for support, saying to the officer, "It's Brody—call me Brody."

"Listen, Brody, it's possible, given the description, that we may be dealing with one of the guys involved in the bank robbery the other day."

"What?"

"Yes, and it's also possible he was part of a shooting that took place yesterday."

"A shooting?" *This guy sounds dangerous!*

"Yes, someone also matching this guy's description shot an employee—a local high school football player—out back of the Dollar General over on Union Street; the bullet just grazed him. I'm not sure how all of this is connected just yet, if at all, but if it's the same guy, we've got some leads as to where he might live."

"Tell me, please."

"Listen, when we finish here, let's go down to the station, and we'll sort through everything we know. The scout leader's daughter—"

"Maddie."

"Maddie has already volunteered to come down and sit with our sketch artist, so we'll soon have a rendering of what this guy looks like. I promise you, we're doing everything we can to locate Abby. We'll find the ones responsible, sir."

Brody was only minimally allayed by the sergeant's assurances. "Okay, Officer. I appreciate it. I need to talk to Brenda now, if you don't mind."

"No. Go ahead. I'll be around a little while longer." David headed over toward the Tahoe.

Brody walked up to the visibly shaken troop leader. On the drive over, he had made up his mind to really lay into Brenda for what had happened, but after Sergeant Jeffries's advice, and noting how distressed she was, he was relenting.

"Brody, I ..."

Here was a woman who cared about his daughter almost as much as he did; his desire to chastise her evaporated. "It's all right, Brenda." He hugged her, and she began to weep.

"I will never forgive myself if anything happens to that child, Brody. Never."

"I heard what happened. We've got to concentrate on locating her now. I know how you feel about Abby. We'll find her; I know we will." He relinquished his hold, retreating to arm's length. "Now tell me all you know."

"Well, we were finishing up the sale, so I had all the girls packing up. One of the girls was ill, so I took her right over there to that trash can. Before I did, I reminded Maddie and Abby to stick together, no matter what. That's what I preach to all the girls—you stay with your buddy. We take that seriously." She was winded from sobbing and recounting the incident several times. "I heard

"Proceed with caution, Unit 73. Suspect may be armed and dangerous."

"10-4." He eased out from the underbrush and headed up to the dwelling.

He parked in front and walked to the steps, casually yet with a savvy patrolman's heed. After knocking, he stood by, waiting. He knocked once more. Nobody came. He stepped down onto the weathered paving stone walkway and moved toward the corner of the house nearest his vehicle. Glancing around the side, he drew his revolver once more and chested it. He swung around the corner, weapon at the ready. All clear. Ducking underneath the twin windowsills, knees bent and his back to the wall, he slid along the brick, stopping at the rear of the house. Pausing, taking a deep breath, he whipped around the corner aiming his weapon at—*nothing!*

He swayed the gun in wide arcs, toward the house and to the detached garage, repeating the semicircle as he moved to the outbuilding. He saw no faces peering from the windows or the back door glass.

As he made it to the side of the garage, perspiration coalesced across his forehead; it dripped down his cheeks, his neck, and the length of his back. As he inched his way to the rear, his heart thumped with abandon inside his chest; his breathing was rapid and shallow, his focus intense. With his gun pointing skyward, the deputy lunged around the back of the garage, dropping the nose down in anticipation of catching Teddy off guard.

But Teddy wasn't there. The garage door was raised, however, and the service van sat inside, exhaust still hanging thinly in the air. A yellow El Camino was stationed beside it, and hanging between the two was a well-worn boxer's speed bag.

Popplewell reclaimed his breath and crossed to the rear of the van. He tested the handle. It was locked.

Suddenly, noises came from inside the van—the sound of movement, along with a frail voice calling out, "Help!" He holstered his service revolver and snatched up his portable transponder hooked to his belt. He placed the microphone to his lips and relayed the following in hoarse, succinct sentences: "Dispatch, this is Unit 73. I am at 311 Downer Lane requesting immediate backup. The vehicle believed to be involved in the Clarksville 207 is parked at the rear of the residence. It sounds like the victim may be in the rear of the vehicle. I am going to attempt to free the victim. Again, this is Unit 73 requesting backup. Over and out."

"Roger that, Unit 73. All units; attention all units. Officer Landon

Popplewell requesting immediate backup at 311 Downer Lane. Repeat: all units in the area, deputy requesting immediate backup at 311 Downer Lane. Please respond. Over."

He reclipped the microphone to his belt and searched for something inside the carport to pry open the door. On a nearby workbench, he found a heavy-duty screwdriver and applied it with some leverage to the crease between the panels.

"Well, well, well—if it ain't Popplewell," Teddy suddenly sneered from behind the deputy. His voice dripped with mock molasses.

Out of the corner of his eye, Popplewell could see Teddy's pistol trained on him, inches away. He hadn't heard Teddy's approach at all.

"Deputy Dawg," Teddy smirked, creeping forward. "Long time, no see."

"Help!" Another muffled cry of distress, youthful sounding, came from within the van.

"Who's in the van, Teddy? What have you gotten yourself into?"

"None o' yo' fuckin' bidness, Deputy Dawg. You best be worried about what's pointin' upside yo' pig head instead of what you hear comin' from inside that van."

Popplewell had an idea what was coming. Teddy had been foaming at the mouth for a nostalgic little get-together ever since their prepubescent milk-money days. The deputy knew all too well that one infraction, one insult, was all it took with Teddy—his grudges were eternal; his judgment days were foregone conclusions. And his payback to Popplewell was looking like it was gonna be a real bitch.

"You got that quarter and nickel you still owe me?" Teddy eased his trigger finger backward.

Popplewell swallowed hard.

"No?" Teddy sighed. "I thought not."

"Teddy, you don't have to—"

"Yeah? And dingleberry pie don't taste like shit, neither. Tell me—was it worth beatin' the tar outta me for thirty fuckin' lousy cents?"

The deputy tensed, closing his eyes. "Teddy, listen—"

"You go to hell now, Popplewell."

"Teddy—"

The report echoed on the wind, carrying quite a ways before fading across the fields of bluegrass. A trail of acrid smoke curled from the barrel of Teddy's gun.

⁓

"The package is secure, El Coronel."

"My courier should arrive shortly. *Heil*, C-zar." The man known as El Coronel settled back into his well-tufted bronze leather chair, smiling, smoke rings drifting to the ceiling like gray jellyfish undulating through the air.

He stroked the flank of Adolph, his sphinx cat, whose tail erected with the touch. The Parteiadler—an eagle clutching a ringed swastika—was tattooed on the feline's naked pink hide.

He blew several more haloes above his chair. *Ja*, Willy had already refueled and departed from Panama.

22

"MISTER! Where are you taking me?!" Once again, buffeted about in the rear of the van, Abby was terrified.

"We're going to visit an old friend, sweetie pie," Teddy gleefully told her. "Sit back and enjoy the ride now, hear?"

Abby had no idea how long they were in transit, but eventually the brakes squealed to a stop. She heard the driver speak to someone with a Spanish accent. Then the van traveled over even rougher terrain, bruising her repeatedly as she bounced. The sound of dogs barking grew louder, and then the van halted once more.

The rear doors popped open at last, and Abby, seeing no constraints, leaped out of the van, stopping inches short of the snarling, slavering snout of a ferocious pit bull that was tugging mightily at the end of its chain. She fell backward, to the cackles of a semicircle of men, some holding flashlights. The one who'd stolen her was laughing among them. They converged on her, and she was dragged by the arm through the corridor of frenzied dogs snapping at her on either side. She screamed as each one lunged at her; the men continued laughing as they kept her from harm's way.

They brought her to a room in the back corner of a big metal structure that had so many loud noises within. A heavyset, brown-skinned man with a rather prominent mustache was sitting behind a desk. As they entered, a youthful, ebony-haired woman rose from underneath the desk, her sheer white blouse was pulled low over both shoulders. She wiped her mouth with her knuckle, smiling coyly at Abby as she strutted across the room, her light-blue skirt swaying back and forth. The man leaned back in his chair and seemed to be fiddling with his pants zipper.

"You got here sooner than expected, Teddy Bear," the mustachioed man said with a sarcastic grin. "Things were still kind of, uh, 'up in the air.'"

The gap-toothed man who'd grabbed her from the storefront, the man referred to as "Teddy Bear," laughed and pushed Abby into the center of the room. The door was closed and locked behind everyone. Her eyes darted here and there—to the men, the fans, the woman laughing, the collection of partially full bottles on the desk. The stale smell of cigar smoke saturated the air. Abby felt overwhelmed by the sheer discombobulation of it all.

Teddy Bear sauntered over and sat in a chair across from the mustachioed one, who motioned Teddy Bear to the array of liquor before him. Seeing the tequila, the gap-toothed man began with that. He swigged the booze, wiping his mouth with the back of his hand. Abby could see he had some letters inked across his knuckles.

The mustachioed man rose to his feet, motioning to the woman to leave. She slid quietly out the door.

He strode over to Abby. She trembled uncontrollably as he put his rough fingertips under her chin and lifted it, turning her head slightly from side to side.

"Very nice; verrry pretty. She'll do."

Do? Do what? Abby's head was swimming.

The man with the mustache motioned to one of the others in the room. "Find her a blanket, Julio. She's shivering."

Tattoo-infested Julio pulled a blanket down from a nearby shelf and unfolded it, draping it around Abby.

She clutched it tightly to herself—a woven shield in her own wishful thinking, like Dr. Griffin's "cloak" of invisibility. How she wished she was in class right then, anywhere but where she really was!

The gap-toothed man's phone rang, and he picked up, putting it on speaker for all to hear.

"Hello, Teddy. Do you have the girl?"

"Yeah," he said.

"Good."

"Yeah? Okay, so now what?"

The person on the other end of the phone sighed. "Make the call, Teddy. Make the call."

The line disconnected.

"Man, why do you let him talk to you like that?" the mustachioed man asked.

"It makes him think he's really in control." Teddy smiled. "Don't you worry, Carlos—his end's a-comin' soon, real soon."

Teddy sang the latter to a tune Abby thought she recognized—it was an old, old song her father had played for her several times in the car, something about a moon rising that was bad in some way.

The man named Carlos grinned. "That's the Teddy I know."

Abby had no idea what was going on, but she strongly sensed it wasn't in her favor.

<hr>

Brody admired the photograph on David's desk as they awaited the latest field reports and the sketch artist's rendition of the kidnapper. "Nice family," he told the sergeant.

"That's Ruthie, my wife." He pointed to the figure on the left. "And that's my daughter, Kaylee."

The word *daughter* initiated fresh stabs of guilt in Brody, like packing salt into an open wound. *What's taking so freaking long?* "David, what exactly do you know about the kidnapper?"

David eased back in his chair. "We have two suspects: one's over in Coopertown to the southeast, and the other's in Kentucky, a town called Guthrie."

"I know where that is," Brody said.

"We had a third lead here in town, but that one didn't pan out. That fella's actually deployed overseas on active duty. We've confirmed his activity with his CO. As soon as we narrow it down between the other two, we'll have our guy."

"When will you know?"

David leaned toward him. "Should know something real soon. And that sketch will come across my desk any minute now."

"Is there anything more we could be doing?"

"Brody, we're doing all we can, I assure you. My men and Sheriff Coonrod's deputies are combing this county; every square foot will be turned inside out within the next twenty-four to forty-eight hours."

"Then what can *I* do?" He felt so impotent; his little girl was out there somewhere, frightened out of her wits.

"I know it's nerve-racking for you to be sitting here, waiting. I'm used to it; it's my job. My advice in these situations is to mobilize family, friends, church members, any volunteers who can help out in search parties. Have them on standby. We may need them tomorrow if we haven't located her by then. I'm confident we'll have some hard leads real soon. Keep your phone charged up and handy. Be watching for my number. I'll call you if we know anything concrete. I promise you we will not rest until every avenue is exhausted."

"All right, good. I'll mobilize as many as I can." Brody headed for the door.

David called out after him, "Hey, Brody?"

He turned in the doorway. "Yes?"

"I know what you do for a living. You … speak to the dead, right? Isn't that what you did the other day on TV?"

"Yes I did. Why?"

"Well … how do I put this?" He thought about it and said, "Have you been in contact with any spirits who might be of help to us in locating Abby?"

"If I had, I'd have already informed you of that or else be on my way myself to find her."

David shook his head. "Stupid question. Sorry."

"No, there's no way you'd've known that. I appreciate your thinking along those lines; it shows me you're considering all angles."

"Sort of. It was worth a try."

"Yeah, it was. Thanks again for thinking outside the box. Keep it up."

As he leaned out the door, the sergeant reminded him, "Have your phone handy. And, Brody?"

Brody stuck his head back in. "Yes?"

"Let me know if you know of or hear of anything new. And check in with me every couple of hours just in case."

"Okay, I will."

Brody tried to head out once more, but David beckoned him back again.

"Brody? One more thing."

Brody leaned into the room again. "Yes, Sergeant?"

"Let us do our job. Please don't try to handle this on your own. I've seen the best of intentions backfire and tragically muck up these situations in a heartbeat."

∽Ϡͼ∽

Standing outside the station, Brody watched the last of the stray gray clouds being chased away. The sun was coming out, warming things slightly—everything except for Brody's spirit.

He decided to start on his phone calls. The first one he placed was to Jennifer. At home and awaiting word about the situation, she begged him once more to allow her to help. He promised to let her know immediately when he knew anything concrete. He'd certainly need her efforts if there was to be a search on Sunday.

Next, he contacted every possible acquaintance about standing by to help out. Lastly, he called in all his markers, pleading with anyone who owed him a favor. Plenty of friends and strangers alike willingly volunteered.

As he racked his brain for more people to call, suddenly it was *his* phone ringing. The caller ID said Unknown, but he picked up; the gravity of the situation dictated he ignore the possibility of a telemarketer and accept the call.

"Hello?"

"Brody Whitaker?"

"Who's this?"

"This is the guy you do *not* want to piss off right now."

"Are you the man who took my daughter?"

"Let's just say our paths have crossed. Now, how you like that?"

Brody waffled over whether to head back inside and clue David in on the conversation. "What do you want?" he asked.

"I have somethin' you want, and you have somethin' I want."

"What could I possibly have of yours?"

"Information. Information not available anywhere else. Where're you now?"

"At the police station."

The man hissed, "Get in your car—*now*!"

Brody, vacillating over whether or not to comply, decided not to test the voice on the other end of the line. "Now what?"

"Good boy, Whitaker. You're that much closer to seein' your daughter again. Now drive."

"Where?"

"Head north on Seventy-Nine."

Guthrie! He's in Guthrie!

"Tell no one, not a soul, or you'll never see your sweet little girl again. I make myself clear?"

"Yes, it's clear." Brody was compelled to comply. He wasn't about to risk Abby's life, regardless of the sergeant's advice. "No one but me."

"Goood," the man cooed.

"Where am I headed?" asked Brody.

"You know where that Bell Witch Cave is?"

"Bell Witch Cave? Just outside Adams?"

"That's it. Get up here now."

"Where's my daughter? Will she be there?"

"Don't you worry 'bout that. You 'n' me got some talkin' to do."

"Now listen to me, you asshole—"

The man cut him off. "*No! You* listen to *me.* If you ever want to see that pretty little daughter of yours sell another box of Thin Mints, you'll get to that cave as fast as your ass'll drag you. You come alone, and you tell *nobody.* If I have just an inkling of suspicion you ratted on me and brought the heat, you will *not* appreciate the outcome. Are we crystal clear?"

Brody simmered. "Yes," he replied softly.

"I can't hear you, bitch. *Put some fuckin'* oomph *into it.*"

"*Yes!* I'm on my way—*alone.*"

As the crow flew, Bell Witch Cave was almost due east of Clarksville, but the fastest way was north into Kentucky on US 79 and then south, on the other side of Guthrie, on Route 11. It was about a two-hour trip; Brody pressed on the gas. Damn the crows—he'd fly anyway.

Officer Malone popped his head inside David's door. "'Scuse me, Sarge. Here's that sketch you were waiting for." He deposited the drawing before the sergeant.

David looked it over. Was this one of the robbers they were looking for? The figure looked rugged, with deep-set eyes and stringy hair, and was definitely missing a few teeth. David was struck by how much the drawing resembled Brad Pitt's grunge look.

"We distributed the image to the authorities within a two-hundred-mile radius. Also heard from the field. It ain't Coopertown."

"No?"

"Negative, Sarge. Fella who owns that El Camino's a car collector."

"And?" David was unconvinced.

"And he's a cripple. Doesn't drive; just shows 'em. Car's been sittin' idle in his garage for near eighteen months, untouched."

David nodded.

"We got the ballistics report back on that full metal jacket from the Tahoe too."

"Yes?"

"Matches the one from the Dollar General, fer sure."

"Thanks, Jay. Good work."

"One other thing, Sarge."

"Yes?"

"The slugs also match up with some other recent posts in the database."

"Really? Our guy's been at it."

"Yeah, the bullets match up with those found on the scene of a cold-blooded murder on the highway, just north of the Red River Bridge, on the afternoon of the bank heist."

"Really?"

"Really, Sarge. This one's a sicko, all right."

"Do the local boys know about that match?"

"Not sure. Want me to verify?"

"Nah, I'll handle it. What about the sheriff up in Kentucky?"

"We radioed 'em about the El Camino owner a little while ago. Said they'd check it out."

"Okay. 'Preciate it, Jay." He gestured to the officer and picked up the phone to call Cletus.

In the middle of his dial, there was a knock on David's door again.

"Yeah?" David called.

Jay reappeared. "Hey, Sarge."

"Yeah?"

"Just got a positive ID on a white van in Guthrie, too. It was headed to 311 Downer Lane. A guy named Teddy Trent. Deputy up in Kentucky just radioed it in. Sheriff's office up there confirms that Trent matches that drawing, the one we sent 'em."

"Thanks, Jay." He quickly jotted the name and address down on a pad from his top desk drawer.

"You bet, Sarge."

As the door closed again, David completed his dialing and waited for the response.

The sheriff's voice came booming over the line. "Hello? David?"

"Clete, hey. Yeah, it's me." With concern, he asked, "How's Billy?"

"He's fine. Chattin' up a storm on the phone with your daughter. What's up?"

"That 207 this morning at Walmart—the little girl who was abducted while selling Girl Scout cookies ..."

"Yeah? I been hearin' about it. What's up?"

"Well, it's the daughter of a guy who was on WCVL Thursday. I don't know if you caught it, but he talks to dead people. Name is Brody Whitaker."

"Really? Yeah, I saw that. Doris had me watch it. I couldn't believe it— how does he do that shit? So it was *his* kid?"

"Yeah."

Cletus's voice grew somber. "Jeez."

"And I think we got a lead on who snatched her. We believe it might be the same guy who robbed Planter's on Tuesday and who also shot Billy."

His demeanor darkening instantaneously, the sheriff thundered, "Shit! Where is the sonuvabitch, David?"

"We believe he's one"—he looked over his notes—"Teddy Trent, who resides at 311 Downer Lane in Guthrie."

"So she's been transported across state lines, huh?"

"It's looking like it. I think we'd better call Johnny over at the bureau."

"Lemme holler at him."

"Okay, and Clete?"

"Yeah?"

"Ballistics positively IDed the bullets as belonging to your murder crime scene on the highway too."

"Shit. This a-hole's a busy little sombitch. 'Kay, thanks for the tip. Now I'm gonna head up to Guthrie myself."

"I'd rather you didn't," David said.

"Why not?"

David said succinctly, "Not by yourself—I'm coming with you."

"David, how are you?" JK asked.

"Good, JK."

Cletus continued, "We can meet you and your boys at the residence."

"Good. You two get to the rendezvous location and wait for my team. Let us know if even a gnat flies in or out of that house. We're mobilizing stat. We'll chopper in to Nashville and hitch a couple of Bucars from there. We'll meet there at twenty hundred hours."

"Got it," David said. "Hey, JK?"

"Yeah?"

"The father—we haven't heard from the father. I told him to call me with any pertinent information or check in, and neither has occurred. I can't reach him either. That concerns me."

"Well, I hope he didn't pass out taking a shit or something, and I *sure* as hell hope he's not going all caped crusader on us."

"Yeah," David said, "me too."

"What's his name?"

"Brody Whitaker."

"The Clarksville Medium?"

Surprised, David asked, "You heard of 'im?"

"They ran a clip about him on the news here in Knoxville. Talks to ghosts, right?"

"That's him," said David.

"Yeah, apparently the station in Clarksville's been spreading the word about that guy. Well, give me his plates, and we'll put the word out with highway patrol for anyone who spots him in that neck of the woods."

"Thanks, JK."

"Yeah, David. But I'll say this—"

"What's that?" Cletus asked.

"I hope he's got better sense. He ain't friggin' Rambo. After today, let's hope we won't need another one of those mediums to talk to *him*."

⸺

The same white clapboard sign, a few yards off Keysburg Road, still marked the entrance to Bell Witch Cave. Like all the locals who had visited the tourist attraction, Brody—and certainly Teddy too—was aware that the cave would be closed, off limits to any visitors, due not only to the time of year but also the recent heavy rains. He and Abby would be isolated there with this madman.

As Brody turned down the drive to the cave, his phone rang. "Hello?" he answered.

"Where are you, man?"

"Just turning off Keysburg. Where are you?"

"At the entrance to the cave. C'mon down! You're our next contestant."

Brody ignored the banal jest. "Where's my daughter? Is she there with you?"

"Let's chat. You alone?"

"I'm alone."

"Don't you dare fuck with me, Mr. Medium. I'm in no mood for it. You best be by yo' lonesome."

Proceeding down the narrow drive, Brody surveyed the grounds, trying to recollect the lay of the property. "It's been a while since I've been here."

"Just keep to the path. Soon you'll come to a small parkin' area and to the path leading down here. It's marked. Good-bye."

Brody rested his phone on his console, noting that the reception in the area was not prime but still present. He drove past the rustic visitor's center—where not a single car was evident, not even the caretakers'—to a small parking lot nearer the path to the cave. There was a white van with the name of a pet shop on it parked there. He pulled up alongside the van and turned off the ignition. Emerging from his Honda, he switched off his phone and placed it screen side against his skin, snugly behind his shirt and the snap of his pants; if he was frisked, it would be less conspicuous there. He approached the van and circled it, checking inside the front windows and trying the doors. They were all locked. He rapped on the rear panels several times with the butt of his fist and called out his daughter's name. "Abby? Abby?" His shouts carried only to the tree line, dissipating beyond on the brisk November wind. But there was no reply, no return of any sound from within or without the van, save for the hooting of a roosting owl. He turned and walked down the meandering path beginning at the edge of the lot, past a low stone wall, careful of his footing.

⌒𝓎⌒

The cave had taken on several feet of water after the recent heavy storms, but with the tapering of rainfall since earlier that morning, the surging waters had

Popplewell should've radioed in long ago, and he wasn't responding to dispatch. His fellow deputies answered his noncommunication by converging on the Trent homestead. They feared the worst when they found his squad car abandoned in the front driveway. They broke down the doors to search the house, but it was vacant, so they turned their attention to the garage.

Blood on the outbuilding threshold indicated foul play. Their fears were confirmed when they discovered the body of their brother-in-arms in the long, low cooler. The yellow El Camino in question was there too but nary a sign of either of the Trent brothers. Both were still believed to be alive and on the lam, traveling in the white Chevrolet van, its whereabouts yet to be determined.

The tragic news found its way to Cletus and David. Dejected, they continued on to the house to meet up with the feds.

Brody closed his eyes for several minutes, focusing his thoughts and energy intensely into willing the spirit of Lyle forward. He kept one eye open a crack—just enough to view any spirit that might step forward in that dank, cold chamber.

"Well?"

Brody held up one hand—his check, for the moment, holding his enemy at bay.

Teddy pressed grumpily back against the cold, hard wall, arms crossed, glaring at the medium. "Okay. Go on."

Unbeknownst to Teddy, close by, the gossamer apparition of a man was appearing. It waxed and waned and then appeared wholly to Brody. The spirit had on bloody clothes and was devoid of his right arm.

"Are you Lyle?" Brody asked.

The spirit nodded.

"What?" Teddy sat up and grabbed his pistol. "What'd you say?"

"Please," Brody admonished. "I'm trying to communicate with your brother; he stepped forward just now."

"Hey, don't jack with me—"

"He's standing near your ledge, down in the water."

Teddy picked up the flashlight and shined it on the surface of the water, all around him. "Where?"

Brody pointed to Teddy's left. Faint surface ripplets in the black liquid signified the presence of *something*, though that something remained unseeable to Teddy.

"He's missing his right arm," Brody said.

"What do you mean? He was never missin' an arm! What kinda shit are you pullin'?"

The spirit spoke to Brody, and Brody relayed the information. "He said it's because of you he's missing his arm."

"Me? What the fuck? I never harmed a hair on his head! That's *bullshit*!" He aimed his gun at Brody.

"He said you left him by the side of a waterway, off the road, on your way home from the robbery."

The gun was lowered.

The spirit addressed Brody with a series of one-handed motions while continuing the dialogue.

"Your brother says that he wasn't dead when you left him."

"Oh, you mother*fucker*! Now you're gonna get it," Teddy warned as he jumped down from the ledge.

Brody steeled himself; he couldn't falter from the task at hand—the stakes were far too high. "You think I'm making this up? Do you want me to continue or not?"

Teddy backed off slowly.

"Then sit back up there while I'm trying to do what you're forcing me to. If you want this to work, then shut the hell up!"

Brody's petulance seemed to stupefy the thug. Teddy frowned and lifted himself back up to his rocky roost, grunting all the while.

The spirit of Lyle communicated more to Brody, who decided to try something risky, what Susan had challenged him with the other evening—throwing his voice. Desperate times called for desperate measures.

He tried to mimic the voice of Lyle's spirit as distinctly as he could. "Teddy!"

The acoustics in the cavern heightened the paranormality of the effect, deepening the bass, making the tone of Lyle's voice sound more resonant.

Brody had become a supernatural loudspeaker; Lyle projected his words *through* Brody. Brody, in turn, was able to throw the sound of Lyle's voice wherever he wanted, much like he'd proved to Susan in his living room. His practice had indeed paid off.

Teddy's eyes bugged. He jerked the light to and fro across the water, trying to pinpoint the source of his brother's voice.

"Teddy, you left me there."

The gunman stumbled quickly to his feet on the ledge in a panic, wanting to distance himself further from the spirit's approximate location. "What? What'd you say?"

"I was *alive*, Teddy."

It was working! This was a first for Brody. He stayed true to the conveyance, maintaining as sturdy a bridge with Lyle's entity as he could; as long as he didn't seek to alter the spirit's message, it seemed Lyle would continue to trust in him and speak through him.

"Lyle? Lyle, is that you, man?"

"I called out to you, Teddy."

"What?"

"I called out to you from the water's edge, but you couldn't hear me. You left. You left me there to die. How could you do that?"

Teddy glanced around, determined to view his brother, but to no avail. Instead, he resorted to shouting, like a creature of the darkness attempts to echolocate its target. "What do you mean? You *were* dead!"

"No, Teddy. I was still alive. You would have seen that if you would've looked hard enough. How closely did you check for a pulse after you dragged me from the car? Could you not feel my faint breath after you tugged me down through the weeds?"

"I did! I checked! I swear!"

"Not very well, obviously."

"What the fuck, man? I was scared shitless, Lyle." Teddy climbed down into the water, moving to a spot adjacent to where Brody's eyes were trained.

"You always looked out for me, always had my back, except when it mattered most, 'brohaha.'"

Whatever the relevance of that statement, it riveted Teddy into the conversation. As he spoke, he rotated, herky-jerky, like a sprinkler head, trying to spray his words in every possible direction in an attempt to land them on target at some point. "Lyle, I panicked. I thought I'd lost you. I didn't know what to do, man!"

"It was bad enough you left me to rot, but that wasn't all, Teddy. That wasn't what took my arm and robbed me, in the end, of my life."

"What happened?" Teddy implored with a whimper.

"A gator is what happened! A big, bad mother of a gator. It came out of nowhere and jerked me off that bank, twisting me and dragging me down into the cold, murky water, where I most definitely drowned."

"No!"

"Yes."

Teddy began to softly sob. "Lyle, I'm so sorry. I had no idea. I never would've left you if I'd—"

"What's done is done. Now you know. You have to live with that, Teddy."

Teddy collapsed backward against the limestone, shaking his head, and then his attention swung back to Brody. "What the fuck, man? What are you tryin' to do?"

"You asked me to call for your brother's spirit. Well, here he is. I didn't manufacture his message; I only delivered it."

Teddy muttered to himself, shaking his head, "It has to be real. It has to."

Brody overheard Teddy's attempt to convince himself of the truth. "Oh, it's Lyle, all right. I believe we've established that."

"Ask him," he moaned. "Ask him about the money, man."

"Will it help me get my daughter back?"

"If you *don't*, you'll *never* see her again—guaranteed!"

"How do I know you have any intention of releasing her to me?"

"You don't." He glowered at Brody. "Now do it."

Frustrated and at wits' end, Brody closed his eyes once more. "Spirit of Lyle, your brother has a question for you." Brody began conversing in both his own voice and that of the spirit, carrying on both sides of the conversation himself.

"What is it?"

"He wants to know where the money is hidden. The money from the bank."

"Will you give him back his daughter?" the spirit asked his brother.

Teddy stood upright again. "Hey! Don't bullshit me! Lyle didn't ask that; *you* did—on your own."

"No, he didn't," Lyle's voice interjected. "Teddy? Do you remember you used to call me Lyle, Lyle, crocodile? Pretty ironic, huh? But it wasn't a crocodile that kidnapped *me*—it was a slightly cheaper pair o' boots!" The spirit continued, "The one *you* kidnapped means nothing to you and everything to this man. Return her to him, and I'll help you find that money."

Teddy was silent.

"Assure me, and I'll tell you where the money is."

Teddy appeared to be mulling over what Lyle's spirit was demanding.

"Well? I won't tell you unless you agree."

"I'm thinkin'! I'm thinkin'!"

After what seemed like eons to Brody, Teddy finally relented, saying, "All right."

"You'll return the girl?"

"I said all right!"

Brody was hopeful once more.

"You promise?"

"Yes, I promise you, Lyle!" he snarled and hunched, wading this way and that, back and forth like a caged hyena. "Now, tell me where it is."

There was a pause in the conversation, Teddy awaiting the response.

"Well?" Teddy finally asked.

"He's sizing you up," Brody told him. "He wants to be sure that you really mean what you say."

"*You're* doin' this." Teddy scowled at Brody.

"And how does that explain the things you heard? How could I possibly know all those personal details? How, Teddy? Was I there? Or could that information have come from only one person? Lyle!"

Teddy visibly caved. "Go ahead. Ask him again."

Brody focused once more on the spirit, asking him, "Lyle, do you know where the money is hidden? Please, Teddy needs your help. My daughter, Abby, needs your help."

The voice of Lyle began, "Look behind the Dollar General—"

"I looked there already; it ain't there," grumbled Teddy.

"To the left of the Dumpsters, in the back wall, by the corner of the building, about eighteen inches from the ground. Look closely; there's a circle-shaped crack in the wall. It's hard to see. Unless you're looking for it, you'd never notice it was there. Push in that piece of wall; it should slide inside, onto a ledge. That's where I put the Walmart bags full of money. *There* you'll find what you seek."

The spirit of Lyle then faded from Brody's view. Teddy peered at Brody; Brody silently returned his stare.

"That money'd better be there."

"Yeah," Brody said, "tell me about it. But that's where your brother says it is."

"Yeah, well … I'm goin' to make a call, and we'll see." He strode through the water over to Brody. "Get down," he ordered.

Brody did as he was told, dipping back into the chilly rainwater. His captor performed a cursory pat down at gunpoint. Brody breathed a sigh of relief that he'd stashed the phone out of view.

Satisfied, Teddy removed two lengths of heavy-duty cord from his back pocket. "Turn around."

Brody rotated a half turn.

"Now, hands behind your ass."

Brody once more complied. Teddy looped the cord several times around Brody's wrists, securely restraining them, and knotted it.

"All right, up we go." Teddy hoisted Brody back up onto the rock ledge. Brody's two hundred pounds, give or take, were relatively easy for the thug to boost; Teddy was apparently quite strong for his stature. Brody figured it was just as well he hadn't tried to take the kidnapper on at the mouth of the cave. It could've ended in debilitating defeat.

"Now lie down."

As Brody reclined onto the hard, damp, uneven surface, Teddy wrapped the other cord around his ankles and tied it snugly.

"I'm going to make a call, and what you said Lyle said had better be true," threatened Teddy.

"Or else?"

Teddy moved to within inches of his trussed-up captive's face. "There better not be an 'or else,' buster. You better hope not."

Brody could smell the tobacco and beer on the hooligan's disgusting breath. He tried hard to remain unflinching. "If what your brother said was true, it'll be there," he said as phlegmatically as possible.

Teddy grunted, waded back toward the tunnel, and proceeded in the direction of the cave's exit.

"Teddy? Does this call mean that we have our information?"

"Where are you right now?" Teddy asked.

"Here in Clarksville. Was he successful in speaking to your poor departed brother?"

My bro has a name, you asshole, thought Teddy. "Yeah, he said he spoke to Lyle."

"Well, did he, or didn't he?"

"He had to've; there's no way he could've known the things he did. No fuckin' way."

"Teddy," the voice chuckled, "you have such a way with words."

Teddy was fuming. *Screw you!*

"Was he able to find out where the money is?"

"He told me. Go to the parkin' lot behind the Dollar General, and—"

"I'm there."

"You're there?"

"Yes, Teddy. I figured it would be a good starting place since your brother only made it from there to a house across the street before dropping. I'm getting out of my car now."

"Go to the Dumpsters."

"Oh, please—tell me it's not in the Dumpsters."

"It's not. Just tell me when you get there."

A brief pause and then, "I'm here. Now what?"

"Look to the left side of the Dumpster on your left, on the wall of the buildin' down near the corner, about a foot or two above the ground."

"What am I looking for?"

"Is there some kind of circle-like crack in the wall?"

"A circle-shaped crack?"

"Lyle said—" Teddy caught himself—that sounded too strange to be saying. It freakin' creeped him out. He started over. "He said it was real hard to see, even in the daylight."

"Let me shine my phone around here on it … Well, well. Yeah, there *is* a crack, a roundish one."

"Push in on it."

"You sure?"

"That's what he said to do. He said the money'd be inside that hole on a ledge. Should be in two Walmart sacks tied together."

"Okay, I'll give it a try."

Teddy listened closely.

The voice exclaimed, "It moved! I'm reaching inside ... I can feel the bags. It's here, Teddy! Yes, sir, yes, sir—two bags full. Good work."

It was so damn rare to hear that voice say anything remotely complimentary to him; the praise was heady, intoxicating, nearly making him forget about wasting the sonuvabitch. He nodded his head in tacit agreement, whispering to the wind, "Thanks, Lyle; thanks, bro."

"Teddy? Hold him until I get there. I'm heading to the cave right now. Understood?"

"Yeah. We'll be here." He hung up and jumped, attempting to kick his heels together but failing due to the suction from the mire. Embarrassed, he glanced around to ensure no one had witnessed the aborted exercise, slicking his hair back with false aplomb, recouping his cool. Satisfied he was alone, he continued on into the night with his celebration, stooping over and pumping his fist in a flurry of irrepressible fervor. "Yesss! Fuck yeah! Woo-hoo!"

Teddy's jubilation funneled into the tunnel. Lyle's spirit had certainly brought tidings of great joy.

24

EL Coronel's Learjet 60 XR touched down at Nashville International Airport and taxied to a remote runway on the fringes of the tarmac. Once the plane came to a stop, the cabin door popped open, and Willy stepped into the crisp evening air. The faint odor of jet fuel hung on the breeze. He took a long, deep breath, savoring the smell.

Carlos's black Escalade was parked below, with three of his henchmen rooted there, sturdy and steady as sequoias, their well-inked limbs crossed before them. They were befitting of a military escort, yet it was not Willy who would require protection.

He lit a cigarette and uncaringly threw the lit match to the ground, fortunate that it didn't hit any stray kerosene. He descended the steps and then stepped over to the waiting car. One of the men, ponytailed and muscle-bound, opened the rear door, and Willy folded his six-foot-four-inch frame tightly into the backseat, Ponytail closing the door after him.

The others piled into the Caddy, Ponytail squeezing in next to Willy, and they headed for the airport exit as the plane was guided into a waiting empty hangar.

The man in the front passenger seat, a rookie on Carlos's team, turned around and flashed a very metallic smile at the pale-faced newcomer. "Have a good flight, amigo?"

"Ja, amasing," he said with a thick Germanic accent. "Tell me, do your teeth interfere viss zuh transmission on zuh radio?"

Rookie's smile disappeared. "Hey, you ..." He made a brief move in the direction of the albino and then relented with a huff, facing forward, his ego smoldering.

Willy smiled wanly at him, cocking his head. "I've flown over four sowsand miles to retrieve ziss package. Let's get on vizz it." He took the last drag of his cigarette and drew the window down far enough to toss the butt out.

"It'll be worth it, my friend," Ponytail promised.

"It had better be." He winked at the Mexican. "El Coronel iss anxious to see zuh package." Willy continued to smile. He always preferred a grin to a scowl; it lulled his adversaries into dropping their guard—a time-tested strategy.

For the past hour and a half of his flight from Panama to Nashville he had indulged in the mile-high club with Sophia, El Coronel's handpicked and horny Brazilian stewardess. The fornication had been epic, given his prowess, his stamina, and his uniquely modified appendage. However, this leg of his journey might prove even more uplifting.

⟶⟶

While the Escalade cleared the vicinity, the FBI's helicopter landed on the opposite extreme of the airport.

Agent Knoxville and his assistant special agent in charge, Tory Basham, ducked under the spinning rotor, climbed into their bureau car, a Lincoln MKZ, and spun around, also cruising to the north exit. They had to make haste to Guthrie.

⟶⟶

Teddy's gaiety continued for quite some time. Brody lay there for nearly an hour, battling monumental fatigue—not always being the victor—and listening to the faint on-and-off whooping from beyond the corridor. He struggled with his binds, but they wouldn't budge. Several times, while drifting in and out of consciousness, he thought he felt a vibration in the cord around his feet, but he chalked it up to exhaustion.

He struggled to a seated position and wiggled over to the outcropping where he hid his phone. Twisting his torso, he stretched behind him for his cell phone, but try as he might, he couldn't contact it with his searching fingertips. Wiggling slightly away again, he gazed down into the shadows while trying to figure out an alternative way to retrieve the device.

He closed his eyes and narrowed his thoughts to summoning forth any spirits that might provide him with assistance or advice. Combatting the urge to fall asleep, he just sat there, trying to concentrate.

When he thought he detected a moan penetrating the far darkness beyond the chamber, he stirred. Was it Teddy again? It came from the opposite direction, though—deeper into the cave. What *was* that sound? Forcing himself awake, he suddenly and unmistakably heard yapping. A pair of little eyes glowed from the darkness behind the outcropping.

He whispered hoarsely, "Ruffy?"

A bark sounded, audible only to Brody.

"Ruffy, is that you?"

Two more barks.

He peered intently as the specter of his dog emerged from the shadows, panting. "Ruffy!" Brody looked in the direction of his phone and back to the apparition. *Whoa—might this work?* Ruffy's spirit had already demonstrated the ability to transport one of Brody's slippers; his cell phone was approximately the same weight. It was worth a try.

Ruffy spun around in a circular dance.

"Go get my phone, boy—my phone." He nodded his head in the direction of his iPhone.

The Pomeranian turned and zeroed in on the prize.

"Go get it, boy. Get the phone," Brody commanded.

And the little spirit was off, moving into the shadows, growling with ferocity.

"Good boy," rasped Brody. "Good boy. Now bring it here, Ruffy."

With great effort, Ruffy nudged it with his nose into the light. He looked over to his master.

"You can do it. C'mon, Ruffy!"

Once more Ruffy pushed it along, whimpering.

C'mon, boy. Lassie could; you can. You just gotta believe! He looked over at Ruffy and solemnly coaxed, "You can do it, Lassie."

Ruffy's ears straightened, and he stood erect, head held as high as a Pomeranian could.

"Lassie—bring me the phone, Lassie. Timmy's in the well, boy."

With strictness of purpose, Ruffy snatched Brody's phone between resolute jaws and elevated it, half-carrying it, half-dragging it arduously back to his master. He deposited it next to Brody, and his tongue began flicking in and out once more.

"Good boy, Ruffy—I mean, Lassie!" Yet the Herculean task wasn't completed. Brody twisted around again, putting the spirit and the phone out of view behind him. "Place it by my hands, boy."

Ruffy nudged it behind Brody's back until Brody could reach it with his fingertips.

Brody leaned backward until he could feel the familiar dimensions of the phone, and then he felt for the power button. He pushed it and saw the glow of his home screen light up behind him. *Oh my word—he did it! What a dog! Yes! Ha, ha!* "You're a hero, boy!"

The canine spirit gave a deeper bark—that same one that had surprised Brody after his slippers had cascaded over the landing at home.

Brody swiped the phone open and touched his thumb on the lock for fingerprint recognition. Then he depressed the main control button until he heard a familiar tone. He said as loudly as he thought he could get away with, "Dial Jennifer Connors."

A feminine, electronic voice responded, "Dialing Jennifer Connors's cell phone. Is that correct?"

"Yes!" he rasped.

Brody waited, listening intently. Faintly, he heard ringing and then, "Hello? Brody? Is that you?"

Thankful beyond measure, he said softly, "Jen! Yes. Yes, it's me!"

"Brody, where are y—" Her voice cut off. A sick feeling washed over him. He slid aside and stared down at the phone. The screen was jet black. *The damn battery's dead! No!*

⌇

"So, Wilhelm—" the driver began.

"Villy."

"Villy," Driver mimicked the big German. "How many hours does it take for that jet to get to Nashville?"

Willy's eyes narrowed at the idiot's snide mocking of the courier's Germanic pronunciation. That pissed Willy off—not that it took much. And he relished the slightest provocation anyway. It was also needless to share such information with peons. "Let me ask you vun. How many Mexicans duss it take to fill a taco?"

Taking a different tack, Driver asked, "Did you stop? Was there a layover?"

"Is ziss a nonstop drive, or vill you be asking me more insipid qvestions?" Willy goaded the two up front.

Rookie had heard just about enough, whining, "Man. Chill, dude."

"As you Americans say, *cool.*"

Ponytail warned Rookie, "I'm telling you, don't fuck with this guy. I know him.

"Shit," huffed Rookie. "The dude looks at least sixty years old, man," he uttered with contemptuous derision.

"Okay—don't say I didn't warn you, and don't let his looks fool you, either. He'd sooner rip off the top of your skull and piss on your brains than have a chitchat. And don't think the khalifa'd give a shit, either—the boss knows better than to jack with this motherfucker."

"I like zuh conversation, fucker uff mothers. It is his greasy hair I cannot stand."

The imbecilic Rookie whipped around, spitting, "All right, that's about enough of this shi—"

Anticipating this, Willy reared his left arm across himself and whipped the back of his hand squarely into the Mexican's forehead with a sickening thud. Blood seeped from the freshly cracked skull, and Rookie slumped over the console.

Driver swerved the car and then recovered. "Dammit!"

Ponytail pushed the limp body back into the front of the car in disgust. "He bitch-slapped 'im! He bitch-slapped 'im to death!"

"He von't haff to vorry about his hair anymore. Ven vee shtop, I'll piss on his brain, ja?" Willy chuckled.

Shaken, Driver asked, "Man, what'd you hit him so hard with?"

"Viss my hand," Willy said.

"Shit!"

"How long before vee get zare?"

"Too long," Driver lamented.

Willy smiled. *One down, one to go.* This little excursion was turning out to be an even more delightful diversion than screwing that lovely young air hostess with the very large coconuts at eighteen thousand feet.

⌒⁂⌒

Teddy had apparently grown tired of waiting at the entrance. Brody could hear him sloshing his way back to the main room. Brody wiggled on his backside to try to cover his phone but couldn't feel it. He torqued himself, glancing behind. Teddy mustn't see that he had the phone in his possession. *Where the hell …?*

A whimper sounded in the shadows over to his right. Ruffy sat half in the darkness of an overhang. Brody spied a corner of his phone lying on the rocks beside the nimble sprite. He winked at the dog and lay back down as Teddy entered the main room again and crossed to Brody's ledge.

"We're good. The money's been found." Teddy chuckled, impressed. "So you really *can* talk to the dead, huh?"

"It appears so," Brody said defiantly. "Now where's my daughter?!"

"Patience, patience."

"I gave you what you wanted! Told you where to find your lousy money. You said you'd give me my daughter back if I did. You promised—on your dead brother's spirit!"

Teddy glanced around, wide-eyed. "Where? I don't see him!" He laughed.

"You son of a bitch." Brody seethed.

"Hey," Teddy said sweetly, wagging a finger at the medium. "Careful now—them's fightin' words."

"Untie me, you jackass. Let's see about that."

Teddy took out his pistol and waved it at Brody. "Ah-ah-ah …"

"You think you're a tough guy because you've got a gun? Put it down, and let's go one-on-one."

"Yeah, right," he sniggered. "You *do* have a death wish. Hey, that's funny for a guy in your line of work, you know."

"Where's my daughter?" Brody shouted at him.

"I'm warnin' you!" Teddy aimed the gun above Brody. "Shut the fuck up!" He fired off a quick round.

Brody cowered as the bullet impacted the rock close by, sending up a tiny cloud of debris, ricocheted up to the ceiling, and then zipped down into the water just behind Teddy, who ducked to avoid being struck from the folly of his own volley.

The second stage of the bullet's journey—the roof of the cavern—was roost to a full colony of brown bats. Startled by the bullet striking within their midst, they scattered, flapping wildly around the cave. Hundreds of beating wings created their own gusts of wind. Their high-pitched screeches petrified Teddy, who dove into the water as the swarming cloud swooped down over him. The gigantic mass of winged creatures corkscrewed into the tunnel and flew toward the night air.

Teddy rose from the pool, dripping wet, dangling the gun that had just been submerged. He shook off the moisture as best he could and then slicked back his hair.

Brody suddenly felt a slight tugging at his ankle bindings and heard faint growling. *Ruffy?*

"That's enough about your daughter," said Teddy.

"So now what?" Brody asked him. "Now what are you gonna do?"

"Shut up."

"Your gun's all wet now, Teddy. May not fire."

"So? Shut the hell up, man." Sopping wet and freezing too, he walked closer to Brody.

"Untie me now, jerk-off!" Brody was baiting him to fight.

Instead, Teddy aimed his pistol right at Brody and pulled the trigger. Brody winced, turning his face slightly, yet nothing happened. As he opened his eyes once more, it was evident that the gun had either malfunctioned or else was out of ammo. Whatever the reason, Brody figured it was now just man-to-man.

⌁

"Listen, Johnny, there's no sign of the suspects here," Cletus said into his radio. "The house is empty, and there's a dead officer jammed into a freezer in the garage out back. Looks like he might've been pokin' around and the suspect ambushed him, killing the poor bastard at point-blank range. See no reason to hang around; we were actually thinkin' about headin' back to Clarksville."

"Why don't you stay there until we have a chance to chew on all of this?" JK said. "Speaking of which, are you fellas hungry?"

David and Cletus looked at each other.

"Yeah, we could eat," David admitted.

Cletus added, "Is there a good Mexican restaurant—"

"Hellll no," Johnny bluntly drawled. "No trigger food on my watch!"

Legend had indeed spread far and wide about Cletus's lax sphincter.

⌐⅄⌐

"Fuck you, man," Teddy said. His abrupt reaction had proven futile, so he reversed direction, retreating to his ledge, drawing himself up onto the rocks to drip-dry.

How long is this going to last? Where's Abby? What's going on here? Brody wondered. He decided he'd had enough. He sat up and slid down from the ledge, almost falling over into the water as he landed but remaining upright. The cord binding his feet suddenly snapped, and his legs were free. *How the hell did that happen?* He glanced over to where Ruffy and his phone were; the dog was panting and yapping proudly. *Could he have ...?* Whatever the reason, now he could move.

"Hey!" Teddy followed him down into the freezing water.

But Brody was twenty yards closer to the tunnel and lurched in that direction as rapidly as he could. Teddy took up the pursuit, and they both swished through the runoff, lifting their knees as gamely as their stamina allowed, seeing who had the will to be the first to gain access to the passageway. Brody was a tall, strong man, but Teddy had the advantage of added propulsion from his wildly swinging arms. He was closing in on Brody fast, his legs churning feverishly.

Gaining the tunnel, Brody felt a hand tug the back of his shirt. He jerked his shoulder, and the hold released. He sloshed toward the exit, splashing water wildly in a heavy spray all around; he was drenched from head to toe. As he high-stepped down the corridor, behind him, Teddy cleared the cavern and closed the gap quickly. He tackled Brody, sending them sprawling into the water and knocking the wind out of them both as they struck the walkway beneath the shallow surface. Brody's face scraped painfully against the submerged limestone, for he had no way to brace his fall with his hands still bound behind his back.

Wincing and struggling to a seated position while trying to regain his breath, he was surprised by Teddy's choke hold from behind. Brody half-stood and backpedaled as rapidly and mightily as he could, toting his assailant and smashing him into the tunnel wall. The jolt stunned the hanger-on, shedding him once more, and Brody, gasping for breath, resumed the race to the entrance.

Suddenly, his right foot was yanked out from underneath him. He fell again, striking his cheek harder this time on the less-buffered walkway. Teddy was on him in an instant, twisting him over onto his back, faceup in the inches-deep water. He straddled Brody and whipped out a hidden switchblade that had been strapped to his waist, inside his shirt. He snapped the knife open and poised it high, pausing before the subsequent plunge into Brody's heaving chest. Brody closed his eyes, fully expecting the pain from the stabbing blade.

"That's *enough*, Teddy!" boomed a voice from the entrance of the cave, shining a light on the two combatants.

Teddy froze the knife in midswing, moisture dripping from the tip of the gleaming steel, and looked up.

Brody opened his eyes and arched his neck, trying to glimpse whoever had issued that decree. Upside down, he watched a figure emerge from the darkness outside, his flashlight illuminating the passageway as he neared.

"Get off him, you idiot," the voice said. Even altered by the corridor's reverberations, it was a voice strangely familiar to Brody.

The figure moved closer, and the light fanned out more around Brody and his assailant. Teddy grumbled something unintelligible, climbing off and backing away, replacing his knife into its leather scabbard. Brody slowly rolled over, raising himself to his knees, his head throbbing from the concussive force of his recent hard falls. He studied the figure; its form and detail became clearer with each approaching step.

"Hello, Brody."

Brody could finally make out the newcomer, and he couldn't believe who he saw standing there, flashing his own gun in the silhouetting light of the passageway: Frank McGuire!

25

THE four lawmen convened at a local barbeque establishment called Red Top, known for its sweet potato and hash brown casseroles and homemade pies. They made it to the restaurant near closing time, but the owners were easily cajoled into keeping their doors and their kitchen open long enough for the group of civil servants to be served. And serve them they did.

Over a large platter of chicken and ribs, David licked his fingers. "Now that—that is good!"

"Yeah, buddy!" Cletus agreed.

JK rested his root beer on the lacquered hardwood tabletop and eased his full belly back. "Has anyone back at the station heard from the kidnap victim's father yet?"

"I told dispatch to patch any calls from him directly to me," David said. He opened up a Wet-Nap and applied it to his sticky fingers. "Dang."

"What?" the sheriff asked.

"I might have to make the drive back up here again for more of this dang-good barbecue! Whoa." He patted his stomach and silently belched twice. Doing so provided room for some more Sprite, so he topped off his tank again.

"How many local men do we have, if need be?" Tory asked Cletus.

"Local sheriff's department has three or four Ninjas."

"You think those deputies are trained well enough in SWAT tactics?" David asked.

Cletus replied, "I've talked to the local boys; they know their stuff. Even though there's not that much in the way of hard-core crime 'round here, they are highly trained for a county this size and are our best option, spur of the moment. You know," the sheriff added, "the killin' of Deputy Popplewell was one of the worst acts of violence against a lawman in these here parts. In fact, this guy Trent—he's one of the worst seeds, a big part of the local problem."

David's radio buzzed suddenly, and he took the call, listening to the station operator. "Yes, put her through." He said to everyone at the table, "Someone named Jennifer Connors. Works at the TV station. Says she's an acquaintance of Whitaker's." He pressed the speaker to allow the conversation to be heard by all. "Ms. Connors?"

"Sergeant ... Jeffries, is it?"

"Yes, ma'am. Dispatch says you're a friend of Mr. Whitaker's?"

"Yes, I am."

"Do you know anything pertaining to his whereabouts? We've been trying to reach him for some time now. Can't seem to raise him."

"He gave me directions to call you. I'm really worried about him."

"Knew it," JK whispered. "He was on his way here; I'd bet money on it."

"Did he by any chance say where he was going?"

"I'm fairly certain that the man who took his daughter contacted him. I think he was on his way to meet up with him—maybe try to get his daughter back. He said his instructions were to come alone and tell no one else."

"Everybody wants to be Batman. Why don't they just let us do our job?" Johnny quietly complained, belching as well.

"When's the last you communicated with him?" asked David.

"About fifteen minutes ago. It was brief. He called, and I picked up, but then I lost the call. He asked me earlier today to give him a little lead time before contacting you, but with that call from him, I *had* to try to reach you—I had no choice. I'm fearing the worst. I'm really worried that he's gotten himself into more than he can handle."

David said with gentle reassurance, "You did the right thing, ma'am. The FBI is here with me now. We're in Guthrie, Kentucky." He glanced at Johnny, who burped again. "We'll find him, but we need your help."

"Of course. What can I do?"

"Where did he say he was going?"

"He said he was going to that Bell Witch Cave."

"Bell Witch Cave?" confirmed the sheriff.

"That's what he told me."

Cletus said in an aside to the other lawmen, "Jeez. That's not far from here. Just a few miles."

"Yeah," JK whispered. "Adams—just down the road a ways."

"Thank you, Ms. Connors," David told her. "You've been a tremendous help."

"You're welcome. My number is similar to his, only the last four digits are 2-3-4-9. Let me know if you hear anything from him. Please?"

David assured her he would and hung up.

Johnny said to the sheriff, "Clete, let's get crackin'."

The driver quickly scrambled from his seat, bailing out of the Caddy. Carlos walked up to the rear door of the Escalade and opened it.

Willy smiled at him. "*Guten Abend*, Herr C-zar. I haff enjoyed ziss trip immensely. Sank you for letting me play viss your boys."

He stretched out of the car, and Carlos surveyed the carnage in the front and rear seats. "I see you spared the driver, Willy. Lucky for him."

"He vass more uff a necessity, really. Anyvay, I hope zay veren't, shall vee say, vital to your organization?"

Carlos grimaced. *That's why I gave them this assignment. God*, he thought, *there's a lot to clean up in there—and so little time!*

One of Carlos's men drove the car into the shop, but the laborious detailing would have to be put on the back burner. With all the local vehicles recently missing and now a kidnapping that could possibly be linked to him, there was far too much heat to hang around. Time to vacate the premises—posthaste—and migrate north.

Willy asked, "Vare iss zuh package?"

Carlos looked up at the German. "You have the money?"

"I haff it here." He patted the breast of his overcoat. "If zuh merchandise iss as advertised, it's yours."

"Oh, it's as advertised, all right. Follow me, amigo."

The men ventured through canine alley, Willy taunting the frenzied pit bulls by extending his left hand within striking distance. One of the dogs bit down hard on his hand, then yelped, two of its teeth snapping off during the attempted gnashing. It sulked away, and the other dogs paid heed, all backing off from this mysteriously powerful new target, growling as they hung their heads in submission.

⁓⁓

Abby was gagged with duct tape and bound to a chair in the office. She had fallen asleep but awoke when the door reopened. She saw the mustachioed man—she had overheard people call him Carlos—again, but this time he was accompanied by a man who had to stoop in order to avoid hitting his head on the doorframe.

He's so weird looking! Creepy! Abby had never before seen an albino, and the intensely unsettling combination of his alabaster skin and snow-white hair caused her to cringe. As the man approached her, an even more frightening feature—his pale eyes—made her squeal from beneath her duct tape muzzle. She tried to wiggle herself away from him, her chair scuffing against the linoleum floor with the struggle. She was instantly fearful of him; he appeared even more menacing than Teddy.

"Zare, zare, my dear," the creepy guy said soothingly, putting his cold hand on her cheek. That only unnerved her more, and she let out a muffled scream. Willy grinned. "She iss a live vire, ja?"

"I told you—she's special. And there's more to know about her than that."

"Yess?" Curious, he lowered his severely squared chin. "Vut elsse?"

"This little girl's father is a medium—he talks to the dead." Carlos folded his arms proudly.

"He does vut, you say?"

"He talks to dead people—for a living," Carlos chuckled. "He's pretty damn good at it too, from what I saw on TV a couple days ago."

"Really? *Un momento, por favor.*" He took out his phone and dialed his superior. "Yess, Herr Doktor. I am looking at zuh package right now ... Yess, Herr Doktor. It seemss to be relatiffly unblemished ... I sink you might reconsider zuh transfer of ziss vun. Ziss iss a more valuable package zan usual ... Herr Doktor. It can be of some benefit, I believe, vizz zuh problems vee are havink at zuh villa. I sink you should trust me vizz ziss." There was a longer pause, and then he said, "You von't regret it, Herr Doktor. Danke. It iss of brilliant quality; mark my vurds, it vill be uff great use to uss."

Abby listened in on the man's conversation. Though cryptic and confusing, it still sounded detrimental for her.

"Auf Wiedersehen." The weird-looking man hung up and placed his phone in his inside jacket pocket, removing an envelope at the same time and handing it to Carlos. "Here. It's all zare."

Carlos stashed the envelope in his desk drawer, locking it.

The weirdo walked over to stand in front of Abby again. Raising his left hand, he gripped it with his right and twisted it forcefully. A connection gave, and Abby heard a *snap!* as the hand swiveled around. She watched in fearful awe as the strange man appeared to unhook his hand at the wrist, unflinching—smiling even. The entire prosthesis unhinged at the base of the joint and released into his other palm. She could see that the fake hand was hollow and of some heft, for it caused the man's coat to droop quite lower on that side when pocketed.

The creepy-looking man then displayed what had been beneath the shell masquerading as his hand. A titanium, four-pronged claw articulated in the light, gleaming like some grotesque appendage out of a science fiction movie. He took a step toward Abby, his rosy lips taut in a devilish pucker, the prongs of his artificial joints flexing open and closed together, and said, "It's time to wrap zuh package."

Abby fainted.

⁓ℳ⁓

Johnny Knoxville stood up. "Time to roll, gentlemen."

The four men rose and grabbed their jackets, thanked the management for their generous hospitality, and hustled outside.

Johnny barked, "Mobilize the Ninjas; tell 'em I've authorized their jurisdiction in Tennessee for this matter. It's too late to secure a squad from elsewhere; we need guys who are close at hand and at the ready. Have the SWAT team meet us at the target—the entrance to the Bell Witch Cave property. Let's move, people!"

Sheriff Coonrod got on the horn and called in the team of Ninjas—so called for their skills of stealth, their jet-black skin-hugging garments, and their advanced weaponry. The squadron headed south toward Adams, David and Cletus leading the way, a blue emergency light flashing atop the roof of their civilian car as they sliced through the autumn darkness.

26

"HELP him up, Teddy," Frank ordered.

As commanded, Teddy assisted Brody to his feet.

"I'd say we got ourselves a shitload of lemons here, Brody? What do you think?"

Brody shook his head at the sour joke, flabbergasted and disgusted. "Frank? How are you mixed up in all of this?"

"Only so much as ... it was my idea," he proudly proclaimed.

"Your idea? *You* did this to Abby? Why?"

Frank shook his gun, indicating they retreat down the tunnel back to the main room. Brody hesitated. He did not wish to retreat from his only means of escape, but he had to find out what these men had done with Abby.

"Tell me," Brody said.

"You wish to find out, then move!" Frank growled. "You're forgetting who has the upper hand here, Brody. Move your ass back down the tunnel." He waggled the gun once more.

With Teddy in the lead, Brody reluctantly began trudging through the deepening water again, trembling harder. "Okay," he grumbled. "I'm moving. So tell me why."

"Why do you think?" Frank asked.

Brody shook his head. "I'm beyond belief. I have no earthly idea why you'd be behind this."

"I want you to come work for me," said Frank.

With those words, Teddy glanced over his shoulder, his nostrils flared, glaring at Frank. "What?"

Brody was confused. "I thought you said the bank couldn't use me right now?"

"Brody, you are *so* naive! Do you think I work for the *bank*?" He chortled.

Puzzled, Brody asked, "Who, then?"

Ceasing his throaty laughter, Frank oozed, "A syndicate—based out of Chicago."

This time it was Brody who shot a backward glance.

"Yes, that's right. We're all in need of a little extra spending money every now and then, isn't that right, Brody? You came to me looking for help, didn't you? I found myself in that position too. Divorce can really put a damper on the ol' lifestyle, can't it? I needed cash, a lot of it. I answered what I thought was a recruiting call from a headhunting firm three years ago, and it blossomed into a full-time career for the mob."

Brody looked over his shoulder again as he splashed into the greater cavern, his bewilderment apparent.

"Oh, yes—the *mob*," Frank lowed, his eyes wide with emphasis. "Do you think loan officers, even vice presidents of measly branch banks earn enough to indulge themselves?" He laughed. "Hell no—it's a pittance! So, when the opportunity came along to finagle things a little bit and earn a pretty little bonus in the process, I snatched that brass ring. Skimming a little here, fudging a trifle there, the money trickling upstream. The miniscule, unaccounted-for amounts were mere pennies to corporate—nothing significant enough to shake a stick at. But over time, they accumulated, especially as more branches in Tennessee, Kentucky, and Arkansas began depositing into the offering plate."

Brody recalled the after-the-fact alterations that Frank had suggested he make on certain applications. They'd seemed a bit questionable at the time, considering standard protocol, but he'd thought little else about them, deferring the rationalizations and explanations of such out-of-the-ordinary figurings for his boss to justify.

"I pointed out those little 'discrepancies' of yours on all those loan documents to my superiors, Brody. They ... took that pass on rehiring you."

That infuriated Brody. Set up and thrown under the bus, his reputation besmirched by this—this *lowlife*. Livid, he wheeled around.

"Not impressed." Frank was pointing his gun at Brody's chest. "Walk, walk."

No match for the weapon, Brody trudged onward while Frank continued his discourse.

"When you decided to leave, Lizzie was next in line. Hmm, now why didn't *her* loan book ever balance? Go figure ..." he sneered. "I pointed out her many, uh, 'errors.' She felt that they couldn't possibly be her fault and seemed so sure they weren't there each previous day when she turned her books in to me—somehow they kept appearing overnight. How on earth could that have been happening?" Frank put his free hand to his mouth in mock shock. "Inexplicable! I mentioned a way for her to have all those 'errors' expunged. A simple solution."

"I'll bet you did," Brody said, his voice full of scorn.

"All she had to do was drive up one night to talk to this guy"—he trained his flashlight momentarily on Teddy—"my so-called 'loan administrator.' Oh, but she had plans to meet his brother, Lyle, for a date that night anyway, so she decided to confer with Teddy beforehand. To kill two birds with one stone, shall we say. Ah, the irony of that little phrase, eh? Lizzie killing two birds? Ah, to kill or be killed ... hmm ... that was her question. The slings and arrows of outrageous misfortune, right?"

Brody said grimly, "Very poetic—just what the hell are you talking about?"

Frank finished his explanation. "Teddy offered the poor girl an antidote to her toxic dilemma—a small stake in our robbery take, for simply looking the other way, for turning the other cheek. But she balked ever so politely, so foolishly. A product of too moral an upbringing, she implied that she might rather contact the authorities about debunking our shady facade, a very unwise faux pas on her part. Her rash decision left me with no option but to prune that pesky, mischievous thorn from the bush—a nuisance more inconvenient but far less difficult to expunge than a bunch of numbers in books. Agony chosen over ecstasy. How tragic indeed."

Brody was sickened by Frank's revelation. Lizzie never deserved any of that; she was such a sweet young woman, a decent and honest person. And her parents certainly had the right to know what had really happened to her. "What did you do to Lizzie?" Brody asked, looking over his shoulder.

"It wasn't me. Ask him." Frank nodded to Teddy, who had turned around for a brief backward step or two.

Teddy shrugged his shoulders, a sardonic smirk on his face. He turned around again and sloshed into the middle of the cavern.

"Did your brother ever find out about this?" Brody asked Teddy.

Without turning this time, Teddy answered, "Hey, dude, let's just say there are some things better left unshared. Even with family."

Brody humphed. "So you set up that robbery, Frank? But why *rob* the bank? Weren't you embezzling enough already?"

Frank continued, "Scapegoats, scapegoats, my dear man—there were no more to be had. And the boss wanted the fix, so it was staged. But with Teddy's brother snuffed during the getaway, that money became untraceable, until *voila!*—through the magic of television—*you* show me how to recover it. How do you like *them* apples?"

"So, where'd you dig up this guy, anyway?" Brody nodded his head in Teddy's direction.

"This baboon? He and his brother were simple to locate and all too hard up for a dime. After skimming all the cream *I* could at the bank, churning the butterfat was best left to … farmhands."

Teddy jerked himself around and gave Frank an icy stare. "So we 'baboons' were just patsies? Fall guys? The hired help gets to take the rap on Old McGuire's farm, huh?"

"What's the matter, Teddy? Did I suddenly say something to upset you?" Frank laughed. "Did you honestly assume you were anything otherwise? You know what they say about *assuming*, right?" He looked at Teddy, who appeared befuddled, as though awaiting further explanation. "Oh, never mind." Frank shook his head and sighed. "Don't you fret; the money's all up there in my car. You'll get your cut."

Brody glared at his once-supposed mentor, shaking his head again.

"Brody, Brody, you seem so shocked. C'mon—welcome to the new corporate America, the new underworld. We're businessmen, more insidious than ever before. We're everywhere and anywhere there's coin to be had! Bankers, brokers, hedge fund operators, politicians, lobbyists. Hell, we're *franchisees!* On every street corner, we're as common as fast-food restaurants. We erode your e-investment portfolios with malignant accuracy. Pilfer your precious PINs with glee. Intercept your indispensable Social *in*-Security checks. Gladly accept your online fantasy sports wagers. And you and your mother's brother's second cousin twice removed never, ever fucking *know*, my friend!"

"That's plain sick, Frank," said a disgusted Brody. "And I'm not your friend."

"No," he conceded angrily, "you're not. Now sit your ass down!"

Brody backed over to the ledge again.

"Time to cut the cord, Teddy."

Teddy took out his blade and flipped it open. He spun Brody around and sliced through his remaining bindings, replacing the knife once more with an expert's twist of the wrist. Frank motioned with his gun for Brody to mount the ledge again.

Brody sat back down atop the rocks. "Where's my daughter?"

"You have one way out, here, Brody."

"Where is she?"

"You'll get your daughter back—"

"Hey, that's not what—" Teddy blurted.

Frank stopped him with the twitch of a finger. "—on one condition. It also happens to be the sole condition of your *own* saving grace. So you can accomplish what Lizzie couldn't—killing those two birds with a single stone."

Teddy fidgeted in the water. "Hey, Rocco, that's not—"

"Shut the fuck up, Teddy. Do you understand that? And don't call me that, you dumbass!" Frank yelled. He turned back to Brody, shrugging his shoulders. "Now then, you can fulfill this one condition, or you can die on the spot, never to see your precious Abby again. Your choice."

Teddy argued, "You never told me not to do whatever I—"

Frank turned on his accomplice. "Not to do what? Circumstances have changed."

Brody shook his head. "What is it you want from me?"

"Not me, Brody. My superiors. What do they want? *You.*"

"Me? What did I ever—"

"To work for them. Personally. Exclusively. No more of that cockamamie television bullshit. No more private readings. Just *them.* They have a need for someone with your specific talents, will pay very handsomely for them, and don't take 'no' for an answer."

Teddy took a step or two toward Frank. "That ain't gonna work."

Frank glowered at the two-bit hood. "Whatever do you mean, worm?"

"I ain't got the girl no more."

Ice water coursed through Brody's veins. He was suddenly disoriented. "What?!"

Frank roared, "What do you mean?"

"What do you mean, 'what do I mean'?" Teddy returned the roar.

The competition continued, with Frank hollering, "I never told you to harm her! We *needed* her! Where the fuck is she? *Sheesh!*" He balled his fists and rotated in place, cursing under his breath. "Do I have to detail *every*thing I say to you?"

"I didn't *harm* her—I sold her!"

Brody was dizzy, sick. "What did you do with Abby?" he shrieked.

"You did *what?*" Frank, in near-total disbelief, shook his gun angrily at Teddy. "What the fuck? That was never the plan! Who gave you the authority to do that, you cretin?"

Teddy whipped out his Hardballer and pointed it at his partner in crime. "Me, motherfucker."

The lawmen and the SWAT team converged at the entrance on Keysburg Road. The game plan was laid down, and the men moved out. The Ninjas, sheathed in their ebony flak jackets and masks, armed with night-vision goggles and semiautomatic rifles equipped with laser scopes, loped down the drive. JK and Tory followed, bringing with them, among other needs, several pairs of infrared binoculars. David and Cletus had brought other items that either the victims or the perpetrators might require on that chilly night—a couple of rolled-up blankets and two thermoses, one filled with coffee, the other hot chocolate. There was enough beverage to go around, in case the lawmen found themselves in a lengthy standoff. Other than the SWAT team, the men each had tiny but powerful flashlights to help guide them if need be, but those would be extinguished when the point men signaled the team to do so.

Cletus was the only one of the group who would have difficulty matching pace, and it was understood that he would move at his own comfortable speed, joining up with the others as quickly as he could.

As they came upon the cabin, the rest of the men held back while the Ninjas circumnavigated the perimeter, checking all windows. One team member tried the door—it was unlocked. He gave a silent countdown from three, and they breached the lobby, fanning out quickly. The goggles afforded them an element of surprise as they probed every nook and cranny. Once the house was deemed all clear, the Ninjas slipped outside and started down the stretch leading to the cave. The other lawmen, their weapons drawn, brought up the rear.

⌁

"You? What the fuck, Teddy?" Frank aimed his gun at Teddy's midsection.

"I needed more money!" he yelled.

Money? Brody thought. These assholes were arguing over money while Abby's life hung in the balance!

"You idiot!" Frank bellowed, writhing a clenched fist.

"Yeah, well—"

"What about my daughter?" Brody cried again.

Frank shook his head, still eyeing Teddy. "*Que sera, sera*, my good man." He and Teddy stared each other down. "This is what you call a Mexican standoff, Teddy. Have you heard about those before?"

"Except his gun won't fire," Brody flatly informed him.

"What do you mean?" Frank asked.

"It fell into the water; it's drenched."

Frank grinned at Teddy. "Well, well. Is that so? Tsk-tsk. Whatever do we do now, Teddy?"

Teddy extended his gun hand somewhat tentatively.

Frank lowered his and shrugged. "How's this going to work, Teddy?"

"You jerk me around," bemoaned Teddy, "call me every fuckin' name in the book, insult me, laugh at me."

"You *are* a fuckup, Teddy. Always have been, always will be. You screwed things up with the little girl too."

"You mother—" Teddy tested the trigger. It clicked, but that was all. He looked at the gun.

Frank laughed. "Ha! You see? You can't even shoot me without fucking that up!"

Teddy squeezed again. Still nothing.

"Let's face it, Teddy, you'll never—"

The third time was a charm. The impact from the unexpected projectile to his chest toppled Frank backward into the water. His gun flew from his hand, striking the cavern wall and vanishing below the opaque surface.

The lawmen had reached the two roughly parallel vehicles.

David pointed to the van. "That matches the suspect's vehicle. The child was likely abducted in that! And that silver Honda looks like Whitaker's car."

The SWAT team rushed down and swarmed over both vehicles, making rapid work of their inspections. They muzzle punched their rifle barrels against the windows of the van, shattering the glass. Their night-vision scopes revealed an empty interior. No one was in Brody's car either.

At what sounded like a gunshot from the vicinity of the cave, the men kicked it into higher gear, trotting rapidly down the pathway. The point man motioned his teammates to hustle up. A single shot was one too many.

Teddy inspected the barrel, sniffing it with bombastic overkill and chuckling, "Huh? Whaddaya know?"

Frank's limp body slowly submerged; only his face and hands remained afloat.

Brody slid down from the rock as inconspicuously as he could, but Teddy caught the movement out of the corner of his eye and summarily addressed his would-be fugitive with the pistol.

"Where's my daughter?" Brody yelled.

"That's for me to know and for you to never find out."

Brody took a step toward the gunman, fists balled. "You tell me, or—"

"Or what?" He chuckled. "We both know this thing still fires, dude."

"Probably," Brody allowed.

"You want to risk it? Make a move."

Brody decided to. If Teddy fired the gun, then so be it. If this asshole harmed a hair on Abby's head, Brody couldn't live with himself anyway. He took another step forward.

The SWAT team reached a point several hundred feet from the entrance staircase and extended themselves, prone, onto the hard path, resting the props of their gun barrels on the rock, their rifles trained upon the railing leading to the mouth of the cave. David and the feds were beside the others. Once Cletus had also joined the group, JK handed out the Ranger digital night-vision binoculars to the police sergeant and the sheriff so they could identify whoever emerged from the cave. While Cletus caught his breath, David peered through the twin lenses and adjusted his contrast control, fine-tuning the correct infrared illumination for the top of the stairs. The Ninjas focused their scopes for the same distance, their guns at the ready, awaiting further instruction.

Something barred Brody. Leaning harder, he met more resistance; an energy of considerable strength was holding him back. Slowly, Lyle's spirit began to coalesce, an expression of determination on his face. His only hand was stretched flat, palm toward Brody, yet a couple of inches from Brody's sternum. Brody eased back.

"Thought so." Teddy grunted, the true cause for Brody's constraint oblivious to him.

Brody began to conduct the thoughts of Lyle, as before. "Teddy, don't do it, bro."

Teddy swiveled his gaze about. "Lyle? Lyle? Is that you?"

"Yes, it's me. Don't do it."

Wild-eyed, Teddy stared back at Brody and yelled, "Don't do what?!"

"You don't need to kill this man. You promised you'd return his daughter if I helped you find that money. You gave me your word."

Teddy blurted out, "What's a promise to a dead man? Huh?"

"You were my brother! Didn't that mean anything to you when you strangled Lizzie Snowden, the one girl who offered me a thin ray of sunshine? Why'd you do it, 'brodacious'?"

"I had to!"

"No, you didn't, Teddy. You never *had* to. There was always a different option. You've always just wanted the easy way out. I covered for you. Made excuses for you. All those years—I had your back. And in the end, where were you for me?"

"You know I loved you, Lyle. I had your back too! You meant the world to me. You were the only thing that really mattered in my fucked-up life."

"Then prove it!" the specter challenged, the words thundering through the chamber and into the outer corridor.

"There's nothin' to prove anymore. You're gone now, Lyle. My words mean nothin' to you."

"Do my words mean nothing to you too, big brother? Didn't I help you find where that money was? Don't you want forgiveness for what you did to me and Lizzie?"

"Yes, but leave me be now, Lyle! Let me do what I gotta do."

"This is *not* what you gotta do! Let him go. Give him back his daughter. For once, put things right. Make amends for all the shit you've done—finally!"

Enraged, Teddy screamed in Brody's direction, "Leave me be, I said!"

Lyle's beleaguered spirit uttered a few more sentences to Brody and then departed.

"Listen to Lyle, Teddy," Brody implored. "Please."

Teddy right-angled himself to Brody and focused with the intensity of a big-league pitcher contemplating his windup. He stared keenly across his right shoulder. Then he raised his arm and extended it, his Hardballer lined up precisely with Brody's forehead. He adjusted his hold on the pistol one last time and sighted down the barrel with his left eye shut. "Say good-bye."

"Say good-bye to whom?"

The question came not from Brody, who stood silently, submissively. The words came from a woman—an elderly one.

"Who said that?" Teddy bristled.

Brody wondered that very same thing, for Lyle's spirit had not since returned.

Derisively, the voice challenged, "Are you going to shoot *me*?"

Teddy peered around the main room and saw no one else. "Who is it? Who's there?" He waded over and grabbed a lantern, hoisting it here and there, and then took a few steps toward the wall housing the face of the Bell Witch. He held the lantern aloft. The formation was gone, just a blank stone wall in its place. He swung the light in an arc, checking the other walls. Transfixed, Brody was baffled as well.

Low laughter crept from a remote pocket of the cavern and reverberated louder, permeating the chamber. Then the voice spoke once more. "What are you looking for?"

Teddy poked the lantern about, circling around in the water, his gun poised, at the ready. An immense dark shadow swooped down from overhead and passed directly over his outstretched arm.

"Are you looking for me?"

Teddy pointed his pistol at the swiftly moving shadow.

"Go ahead; shoot me! See who it hurts—me or *you*!" The laughter repeated, tapering as the shadow drifted away.

"Who the fuck *are* you?" Teddy demanded, wide-eyed, suddenly shivering.

"Like my flying friends you disturbed from slumber, you have awakened me as well. Some call *me* Batts, Kate Batts. Unlike those bats that scatter when scared, *nothing* frightens me!"

Brody thought, *It is the witch!* Only this time she was a full-on apparition.

The shadowy spirit shifted lower on her next pass, enveloping Teddy and spinning him like a top as she uncoiled and whipped to higher altitude. "Leave this place while you still can. You defile my home!"

Teddy, dizzy and panicked, fired an off-balance round above him.

There came a bloodcurdling, wounded shriek. "How *dare* you! Mortal being, you won't leave well enough alone! Like that insipid daughter of John Bell. She and her father tried to cast me out more than once, but they failed! I was *too strong*! Now *you* shall rue the day you awakened the vengeance of the Bell Witch!"

The shadow struck into the water, just beneath the surface, torpedoing toward Teddy. With a ferocious spectral uppercut to Teddy's midsection, the spirit catapulted him backward. He splashed down, extinguishing the lantern. His gun submerged again before he could manage, sputtering and spitting, to right himself.

The witch roared, "For years I've waited, biding my time, until someone gave me due cause to reappear. And now you have!"

The witch whorled herself next around Brody, sapping his body's heat. She slithered in front of him, fully facing him, assuming the same menacing side-to-side sway she had employed years prior on that fateful college trip. "You return?" the crone snarled. "Once before, you insulted me here, yet I spared you and your lady. I left my mark—a sign of your intrusion—in the only photographs you had from your visit here."

The smudges in those photos! It was her!

"Those marks were to serve as a reminder to you to never return here. You came again today of your own volition?"

"No. I was forced here by him." He jutted his chin at Teddy.

The witch opened her black maw wide, baring rotted gray teeth; slackened sinews framing her gaping jaw vibrated from each of her spoken syllables. "For what reason, medium?"

"He kidnapped my daughter to blackmail me into helping him retrieve some stolen money his dead brother hid."

The Bell Witch swiveled her head in the direction of the terrified Teddy, who took several steps back. She peered at him, as though scrutinizing his very soul, and hissed at him, "*You* brought him here? You foolish mortal! You sabotaged yourself before you even began."

The apparition swung back to Brody. "Begone! Leave and never return! Before I change my mind again!"

She turned once more and growled a deep, ominous rumble at Teddy, like the sound of distant, cumulating thunder. The sound sent shivers up Brody's spine. "All of this, over money? Ha! You're no better than John Bell!" the phantasm hissed, rising higher, towering over Teddy. Then it barreled down at him.

With Teddy occupied, Brody seized his opportunity to flee. He splashed over to the ledge, fumbling through the shadows with cold, numb fingers for his phone. Something nudged it toward his probing hand. A yip came from the darkness, and he whispered, "Good dog, Lassie!" He jammed the phone into the pocket of his jeans and then churned feverishly to the tunnel.

The specter rammed Teddy full force once more, and he crumpled, struggling to keep his pistol above water. He saw Brody gain the passageway and took aim. As he fired, the witch grazed his arm again, altering the bullet's trajectory enough that it struck harmlessly off the limestone wall, a foot away from his fleeing captive. Brody made the bend into the outer portion of the tunnel and was gone.

"Let him go. Do not test me again, kidnapper—I'll be watching you!" the witch cackled as she circled upward, spiraling tighter and tighter. And then she vanished, her laughter bounding off the walls in the distant tunnel.

Teddy sat in the water, scared out of his wits, attempting to recalibrate his internal gyroscope. He rose slowly and sloshed over to retrieve another lantern and then moved to the wall where the witch's portrait had been, not half an hour ago. He held up the lantern, and it was back, in exactly the same spot as before! That infernal image was *taunting* him. He pointed his gun at it and pulled the trigger—once, twice, three times—but his cartridge was spent.

A series of eerie, abstract sounds began emanating from the far reaches of the outer chamber. They rose in ghastly amplitude and frequency, merging into a spate of monstrous, deafening bellows—sonic booms. Hunching over, he covered his ears with his trembling hands until the horrible noise faded away.

He then flung the lantern against the wall. It burst, sending blazing fuel across the patterned stone, etching ebony scorch marks across the surface of the rock. Another hideous shriek rang out from the darkness and then shriveled into a moan, echoing off into the innermost remote recesses of the cave system. The flames peeled harmlessly off like chunks of seared flesh, falling and extinguishing in pinches of steam as they tapped the water below.

While the stone surrounding the face had been visibly charred by the searing gas, the face itself was utterly, confoundingly unscathed.

The apparition suddenly exploded from its likeness on the wall and plowed into Teddy near the opening of the outer corridor, forcing his head underneath the rainwater, with the intent to drown him. He struggled against the incredible power of the Bell Witch until he managed to gain purchase on the limestone floor. Bracing himself, he pushed along the walkway with all the strength his arms and legs could command. All the while, the witch had a stranglehold around his neck, stealing away his consciousness. He fought feverishly, inching his way along the tunnel, until finally the witch disengaged herself and withdrew back into the cavern, leaving him there.

Coughing and gasping, he crawled several more yards and then found the stamina to lift himself halfway erect, stumbling to the mouth of the cave. He fell once more onto the lower plank of the stairs, pausing to gather some strength and force more fresh air into his burning lungs. Then he heaved himself up the remainder of the staircase.

When the booms drifted from the cave's entrance, the men tensed, watching for any trace of movement. A lone figure dragged himself to the top of the staircase, into the chilly night air, collapsing there.

David focused his binoculars and alerted the snipers, "Hold your fire! *Hold your fire!* That looks like the missing girl's father!"

"Stand down, men. Repeat: hold your fire," JK ordered.

Brody lay on the path, his chest heaving, and David rushed to his aid. Assisting the medium to his feet, David could feel the poor guy shivering uncontrollably. The officer assisted him back to the group.

"Can we get this man a blanket or something? He's freezing. And how about a cup of coffee?"

One of the felt blankets was produced, and Brody encased himself in it. He reached for the cup of steaming liquid and drank several relishing sips.

JK approached and asked, "What happened in there, Mr. Whitaker?"

He shook his head slowly. "I'm not quite s-sure, but the men who robbed the b-bank are in there."

"Is one of them Teddy Trent?" asked Sheriff Coonrod.

Shuddering hard again, Brody said through chattering teeth, "Yeah, h-him."

"Is the other his brother?" Tory asked.

"No, he's dead. Killed in the g-getaway on Tuesday."

"That must've been whose blood I found on a neighbor's lawn," David explained to the feds.

Brody added, "But the other man in there—I think he's d-dead too. Teddy shot him. He g-g-goes by Frank McGuire, and—"

David interjected, "Hey, isn't he the bank VP that I questioned after the robbery?"

"Yeah," Brody said. "He apparently set the whole caper up, working from the inside. He's p-part of some Chicago-based syndicate. Teddy called him 'Rocco' one time in the cave. I d-don't know if that's his real name or a n-nickname. He was set up at the b-bank a couple of years ago to skim money off loans. He bragged that this was going on at several other Tennessee b-banks, Arkansas and Kentucky too—you guys need to look into that."

Tory nodded.

Brody gulped some more steaming liquid and continued, "And he hired those two brothers to rob the bank for a bigger haul. The money f-from the robbery is in his car up there." He tipped his head in the direction of the main entrance.

Cletus asked, "Where's your daughter, Whitaker?"

The question seemed to jar something in Brody. He stood abruptly, the blanket sliding from his shoulders. "I know where she is!" He released his fingers from the cup, dropping it to the ground, spilling the remaining coffee. "We've got to hurry—please!"

"We've got movement!" one of the Ninjas called, pointing down the path.

Through his binoculars, David spotted a lone figure resembling the police sketch mounting the uppermost stair. "That's the kidnapper. It's Trent!"

"Is he armed?" Johnny asked.

"Affirmative!" the Ninja replied.

JK reached for his bullhorn. "Teddy Trent!"

Chilled to the bone, Teddy flung himself onto the path, physically spent, emotionally drained, and psychologically reeling from God knows what he'd experienced in that cave. He was convinced that Brody was long gone, but suddenly he became aware of further company.

"Trent, you are outmanned," someone warned from somewhere up the path, using a megaphone. "Drop your weapon."

He squinted into the night but couldn't perceive anyone. Empty and broken, he could summon only a verbal retaliation: *"Fuck you!"*

The loudspeaker voice calmly said, "Teddy, put your weapon down. No need to try anything foolish. Place it on the ground."

I'm sooo tired, Teddy thought. All the events of the last few days fell like dominoes, one by one, through his tortured mind: the robbery, Lyle's death, the highway homicide, the run-ins with Big Jim and his goons, the killing of Deputy Popplewell, the kidnapping of that medium's little girl, and the cherry on the top—that *bitch* of a witch!

"Drop your weapon, Teddy. Put it down, and walk slowly up the hill. There's a blanket and some hot coffee for you. You're outnumbered. Do it now!"

Damn, that coffee and blanket sure sound good! Teddy laughed; he could barely stand, let alone walk up that path! He lay there and kneaded his haggard brow with waterlogged fingertips, staring up at the stars twinkling above. *The money—surely they have the money by now.* It was all lost, all for naught. And worst of all, Lyle was gone. Teddy found the strength to rise to a sitting position on swollen knees. He slicked back his hair and began to lift his gun.

In that crystallizing moment, everything from Teddy's shoulder down to the fingertips of his shooting hand felt as overweight as his total sense of failure. Every episode in his life had either been a letdown, a put-down, a travesty, or a turn for the worse—*everything.* Now he'd even managed to botch this. Maybe Rocco had been right. *I fucked up everything just by bringing that medium into this cave!*

As he tried to level his arm, something of formidable force opposed him. Whatever it was, it was trying to prevent a fatal outcome. One possibility sprang to mind: *Lyle?*

"Don't do it, Teddy. Drop the gun!"

Surely that suggestion came from the ridge. *Or from right beside me?* Teddy glanced to his right but saw nothing. He lowered his weapon, dog tired. He laid the Hardballer on the ground and looked at his palms, moist and clammy, bleeding, weathered beyond their years. He rolled his hands over and studied his ink-stained knuckles—the two upside-down words summarizing the distorted philosophy that had propelled him through the years: destiny … absolution. Back and forth, he surveyed one and then the other, repeating the words to himself.

Teddy reached for his pistol again with his right hand and braced the muzzle onto the rock—a lethal crutch—steadying himself. Lifting his chin to the heavens, he sniveled, "Lyle, Lyle, why'd you leave me, bro? Why?"

There came a whisper on the wind. "I'm right here, Teddy."

He raised the weapon, perusing its sleek, metallic exterior. Out of ammo, he knew it was his apt destiny for this chapter to end thusly.

Only one thing left to do, thought Teddy. *One fuckin' thing.* He had to atone for his sins and the sins of his father. He shuffled the gun over to his left hand, his nonshooting hand, rose to his feet, and extended the pistol out to the darkness. *Absolution.*

Something clamped onto Teddy's hand, pushing it downward. Teddy fought to resist whatever was applying itself against his left hand, bringing his right hand up to help steady the other. "Lyle? Lyle? What the fuck? *Stop* it!"

"Who's he talking to?" asked Tory.

"My guess," Brody said flatly, "his brother."

The men all stared at him, confounded. The Ninjas then adjusted their sights, reacquiring the target, their fingers at the ready.

Johnny was likewise confused. "But I thought you said …?"

"I did," Brody replied. "He *is* dead. But Lyle Trent is reaching out, one last time, trying to save his brother from himself."

◆

"This ain't up to you, Lyle!" Teddy shouted, overwhelming the spirit of his brother and regaining control. He leveled his firearm in the direction of the sound of the negotiator. Squeezing the trigger, he cried out, "I love you, bro!"

A hail of bullets pierced Teddy in the arms, chest, thigh, and head, collapsing him to his knees. His shoulders hung from the weight of his entire world crashing down upon him, and he released his gun to the cold, moist stone and then tilted backward, sprawling on his back down the stairs, sliding lifeless to the mire.

◆

The team charged in and stood over the body, training their flashlights on the dead man's head and the surrounding runoff. Teddy's empty brown eyes could now merely reflect the twinkle of the stars as his blood slowly drained, darkening the trickle emptying from the mouth of the cave.

Cletus redirected their attention. "Hey. Watch those leaves, fellas."

Everyone followed a few wayward leaves as they drifted with the flow of the rainwater, moving around the body and away from the cave, heading toward the cliff.

JK picked up on what the sheriff was referring to and shook his head. "Holy shit. What do you make of that blood, guys? Ever seen anything like that?"

In one final act of defiance—contrary to the physical laws of nature—the last vestiges of Teddy's earthly existence seeped upstream, back into the mouth of Bell Witch Cave.

27

ALL units responded, converging at Hadensville Road—for, in the cave, the spirit of Lyle, out of sympathy, had divulged to Brody the destination he'd so sought. With the aid of a departmental chopper, the maze to Carlos's hideaway was solved in short order and a clear path marked. The convoy quickly dispensed of the chained gate and sped down the gravel path to Carlos's lair.

They met no resistance as they approached, and everyone braced themselves for the worst. Except for Brody. He'd come that far, been through so much—he couldn't fathom his quest resulting in failure. His mind couldn't wrap itself around such a grim possibility.

Empty posts in twin rows lined the compound, their iron rings all idle. The place was sickeningly still, save for the footfalls of the intruders, who hurried to the larger of the two buildings.

With a battering ram, they broke down the door to Carlos's office, which was devoid of trappings and of the trapped. There was, however, a small rectangular scrap of paper taped to a blade of the slowly revolving ceiling fan. One of the agents switched off the fan.

Cletus grabbed a chair and slid it below the fan as the blades abated their merry-go-round. He snatched down what appeared to be a calling card. He looked it over and read the engraved inscription aloud: "EC was here." He next read what was scribbled below that in black ink: "Adios, pendejos!"

Johnny translated for everyone, "'Good-bye, dumbasses.'"

"Who's EC?" Cletus asked.

David asked Brody, "Do you have any idea who that might be?"

Brody shook his head dejectedly. "I haven't the foggiest." His knees weakened but not his resolve. Not yet. He helped scour the entire garage and then the house.

They searched the immediate grounds, but not another soul was discovered.

It was time for Brody to finally surrender. He sank to his knees and wailed.

⌁

Willy stepped out of the Escalade and looked into the back seat. The girl was unconscious. She'd awakened from her swoon and then put up a worthy struggle for one so small, but in the end, the chloroform had proved the victor. He lifted her out of the vehicle and kicked the door closed with his foot. With the package draped limply over his arms—her head bobbing along to his gait—he carried her through the open bay door of the hangar.

Sophia opened the cabin of the jet. She waved to her *muito viril* albino and blew him a kiss from her plumped crimson lips. Willy ascended the steps and stared at the canyon of cleavage between Sophia's partially exposed, sun-kissed twin peaks. As he passed her, he kissed her full mouth and bit her pouting lip, a satisfyingly acrid taste coating his tongue. Her lipstick and blood exaggerated the rouging of his lips.

They entered the Lear and sealed its hatch. The plane then taxied from the hangar, toward an open runway. As they lifted off, Willy smiled down at the expanse of Tennessee lights dimming in the distance.

The girl was strapped in on the sofa behind him, unresponsive still. Sophia, taking full advantage of the situation, straddled Willy, unbuttoning both of their shirts. He reached beside her, grabbing an open Dom Pérignon from a silver ice bucket, and poured them each a glass while Sophia busied herself with unfastening his trousers, her brown locks spilling over his toned abs.

"A toast," he said, raising her chin, and his glass to hers. He smiled. "Here'ss to a long, eventful flight home."

⌁

Without patrol dogs, the law officers decided to search the surrounding acres at first light. Brody was to have his search-team volunteers there by midmorning.

On the ride home, about a quarter of an hour away from Clarksville, Brody reined in his raw nerves and fevered thoughts and dialed Jennifer's number. David had provided Brody with a charging cord. The sergeant was at the wheel of Brody's Accord, for the suffering fellow was still in no condition to drive.

"Hello? Brody?"

"Hi, Jen."

She choked up. "You're okay?"

"I'm fine," he assured her.

"When your phone cut out so abruptly, I thought ..."

"I know how you must have felt. It frustrated me too."

"Abby? Did you find Abby?"

He hesitated. "No."

She gasped.

"We have no idea where she is."

"Oh my God, Brody. What can I do?"

"What can any of us do, Jen?" He began to weep anew. "My little girl's gone!"

David, his voice full of resolute determination, vowed to Brody, "I won't rest until Abby's found. After I drop you and your car off at home, an officer'll pick me up. I'll be headed straight to headquarters from there so I can begin the search immediately. I'll have the whole damn department involved. Bet on it."

"Brody ... Brody ..." was all Jennifer could say.

"Thank you for notifying Sergeant Jeffries, Jen."

"Of course." Finally, after his crying slackened, she said, "Listen, I'm here if you need me. You call me, and I'll help. Anything. Please promise."

He sniffled. "Yes. I will. I've got to go now, Jen."

"Okay. Remember what I said."

"Yeah, I will. I'll call you in the morning. Promise."

And he hung up.

28

BRODY slouched askew in his recliner, with his eyes buried beneath his right forearm and his left arm dangling limply over one edge of the chair. He was all cried out; his spate of tears had persisted late through the midnight hour. He picked up the water bottle on the end table next to him and swigged from it, replenishing his spent moisture, never budging his blindfold. Even in isolation, he was ashamed to show his face.

The sun would be interrupting soon, and the more he retraced the previous day, the more painful the recap became. And the stronger his desire to hide.

When Brody's eyes reopened, dawn light was creeping through the rear french doors. In stark contrast to his melancholy, the backyard finches had initiated their gay wake-up warbles, and the aluminum wind chimes that Abby had coerced him into hanging—in homage to Susan—were ringing their lilting melody, as though signaling some musical Morse code. He listened intently—perhaps he might decipher something cryptic in the mélange of miscellaneous notes. *Maybe a message from Abby? But that would mean ...*

He banished the unthinkable thought and then rubbed the sleep from the corners of his eyes and stretched in the chair, yawning. He was stiff all over—his hands, his legs, his back, his neck, his hips. He was a mass of bruises, knots, and inflammation—another excuse for not showing his face. As he eased himself gingerly to a fully upright position, he noticed Susan waiting there, perched on the hearth.

"Hey, Giff," she said.

Gushing a fresh stream of tears, he sobbed, "I'm sorry, Susan; I'm sorry." He lowered his head into his hands, unworthy to gaze upon her.

"Brody. Brody," she called to him, softly, sweetly.

He raised his chin, wiping his nostrils with his shirtsleeve. "I'm so sorry," he whimpered again.

"Brody, you can't believe that what happened was your fault?"

"It *is* my fault. If I'd have been there—"

"Stop right there," she scolded. "Don't you dare do that."

"But I was somewhere else—somewhere with Jennifer."

"My dear, sweet man. This is foolishness, what you're subjecting yourself to."

He gazed at her face, radiant in the early-morning light. "I wasn't there for her."

Susan's form rose and spoke as she drifted slowly to him. "We both know it's impossible for you to always be there. You can't. And you can't shield her all her life from being a normal child—from being *herself*—this newfound talent of hers aside."

Her validation was so vital to him in his fragile state of mind.

"*I* was there," she said.

"What?"

"I attempted to present myself to her."

"You did?"

"Our bridge wasn't strong enough yet to connect with her in full form."

"How? What did you do?" he asked.

"I manipulated the branches of a tree, bending them so that they resembled my face. I tried to warn her, but the event was too fragile, too fleeting. It failed; I failed."

"But at least you *tried*."

She nodded. "So did you, my dear."

"Yes, and I've tried to summon Teddy's spirit, the man called Frank McGuire's, and even Teddy's brother, Lyle, again. But no response. None of them will step forward." He felt overwhelmed with simultaneous grief and vindication. A lump rose in his throat. "At least I haven't been able to summon *Abby's* spirit forward. I've tried on and off throughout the night. Nothing. That's something." He chuckled at that.

"And I've felt no setbacks in the energy forming between her and me. That can only be if her soul is still among the living."

"Do you have any idea where she is?"

"My attachment to her isn't such that I can reach her in her own touchpoints yet—if you hadn't been to that Walmart so many times, I'd not have had the chance, the opportunity there. But Grampa Eddie's attachment *is* strong enough. He was there at Walmart too."

"Gramps?"

"He tried to stop the abduction too but ultimately was unable."

"I'll just summon him forward then," Brody said.

"You can't. Because of his attachment to her now, he's able to shadow her. He won't stray from her side as long as she remains in any sort of danger. Even I cannot reach out to him, for he is no longer present in this spiritual plane. He is far from here, with her."

She put her hand upon his arm; he felt a coolness where it rested.

"Keep faith, Brody, and be assured: to paralyze yourself with guilt and doubt will sabotage what she needs most right now. She needs you—more than ever. Your focus must be on finding her and bringing her home."

He looked into her angelic eyes. "You're right—*focus*. I've got to find Abby."

"Gather whatever facts you can from the material world, and again seek out those spirits nearby who have knowledge of where she might be. That is where your search begins." Before she faded from view, her intervention complete, she smiled and said, "*I* have faith in your abilities, Giff. From the moment you revealed them to me, I always have."

Jennifer offered Brody the resources of the station once more, and early that morning he recorded a plea to be broadcast later in the day. In the plea he mentioned the mysterious calling card and offered a reward of $10,000 for any information that might shed light on who EC or the owner of the unidentified jet might be. A hotline number for the task force set up at the precinct would be left on-screen throughout the plea.

Then both Brody and Jennifer rounded up all the idle hands they could for the search party. Folks from Brody's church and many of his clients volunteered. Bank employees and everyone available from the Girl Scout troop—Brenda and Maddie included—and Abby's school all offered their services. K-9 units were brought in, and David and other officers from the Guthrie and Clarksville police departments, as well as JK and several of his field agents, contributed to the effort. The search party combed the woods surrounding Carlos's vacant garage. Everyone's collective time and toil, though essential, proved fruitless, and the search was halted around noon.

Brody and David thanked every volunteer personally for their effort, and David showed each one a photocopy of that calling card recovered at Carlos's lair—the only clue as to Abby's whereabouts that they had to offer. But no one had any inkling about whom or what it referred to.

In the early afternoon, Brody received a call from Sergeant Jeffries with the latest progress from the Clarksville station's investigation.

"What have you found?" Brody asked, putting his phone on speaker so that Jennifer, who was by his side, could hear as well.

"An unidentified Learjet landed at Nashville International sometime late yesterday afternoon and departed last night around eleven forty-five. What was strange about this particular aircraft was that the registration didn't coincide with anything in the FAA database."

"Really?"

"Yes."

"How could that have happened, especially at a fairly decent-sized airport?"

"We don't know yet. The FBI and the FAA are looking into whether or not anyone in air traffic control there is involved. Regardless of that, the Learjet's flight plan was also squirrely."

"What do you mean by that?"

"Well, their itinerary indicated they were scheduled to arrive at Brownsville—South Padre International. But they never landed there. At least there's no record of that either. Not a single private plane has flown in or out of that airport over the past three days, which is actually a bit peculiar in and of itself."

Jennifer asked him, "Why, Sergeant?"

"South Padre's a beachfront resort, and Brownsville's a border town. Normally, there's a lot of air traffic through there, from tourists to the cartels—

border breachings and all. So, we've got a plane with a falsified flight plan and clandestine arrivals and departures. That plane never made it to Brownsville, apparently."

Something sudden and frightening dawned on Brody. "My God, could it have crashed?"

Jennifer took his free hand, squeezing it. They looked at each other.

"The thought crossed my mind too, but don't worry, Brody. There have been no reports of any aircraft mishaps across the entire state. No distress signals, nothing. I've checked that out as well. So it's extremely unlikely."

"The people on board such a flight would probably be incommunicado, though, wouldn't they?" Jennifer asked.

"True, but the FAA hasn't received any reports from that region of a downed aircraft. Nor have any of the media outlets. In this case, no news is good news."

"Then where could it be?" asked Brody.

"That's the million-dollar mystery."

"What do you mean?"

"Well, somewhere out there is a private aircraft—unregistered with our aviation agency yet able to fly into and outside of our borders unscrutinized—and not a damn soul knows what direction it took off or where it eventually landed. It has essentially vanished from the grid, Brody."

Late that afternoon, Brody was toweling off from a soothing, languid shower when the doorbell rang. He hurriedly slipped on his robe and went downstairs.

Jennifer stood there bearing a pot roast in her outstretched hands. "Thought you could use this," she said, handing him the Crock-Pot. "It's been slow-cooking all day."

He showed her inside and headed to the kitchen, where he deposited the entree on the stove. Then he grabbed her and hugged her tightly. "Thank you for helping today," he told her. As she stepped back, he let his hands linger on her soft shoulders, caressing her with his thumbs.

"Thank you for calling," she said. "I told you, anything you need, just tell me."

He leaned and gently kissed her, his sore cheekbones forgotten for the moment. "I've needed that."

She echoed his sentiment, leaning in for another soft, lingering kiss. Following their embrace, she said, "Mmm, that was nice. Listen, there's more to eat. Let me go and get the rest out of the car."

As they sat and ate Jennifer's savory meal, Brody's tension dissipated. Her visit was truly cathartic; it was permitting him to internally unwind. By the time they'd finished, he was gaining a stronger sense of clarity, of purpose. His forthcoming plans were taking shape in his troubled mind.

Brody also realized there were details that Jennifer would rightfully inquire about, such as, "What really happened in that cave?" and "How did you manage to escape?" He would discuss all that in time with her, but he didn't wish to share his encounter with the spirit of Kate Batts with either her or the authorities just yet. Certain aspects of his story might actually endanger any one of those individuals, should they seek to substantiate his story about the Bell Witch or syndicate ties to the bank on their own. And with Jennifer's propensity for journalistic inquiry, well, he had enough to be worried about without inadvertently placing her in harm's way.

"Brody, listen—" Jen started.

"Jen, I—" Brody said simultaneously.

They chuckled together.

"You first," Brody said.

"Okay. About the show ..."

"Yes?"

"The station decided to pull Monday's segment, at least for now; we're not going to run it in the morning."

"Why? What do you mean?"

"With Abby—" She caught herself and opted for another avenue. "We couldn't in good conscience run the next session. Not after what's happened."

"Jen, I appreciate what the station is trying to do, really."

She arched her eyebrows. "But?"

He looked her squarely in the eyes. "I believe that airing the session now is the right thing to do."

"You do?"

"For several reasons."

"Yes?"

"For starters, I intend to honor my commitment to you and Jack, but that's the least of my reasons."

"Brody, you don't—"

His expression gave her pause, and he thoughtfully explained, "I believe it's important to get back to a state of normalcy—*routine*—as quickly as possible. Not for me to disregard Abby's plight"—he gulped—"because she's still out there. I *know* it. Knowing that you're running the segment and continuing what we've started will give me one less thing to worry about and help me direct my thoughts on finding her and bringing her back."

"Well, you'll need some time away from recording further sessions until you've found Abby and returned her safely home. Jack's suggestion. We're officially on hold with the project, not off the air with it."

"Jack's suggestion?" Brody was surprised.

"Yes, you have him firmly entrenched on your side now, although he *is* still a bit skeptical."

Brody smiled.

"Really," Jennifer said, "he wants you to know that his thoughts and prayers are with you and with Abby."

"Thanks. I know you'll understand this, having fought so hard to find yourself after your daughter succumbed to her illness." Brody knew that it had taken months and her daughter's indomitable spirit for Jennifer to right her own ship.

She nodded. "Yeah, I do."

He reached out for her hand, and she clasped his; her touch imbued him with renewed hope and vigor. "And also ..." he began.

"Yes?"

"Let me see if I can explain this clearly. All my life, for as long as I can remember, I've dealt with this ability. Some call it a gift—I have too, at times. But it can also be a curse of sorts. Like when you have to hide it from your friends at school or else face ridicule and be branded a laughingstock. Or when you yearn so much for a brief respite, but someone's spirit just won't comply. When you receive a message from the other side and choose to look the other way, supposedly in the best interests of someone you care very deeply about, but then the worst befalls him or her." The serious self-doubt in his expression intensified. "Well, maybe it really *is* a curse and not a blessing after all."

Brody had her firm attention, so he continued, "I always thought that if I kept pursuing this path, I might eventually derive some sort of fame from it. It was always in the back of my mind, and I even wished for it at times. But I also feared that such a day as *this* might come—when someone, somewhere, would see what I was capable of doing and seek to pervert it. To convert it into something foul, for their own twisted, ill-gotten gains, and with someone else hurt in the process. I never guessed it would happen so soon; it was always a down-the road type of possibility—something to worry about tomorrow or the next day or the next. And the worst part about this? As afraid as I was that this might happen to me, in my wildest nightmares, I never dreamed it would involve my *daughter*—my precious Abby. Yet now it has."

"Brody, you never could have known this was going to occur. Wasn't she chaperoned?"

"Yes, but the troop leader was called away, and in that precise window of time, that evil man saw his opportunity to take her."

She pressed his hand. "Which *no one* could have foreseen. Not you or anyone else. It wasn't your fault. You are a loving, responsible father. What happened was totally beyond your control. You must realize that?"

He chuckled again.

"What?"

"That's the same thing Susan said to me this morning."

A great many women might've been taken aback by all that talk about the spirit of a man's departed wife, but Jennifer merely smiled, saying, "See? Great minds think alike, huh?"

He returned her smile. "A voice of reason. I'm lucky to have you in my life, Jen. I really mean that. I'd be accomplishing very little right now if you weren't here."

"I'm here for whatever you need."

"Then, please," he urged her, "run the segment tomorrow. For me? For Abby?"

"If you're absolutely positive about that."

"I don't want to be afraid of who I am, to feel the need to shy away from what I'm capable of, just because some miscreant might seek me out for all the wrong reasons. I can't do that—it's not my nature. And I don't want that at all for Abby either. What am I saying to her if that's the kind of example I set? We can't live our lives in fear, or this gift really *will* become a curse."

"Then don't be afraid. And if you want WCVL to run the session, I'll convince Jack. It'll air as scheduled in the morning."

"That's what I want."

She took both of his hands in hers. "Then that's what we'll do."

It was a pleasantly dry early Monday morning, and David pulled up to the curb nearly a block away from Irv's house—it was too crowded to park nearby. He removed the heavily laden shiva tray of baked goods and brunch fare from his trunk, walked along the row of cars back to the Crossman residence, and rang the doorbell.

A tall, handsome young man with a custom-trimmed burnt-umber beard, matinee idol smile, and bright yet piercing eyes answered the door. "Hello."

"Hello," David replied. "I'm a fairly new friend of Mr. Crossman's from the temple."

"I'm Mr. Crossman's grandson, Aaron Rubenstein."

"You're the fellow from Israel?"

"Yes," he chuckled, "I am. Thank you for coming by. And you are …?"

"Oh, I'm sorry. David Jeffries."

"The police sergeant?"

"Why yes."

They shook hands, David trying to match the young man's strong grip.

Aaron chuckled once more. "He's told me about you."

David raised an eyebrow.

"He said he was hoping you'd stop by."

David's eyebrow rose further.

"Please, come in."

He handed the grandson the weighty tray. "This is from our family to yours."

"Thank you." Aaron took the tray, which seemed light as a feather balanced on the young man's fingertips. "Grandpapa," he said, pronouncing *papa* as *pawpaw*, "will appreciate it very much."

He deposited the tray on Irv's dining room table among all the other dishes prepared by friends and neighbors and showed David into the living room. A group of nearly two dozen mourners were seated or standing opposite

Irv. The elderly man—his yarmulke balanced atop his head, a blue-and-white tallit draped over his shoulders, and his Old Testament resting in his hand—led the group in the Kaddish prayer. Irv noticed the new visitor being escorted in, and he beamed.

Once Irv had ended the first session of prayer for the day, he directed his guests to the table for some nourishment. He sequestered David, shepherding Aaron along with him, off into a corner of the room.

"I see you've met my *eynikl*, my grandson, Aaron?"

"Yes, he's quite a strapping young man."

"Strong as an ox!"

"Grandpapa ..."

"Well, aren't you?" Irv said proudly, turning back to David. "Thank you for coming by. Can you stay?"

"Well, actually, I'm working on a case that came up over the weekend, so I'm afraid I can't stay much longer."

Irv nodded. "Sounds serious if it has that much of your attention."

"Well, this type of case is extremely critical in its first few hours. It's an abduction, I'm afraid. A little girl."

Irv covered his mouth loosely with his hand and gasped, "Oh no. That's horrible!"

"Terrible." Aaron shook his head, agreeing.

"Yes, it is. It's the daughter of a fellow who's been on local television recently. He calls himself the Clarksville Medium."

Irv's face blanched a shade paler. "No! Really? I just phoned the TV station late last week after Marie passed. I saw him on the *Daily Show*, and I had to try to see him. I'm supposed to have a reading with him, so they told me."

"Grandpapa, you hadn't mentioned that to me."

"I was going to, as soon as we'd finished mourning. I thought you'd think me foolish, I guess."

The young man wrapped his arm around his frail grandfather and squeezed a wheeze out of him. "I think it's lovely that you'd try something like that. I'm not a big believer in things of that nature, but so what?"

"Well, you should see this guy. It sure looks as legit as *I* can tell," David said. Turning to Irv, he added, "But it looks as though your session with him will be on indefinite hold."

"What happened to the girl?" Irv asked. "I haven't had my TV on all weekend, so I haven't seen the news."

"Well, this is already public knowledge, so I'll fill you in. She was abducted in broad daylight on Saturday morning at Walmart. She was selling Girl Scout cookies with her troop when a white van pulled up and snatched her away. She hasn't been seen or heard from since."

Aaron shook his head. "I'll bet that poor father is going bananas."

"Yes, he's beside himself. We finally located the place we thought she'd be, but whoever was holding the girl had vanished, along with any trace of her."

"Well," Aaron said, "I hope you find the bastard responsible. People like that deserve whatever it is that's coming to them."

David regarded the young fellow and his bold statement, silently sharing the same sentiment.

Irv steadied himself on his grandson's sturdy wrist. "Do you know anything more? Were there any clues left behind?"

"Yes, as a matter of fact." David removed the folded piece of photocopy paper from his pocket and showed it to the pair of men. "This card was taped to a ceiling fan blade in the room where we think she last was."

Irv put his glasses on and took the paper, looking at the reprint. He gasped and then covered his open mouth once more, handing the paper over to Aaron. The grandson stared at the copy and then back into his frail grandfather's suddenly steeled eyes. They both shook their heads.

David noticed the exchange. "What? What is it?"

Irv handed it back to David, advising him through clenched teeth, "Hurry."

"What?"

Aaron reiterated, "He said *hurry*. Hurry and find her."

Irv said earnestly, "You must locate this child as soon as you can, Sergeant. She is in grave danger."

"Why? What does this mean, this card?"

"It means," Irv said, grabbing David's wrist with both hands as tightly as talons clamping a bough, "she was taken by a *monster*—the Devil himself!"

⁓

Following a fitful night's sleep, Brody got up early to await any news regarding Abby, but by nine o'clock he had received nothing more concrete from anyone involved in her case. He'd packed a suitcase to the brim with various odds and ends of clothing—prepared for any possible clime. He'd placed the suitcase by the door, figuring he might have to head to the airport at a moment's notice—whenever he was granted the location of his destination.

The sun shone brightly as he drove to Planter's Bank, where they were already scraping Frank McGuire's name off the glass. He greeted Tony Polino, who was back at his security post, a bandage still spanning the bridge of his proud nose, and they chatted briefly about the robbery and the men behind it. Lucy Smalls gave him a warm hug and then helped him retrieve his passport from his safe deposit box. He didn't overwhelm them with the details of Lizzie Snowden's disappearance; he'd let the authorities break that news, as they had already done so to Lizzie's devastated parents.

Back in his Accord, he put in another set of calls to David and Cletus, both of whom had been summoned away. To Brody, it seemed that the wheels of justice were turning extraordinarily, excruciatingly slow while encountering far too many bumps in the road. They needed greasing. And a precise, professional alignment.

So as he made his way home, he had only three certainties: one, whoever was holding Abby captive had scattered to the four winds like the cockroaches he, she, or they were; two, Abby might have been taken aboard a private plane that had been bound for Brownsville yet never arrived; and three, his daughter was out there, somewhere, terrified, depending on him to rescue her.

Once home, he took the suitcase out to his car. Stepping back inside the foyer, he snatched his jacket off a coat hook, slung it on his sore shoulders, and locked up.

Brody Whitaker was being summoned down a path, hopefully one that would lead him to his little girl. As long as there was breath entering his lungs, he would not let Abby down. He was going to find her by doing things his way—the only way he knew.

Printed in the United States
By Bookmasters